Desperate times…

"Hey, are you—" He looked back down and tried to not immediately panic.

There were two ugly wounds on her neck, and the blood dripping from them was clearly the wrong color. Worse were the dark tendrils seemingly spreading from the wounds under her skin. He had clearly released something inside her, and it was spreading fast. John was starting to understand why he had fled so easily.

Danielle's eyes were shooting around quickly, and John could see the fear and awareness in them, but she didn't appear able to move her body. He quickly crouched next to her even as she started convulsing. It appeared similar to a normal seizure, but there was nothing normal about that happening to a vampire. Blood was starting to pour out of her mouth, and he couldn't think of anything to do beyond trying to hold her still.

"Dani, you have to heal!"

Despite what she was going through, Danielle managed to give him a nasty look at his stupidly obvious instruction.

"Sorry, but I don't know what to do." He was trying to stay calm for her sake, but he wasn't fooling anyone. The only way either of them could help the other heal was by giving them more blood, and he doubted she had the ability to drink.

Small broken sounds were coming from her throat as she tried unsuccessfully to form words. He knew she was trying to tell him something, but beyond her eyes, there was no control. Holding her head still, he tried looking into her eyes more clearly, and she was looking hard back into his. An image slowly formed in his mind as she gave him instructions.

"Jesus, Dani, I can't!"

Her idea was insane. There was no way he would risk it. Even as he said it, he mounted her and tried to distribute his weight in a way to keep her upper body still. He could feel her muscles straining underneath him, but at least he was stronger than she was. Her eyes were pleading, and he watched in horror as tiny black fingers started invading her irises.

Do! It! Her thoughts were so weak, but the desperation was clear.

John forced himself to focus carefully as he pushed Danielle's head down firmly. Pushing against her forehead with his right hand, he was able to reduce the movement to an acceptable amount. He then positioned the claws of his left hand very precisely, hesitating slightly as he saw a single red tear drop from her right eye.

Lowering his gaze from her face, John ripped out the source of the infection, along with almost three-quarters of his wife's throat. The feeling of her body going completely limp the instant her spinal cord was severed was unnerving—although, technically, *severed* was far too clean a word to describe what he had done.

Almost four vertical inches of her throat were gone, with barely more than skin and some muscle on the left side keeping her head attached. He had exactly no idea what would happen next, only that he had to hold her head very, very still. Not being ash yet meant nothing under these circumstances.

ETERNAL NIGHTS

BOOK II - ORIGINS

RICHARD SPEGAL

Published in the United States of America

ISBN 979-8-9998996-8-2 (SC)

ISBN 979-8-9998996-9-9 (Ebook)

For Book Rights Adaption and other Rights Permission.

Call us at toll-free **601-914-6178**.

OTHER BOOKS BY RICHARD SPEGAL:

Eternal Nights Series

Prequel:
Book 1 – Redemption
Book 2 – Origins

Series:
Arrival – (forthcoming)

Wolves and Ravens Trilogy

Book 1 – The First Law
Book 2 – Choice
Book 3 – Broken Angel (forthcoming)

DEDICATION

To my children, including the one still being cooked at the time of this publication (perhaps one day I will write something appropriate for even them to read), but mostly to my wife. Being forced to deal with long periods of separation, always thinking she isn't enough and never understanding she's everything.

PROLOGUE

Before Recorded Time

Humans had not yet begun to form their first settlements when the creature first arrived in this world. The arrival was rather unexpected—more of a crash, really—but the creature was naturally adaptable and willing to make the most of its untenable situation. There was little chance of it being able to leave the world for the foreseeable future, so the creature made the only choice it could think of. If one couldn't leave, then one might as well be in charge.

It was strange how similar the humans were to its own appearance. They averaged a bit smaller, and their heads were not as elongated as its own, nor were their ears pointed. The most obvious difference, however, was the creature's teeth. Designed to be the purist of carnivores, it boasted a mouth full of canines each about half again as long as the average human's.

Humans of the time were not organized enough to offer proper resistance to the power and technology it had access to. The fact that the humans also represented a viable food source was simply an added bonus. Life had not been great, but the possibilities had been acceptable, until something strange began happening.

No one would ever call the creature "good," and it would have never claimed to be. On the other hand, the creature did not consider itself to be evil—merely focused on looking out for itself and taking whatever advantages from any given situation it could get.

When the bodies of the humans the creature had used for food began to start walking again, it became a cause for concern. The creature was immortal, but it had known all along that the humans were not. Dead humans were supposed to stay that way.

1

Some time spent studying the phenomenon caused the creature's concern to grow. The newly risen corpses were not mindless beings but seemed to somehow display a shadow of the creature's own power along with total sentience. They began displaying signs of bloodlust, feeding upon and killing their fellow humans. When some of those fed upon began rising themselves, the creature began to panic. The creature might have wanted to rule this primitive culture, but the idea of releasing some sort of dark plague in the world had never been part of the plan.

Its new path became painfully clear. The creature spent years hunting down and destroying every one of the abominations that were to be found until it was sure the job was done. Knowing that living among the humans could risk another outbreak, the creature then did the only thing it could and secluded itself within a cave that no human would dare enter. Sorrow and remorse had been unknown feelings, yet once the creature got a taste of them, all thoughts of ambition fled its mind. The creature refused to ever feed again, not when the cost was so high, so it vowed to remain in the cave where it could do no harm.

Immortality kept it alive, but without sustenance, the creature's body began to age and weaken. When decades, centuries, and finally millennia began to pass, the creature's very flesh began to merge with the walls of its new domain. Unfortunately, not only could the creature not die, but its mind continued to grow in power, even as its physical body withered away. It was logical, given that age brought power to its kind, but it was an unwanted consequence.

Within the first few millennia, the creature's mind had grown strong enough to reach out through the world. It was an interesting development, but it brought a horrific discovery. Humans all appeared the same to the creature's mind. But there was something that seemed different among the background of humanity, something that appeared to taste more familiar, and the creature was forced to realize its failure. The abominations had not been completely wiped out. Some had escaped, and the scourge had spread.

The creature's mind writhed in torment at the discovery. Physically, it was no longer able to do anything about the problem. Throughout the ages, the creature attempted to use its mental abilities to influence humanity in order to give them a chance against the scourge, but the results were always disastrous. It was not easy to influence events on such a detailed scale, and most of the creature's attempts ended in bloody, widespread warfare.

Eventually, the creature had to accept the damage was done. As powerful as it had become, successfully steering humanity into any direction was not possible, nor was it appropriate. There was nothing to do but sleep. Slumber helped to quiet the creature's tormented mind. There was always a possibility of future opportunities to undo the damage, but sanity would be necessary to make proper use of those opportunities, and sanity was rapidly slipping away. So the creature slept. If nothing else, perhaps one day there would be a way for it to die.

AD 1970

Hope. It began as a small fire in the back of the creature's mind but continued to grow until it eventually glowed brightly enough to wake it from its long slumber. The creature did not wake easily. The unknowing and uncaring dark blanket of sleep was not something to be cast away lightly. The fire would not be denied, however, and the creature was forced to confront what had awakened it after so long.

The humans had built quite an impressive civilization compared to what the creature remembered, and its mind longed to reach out to it. At times the loneliness was even bitterer than the despair, and it was just another reason to wish for death. With effort, the creature was able to keep its power under control and consider the situation. Much had changed, but in the end, what difference did it make?

The humans had grown much more powerful, but it was also obvious that the scourge had survived. Anger began to grow and vie for position with the hope in its mind. To wake from slumber just to be mocked by its failure was torture even the creature should not have to endure . . . But what was that? On the very edge of its awareness, the reason for the hope began to clear up.

It was still possible for the creature to be killed, but its power was so great that even suicide was no longer an option. Any weapon the humans possessed that would be strong enough to destroy it would also destroy a great many innocent lives, and the creature would not allow such a destructive gift to be his last interaction with humanity. There was only one way, but it was unthinkable.

The creature's children—it shuddered to think of the abominations in that way, but it was no less true—had the ability. In battle, none could hope to prevail, but if the creature chose to not defend itself, the link it shared with its children should allow them the ability to kill it. Unfortunately, this potential salvation carried a grave risk. It was possible

3

that whoever killed the creature in that fashion would inherit its power, and that was a risk that could not be taken. Not after the damage the creature had already done to this world. So why was its mind torturing it so by dwelling on hopeless thoughts?

There it was again.

Something was different. No, wait, *someone* was different. Was it even possible that the abominations themselves could have evolved, much as the humans had done so as a whole? Even if that were true, it did not mean any were capable of killing the creature without becoming even more corrupted. All humans had the capacity for good; the creature understood and believed that. Unfortunately, every one of its children had the same capacity for evil, no matter how the individual abomination might act. Still, any chance, however small, was worth examining.

The creature had learned from its previous mistakes. This time it would take the time to approach things carefully and use only the most delicate of touches when influencing the minds of others. There had to be absolute certainty before any decision would be made. What were another few decades of waiting on top of the countless millennia that had already passed?

CHAPTER 1

Present Day

"Don't listen to him, Priest. He knows his only hope is to divide us," Marcus pleaded with Jenkins, his bald head reflecting the room's light in an amusing fashion. The large, well-muscled ghoul had begun shaving his head two years before and refused to admit that the "bald look" simply did not work for him.

"Now, now, Marcus, Jenkins is an intelligent man who knows the way the world works. Let him make up his own mind," Sam said, smiling sweetly. The young vampire was careful to hide his fangs as he eyed the dark-haired priest, who even in this setting refused to take off the noticeable white collar of his office.

"You know what Sam, you're right. I'm way too intelligent to fall for your tricks." Father Jenkins gave no notice to the several discarded weapons within easy reach of the other two. It would have been a bit hypocritical of him to do so since his own handgun lay next to his beer. If it seemed odd for a priest to carry a weapon, well, Jenkins wasn't a normal priest.

"Oh, really?" Sam replied, narrowing his brown eyes slightly.

"Hey," Jenkins called out as he felt something begin to tug at the edge of his awareness. "We agreed on no mind control, so knock it off." He had been experimenting with letting his blond hair grow out a bit, and he scratched at it as the odd feeling made his head itch.

"What, me?" Sam winked innocently. "I have no idea what you're talking about. Surely, you aren't accusing me of violating our gentlemen's agreement?"

5

"That's it. I'm attacking Argentina from Brazil. Defend yourself, and kiss South America goodbye." As the dice rolled across the game board, Sam knew he had been beaten.

"It's not over yet, you two. I still have Australia." The defiance was clear, but there was a decided lack of hope.

"You may as well just surrender now."

"Fool, Australia is the key to the entire game, you know that."

"Sure," Marcus answered. "When you control Australia early and use it as a launching point for further attacks, but not when it's all you have left at the end of the game. That pathetic continent will be your tomb."

Sam glared daggers at the ghoul but could do little to prevent his eventual doom.

"You guys do realize that's just a game, right?"

The competitors' banter had allowed John and Danielle to enter the room unnoticed, but Danielle's question caused a small stir as Marcus nearly toppled the game board, trying to jump to his feet.

"Oh, calm down Marcus."

"Yes, milady," he responded as Danielle rolled her eyes.

Marcus had made it clear he would never drop the formality, and they had both long since given up trying to force him.

"How are you this evening?"

"I'm fine Marcus, thank you." She did her best to sound pleasant while John walked into the kitchen chuckling.

"Do you require anything, milady?"

"No Marcus, thank you." She was beginning to sound slightly less pleasant.

"You will let me know should you change your mind, milady," Marcus phrased the question as a statement.

"Yes Marcus, *thank you.*"

"You sound upset, milady. Have I offended you in some way?"

"Okay, enough is enough, you annoying—"

In a moment of clarity, Danielle realized what was going on, and the stupid grin beginning to touch the edge of Marcus's lips confirmed it. The "oh so formal" commander of their ghouls was playing her, and she fell for it.

"Oh, I should gut you, you little twerp."

"Of course, milady."

Danielle displayed her middle finger in a very human, albeit unladylike, gesture of defiance as Marcus retook his seat. Of course, what would have been a normal finger for a mortal was morphed into a wicked-looking vampiric claw. Any appearance of menace was lost, however, as John returned from the kitchen laughing so hard he was holding his sides.

"I . . . I can't b-believe . . . ," he said and paused a few seconds to draw a breath his body only required for speech. "I can't believe you fell for that. I read his intentions like a book the minute we stepped in and had to run into the kitchen since there was no way I would have kept a straight face. You should have seen the look on your face. Hah, I thought for a second you might attack him!" John threatened to start laughing again, but Danielle shoved him before he got the chance.

"Anyway, if everyone is done laughing and making fun of each other, do you two have any special plans this evening?"

"Nah, Sam, nothing beyond a nice midnight stroll. The night sky is so much more beautiful out here."

"Leo," Marcus called one of the ghouls who had been relaxing on a loveseat watching the game and nodded toward the kitchen. Minutes later, the ghoul returned with a pair of blood-filled thermoses, which the vampires accepted gladly.

"Mmm, you warmed it up. Thank you, Leo," Danielle said, smiling sweetly.

The ghoul blushed and bowed slightly, returning to his seat. Jenkins knew that despite appearances, the ghouls were not the simple servants they appeared to be. It could be argued that the term *slave* would better define the ghouls than *servant*, and many "experts" would have called them that, but Jenkins knew differently.

It was true that ghouls relied on vampiric blood for existence, so they literally lived or died at John and Danielle's whim. In that way, they were very much like slaves, but John and Danielle treated them like family. Each ghoul had a specific job, but the overriding responsibility they all shared was to the safety and security of their masters. Jenkins did not believe John and Danielle were the types of people—and to him, they *were* people—who considered being waited on hand and foot part of "safety and security." The fact was, every one of the ghouls did so because he or she *wanted* to dote on their masters' every need.

He had come to realize it was true loyalty, not fear or force, which spurred the ghouls to act this way. By not accepting the attention, the vampires would only succeed in insulting them.

So it was that John and Danielle had waited patiently for Leo to fetch the blood they were more than capable of retrieving for themselves and even pretended they would both be lost without the careful attention

7

of their many keepers. Being undead creatures of the night was no excuse for rudeness after all.

Jenkins could no longer even believe that at one time he had considered these two to be abominations of the night, bent on the destruction of innocent life. Though it had only been a handful of years, it seemed like another lifetime when he had not only been on the other side but had helped in the hunting of these very creatures. God himself, so to speak, had opened his eyes to the good that resided in them both, and he had suddenly realized he was on the wrong side of the conflict. His new vocation, thrust upon him by the pope himself, was to see that the vampires one day recognized that good for themselves.

"Back to the original point my darling wife was making," John's voice pulled Jenkins back to reality. "I'll admit that is a fun game, but to hear you guys talking, you would think lives were at stake." John chuckled slightly at his own comment while Danielle's eyes narrowed at the serious expressions of the three players.

"It is just a game," she chimed in. "The loser doesn't really die or anything."

"Well . . . ," Jenkins began but cut himself off.

"Well, what?"

"Well," he began again, "we sort of made a small wager to make it more interesting."

"Oh," Danielle shrugged. Gambling could make even the most childish game far more serious. "Whatever makes you happy, I guess. Out of curiosity, though, how much are you playing for?"

"Oh, we don't play for . . . ," Jenkins broke off when Marcus and Sam suddenly threw menacing glances in his direction, and he wore an expression that suggested he had said too much.

"For crying out loud," John took over. "Okay, spill it. What stakes did you crazy kids set for yourselves?"

The cat was out of the bag, and they had no choice but to come clean now. As the vampire, Sam had seniority, and he spoke for the others.

"Well, you see sir, money has no real meaning for us, so we came up with a wager that was not only better but much more realistic to the game."

John arched an eyebrow to encourage Sam to get to the point.

"The winner gets to shoot the losers."

"What?" John shot a look at his wife.

She nodded, confirming that Sam was being completely honest.

He then speared Jenkins with a glance. "You agreed to this insanity Priest?"

"Sure, why not? The winner gets to march the two losers out back and execute them. Sounded like fun to me."

"If you have a death wish, we can find more pleasant ways of ending your existence."

"First of all, I plan to win. Secondly, we obviously aren't going to kill each other. Since Marcus and I are mortal—well, sort of," Jenkins said, glancing at the ghoul, "we'll be wearing body armor." He added, "Sam, on the other hand, has to take it in the flesh. See? No killing, just pain and humiliation."

John had to remind himself that the man speaking to him was a devout priest.

"You're all sick, you know that?"

"Yes," came three near-simultaneous answers.

"Come on, husband." Danielle was getting bored with the insanity, "We're wasting moonlight."

While they walked past the board, she couldn't help but notice Sam was truly doomed and said, "Hey, whoever shoots Sam, I don't want any blood or guts on my flower beds. Understood?"

"Yes, ma'am."

She shook her head at her surrogate, and rather dysfunctional, family members and followed John out the door.

Danielle had to admit that her husband had a point about the night sky around their new haven. The light pollution, which was a given in any city, had obscured the sky from even their enhanced vision. It was still an issue in the suburb they now called home, but at least here their vision could pierce it well enough to properly enjoy the beauty of the stars. Unlike the mindless animals most vampires became, John and Danielle had never lost their appreciation for that beauty, which they enjoyed this night as they waved to the occasional neighbor.

Their vampiric eyes were able to see the stars as no mortal ever could—a clarity seen only by astronauts, mixed with the same twinkle of atmosphere that could never be enjoyed from space. Gone too were the annoying scents of garbage and too many mortals in a single place that pervaded the city air, replaced instead by the lovely smells of fresh cut grass and the flowers Danielle would never admit to loving. It would do no good for her reputation to admit to being enamored with something so "feminine" as flowers. Unfortunately, it was obvious that her feelings on the subject were well known. Why else would every single house in their new haven boast such beautifully maintained and extensive flower beds?

It was times like these that she could not help but think of how odd their current haven was, especially when compared to the obtrusiveness of the exclusive 5-star hotel that had been their previous home.

Subtlety was neither of the vampires' strong suits. However, since the hotel had come so close to becoming their final resting place, they had both decided to give subtlety a chance. It had taken three annoyingly boring years of living in a safe house to set the plan fully into motion, but the time was well worth it.

Jenkins had to get the credit for the initial idea, but it was Marcus's planning that had made it all come together.

One of the reasons having a hotel worked so well for them was that it satisfied the need for a large amount of living space. Two vampires did not need a significant amount of space, but they had over seventy surviving ghouls to worry about as well. Jenkins had suggested an interesting solution to the problem.

Why did they all have to live in the exact same building? As long as they were all close together, what difference did the living arrangements make? This led them to the horribly complicated, and yet unbelievably simple, solution of taking over an entire housing development in one of the distant suburbs of New York City. John and Danielle had both been against the idea initially, but after listening to Jenkins's argument, neither of them could fault the logic.

New housing developments were under construction all the time throughout the United States, and it was relatively common for large investment or real estate firms to buy and sell entire developments as if they were small commodities. It was not uncommon for a plot of land to change hands several times before construction was even started. With a bit of research, it was easy to find just such a development under construction about thirty miles outside the city limits of New York.

The real estate company had been hesitant to sell at first as the properties were in a prime location and expected to fetch quite a price. Offering them triple their already-optimistic projection of the total property's value, however, had quickly changed their minds. With the land firmly in their possession, construction continued as normal, and the rest was simply a matter of very complicated paperwork.

Posing as an investment firm, the vampires sold the properties one at a time to potential buyers over the next few years. Of course, every buyer who secured a successful purchase was a ghoul. The ghouls all used funds that had been given to them by the vampires themselves to get valid mortgage loans from real banks and close the deals on the homes. It seemed overly odd and unnecessarily heavy with paperwork, but the result was a legitimate paper trail that marked them all as valid homeowners with very real mortgages.

Some of their ghouls moved into houses on their own while some did so as couples, but there was plenty of space for them all. It had been a slow process, which was necessary to maintain the illusion, but it was worth it. This new haven was far more secure than any the vampires had ever enjoyed.

With every neighbor and passerby being an ally, they did not have to worry as much about prying eyes, and the entire development was blanketed with the latest and best surveillance equipment money could buy. It was nearly impossible for anyone, or *anything*, to get anywhere near the ancients without them being alerted, with plenty of time to prepare a defense. Even the roads were under strict control.

Housing developments were quite often separated from main roads. The side roads winding throughout a development generally did not go anywhere except to the houses within the specific development, with very few connections to the main roads. This being the case, the existence of only one single entrance and exit from their development did not seem unusual despite how large the overall development was.

In other words, there was absolutely no reason for any vehicle to ever enter the development without having strict business inside. The entrance and exit were both well seeded with electronic sensors that corresponded to tags attached to every one of their vehicles. An unknown vehicle could not so much as enter the development without setting off multiple silent alarms. The only problem with that system was the daily mail truck and other types of delivery vehicles, but that was what the cameras were for.

The entire project had taken years to finalize and cost more money than most millionaires would ever see in their lifetimes. The money was a nonissue, though, as the vampires had access to enough resources to make the richest man in the world a pauper by comparison.

The problem was in the logistics, and only Marcus's skill with paperwork made the entire project work so smoothly. He even turned the inside of the house intended for Jenkins into a beautiful chapel. The outside had to remain plain, of course, but Jenkins still wept with joy when he had been presented with the gift.

The need for a new haven was only the first of the two major problems the ancients had to contend with after the conflict with the Sword of God. While they had emerged relatively unscathed, their force of ghouls had been severely thinned.

Technically, it was not difficult to create new ghouls, but Danielle and John both refused to turn mortals against their will. Even if they were actively looking, it could take years to find a single mortal who both possessed the qualities they were looking for and desired the transformation. This problem was potentially more dangerous than the lack of a secure haven, for the ghouls were not only their faithful servants but their daytime protectors.

The solution to this problem came in the form of a mixed blessing.

While the SOG failed to destroy them, the final attack on their haven successfully sent one of their friends to his final death. As with any vampire with ghouls, Jose's destruction doomed them all. Without his blood to sustain them, there was no other possible result—that was, until Jasmine, Danielle's lead ghoul and easily the smartest individual they had ever come across, came up with a radical idea.

Since no one knew where vampires came from, there were certain things that were not quite understood. Certain things worked simply because they worked. No one knew why a ghoul was eternally linked to the blood of the vampire who created it; that was just the way it was. Jasmine proposed that it might be possible for them to sort of . . . redirect . . . the link of Jose's ghouls to themselves.

Power came to vampires with age. There were many things a vampire could learn to increase his or her abilities, but age was what increased the power of their blood and hence their entire beings. John and Danielle were much older than Jose, so their blood was so much more powerful that maybe the ghouls could be linked to them instead. No one really expected it to work, but considering that every one of the ghouls would die anyway, it was worth a shot.

The experience turned out to be rather unpleasant. Many of the ghouls did not want to try. They saw Jose's destruction as a personal failure, and many simply wished to die as punishment. Eventually, they were all talked into rolling the dice, and the process of weaning them onto John and Danielle's blood began—a process that could only be described as horrible.

Every ghoul was ravaged by horrid pains and retching, and all became comatose. Roughly half of them never regained consciousness and simply began rotting from the inside out. As horrible as it was, however, half the ghouls survived and slowly regained their strength. Since the initial prospect had been a long shot, this was counted as a tremendous success, and the ancients suddenly replaced some of their losses.

Danielle also found a willing subject in the form of an aging weaponsmith, after being impressed with his work. A combination of cancer and lack of ties to the mortal world convinced him to accept her rather unbelievable offer, and he seemed to be enjoying his newfound strength and vitality. The basement of his house was a bit larger than the others and was converted into a workshop based on his exact specifications, and he even found a willing apprentice among the older ghouls.

All in all, Danielle reflected, it was difficult to find anything wrong with their current situation. They were even in the process of setting up a new blood bank in the city. Surprisingly enough, the blood bank was turning out to be the easiest thing of all to take care of, and it was only a matter of time before that loose end would be tied up. It was hard to believe how well everything was falling into place when it had been barely a decade ago that they were facing almost certain destruction.

"Where are you, love?" John's query pulled her mind back to the present.

"Hmm?"

"You've been staring off into space for a few minutes now. I was just wondering where your mind was."

"Oh, I'm just thinking about how we got here and how things worked out all so well," she answered honestly.

John shuddered at his own memories of their recent conflicts, and his arm involuntarily tightened around his wife's waist.

"What's important, my darling, is that we are here now and as safe as can be expected for the likes of us."

While his comment rang true, he could not help but briefly relive their recent battles in his own mind. As harrowing as it had been for them all, it was Danielle who bore the brunt of the injuries. Despite not sharing her misgivings about their current security, it was only natural for him to want to comfort his wife.

They both knew how impossible their situation was, but like many other things, it was the way it was. While they were slowly coming to terms with the possibility that being a vampire did not necessarily make one evil, they both knew that every vampire had a very real demon deep inside, in the form of the bloodthirst they all felt. That same thirst caused so many of their kind to revert to a near-animalistic state and prevented even the best vampires from reclaiming many human emotions.

Most vampires had to spend eternity fighting to prevent being overwhelmed by their bloodlust. This struggle caused many vampires who lived long enough to become ancients to go thoroughly insane. In fact, the best a vampire could realistically hope for was contentment in what had become of their lives and maybe even appreciation for certain things, but love was an impossible goal.

They had met countless vampires in the near millennium since they themselves had been turned, and while most were demons in their own right, some were rather respectable beings. Even the good ones, however, admitted to being unable to love anything—at least anything positive—regardless of how hard they might have tried. Love was a trait of humanity, something a vampire could perhaps strive for but something they would never again attain.

John and Danielle were the exceptions to the rule. They loved each other fiercely with feelings that had only grown stronger over the centuries. The only explanation either of them could think of was the way in which they were turned. As mortals they were married, and it was on their honeymoon that they had been captured and turned.

Their love for one another had provided a sort of anchor for them as they clung to one another in the face of the monsters that they had become. Their inability to leave one another had also been the only thing that kept them from destroying themselves. As foolishly romantic as it all sounded, it truly was the only difference they could find that might explain their current situation. Even stranger was that their love even extended into the physical realm.

Physically, vampires were technically nothing more than very powerful walking corpses. Many vampires used sex as a lure for prey, but the physical enjoyment that was so much a part of sex was lost on them. They could mimic the act perfectly by directing their blood flow to the necessary areas, but their bodies were still dead. In this area, John and Danielle were again the exceptions to the rule.

Their bodies were no longer capable of producing the particular fluids associated with sex, of course, but they still derived considerable pleasure from the act. In fact, even after more than nine hundred years, their sex life was healthier than most newlywed couples. It was one more thing they were unable to explain, and they simply attributed it to the odd

14

circumstances under which they were turned. Explainable or not, they were both grateful for the seemingly impossible situation of which they were both a part.

They were both very curious to see if Sam would exhibit any of their irregularities as well. After leading their force of ghouls for over a century, he had become the first vampire they had ever created. Would sharing their blood, and having them setting the example for him for that long, cause his vampiric life to be as different as theirs? It was a question only time would answer. Whether he would be capable of ever experiencing true love for himself or not, at the very least, it should be far easier for him to remain one of the "good ones."

"I know it seems like we're safe and secure, husband, but I just can't convince myself that it's over."

There was no need to elaborate. John knew exactly to what his wife was referring. Nearly ten years ago, their existence was discovered by a militant branch of the Catholic Church known as the Sword of God.

The SOG had been created many centuries ago for the purpose of combating the physical manifestations of evil. The group was ordered disbanded when it was decided they were going too far by wanting to enlist the aid of werewolves to combat vampires for them. Unbeknownst to the Church, however, the group simply went into hiding, spending the next several centuries secretly building their power.

Through a series of desperate battles, the vampires were able to barely hold their own as the SOG poured ever-greater resources into what was fast becoming a war of extinction. John and Danielle sought out the pope himself in an effort to force them back, only to discover that he was as surprised as they were to learn of the organization's existence. In a final bid for victory, the pope actually held a press conference admitting the SOG's existence to the world and providing authorities with the extensive amount of information the vampires had acquired.

In a move that shocked them all, almost immediately following the press conference, the entire SOG simply gave up. Hundreds of thousands of individuals simply turned themselves in, confessing to being members—including the SOG's entire leadership group—almost overnight. It took months to straighten everything out, but by all accounts, the whole organization had simply dissolved.

The vampires were not about to look a gift horse in the mouth, but the whole incident raised many questions. They had been convinced then that there was something else going on, and the more information they got, the more convinced they became. It wasn't just that the SOG was dissolved, but when all the interviews and reports were finally gathered and reviewed, they made a frightening discovery.

The confessions and stories told by the various members throughout the world were nearly identical. Whether the individual was a simple foot soldier or one of the thirteen head cardinals, they confessed to the same exact things in almost the same exact way. Lie detector tests were even set up, yet no one failed. Church authorities eventually just shrugged their collective shoulders and proceeded to take them all into custody.

To confuse the situation even further, roughly six months after the incident, every single individual who had confessed suffered complete and simultaneous amnesia. Convinced some sort of conspiracy was underway, every test imaginable was done, but no explanation was ever reached. Everyone who had once been a member of arguably the most powerful organization in the world was now a little more than a raving lunatic. Whether or not something else was going on was no longer a question—but what?

The vampires waited years for the other shoe to drop, but nothing ever surfaced. They continued watching every avenue they could think of and even maintained regular contact with the pope. No explanation was ever discovered, and no evidence of outside involvement was ever found.

John was content to simply go about their lives, while remaining extra vigilant, but he knew Danielle's obsession would never cease.

She continued to blame herself for the entire situation. The SOG had made its first move against her, and her decision to allow her attacker to live and report back had caused the ensuing conflict. She missed the signs and assumed her attacker to be nothing more than a foolish lone hunter. She allowed pity to override good sense. John feared she would never forgive herself for that decision.

"I know, I know. Honestly, I find your obsession with this rather comforting."

She eyed him warily.

"Seriously, love. If someone did miss something along the way, I'm sure you'll detect it before it bites us in our collective asses."

"Well, thank you for at least making it sound positive."

"Of course. I am, after all, the big, strong man trying to comfort his wittle-bitty wife."

She elbowed him in the ribs before he could say anything else.

"Seriously, though," John said, making an overly dramatic show of rubbing his imaginary bruise, "I know you're right. I just don't see the situation as negatively as you do."

"What do you mean?"

"Well, I said it myself nearly ten years ago. Something else is out there, and it appears to be pulling the strings."

"Yes, I do remember you saying that, but you're telling me that doesn't bother you?" She eyed her husband with some confusion.

"Well, I guess it does a bit," John shrugged. "But here's the way I see it. There's an unknown player on the field with far more power than either of us can imagine. Whoever or *whatever* this new player is, *his*, *hers*, or *its* first open action was literally to save our asses from a bunch of religious fanatics. That's okay by me."

"Yeah, well, the enemy of my enemy is *still* my enemy until proven otherwise," Danielle hissed slightly at the end of her statement.

"How characteristically pessimistic of you, dear," he grinned. "I will say that I am certain of one thing. As sure as I am that I love you, I know we'll have answers eventually."

She cocked an eyebrow at him.

"Well, for good or ill, this person or thing saved us. It makes sense we'll eventually know why," he concluded.

She nodded in agreement to his final point as they continued their stroll through the night.

The creature was growing weary of waiting and had to constantly remind itself of the dangers of rash action. Eliminating the threat posed by the SOG was a calculated risk, but it appeared to have worked. The organization's interference was unforeseen, and they were nearly successful in destroying the creature's potential saviors. This could not be allowed. Influencing so many minds at once was not easy, however, and the creature was certain many innocents were touched as well and confessed to crimes they had nothing to do with.

The humans had a phrase for such occurrences. They called it "collateral damage," and the creature was content to leave it at that. The amnesia suffered by the victims was a necessary evil as well. It was the only way to ensure none of their minds reverted back to what they were. Wiping a mind clean was always easier than maintaining an illusion.

Unfortunately, there was another problem the creature had not foreseen. It had already made the decision to bring the vampires to its domain, but its summons was going unanswered. It had been calling to the vampires for years now, with no apparent effect. Either the creature's summons were being ignored or it wasn't being heard at all. Either way, it was faced with a dilemma.

More power was needed, but more power made it more difficult to focus the effort on the two he wanted. The minds of vampires "tasted" different enough from mortal minds that the two would never be confused regardless of the power used, but the creature only wanted two vampires, not all of them. There was a risk that if the summons was increased in power, it would touch all vampiric minds. Such an occurrence would be problematic.

So the creature had been slowly increasing its call, but to no avail. The vampires it wanted either had powerful mental defenses or heard the call and decided they did not care. Too much time and energy had been wasted already, and the creature saw no other option but to use all its power for a summons that could not be ignored. The consequences would be dealt with later; the first step must be taken.

Come to me! Come to me NOW, my children!

CHAPTER 2

"*AAH!*"

John and Danielle clutched at their skulls that felt ready to explode as they shrieked in agony and nearly fell out of bed. Unfortunately, being awake did nothing to silence the freight train screaming through their respective brains, and the thrashing merely succeeded in destroying a perfectly good down comforter.

"*AAH!* What the f—AAH!"

John briefly considered driving a claw through his own brain, but he couldn't concentrate hard enough to fully morph his finger into one. A loud thud announced his wife's failure to remain on the bed, and he could hear her thrashing about on the floor.

He was convinced they were under some sort of attack when, as suddenly as the pain had occurred, it vanished. John lay motionless for a moment, half expecting the pain to return or some sort of attacker to burst through the walls. When nothing happened, he carefully freed his legs from the sheets, where they had become hopelessly tangled.

"What the *hell* was that?" Danielle gasped, slowly pulling herself back onto the bed.

"I don't know, I'm just glad it's over," John answered, reaching to pull his wife closer to him. He opened his mouth to say more, but he was cut off by the sound of their bedroom door being kicked in.

Without thought they both pointed in the direction of their would-be assassin but held their attack when Marcus's face came into view.

"Masters, what happened?" he shouted the question even as he jumped through the ruins of the door, weapon at the ready, followed by the rest of his team.

"Relax, Marcus. We honestly have no idea, but it's over now, so there's no need to do any additional damage to our room." John eyed the broken door, which drew a small blush of embarrassment from the ghoul.

"My apologies, master, but we were unsure of what to do. At first, we believed the noises to be . . . um . . . normal." He coughed slightly, and it was Danielle's turn to blush. It was true that they tended to make considerable noise when left alone in their bedroom. "Anyway, it began to sound distinctly like you were both in pain rather than pleasure, but we were still unsure, so I called out to you. When no one answered, well . . . ," Marcus trailed off and shrugged his shoulders.

"No, you did the right thing," John said, waving off Marcus's apology. "I just wish I knew what that was. It felt like someone just drove a railroad spike through my skull," he absently rubbed his skull as Marcus ordered the other ghouls back to their positions.

"More like a steam roller just flattened my brain," Danielle countered. She had a haunted look in her eye, and John held her a bit closer.

He knew that his wife's more powerful mind also made it more receptive. Something that breached their mental defenses would always hit her harder and faster than him. For John, it was just a matter of tremendous pain, annoying but simply a symptom of life. For Danielle, it was a matter of control, and there was an element of fear added to the pain.

"I'm getting confirmation now for the all-clear," Marcus said, tapping his earpiece.

John knew that meant all the security checkpoints throughout the haven were reporting any disturbances, or lack thereof, to their commander. Of course, since disturbances were always reported immediately, Marcus's need to request updates was in itself a sign that there weren't any. Still, proper discipline and protocol had to be maintained, and it was always possible that a team or checkpoint could have been overcome before signaling a warning.

"All stations confirm, nothing to report," Marcus gave an unnecessary thumbs-up, as if they hadn't heard him. "I'll have that door replaced by the end of the night."

John hadn't even noticed the ghouls had already cleared the fragments away.

"Milord, milady," Marcus nodded briefly to each of his masters before turning to leave and nearly colliding with Leo, who had apparently charged into the bedroom at nearly a full sprint.

Marcus intercepted the seemingly insane ghoul while John chuckled quietly. Their ghouls tended to be so jumpy at times; it really was rather amusing. However, he felt his wife's body stiffen slightly, and all humor immediately vanished from his mind.

"What is it, love?" he asked.

But her eyes were locked firmly on Leo, who was still trying to catch his breath and speak at the same time.

"Leo?" Danielle called to the ghoul calmly but firmly until he finally looked up at her. "What's happened to Sam?"

"We were hoping you could tell us, mistress," Leo confirmed Danielle's insight into his thoughts.

The vampires quickly followed the ghoul across the housing development to check on their friend. They entered his bedroom to find a pair of ghouls keeping a confused watch over him, hoping to detect some sign of the problem.

"I heard a sharp cry of pain. There was no answer to my call, so I came in and found him simply lying in bed. He's been like this since we came to check up on him."

"You entered the room?" John made a show of looking at the intact bedroom door. "I don't see any shattered door fragments littering the floor."

Leo appeared confused by the statement and said, "Well, no, master. I just opened the door and rushed in." Leo was beginning to wonder if he had done something wrong.

"Interesting how easily you found it to simply open the door to check for threats rather than breaking it down." John looked rather pointedly at Marcus, who suddenly found the carpet to be rather fascinating. "Anyway, please continue."

Leo nodded curtly, dismissing the interplay at work.

"Well, at first, we were not concerned. As you can see, he appears to just be sleeping peacefully, but we were unable to wake him. It was possible he simply had some sort of nightmare." He looked questioningly at John, who nodded slightly.

Vampires tended to have dreams and nightmares just as mortals. A human brain was a human brain, after all, regardless of what changed about the body carrying it.

"We wanted to play it safe, especially when I noticed his eyes were still open. When we were unable to wake him, I got concerned, and when I heard Marcus's call, I knew something bigger had to be going on."

21

John nodded his understanding and looked at his friend once again. He had to admit, the scene was rather creepy. Vampires did not need to breathe unless talking, so Sam had all the appearances of a corpse with the sole exception of his eyes, which were eerily open and still full of life.

"Why didn't you report this when I called for the all-station check-in?" Having recovered from his brief embarrassment, Marcus asked a very good question.

"I'm sorry, sir. I thought the situation was potentially very serious and wanted to deliver the information as quickly as possible. Since there was no physical threat to be reported or need for backup, I thought speed and clarity were more important," Leo answered his commander's challenge.

"So rather than push the Transmit button on your radio, you left it here and ran across the entire housing development to find us, all in the interest of *saving* time?"

Leo opened his mouth to respond and shut it immediately. There was almost a visible light bulb winking above his head.

"Sir, I . . . I mean, I didn't—"

"He just panicked. Let it go, Marcus," John commanded. "We're here now, so let's get this thing figured out."

Marcus continued to hold Leo under visual scrutiny until the ghoul appeared properly chagrinned.

"Yes, master."

"Good. We're all thinking the same thing. Whatever happened to us must have happened to Sam at the exact same time. My guess is that while we were strong enough to come through it, it appears to have shut Sam down. What are you getting from him, love?"

Danielle had been ignoring the conversation since they arrived, instead concentrating on finding any clues that might be lurking in Sam's mind.

"Not much. He's in there, but that's all I can say. I will say that it doesn't feel like he's under attack. Whatever happened, it's over now. It just mentally overwhelmed him. I'd call it a coma if he was mortal, but as a vampire, I honestly do not know whether or not we should be concerned."

As peacefully as Sam appeared, it was difficult to believe anything was wrong.

"You are certain?"

"Yes. There is no conflict in his mind, no ebb and flow of thought, power, or emotions. If an attack were occurring, it would be easy to sense, even if he were losing."

The ghouls would not dare question her assessment, but John was still not convinced.

"What if it was an attack, but he already lost?"

"You don't understand. Mind control isn't as simple as just taking over someone's mind and leaving it at that. The mind gets suppressed and forced to obey your will, but somewhere in their subconscious, the victim is still fighting against you. As obedient as my victims may appear to you, the mental fighting never ceases until they either die or are released.

"True and absolute mind control is a myth. It is not a question of power, it's just the way the mind works. If you want the subject to obey you, something of themselves must remain in order to carry out your directions. You can choose to completely wipe a person's mind, but that's rather foolish since the result is a completely useless hunk of flesh. In that case, it would take far more effort to even force the empty shell to walk than it would be worth."

John was listening intently, for even after all this time, he did not completely understand how his wife's mind control worked.

"Wait a minute." A thought had occurred to John. "You're saying all our victims weren't the happy puppets you seemingly made them? They were actually writhing in mental agony the entire time?" John was suddenly very understandably concerned and upset.

While they continued to hunt mortals for blood, it had always been very important to both of them to make the experience as pleasant and safe for their victims as possible. After all, they weren't monsters. If what Danielle was saying was true, it meant all those happy faces they had fed on over the centuries were actually shivering in terror within their own minds.

"No, that's not what I'm saying." Danielle saw the confusion in her husband's eyes and sighed. "Look, just because you think all mind control is the same doesn't make it true. A mortal's mind is so weak that I don't need to actually take over it in order to force it to do my bidding. Powerful suggestion is all that I need in those cases, which results in the mortal agreeing with me rather than fighting me. Our enemies, on the other hand, aren't worth the consideration, so I flay their minds if necessary. You understand? Mind control equals bad things for the victim while mental suggestion can be quite pleasant."

"Okay, I get it." At least he thought he did. "And you already said that you did sense something in him, so we know his mind hasn't been wiped, and you sensed no conflict, so no ongoing attack or attempt to control. So what's left, and what do we do with him?"

"Honestly, he's most likely in no danger at all. There's nothing physically wrong with him, so there's not a drop of blood loss, and that's all that matters to us. My guess is that he'll recover on his own eventually. We should keep an eye on him. Maybe force-feed him a cup of blood a night, more if his skin pallor changes." She shrugged her shoulders, and it was clear she didn't find his condition serious.

"You heard her," was all John needed to say to get the ghouls to begin the necessary preparations. "Come on," John said, directed at Danielle. "I'm thirsty."

Back in their own kitchen, cups of blood in hand, the vampires pondered the situation. Realizing that Sam's condition was strange but not serious convinced them that the only way to help him was to figure out what had happened. As exciting as the night had begun, John was forced to agree with his wife that there seemed to be no threat. The incident had been tremendously painful and shocking, but it was too brief and lacked the follow-up an attack would have had. Had it happened to any one of them, it would have been easily dismissed as a quirk of being an incompletely understood powerful being. Happening to all three of them at the same time, however, spoke to another less random cause. But what?

"Communication," Danielle spoke the word softly, seeming to be talking to herself.

"Hmmm?" John, lost in his own thoughts, wasn't certain of what he had heard.

"What if someone is trying to tell us something?" his wife suggested.

"By giving us both a splitting migraine? I can think of better methods, but I'll bite. What makes you say that?"

"Well, I can't explain what that was, so I've been thinking over the last few years, and something strange *has* been going on."

John sat up a bit straighter and gazed at her more intently.

"I have felt something, call it an itch at the back of the mind, for quite some time now. With everything that has happened to us, it was simple for me to dismiss it as nerves mingled with some uncertainty over what happened with the SOG. After tonight, though, I wonder if it might be more than that. Tell me, husband, what would you do if you tried calling someone once a day, every day, and they never returned your call?"

"I don't know. Send them an email, or maybe just take the hint and leave them alone."

Danielle rebuked his flip demeanor with a sharp glance, but she shouldn't have been surprised at his answer. It was technically correct while purposefully missing the point he had to know she was trying to make.

"Fine, I'll rephrase the question. Assuming you had already decided that it was absolutely necessary to speak to the individual, what would you do if your calls and messages were consistently unanswered?"

Having already gotten in his joke answer, John considered the question more seriously.

"It depends. I guess if I knew where the person lived, I would try to visit them in person. If not, I would try to figure out some other method. Maybe call them at work where they would have to pick up the phone or something like that," he said as he shrugged and refilled his glass.

"In other words, you would strengthen your efforts?" she said and paused, waiting for him to nod before continuing. "Well, what if that is what is happening here? What if this itch I have been feeling is someone's attempt to communicate, and what happened tonight was the response to my lack of response?"

"It's creative, I have to admit, but I'm still inclined to think you're grasping at straws, except . . . ," he paused to consider his words while Danielle waited impatiently for him to continue. "I've been feeling the same thing as you, and probably for exactly as long."

Her eyes grew a bit wider at his response. "Why haven't you said anything about it?"

"Hey, first of all, neither have you. Secondly, I simply don't care. I admit to having felt this for quite some time, but when I initially established there was no threat, I simply began to ignore it." His tone made it clear that he was surprised she would ever expect him to do anything differently.

"To this day, the depths of your apathy continue to amaze me," she muttered.

"Apathy and ignorance, definitely the best way to spend eternity." John raised his glass in a mock toast, clearly taking her comment as a compliment.

"That wasn't meant as a compliment, but my point is, I think I'm on to something with this theory."

"In all seriousness, maybe you are, but two examples are not sufficient to establish a pattern. You know that two points . . ."

"Make a line, a third is necessary to establish a pattern," she finished the comment he was obviously going to make. "You're right, I do know, but what about Sam?"

"True. While he can't comment at the moment about any strange feelings, he was affected at the same moment we were. Okay, let's say you are right. What do the voices in your head tell us we should do?"

Danielle chose to ignore his phrasing while John chuckled at his own clever wording.

"I feel like we should go somewhere, but I can't be sure, and I definitely have no idea where."

"Marcus?"

"Master," answered the ghoul, never too far away.

"A world map please, and make it a big one."

"Of course. One moment, master." The ghoul hurried off to the vampire's library.

Danielle had an idea where her husband was going with his request, and she began to clear off the rather large, fixed table that stood as a centerpiece in their kitchen.

An outside observer might have found the sheer size of their kitchen strange, considering vampires had no need for solid food. The extensive assortment of expensive appliances and implements—the best money could buy, in fact—simply added to the mystery. In truth, Danielle rather enjoyed cooking, and her heightened senses gave her an advantage no mortal chef could match. The one disadvantage was her palate's lack of sensitivity, but there was never a shortage of volunteers to assist her in tasting the creations that came out of her kitchen. Even if it was true that actually eating was more trouble than it was normally worth for her, there were dozens of ghouls, and one mortal priest, who were more than appreciative of her talents.

Marcus returned, shortly after the tabletop had been cleared, and handed the map to John. Quickly unfolding the large map, he flattened it against the smooth surface of the table and oriented it so it would face his wife. The map was fairly big, but the world was a rather large place. Many of the countries appeared extremely small, but John figured if they could just get an idea, it would be easy to get a better map of the indicated area.

"Okay, Dani, you thinking what I'm thinking?"

"I believe so," she answered, examining the map.

"Could someone explain it to me please?" Marcus had been following the earlier conversation and could no longer hide his interest.

They both encouraged their ghouls to be inquisitive, so they couldn't very well fault his question.

"If we're right, something wants us to go somewhere. If that's true, it would make sense for that location to be told to us, otherwise we would never get there. It's quite possible the information has been repeated to us hundreds of times but we weren't listening. I'm hoping that since Danielle is the more sensitive one, if she relaxes and lets the information come out, we'll get some sort of sign."

Marcus nodded uncertainly, not wanting to point out how many assumptions were mixed into his master's reasoning.

"Okay, sweetheart, you're on. Pick out our next vacation spot."

He waited while Danielle began studying the map section by section. They both had the same idea but weren't sure how to go about acting on it.

"This isn't working," she declared after what felt like several hours but in reality had only been a few minutes. "Maybe I'm thinking about it too hard, like my conscious mind is overwhelming the small voice trying to give me the answer. What if we just wait? Now that we know to remain open to the possibility, we may be able to establish contact the next time whatever it is tries to communicate with us."

"Um, sweetie," John said, pointing at the map.

Danielle, following his gesture with her eyes, was astonished to see that not only was one of her fingers firmly pointing out a location, but the tip had morphed into a claw and made a very precise hole in the paper. Her jaw going a bit slack, she snatched her hand back as John leaned over the map.

"Marcus, get me every map we have on the Ottoman Empire."

The old vampire stared wistfully into his jeweled goblet before taking a long drink. He savored the overwhelming ecstasy that immediately coursed through his body. Allowing himself to enjoy the moment, he couldn't help but glance mournfully at the body of the young woman whose life now filled his cup.

Perhaps he should have exerted more control when draining her, but he had overindulged himself. It wasn't that he cared for her life, much to the contrary, but she was absolutely delicious. The young ones always were, and had he taken more care, this one could have easily lasted another few nights. On the other hand, he considered as he gazed into the ruby liquid, he was planning a trip, and the less baggage, the better.

"Igor, come out of there," the vampire spoke softly, but his voice carried to the far corners of the large room, and its command could never be ignored.

"Yes, master?" came the raspy reply as a hunched figure emerged from the shadows that permeated the room. The shadows did not, however, take away from the regal appearance of the vampire's throne room.

Rare paintings and various sculptures were placed in visually appealing locations, and gold reflected the small amount of light allowed into the room rather splendidly. The vampire's throne was worth a king's ransom in and of itself, but it had been carefully designed to not draw the eye away from its occupant. Gold and platinum had been seamlessly blended together and inlaid with jewels to create the rather exquisite throne, and it had the added effect of making it weigh as much as a small vehicle.

"Igor, you will prepare transportation for me immediately."

"Yes, master. Where is it you wish to go?"

"Insect!" He did not raise his voice, yet the word seemed to carry the weight of a physical blow, and anger flashed in the vampire's eyes as he snapped his gaze to focus on his servant. "You presume to ask a question of me? Do as you are instructed, or I shall rip out your throat."

"Yes, master, apologies, master." Igor quickly averted his eyes from his master's piercing gaze and began to cower. Arms too long for his body rose to defend his disfigured face from the expected punishment. When his master refrained from attacking him, Igor resumed his former position of deference.

"Just do your duty, and inform me when all is ready."

"Of course, master."

"Oh, and Igor," he said, indicating the young corpse with a wave. "A gift, dispose of it as you see fit."

The servant's mismatched eyes went to the corpse with excited longing. It was rare for the master to grace him with such a treat. His senses detected that the body was even still warm, and Igor's mind began to fill with the pleasure of expectation.

"Oh, thank you, Lord Dracula." Igor immediately began shuffling toward his prize.

Dracula observed his faithful servant with barely concealed contempt. Even though he could control all his servants' very thoughts, it was still good to give them the occasional gift. He was also in very good spirits this evening because he had just received an invitation to a party. He had suspected the call for months now, but last night had erased all doubts. The pain had been unpleasant but was easily forgotten.

He would finally have his answers.

CHAPTER 3

Gaziantep Ili, Turkey

The journey to Turkey, which John had to keep reminding himself was the Ottoman Empire's new name, had been thankfully uneventful. The recent security upgrades and procedures the world had adopted over the last few years made traveling by plane especially problematic for the two vampires unless they planned everything out well in advance. Of course, there were ways to circumvent even the most stringent of precautions, and having access to their vast resources had a way of helping things along.

Leaving the Continental United States was normally the only difficult portion of their journey, since once airborne they had the freedom to land at any private airstrip they could find. Their jet was customized for extra speed and to carry spare fuel, so they had a much greater range than would have been normal. A smaller jet could also make use of a greater number of airfields. John and Danielle would normally stow away aboard the jet early and simply wait in their adapted quarters. Their ghouls had more than enough skill and experience to handle the security measures and piloting without interference. The vampires would simply provide a destination, sit back, and wait.

This time around, they found a private airstrip outside of Gaziantep in the Gaziantep Province of Turkey. The airstrip was intended mainly for local use, and the appearance of their jet caused quite a stir at first. Of course, a liberal amount of currency quickly calmed the locals.

It was fascinating how easy it was to make friends in the private sector when one had money to spend. In a matter of hours, their jet had been elevated in status from an unwanted oddity to a local treasure. The promise of more currency also guaranteed that their ghouls and property would be left alone and well-guarded for as long as they needed.

The vampires had spent the last two hours following the "scent," which had brought them this far, and were currently strolling more or less east along the Merziman Brook. They seemed to be getting no closer to their goal, but they had at least seven hours of darkness remaining before a decision would have to be made. Danielle had wanted to move faster, but John had advised caution and received grudging agreement to his point.

"What do you think?" Danielle interrupted the long silence of their stroll with the simple question.

"This place is boring as hell if you ask me."

"Boring? I think it's beautiful out here," she said, frowning at his negative response.

"You always say that when we're in the middle of nowhere. I admit that it's clean and the air smells rather fresh, but you know I hate these arid climates."

She knew that John's comment wasn't directed at the weather or temperature, neither of which affected them anymore, but at the resulting plant life. Plant life was in abundance all around them, especially this close to running water, but anything larger than a bush was rare to find. Small plants and flat ground meant there was very little cover for them to use if needed, and that was what bothered her husband the most. They were stuck out in the open. Exposed.

"True, but even you have to admit the stars are nice out here."

John only grunted in response, but she did notice him looking up for a time. The cloudless sky and being in another hemisphere gave them a different view than they would have had from home, and they were both enjoying it.

"Hey, Dani, you remember that myth that vampires can't cross running water or something like that?" Gazing into the Merziman had brought the thought to mind.

"Um, I think so. Why?" She had grown accustomed to her husband's seemingly random mental wandering. It was easier to just go along with it.

"That never made any sense to me. I mean, why would we care about water, and how could water hurt us? Does that mean vampires aren't supposed to go out in the rain?" John's questions were annoyingly serious.

"How should I know? Are you telling me you're afraid of water now?"

31

"No," he said, sounding slightly defensive. "I was just wondering where that particular myth came from. I mean, most myths are based on at least a tiny bit of truth, so what kernel of truth is that one built around?"

She rolled her eyes. "Who cares? Mortals are stupid, there, is that good enough?"

"Want to go for a swim?" John said suddenly.

"What?"

"Let's go for a swim. Can't you smell how clean that water is? It'll be fun."

Danielle had already figured out where her husband was going with this and decided it would be easier to just play it out.

"Neither of us brought swimsuits."

"That's why I said it'll be fun," he responded with a mischievous grin, and she rolled her eyes again.

"Aren't you clever? Now that that's out of your system, can we please focus on the task at hand? Something doesn't feel right."

Her soft warning succeeded in killing John's levity. "What's wrong?"

"I don't know, but haven't you noticed that there's nothing else living around here other than plants?"

It was both true and mildly disconcerting. While large game was rare in areas like this, there should have been a myriad of smaller species present in abundance. Arid climates tended to have very active nocturnal life since the temperature was so much more pleasant once the sun went down, but there wasn't as much as a single insect or lizard for miles. It was possible that it was in response to the two predators traveling through their domain, but having learned from past mistakes, they were masking their presence.

"You're right, but we're far from alone. I'm guessing that our friends' presence answers that particular mystery."

Danielle cast a surprised sidelong glance at her husband, then narrowed her eyes slightly as she extended her senses. It wasn't long before her eyes shot wide in shock, and she bared her fangs reflexively.

"How long have you known?"

"About thirty minutes so far."

"And you were going to share this information with me *when*?" she demanded accusingly.

"Sorry, but they're acting very strangely. I wanted to analyze their movements for a bit to be sure my theory was correct before concerning you."

"Fine, but if we're going to divide responsibility for watching our surroundings, I would expect that we would point out oddities immediately, not after they've been *analyzed*," she nearly spit the last word.

John nodded his apology. His wife was still a bit jumpy about having been taken by surprise more than once by the SOG years back. He should have kept that in mind and told her about what he had sensed.

They had decided to play it safe and divide their efforts. Rather than both of them keeping watch on everything, Danielle concentrated her efforts on their immediate surroundings while John focused on everything long-range. To take them by surprise, an attacker would have to first escape John's concentrated senses (which no one had ever done before) and then breach Danielle's (which had only technically occurred twice before and neither time had she been properly applying herself).

So it was that John had noticed the rather large gathering of vampires that seemed to surround them nearly half an hour ago. He was being serious when he said that they were acting strangely, so he made the decision to keep the news from his wife on purpose. Tracking their movements was simple for him, but there were so many it was difficult to tell if they were getting any closer. He had been waiting to see if Danielle would notice them, and since she hadn't, it meant they were keeping their distance.

"Well, I think I know what's going on, but I can't say I like it."

"Obviously, we're surrounded."

"Yes and no," John corrected.

"Sorry, husband. Being in the middle of a mob seems pretty surrounded to me. Damn, there must be hundreds of them."

"Exactly, we're in the middle of a mob. We're not being surrounded by an attacking force, we simply ended up in the middle. We're traveling using every active defense we know of. The reason we're in the middle is that our defenses are keeping everything at a distance without them even knowing it."

Danielle considered it briefly but then shook her head. "It makes sense, but we're not strong enough to hold back that many vampires."

"True, but they *don't know* we're here. They're all following something, probably the same something we're following, and they aren't close enough to see us. With all our defenses up, even another vampire would have to be very close to see or sense us, and that's only if the vampire is actively looking. Since none of them are, they're sort of being guided around us. I bet if you looked down at us, you would see the two of us surrounded by hundreds of others but with a perfect bubble of open clear space in between."

She was slowly nodding along with his explanation. It seemed plausible, and she couldn't think of anything better.

"Okay dear, but that's not our only problem."

John turned at his wife's comment to see her pointing rather threateningly at a nearby bush.

"Um, that bush is a bit dry and scary-looking," he began in a slightly mocking tone, "but I don't think it will attack."

"Moron. That bush should be a pile of ash right now."

John suddenly turned serious at the implication and gestured at the scraggy bush himself, intending to send a stream of fire into it. Nothing happened.

"Our magic isn't working," he couldn't help but state the obvious.

"No, we're being suppressed. Nothing elemental is responding. My mind control still works, fat lot of good it'll do us though. This changes things."

John nodded in agreement to his wife's understatement.

They were outnumbered literally hundreds to one. Even against mortals, those would be steep odds due to the attrition factor. Against other vampires, fledglings or not, it could mean certain death. Magic could level the playing field by sheer crowd control, but without it, they could be easily surrounded and overwhelmed. A new tactic was needed, and quickly, while they still possessed the element of surprise.

"All right, I have an idea. Do you—"

"Wait," Danielle cut him off. She had stopped moving and was facing him directly. "I don't like this at all. At first, we thought we were just going to find some answers, at worst more questions, but this is starting to smell very wrong. Hundreds and hundreds of other vampires, something very powerful suppressing our magic, and who knows what else lies ahead? What if you're wrong about the other vampires not being aware of our presence? What if someone or something else is just making it appear that way? We're walking into a trap."

The uncertainty in her voice was an unfortunate by-product of their encounter years before. Being caught off guard twice, and nearly destroyed once, had left his wife scarred and paranoid. Still, it didn't mean she was wrong.

"You might be right," John acquiesced. He motioned for them to start moving again.

The rear of the mob was getting too close for comfort, and proximity could undo their shrouds at any time.

"But we've come too far to turn back now. I want answers, and I'm not leaving until I get some." There was no room for argument in his voice, and she knew it.

"I want answers too, but I'm tired of fighting for my survival. We're strong enough to stay hidden forever, and yet we end up running around and attracting attention from the only things in the world that can actually threaten us. I don't want to fight anymore." Her statement was more of a plea, and a large part of him was on her side.

"Okay, my love, here's the deal. We can't turn back without a fight now, but this is it. We get to the bottom of this, find our answers, and then we're done. Next monster or hunter we see, we turn around and run the other way." He mimicked turning and running with his fingers. "Just you, me, and margaritas on the beach."

"Margaritas on the beach?" she sounded unconvinced.

"Okay, maybe cups of blood on the couch." He thought for a moment then added, "And Sam, Marcus, and the others will probably be there, but we can watch a beach scene on the plasma at home."

His effort was rewarded with a small giggle.

"Promise?" Danielle said.

"I promise, honey."

"Deal," she said and took an unnecessary deep breath. "So what's your idea?"

John smiled, satisfied that his wife's head was back in the game.

"Well, can you tell where we're headed yet?"

"Yes," she nodded in the darkness. "You were right, we're heading directly for Rumkale settlement. It's about fifteen miles ahead of us."

John wasn't surprised, but he had to make sure.

The fortress at Rumkale was older than both of them combined, and its age alone accounted for the area being steeped in mystery. Originally built around 840 BC by the Hittites, the fortress had changed hands more times than anyone could keep track of. Having been built on top of a cliff on a small peninsula overlooking the Euphrates River and Merziman Brook had given the fortress major strategic value. It was even said that St. John, one of the original apostles, had once used the fortress as an outpost when attempting to convert the area to Christianity.

Little remained of the original fortress today except for the main walls, a few small structures, and a lot of rubble, but it was still the largest fortress in the province. Few locals would go near the area, even during the day, and even tourists avoided the fortress at night. Since he had seen the fortress on the map, John had known it would be their destination.

"Okay, our best chance is to simply assault through. We can move faster than any of them, and we have the element of surprise. So just charge straight toward our destination, and kill anything in the way, but don't deviate. We should leave most of the mob behind us."

"Got it," Danielle nodded. "But what happens once we get there?"

"One problem at a time, sweetheart. Ready?" John drew his sword and extended his claws.

"Ready," Danielle answered, mirroring his actions and baring her fangs as well.

Now, John issued the silent command, and they both blurred into motion.

There was no need for Danielle to lead anymore, so John stayed a step ahead in order to bear the brunt of the pending attack. They knew it would only be seconds before they made contact, and most likely, every vampire in the area would immediately sense them. A few might avoid the ancients, sensing the pair's power, but for most, that power would attract them like moths to a flame.

The first engagement was a simple slaughter as three vampires sensed a presence behind them and then simply ceased to exist. As the first strike went home, it was as if a switch had been flipped throughout the mob. Hundreds of vampires suddenly changed direction and charged the ancients as one. Most were already too far behind to affect the outcome, but there were still more enemies ahead of them than they could count, and every brief encounter could potentially slow their progress.

John plowed through the mayhem, sword flashing and claws striking at any target unfortunate enough to be in range. He could hear Danielle hissing challenges and engaging her own targets off to his right. Their elemental magic was useless, but he could feel her increasing the power of her sheer presence. Many of the younger vampires were unable to close in to attack as they were stunned in awe by her dominance of the area.

The pair continued charging on a straight path, but as more and more of the mob turned to engage them, the scene quickly dissolved into utter chaos. Heads and limbs were severed, bodies were gutted, and ash filled the air, but they were beginning to get bogged down. The rush of attackers was thickening rather than thinning, and John quickly recalculated their odds.

So far, their injuries were rather minor, the occasional claw or fang that managed to slip through. Nothing that couldn't be quickly healed, but there was no end in sight. If the rear of the mob caught up to them, they would be overwhelmed and overrun.

Too slow. More running, less fighting.

Danielle responded to the order with a burst of speed that put her quickly into the lead.

Not wanting to be outdone, John followed suit, and they charged directly into the center of another wall of vampires side by side.

Dispatching the four vampires in reach had been easy, but the sides of the enemy line had folded backward in an obvious attempt to encircle them. The maneuver had been too slow to be effective, but the attempt had come as a surprise. Ganging up on the two strongest vampires in the area was relatively normal, but actually working together was a far more disconcerting story.

This doesn't make sense. Why are they working together? Danielle asked.

I don't know, John replied. His wife's earlier warning about a trap began to echo in his mind, but John ignored it. *Focus your control ahead of us. Confuse them.*

I've been trying. The resistance is too strong, she responded.

John's eyes narrowed in suspicion. There was no way any of their attackers were strong enough to resist Danielle's focused control. The unknown variables in this battle had reached an unacceptable level, and disengaging was starting to seem like a good idea, but it wasn't a viable option. Mist-form would be the only true way to escape, but there were a few stronger vampires scattered through the mob that could possibly track them until they reformed. It would end up being an enormous waste of blood they couldn't afford to lose.

Follow my lead, he said.

Without waiting for a response, John deviated from their straight-line path and charged the nearest cluster of opponents. Rather than moving straight through them with surgical strikes, he expended extra effort to rip them all apart. Danielle quickly understood the new strategy and moved to find her own prey.

John's idea was simple. Something had to be controlling these vampires, but they were still vampires. The more violence, and especially the more blood spilled, the greater the chances of a vampire entering into a blood frenzy. It was difficult for Danielle to control even a single vampire whose mind frenzied, and there were hundreds being controlled at once here. If enough of them could be driven over the edge, it would certainly shatter whatever control was forcing them to work together. Once they began turning on each other, John and Danielle could use the ensuing madness to cover their escape. The only true risk was whether or not they could hold out long enough for the plan to work.

Seconds seemed like minutes, minutes like hours, hours . . . well, John had a feeling they wouldn't last long enough to know what hours felt like. The pair slowly moved closer together in order to better support each other's attacks, and before long, husband and wife were fighting back-to-back. They were far faster than any of their attackers, but there were so many of them—too many to keep track of, John realized as he felt a sharp pain in his shoulder. He spun to decapitate the offending vampire and noticed Danielle's face was marred by an ugly gash.

Movement in any direction was now impossible, and the couple abandoned aimed strikes in favor of sweeping attacks. They couldn't keep track of what was happening anyway, so it made more sense to simply swing their swords and claws in wide arcs and random directions. The change in tactics paid off as they were now hitting multiple opponents with each strike.

Unfortunately, John and Danielle began to feel another opponent in the distance. So much violence and blood was beginning to have the same effect on them that they were trying to force on their enemies, and John could already feel his thirst growing. As much as they both needed blood, there was no time to drink, and being surrounded by so much of it was making it even worse.

The tide finally seemed to be turning. However, as John could at last see past the thrall of attackers, what he saw instead caused what was left of his undead heart to break. Scores, if not hundreds, of additional vampires were mere seconds away from joining the attack. They had been immobile for too long, and the rest of the mob had caught up. No fresh power or clever trick could save them from a fresh onslaught of so many.

I was wrong, he said to her in his mind. As his heart broke with the knowledge that he had led his wife to her final death, not to mention his own, he could think of nothing else to say.

Don't be so quick to apologize, she replied.

The levity in her thoughts caught him off guard until he finally sensed what she had already noticed. The new wave wasn't rushing in to attack them specifically; they were simply rushing in to attack. John even saw some of the lead elements already tearing into the rear of their current opponents.

Insanity was the only way to describe the next few moments. Blood was so thick in the air they could almost drink by simply inhaling, and the other vampires were beginning to go wild with frenzy. It started happening slowly at first, but the sight of other vampires in a blood frenzy sent the others over the edge, and before long, it was every undead creature for itself.

The situation was far from safe, but it was no longer desperate. They redirected their efforts away from the bulk of the mob and before long broke free from the mass of bodies. After covering a few miles, John slowed to a normal walk to ensure nothing was following them. Reasonably certain of their safety, he felt it was a good time to take stock of their injuries.

"Well, that was fun," he mumbled to no one in particular. "You okay?"

"Nothing that won't heal, but you owe me a new shirt."

John noticed the right side of her shirt was badly torn, exposing the sports bra she preferred for combat, and he cocked his head slightly.

"No problem, I can fix that."

Before she could move, he deftly tore the shirt off completely, making sure to sever one of the bra's shoulder straps as well.

"There, all better," he said with an evil grin.

"You're such an ass," she growled while fishing another black shirt out of her pack.

"Yep, and you're sexy," he responded, still grinning.

"You knew I only brought the one bra." She refused to give him the satisfaction of taking it off, preferring instead to tie the severed strap together.

"That looks uncomfortable."

"Whatever," she said, rolling her eyes. "You know, I had a gift for you, but you can forget it now."

"Aw, don't be—"

He spun around suddenly, claws out and ready, as a pair of vampires ran toward them.

"Calm down, they're with me," Danielle warned before he could strike.

As the vampires drew closer, John was able to see the oddly vacant expressions they were wearing.

"How did you control them so thoroughly after they frenzied?" John wondered aloud, all lewd thoughts suddenly leaving his mind.

"I didn't. I just wiped their minds completely. It was rather simple actually and, I imagine, extremely painful for them. Making them follow us was a bit more difficult, and I couldn't make them move very fast, so it took a bit for them to catch up. I figured we could use a snack."

"Can I have one?" he asked. A gallon or two of vampiric blood would go a long way toward easing his thirst.

"Well, I did bring two for a reason, but that was before I was brutally sexually harassed. In fact, I think this could be classified as sexual assault. I think I need the extra blood now to heal my mental trauma." She crossed both arms and began tapping her foot.

"You're not serious, are you?" He wouldn't put it past her to try and teach him some sort of lesson.

"That depends. Apologize."

"For what?"

"I'm waiting, and I don't think we should stand here much longer."

"Fine," he exclaimed, a bit exasperated. "I'm sorry I tore your shirt off and ruined your bra. I'm sorry you didn't have the foresight to know I would probably do something like that at some point on this trip and pack extra bras. A woman's body is more than just some plaything, and I should respect that, no matter how much fun playing with the particular body in question is," he said, trying to appear contrite and raising an eyebrow.

"Your apologies need work, but good enough."

The pair wasted no more time on banter and leaped on their meals. The vampires were fledglings, but vampiric blood was so much more potent than that of mortals that it did wonders for them. Injuries completely healed, their pallor changed back to normal, and finally, they felt far more energized and prepared to meet whatever came next. Not wanting to waste a single drop, they drained both vampires quickly and completely. The two hadn't been old enough to turn to ash, but the bodies were noticeably desiccated and partially decayed when the ancients were finally done with them.

"Ah, much better," John said.

Danielle was too busy licking her lips to comment.

"Let's get moving, we still have a few miles to cover," he urged.

With that, the couple left the raging melee far in the distance.

Dracula had been watching the entire scene below with considerable interest and was more than a little impressed with the couple's abilities. When he first arrived in the area several hours ago, it was quickly apparent that he was not alone. Being in no particular rush, Dracula explored the area and came across the vast mob of vampires some time ago. He also noticed the pair of ancients traveling in the center.

This was not the first time he had encountered vampires not of his own creation, but never before had he seen so many. The couple in the center were also far more powerful than any other vampire he had ever met, excluding himself. Were they the sires of this other vampiric family? Was this their army? Had they struck their own deal with the same dark creature who had visited him so long ago? Why were there two of them? So many fascinating questions.

He realized that they must be here for the same reason. The call he had heard had not truly been meant for him alone but apparently all vampires everywhere. It was a bit disheartening, but he simply adjusted his plans and moved on. The wise quickly learned that not all information was welcome but all information was power, and plans needed to be adjusted immediately upon learning new things.

Whatever was at the end of this particular journey, Dracula had no intention of sharing. The mob was laughable, but the couple at the center were older than even he, and he was marveling at their power. It surrounded them like an aura, and he couldn't help but reach into their minds to learn more. It was too risky to reach far, so he was careful to limit it to just a taste—but what a taste! The instant he felt the pleasure, Dracula was quick to withdraw his mental touch, wary of going too far. It was enough to confirm that the other vampires weren't their direct minions as he had originally assumed.

The couple gave no sign of being aware of his touch, which confirmed one of his suspicions. Individually, he was still the stronger. If they fought together, however, his victory was no longer assured. He wondered again what two vampires of their power were doing traveling together in peace anyway. Oddities were quite entertaining in theory, but in reality, he preferred things to make sense.

Vampires were not always solo creatures, but there was always a hierarchy involved—one leader with younger, less powerful minions for example. He had even known vampires of the opposite sex to join together on occasion to try in vain to rekindle some lost aspect of their former humanity. Even in the latter cases, however, there was always a leader and a subordinate. Vampires simply did not know how to work and play well with others. In order to travel in groups, one had to demonstrate his or her power, and the others simply followed through fear and necessity—safety in numbers and all that. At least that's what his limited experience with this other vampiric family had told him.

The giant mob was odd enough, but that could be explained by the pull that he even now felt himself. The pair in the center obviously felt it too, but they were strong enough to not be overpowered by it. They were traveling together by desire, not happenstance. The male appeared to be the stronger and the one in charge, but the female was not interacting with him as a subordinate should. They were acting as equals, and Dracula was decidedly baffled by the situation.

Still, the missing information could be filed under "interesting but not relevant" since it did not change what he intended to do. The two would have to be dealt with if he wanted to finish this journey unhindered. Unsure of his abilities against both of them united, he contemplated how to best turn the mob against them. It was obvious that their power was keeping the mob at a distance, so how could he interrupt that without exposing himself to the inevitable battle?

As it turned out, he didn't need to do anything. He saw the pair suddenly dash to one side of the mob in an attempt to break free. Maybe they realized being in the middle of the mob was too dangerous. Perhaps they never intended for that to happen, and it was merely a result of their power, causing the others to flow around them. Being forced to remain on the ground did tend to have unfortunate travel consequences, and Dracula was once again thankful for the extra powers granted to him by the cape he wore.

Mortal eyes could never track the ensuing struggle, but his could, and they widened in appreciation. They were good—and faster than he expected. Every strike was surgical in precision, and every move one of them made was done to support something the other one did. He amended his earlier hypothesis. There was no way he could best them both at once in a purely physical encounter. They fought as one supreme unit, almost as if they had practiced this exact battle before arriving, which was, of course, impossible. Dracula had no experience fighting side by side with anyone, much less the same person, for centuries, so he could not fully understand what he was watching.

The male was naturally taking the brunt of the assault, but the female was no slouch. Dracula was beginning to appreciate something else as well, as he considered the female a bit more carefully. He had often wondered what it would be like to have a queen at his side, and what better match could there be? Her appearance was as delicious as her power, and she clearly had not turned into the ravening animal so many vampires were destined to become. With enough time and effort, he could easily subvert her mind and make her his pet. It would be quite the unexpected reward for his journey, but the male would have to be dealt with first.

As the mob began focusing its attention on the couple, Dracula began focusing his attention on the mob. Slowly and subtly, he extended his influence across hundreds of minds. It was a strain, even for his power, but Dracula knew what he was doing. He was not trying to control any of them, simply directing their efforts. The mob was already heading for the fight; he was just controlling various groups' speeds and directions. His influence also had the added benefit of protecting most of the mob from the female's mind control. That power had been unexpected, but he should not have been surprised. They were, after all, even older than he was. It made sense they would have a few tricks up their sleeves.

As the battle raged on, he directed more and more attention to the male. The couple's strikes lost their precision, but Dracula was experienced enough to refrain from claiming victory. It was simply a change in tactics on their part, rather than exhaustion. Their powers, on the other hand, had ceased to impress him. They were extremely powerful, but the powers themselves were nothing special.

Strength, speed, claws, and a little mind control were all he had witnessed, and almost every vampire could do those things. To be fair, these two were doing those things on a level he had never before witnessed, but he had been hoping to see something . . . special or different. As far as he was concerned, the battle was over since it was merely an endurance test now. Even if they both survived the mob, he would simply swoop down and destroy the male while he was still weakened.

Dracula spent the next several moments watching the battle and delighting in the thick scent of blood in the air. The pair were no longer healing their minor injuries, a sign of exhaustion among vampires, and it was clear their end was near. It was then that Dracula felt something odd in his mind. It was absurd, but his hold on the mob was weakening. Earlier he had felt the female's weak attempt at control, so how could she be winning now?

The problem with being at the top of the food chain for so long was that one tended to forget how to recognize failure, assuming they'd ever learned in the first place. Dracula had no idea what was happening and the fact that the female had nothing to do with it, at least not directly. No one he had controlled had ever broken free from him, so he had no idea what it felt like when the victim's mind fought back after having already been broken. It never occurred to him that vampires in frenzy were harder to control, simply because he had never been in that situation before.

So when the couple enacted their latest plan, Dracula did not realize what they were doing. If he had understood, he would have had plenty of time to sever the mental link on his own and save himself. Unfortunately, information was, indeed, power, and this was information he lacked. So when the mob frenzied, he was unprepared for the mental backlash that smashed into his skull like Thor's own hammer.

He reeled, as if from a physical blow, and immediately lost control of his cape. The impact was more painful than anything he had experienced in recent memory or would have been, had he not already been clutching his skull in agony. As intense as the pain was, it was shock more than anything that had stunned the old vampire. The couple had somehow mentally defeated him without even knowing he was there, and he was certain that his presence was still unknown. The raging melee had easily covered his screams and fall.

Not wanting to take unnecessary chances, however, he quickly gathered himself and levitated back to a safer altitude. Once secure, he watched as the mob continued tearing itself apart with his main targets mysteriously absent. They had not gone far, but Dracula had not survived this long by rushing in hastily. He still had no idea how they had escaped, nor did he have an idea of their endurance limits.

Certainly, attrition must be taking its toll on them, but there was no way to tell how much. It was also possible he had misjudged their overall power. It would be best to remain hidden as long as possible to ensure rapid escape, should it be required. No, what he needed right now was cannon fodder to run a test or two. Fortunately, that was exactly what minions were for.

CHAPTER 4

Rumkale Settlement, Turkey

"Great, now what?" John mumbled in annoyance.

Danielle simply groaned. They had just arrived at what could be considered the front doors of Rumkale to find the entire fortress bathed in pure darkness. The sky was clear, and the moon was full. It was the vampiric equivalent of high noon, so the darkness was obviously supernatural, which meant this was clearly another trap.

"Maybe we're simply being tested?" Danielle offered.

"Come again?"

"Well, you said yourself, anything this powerful could just come right out and kill us, so why bother with all this? Maybe we're being tested for worthiness or something like that?" she said, curling her lip a bit, as if she didn't much believe her own theory.

"So we're being philosophical now?"

"You have a better idea?"

"As a matter of fact, I do." With that, John immediately turned and charged the entrance, claws and sword at the ready.

"John, wait!" Danielle tried calling after him, but it was pointless.

He was in one of his moods and was immediately enveloped in darkness upon crossing the fortress's threshold.

"Whatever, guess I get to bail your ass out," she muttered while literally stomping into the darkness after her husband.

"Kinda freaky actually, but I have to admit, I sort of like it."

Danielle just shook her head and examined their surroundings. The rubble-strewn dirt floor was clear enough, but blackness permeated everywhere else. Their senses were too confused to be helpful, and not even moonlight was shining through from above. It was easy to dismiss the darkness as simply an odd pattern of shadows, but their earlier suspicions were quickly verified.

The darkness was too complete, too solid-looking, and it extended everywhere they looked. It was as if the pair had been dropped into some sort of black bubble. There was no obvious threat at first, but it was clearly another trap. The vampires reflexively looked at one another, only to see nothing but more blackness.

"Dani?" John called, his voice having an edge of uncertainty to it. Situations wherein he could not clearly visualize his enemy tended to make him nervous.

"John," Danielle answered, hearing his call and feeling his growing anxiety. "Calm down, I'm right beside you." She reached out to her right until she felt his arm.

The physical contact immediately dispelled a portion of the illusion, and they were once again visible to one another. Danielle could see the obvious relief in her husband's eyes, but their overall situation remained unchanged.

She slowly released John's arm and sighed in relief as the wall of darkness that had previously separated them failed to reappear. Having overcome the first obstacle, the pair began a more careful examination of their surroundings. Upon closer inspection, they could see the darkness was actually moving all around them. The density seemed to be shifting constantly, and certain areas were moving in and receding seemingly at random. Unsurprisingly, John began attacking the closer shadows with both sword and claws, although neither seemed to have any real effect. The shadows would simply dissolve back into the mass surrounding them.

"John, you're wasting energy. It's all just an illusion."

John lowered his sword in response to her comment, and the shadows attacked without warning.

A tendril of darkness shot from the wall and speared him through the shoulder before he had time to dodge. His answering cry carried more anger than it did shock and pain, but the shadows were clearly unimpressed. The tendril lifted John off the floor and began shaking him like a rag doll before Danielle dissipated it with a strike from her sword.

"Just an illusion," he growled, picking himself off the floor while clutching at his bloody shoulder.

Danielle felt guilty for being fooled, but she only had enough time to shrug meekly before one shadow became a dozen and attacked together.

Knowing now to take them seriously, the pair began quickly counterattacking anything that came within reach. The situation seemed confusing and desperate, but the battle, in reality, was very simple. It was never good to be trapped and on the defensive, but the actual combat lacked the challenge they had both expected. Even more confusing was that despite the number of shadows, which was continuing to increase, the fight was getting easier for them.

"Why does this seem so easy?" Danielle shouted the question, not wanting to waste energy focusing on mental communication.

"I think you were partially correct before. This is some sort of illusion," John answered in between strikes.

"Pretty damn painful for an illusion," she muttered as another shadow slipped by her defenses.

"I mean these shadows aren't real. Someone or something is creating them. We're only fighting one attacker. That's why the shadows get weaker as their numbers increase." John had to cut his explanation short as the shadows redoubled their efforts. It was as if their true attacker heard him and was beginning to get nervous.

Danielle had heard enough, however, and his theory made enough sense to act on.

She took a step behind John and allowed him to reflexively defend her as she began to concentrate on finding the real threat. Danielle focused and began reaching out with her mind to the area around them. Her reach was blocked when it encountered the barrier of darkness, but she knew she had to see past the barrier in order for them to escape the trap. Rather than expanding in all directions, she tried picking a single point and focusing her efforts on a narrow band.

Danielle wrestled with the barrier for what seemed like an eternity. All the while, she was shutting out the sounds of battle and trying to ignore the fact that John was fighting alone and trying to protect the both of them. He had no idea what she was trying to do, but he never asked. He knew that if she wasn't fighting, there was a reason, and he would defend her as long as he was able.

Finally, Danielle let out a mental cheer as her senses broke through. The moment was rather anticlimactic as there was nothing on the other side except a stone wall, but that was not unexpected. If John was right, she was looking for only a single attacker, who could be anywhere outside the barrier. Fortunately, having created a hole in the barrier's power, it was easy enough for her to funnel her senses out and around, and within seconds, she had located the source of the attacks.

47

A lone creature was standing suspiciously close to the barrier on the right side. Not human, but beyond that, she was unable to tell. A second check verified the creature was the only living, or unliving, being anywhere around them. It wasn't quite cold hard proof, but it was good enough under the circumstances. She locked onto the location with her mind and pulled her senses back to the battle at hand.

"There!" Danielle wasted no time in shouting the command and charging the barrier.

It was possible the creature had noticed her mental probing, and she wanted to attack before he, she, or it could react. To John's credit, he never hesitated but simply slid into motion behind her at the sudden command.

He had no idea what was going on, but since Danielle was suddenly charging the darkness, John knew they weren't fighting the shadows anymore. The shadows responded to their sudden change in tactics by doubling yet again and increasing in speed. His wife was ignoring the new onslaught, and he followed her lead while taking notice of the air of desperation that seemed to hover over the new attacks.

John barely even felt the impact as several shadows struck him in the back. It was as if the puppet master was losing focus, and that was enough to tell him that she was on the right track. Danielle shrieked, striking out with her claws, and John followed up her attack with his sword. He hesitated for a fraction of a second to ensure his attack hit the same seemingly random spot she had chosen. The results were immediate.

Danielle's claws were turned away with seemingly no effect by the black barrier, but she must have weakened it significantly. His sword met only token resistance before sliding through what was now truly just a simple illusion. John could actually feel the barrier lose solidity in response to his attack. The instant his blade went through the darkness, he felt it sink into flesh, and a cry of agony split the night. The darkness faded almost instantly as the illusion's creator died, and the vampires were once again bathed in very normal moonlight.

"What the hell is that thing?" Danielle was clearly referring to the rather small but horrifically disfigured creature lying at their feet.

"Who cares? It's dead now," John said, flicking his sword to remove most of the gore before replacing it in the scabbard.

With the illusion gone, they could see that they were standing roughly in the center of the fortress ruins.

John looked back and forth and asked, "So any idea which way to go now?"

"His name was Igor," a soft yet remarkably loud voice proclaimed, cutting off any reply Danielle might have made.

The two vampires turned as one and immediately saw a figure standing atop one of the ruined walls.

"He is as easily replaceable as any of my minions, but he was one of my favorites. His loss will be punished."

"Uh-huh, and who the fuck are you?" John was in no mood for any more traps or games, and the silent anger radiating from his wife was a sign of her agreement.

This asshole appeared to be pulling the strings, and the faster they killed him, the better.

"As appalling as I find your language and lack of respect, boy, you may call me Lord Dracula. If you prefer, I will also accept *master*."

As ready as they were for anything, John and Danielle couldn't help but glance at one another in disbelief. Naturally, they had both read that book long ago and had shared quite a few laughs about how wrong it was about everything. It had to be some sort of stupid joke, but John examined the figure more closely.

Long, styled black hair drifted softly in the light breeze complemented by an overly styled black mustache. His clothing was obviously custom-fit, from the intricately stitched black leather pants to the clearly ceremonial black cuirass he wore over an elegantly quilted bloodred shirt. John even caught himself admiring what looked to be cuffed, knee-high riding boots that had a natural sheen that seemed to draw the eye. Of course, the most obvious article of clothing was the overly large black cape with a red inner lining. Even now, the cape flowed at roughly hip level, clearly due to something more supernatural than simple wind. As ludicrous as it seemed, it appeared John was looking at a medieval warlord.

"John, as crazy as it sounds, he's telling the truth," Danielle commented.

"I gathered as much," he responded to his wife.

Dracula had yet to make a move and was simply studying them as a human might study a pair of interesting-looking insects.

"All right, Dracula," John continued more loudly, practically spitting the name. "Anything in particular you need before we kill you?"

"Dear boy," Dracula began, baring his own fangs with a smile. "All I require from you is death. From her, however . . ."—his gaze shifted to Danielle—"my dear, I have much higher expectations of you."

As expected, both vampires responded to his taunts by drawing swords and launching into their attacks. Before they could take more than two steps, however, the darkness consumed them once again.

Dracula's earlier excitement and anticipation were beginning to get tempered by his annoyance. Igor's destruction had not been part of his original plan. It was true that any of his creatures could be replaced, but Igor had been with him from almost the beginning, and he had always felt a certain amount of affection for that particular minion.

His original plan had called for him to intervene before Igor failed, but he had become too engrossed in watching the struggle. The female in particular had been quite impressive. The ease with which she had seen through the illusion had been remarkable. Just thinking about making her his queen had been so distracting he had missed his cue to intervene, and Igor had been thoroughly dispatched.

Dracula's overall objective remained the same, and attrition had clearly taken its toll on his opponents. Still, the male was far too powerful for him to combat while simultaneously trying to subvert the female. Now that he had intervened personally, however, it was an easy-enough obstacle to circumvent.

His plan was relatively simple. He threw a shroud of darkness around the pair the instant they appeared ready to attack. The momentary confusion would allow him to flay their minds and learn everything he would need to know about them both. As a pair, Dracula knew they were too powerful to be overcome immediately, but with enough focus and effort, he was certain the male's mind could be erased before either of them could react. After that, it would be simple enough to subvert his new queen.

Seeing her companion fall so suddenly would certainly shock her. Add to that the fact that she was clearly the weaker of the two, and there wouldn't be much fight left in her. Holding her off physically while he mentally subverted her would be rather simple. He could simply leave the male's empty shell for the sun to finish.

Satisfied he had the situation well in hand, Dracula focused on raping his opponents' minds.

When the darkness engulfed them yet again, Danielle immediately prepared herself for another shadow assault. She quickly realized, however, that this time the darkness truly was just an illusion. The slight tug she began to feel in her mind confirmed where the real attack was coming from.

Even as she threw up every mental defense she had; Danielle knew it was ultimately futile. If Dracula truly was the one behind what was going on, she already knew his mind was far more powerful than hers. His ability to control the horde of vampires earlier that evening had proven as much.

As her barriers began to fall one by one, an idea occurred to her. In mental combat, defense was far easier than offense, and she was not alone. If she could join her mind with John's, it might be possible to link their efforts together. Rather than two powerful but separate minds, they may be able to act as a single, exceptionally powerful mind.

With no better ideas presenting themselves, she mentally reached out to her husband. Unfortunately, what began as a rather simple plan turned into a matter of concern when her reach failed to find anything where John's mental presence should have been. Whether it was an effect of the darkness or a sign that John's defenses had already failed, she couldn't tell, but where her husband's mind should have been, there was only empty space.

Having no backup plan, Danielle gathered her remaining strength to both counterattack and reach out to John once again. She felt a weak contact that had to be him, but she couldn't link with it. His mind didn't have enough strength to meet her halfway, and she no longer had enough strength to make up the difference. At that moment, her last barrier fell, and Danielle could feel Dracula's influence rampaging unchecked throughout her brain.

She screamed in defiance, knowing it was useless. He was simply probing for information rather than trying to control her. This meant there was no direct confrontation—not that she could win, even if there was one. Any time she sought to challenge his influence, Dracula would simply retreat to another part of her mind, and the chase would begin again.

This mental cat and mouse went on for a two-minute eternity before she felt his influence leave her mind. Considering her failure, that could only mean he had learned all he needed and was preparing for the next attack. Aside from the anger of being mentally raped, she was unscathed, and as the darkness faded, Danielle knew she and John needed to stop wasting time and proceed with the killing.

"All right, I've had enough," she announced as she could once again see her attacker. "Let's just kill this piece of shit and go home."

Dracula was standing atop the same wall, cape still fluttering unnaturally behind him. He made no response to her obvious threat, and the smug expression on his face was infuriating. Danielle also noticed that John hadn't answered.

"Come on John, you charge left, and I'll take the right. He can't take us both."

There was still no answer from her husband.

"That may be true, my dear lady, but I no longer have to."

Dracula's comment was like an icy fist clutching onto her insides, and she reluctantly looked to her left. Had she been breathing; it would have caught in her throat the instant she saw her husband lying face down on the rocky floor.

"John!" she screamed, Dracula's presence momentarily forgotten as she rushed to her husband's side.

Dropping her sword without thinking, Danielle used both hands to roll him over. Looking into his now empty and truly lifeless eyes was by far the most frightening thing she had ever done.

"John, wake up," she instructed as she started shaking him with no effect.

"He is, as you can see my dear, quite dead . . ." He continued after a brief pause, "Well . . . I should probably clarify and say, 'permanently dead,' considering that we are all technically dead already."

She refused to listen to or accept that and began shaking John harder as Dracula sighed and began examining his fingernails.

John, this is a trick, right? John! Danielle screamed at him mentally but got no response. She didn't even sense his mind at all, and there could be only one explanation for that.

Fear and anguish began to slowly creep into her dead heart as her husband's death sank in. She was no longer shaking the lifeless body, but she refused to let him go.

"Please, baby, please wake up," she mumbled softly as the tears began to flow.

In the back of her mind, a tiny voice of rationality tried to get her attention. The situation didn't make sense. Vampires didn't simply lie down and die. As long as there was blood in the body and a head on the shoulders, physical recovery was inevitable. They had both had so many head wounds in the past; they knew from experience that even their brains could regenerate rather quickly as long as their heads were still attached. Even more obvious was the question of ash. Had John been mysteriously killed, he would have become a pile of ash almost immediately.

All these facts and more were being repeated in the back of her mind, but the voice was too small next to the size of her grief. Danielle the rational thinker was currently unavailable, and Danielle the wife could do nothing but cry over her husband's body. How could Dracula's attack have done this?

He had raped her mind, sure, but she was fine now. Unless . . .

Realization slowly dawned as she truly processed his last few statements. John had been the true target. Dracula's intent had been to eliminate him quickly so he could deal with her unhindered. She had not reacted fast enough, and John had to face the brunt of Dracula's assault alone. Even if his body was intact, what if Dracula had wiped his mind?

"Dear girl, I sympathize with your loss." Dracula stepped from his perch and seemed to ride an invisible elevator to the ground. "Truly, I do," he continued as if Danielle cared what he had to say. "But I am not prepared to spend any more time waiting. The two of us have much to discuss before the dawn interrupts us."

He was on the other side of what had at one time been the fortress's courtyard, barely thirty meters away, but as far as Danielle was concerned, it could have been thirty miles. What could she do now? She didn't want to spend eternity alone any more now than she had nine hundred years ago, but was she brave enough to welcome the sun?

Despair warred with grief as the hopelessness of the situation truly sank in. John's murder demanded vengeance, but again, what could she do? Dracula had killed him so easily, and she felt so weak. What hope was there now that she was alone?

She was considered by all who knew her to be a powerful and ancient vampire, second only perhaps to John. But look at her now, just another widow who couldn't stop crying over her husband's body. She had to do something, anything, but the tears of precious blood just wouldn't stop flowing. The rage, anger, and power were there, but they were worthless next to the grief and despair.

The whole time she could hear Dracula's soothing voice coming from across the courtyard. What was his problem? This whole mess was his fault, so why couldn't he just shut the fuck up? The least he could do would be to kill her as well, but he just wouldn't stop talking.

"My patience is not infinite, girl," Dracula began slowly approaching. "If you are to be my queen, you must learn obedience. Leave him and come to me." He continued his approach as one would approach a wounded animal.

Danielle didn't respond to his taunts and was still unable to even look away from John's body.

He's gone, the thought kept rampaging through her mind as she kept waiting for him to wake up. She couldn't accept what was happening, but his skin was so very cold.

As the initial shock began to wear off, it was quickly replaced with pure grief and anguish. Underneath it all, however, anger and rage on a level she had never experienced before built their way to the surface. Her senses once again began reporting information about her surroundings, and she became aware of Dracula's approach.

She heard his words and finally realized what this monster truly wanted. He wanted *her*. John had to die because some sick, narcissistic fuck wanted to make her his queen. It was too much for her rapidly failing sanity to process. Rage mixed with anguish, and something inside her mind snapped.

Danielle's head snapped up, tearstained face looking at Dracula with such suddenness he paused in midstep before she looked to the heavens. Anguish and rage forced their way out in a wail no words could describe.

For miles in all directions, every living creature was reduced to ash upon hearing what could only have been a cry from the depths of hell. Religious leaders in nearby cities made various signs of warding in response to what they perceived as a sound of demonic foreboding. Crying children ran to the arms of equally frightened parents as it sounded like heaven itself was screaming in anguish.

Back at the settlement, Danielle's wail went on. Having no need to save oxygen to sustain herself, her entire lung capacity, further enhanced by the power of her blood, was devoted to her wail. In those moments, her voice carried enough power to blow a hole through a mountain, had she been focused. Mad with rage as she was, the result was akin to a bomb blast erupting upward and outward in all directions.

The shock wave took Dracula completely off guard and threw him into the nearest wall with enough force to reduce even his spine to jelly. Danielle was in motion instantly, launching herself at him with superhuman speed. Her wails turned quickly to a battle cry, but there was no longer any true power behind it.

He managed to throw up some sort of dark shield, but Danielle scoffed at his defense. Streams of fire left her hands and quickly dissipated the darkness. Dracula had barely enough time to stare in shock before she was on him. Before he could move, she had wrapped her legs in a viselike grip around his waist and began slashing madly with her claws.

Danielle's sword was still lying forgotten on the dirt as she focused on getting up close and personal with her husband's killer. Strategy and tactics never entered her mind as she was overwhelmed with the need to draw blood. It was an error on her part that she was incapable of recognizing.

Dracula had been taken so thoroughly by surprise that she could have cut him to ribbons several times over. Unfortunately, she was stuck in a frenzy the likes of which she had never experienced before. Instead of trying to kill her opponent, she only wanted to see blood and cause pain. Her slashes and cuts were many, but they were shallow, and while her claws were covered in Dracula's blood, the injuries themselves were a mere annoyance to a vampire of his power.

Once the initial shock of her insane attack wore off, Dracula was easily able to deflect her strikes. Counterattacking was still problematic for him, but Danielle could see his injuries healing as quickly as she could inflict them. She tried to correct her tactics, but it was useless as her body continued responding like a rabid animal.

Dracula's increasingly successful deflections were feeding her rage, and she began hissing and screaming like a banshee directly in his face. He was clearly unimpressed, and her attacks began going wild with anger. She was trying desperately to get back some semblance of control when an explosion sent her flipping away to the other end of the courtyard.

Dracula had made a grave tactical error—more than one, in fact— and he recognized how lucky he was to have not been destroyed. All signs had pointed to the male being the more powerful of the two. He had done most of the fighting, and the female appeared to follow his lead throughout their encounters. However, the unbelievable power that was effectively radiating from the female made him wonder if he had been mistaken. Power and energy were emanating from every pore in her skin, and had Dracula needed oxygen, he wondered if he would even be able to draw a breath through the pressure.

There had been no chance to defend himself against the power of her shock wave, and he had felt his bones crushed when he impacted the nearby wall. Instinct, more than any visual cues, caused him to throw up a shield of darkness while he worked quickly to heal himself. Danielle's immediate charge had been no cause for concern since his defense was in place, but when the flames left her fingertips, he was uncertain how to respond.

Mortal magic?

Dracula had never seen a vampire utilize elemental magic, and there had been no way to know if his defense would hold. If she had possessed this ability, why had it not been used earlier? The fire weakened the dark shield enough that Danielle broke through easily, and before he could react, she had her legs wrapped around his waist in a death grip. He had no choice but to divert a large amount of power to prevent his lower body from being crushed. As if that hadn't been enough, she had begun wildly raking her claws across his face and upper body.

He had been able to ward off most of the blows but was unable to mount a successful counterattack. As blow after blow opened his flesh, he had to expend even more energy on simply healing himself. The pure rage and animalistic nature behind her assault had surprised him, and Dracula did not like being on the defensive.

On a whim, he tried a mental assault to gain the upper hand, but it had been a grave error. Her mind was in such utter turmoil that the instant his eyes had locked onto hers, he almost cried out in agony. If the eyes were truly windows to the soul, then her soul was on fire and desperate to consume anything in its path.

Dracula forced himself to fight the brief panic stirring within and focused instead on her attacks. While her sheer power was creating physical pressure all around him, the attacks themselves were wild and far from fatal. It was as if, in her rage, she wanted to merely hurt him rather than outright kill him.

They were deadlocked, and it would only be a matter of time before she was able to clear her mind enough to attack him properly.

Dracula abandoned his defensive efforts on the theory that superficial wounds could be easily healed later. He ignored the pain as her claws continued to rake his flesh and speared his own claws deep into both her thighs.

She cried out, more out of anger than pain, but did not release her hold. No mythical banshee could have matched the hissing and shrieking as she began to grow even wilder. Her head was so close to his that Dracula could feel the spittle on his face. There was little supernatural power behind her voice, but the sheer volume and pitch ruptured both his eardrums, and he felt blood pouring from his ears.

He ignored the pain and moved to take advantage of her insanity. He quickly placed his left hand on her chest and sent a bolt of darkness into her flesh before she could react to the touch. Such an attack was not intended to be used at such close range, but it was the only idea he had. The explosion injured his hand badly, but he was rewarded with the sight of his attacker cartwheeling through the air until she crashed into the opposite wall. He also noticed the trail of blood and gore she left in her wake with a great deal of pleasure.

Something else he noticed earlier, but dismissed as unimportant, was coming back to haunt him. Both vampires were wearing simple golden bands around their left ring fingers. The idea of two vampires being married was ridiculous, so he had assumed it was some sort of cover. They were obviously traveling companions, and passing as husband and wife was a good idea for several reasons. The strength and depth of the female's reaction were causing him to think the impossible.

One did not break down in grief and anguish over the death of a simple traveling companion—at least no vampire would, anyway. A degree of anger and shock was understandable, but the female's emotions were out of control. When she had raised her head before, Dracula had barely enough time to notice the bloody tears streaking her face before her anguished wail hit him. She was acting exactly as one would expect for a wife who had just seen her husband murdered. Now that he had a moment to spare, he began analyzing what he had pulled from their minds and nearly vomited in revulsion.

They were married!

Somehow their feelings had survived their transformation, and they'd been inseparable for over nine hundred years. Dracula was disgusted but could not ignore the facts. His plan was flawed. The shock of seeing a companion murdered could leave one weakened and open to subversion. The shock of losing a lifelong mate would more likely lead to the anger and rage she was exhibiting now. Even once she was defeated, she would be even less susceptible to subversion since she wasn't an average vampire interested only in self-preservation.

He was certain that he was still strong enough to defeat her, but he did not want to destroy her. Unfortunately, hammering her into submission might not work. In her clearly deranged state of mind, she might keep coming at him until he was forced to destroy her. It might be simpler to just end things now and get back to the original reason he had come to the place, rather than take the risk. On the other hand, what were the odds he would encounter another vampire like her?

In the end, Dracula decided it would be worth the risk. He could always choose to kill her later if he had to. Having broken the assault, he hovered to a safe distance to wait and see if he had done enough damage to allow him to begin subverting his future queen.

Danielle dug herself out from the rubble while she worked to heal her chest and legs. She shook her head briefly, thinking at least the shock of Dracula's brutal attack had broken the frenzy that had overcome her. Being angry at herself for the failure would solve nothing, but it was hard not to feel that way.

It was easy to sense that Dracula was more powerful than she, yet he had underestimated her more than once. She could have killed him at least twice by now, had there been any control or thought behind her actions, but there hadn't been. Of course, missing probably her only chance to win the battle did not change the situation. Her husband's killer could not be allowed to leave.

It was hard not to appreciate his ability to hover and fly, and she couldn't help but wonder how much of that ability was his and how much was due to his cape. Of course, she bared her fangs and claws; two could play at that game. After leaping on a nearby wall to gain some height, she quickly hurtled toward him.

Danielle's ability to leap extreme distances and exert some control over local air currents resulted in limited flight capability. It was closer to gliding than true flight, but it should suffice to at least get her into attack range. It did. Just before she attempted her first strike, she was sure there was a note of genuine approval in Dracula's eye.

The aerial combat was interesting to watch, for any onlooker who could keep track, but was not accomplishing much for either party. Both combatants were expending so much energy remaining airborne that there wasn't enough left for the combat itself. Blows were exchanged and deflected with relative ease, and any strike lucky enough to land unopposed simply knocked the victim through the air. Soon enough they realized their efforts were being wasted, and they returned to the courtyard floor, where the combat reached a new level of ferociousness.

Danielle and Dracula were attacking and defending with blinding speed. Claw met claw, sword met darkness, and occasional sparks of fire topped off the hellish melee that even other vampires would have had difficulty following. She knew she was outmatched, but her sword gave her an advantage in reach, which she pressed for all she was worth.

She was also using a tactic John had taught her and abandoning any pretext of defending herself. When facing a more powerful attacker, one could easily make up the difference by focusing all energy and power on the offense. As long as your opponent continued to divide his or her energy between the offense and the defense, there was a chance for the weaker combatant to overpower the stronger.

Unfortunately for her, Dracula was powerful enough that he could still defend himself while matching her blow for blow. As ferocious as their attacks were, neither of them was inflicting any injuries that weren't able to heal almost immediately. A standstill was bad news for her. She was expending far more energy than Dracula, and he seemed content to simply allow her to exhaust herself.

"Come now, Dani, there is no reason for us to struggle this way," his soothing voice oozed with supernatural intoxication. Danielle was not sure if it was that he was speaking again or the use of her name in such a familiar fashion, but she felt her anger spiking once more.

"*Monster!*" she hissed, redoubling her attacks. "You have no right to call me that!"

"Very well, milady," he responded sweetly, easily twisting out of the way of her sword. "I can call you Danielle for the moment."

"*No!*" It was like Dracula was not even taking her attacks as a serious threat, and she felt her eyes begin to redden with true frenzy.

"Hmm," Dracula sounded mildly annoyed at her antics. "I must protest this foolishness, milady," he sounded more like a scolding parent than a vampire locked in intense combat. "Is that not your name? Why should I not call you by your name?" He arched an eyebrow inquisitively, while at the same time his claws opened a series of wounds across her shoulder.

Wincing in pain, Danielle refused to be further baited. Fighting her frenzy was difficult enough without wasting effort verbally, and

Dracula shrugged his shoulders almost uncaringly as if finally making up his mind. He clamped down on both her wrists, before she could react, and twisted around until she was pinned against the wall.

The harder Danielle tried to break free, the tighter his grip became. Feelings of entrapment caused fear to mix with the feelings of frenzy building within. As useless as it was proving, she couldn't help but continue struggling with all her remaining might.

"If you are to be my queen, you must learn obedience," he said and leaned in until his face was barely an inch from where her own was struggling. His smile was innocent, and his expression as a whole seemed to give no indication that he was even aware that there was a struggle going on. She continued straining against his hold, hissing and gnashing her teeth. If nothing else worked, she seemed determined to at least sink her fangs into his face.

"Do what you will, bastard, but don't pretend to know me," she hissed. "Just because you raped my mind to learn my name, don't expect me to ever answer to it for you." Her hisses were turning to growls as her eyes became even more dangerous.

"Very well then." He leaned in even closer, the tip of his nose brushing hers. "What shall I call you?"

"*I am Shiva*," she growled in a voice no longer completely her own. "*Destroyer of Worlds!*" Her eyes were twin red flames as she lunged forward unexpectedly and managed to sink her fangs into Dracula's cheek.

He cried out, more in surprise than pain, and pulled hard on her right wrist. Not expecting the sudden move, she was thrown briefly off balance, and Dracula was quick to take advantage of the opening. Still holding her right arm straight out, he released her left wrist and used his now free claws to sever her sword arm midway between the wrist and elbow. As the appendage turned to ash and the sword skittered away, he simply tossed her aside as if she were made of straw.

Disarmed and seriously wounded, there was little chance of Danielle continuing to struggle successfully. Dracula had clearly learned a harsh lesson about underestimating her, however, and he wasn't about to take any chances. He still hadn't given up trying to subvert her, but as he approached and reached out with his mind, he remained ready for anything.

She could feel the tugging once again at the edges of her consciousness, but she was far from out of the fight. The explosion of fresh pain had cleared her mind of frenzy, and with that clarity came an idea. She quickly shoved herself up and charged, with a wail of battle that brought nothing but pain to already-ruptured eardrums.

As she reached attack range, Dracula appeared disappointed but relatively unsurprised. Danielle spun and executed a perfect reverse roundhouse kick. The maneuver was beautifully executed and had enough power to remove his head. It was also a maneuver anyone but a fool would be able to deflect, and as he twisted to the side to easily avoid her strike, her grin was far more demonic than anything out of the netherworld.

What he had not noticed was the way she had been hiding the stump of her right arm from the moment she had stood back up. She had forced an incredible amount of blood and energy into recklessly healing the appendage and accomplished in seconds what should have taken several minutes. The result was a disgusting mess of muscle and bone, but it was the proper length. Most important was that she was able to reform her claws.

He was too fast to get through with a solid attack, unless she managed an attack he wouldn't think to defend against. An attack perhaps from an arm that should no longer be there? Her kick was a feint to get Dracula to move and an excuse to turn her body away before he could see what was coming. It was perfect, and she completed her spin by burying full-length claws into the flesh below his right shoulder and opening his chest and torso down to his left hip.

There was an almost-imperceptible pause as both combatants seemed frozen in shock—Dracula, from the pain, and Danielle, from her first success in the battle. The pause did not last, as he quickly launched himself to hover out of reach, and she noticed his chest already starting to heal. It was hard for her to not start cursing in anger after realizing her perfectly executed plan failed.

The failure was not total. She could see a sheen of blood-sweat covering Dracula's skin, a clear sign of stress and exhaustion for a vampire; but her attack was supposed to destroy him, not simply tire him out. The battle was taking too long, and it was obvious how a war of attrition would end for her.

Moments ticked past with the combatants simply staring at one another, focusing on healing and considering their next moves. Danielle was tired. One way or another this had to end, and it needed to end now. The next attack would be her last. There was an almost-imperceptible nod of agreement from Dracula, but not because he had read her mind. The conclusion was easy enough for him to reach as well, and he purposefully lowered himself to well within her attack range. For the smallest fraction of a second, Dracula was simply her opponent, not her husband's murderer, and she returned his nod.

Both prepared for the final strike, and it was obvious who was going to attack whom. Danielle retrieved her sword, crouched down, and began gathering every bit of power she could find within herself. At the same time, Dracula braced himself for the coming attack, throwing up every defense he had at his disposal and hoping the whole time that this wouldn't result in the female's destruction.

She sneered as he disappeared behind a cloak of darkness, but she knew he was still there. Just as she knew that she was leaping to her own death, she knew Dracula was in for a surprise. She accepted that she couldn't win, and that gave her an advantage. No blood would have to be saved for healing later, and no regard had to be given to keep her own abilities from injuring herself. The result would be an attack far more powerful than anything Dracula could possibly expect out of her, and if there was any god above, observing their struggle, they would both be dust on the wind in a simple matter of seconds.

It was with that pleasant thought in mind that Danielle leaped to exact vengeance, leaving a small crater in her wake; such was the power she was now capable of. The only thing that could match her strength and speed was the cry of defiance that both accompanied her and split the heavens.

So it was that the unstoppable force met the immovable object, and the ensuing shock wave would have leveled a small village. Thankfully, the bleak desert landscape was largely unaffected, but tremors would be felt in many settlements and towns throughout the area. As for the two combatants, neither would be able to later describe exactly what happened at the moment of impact.

Both were violently hurled from one another, grievously wounded perhaps but not destroyed. Danielle had been successful in running her sword through Dracula's chest, but her angle of attack was now quite literally her downfall. While he was thrown backward through the air, quite harmlessly, she was sent streaking back toward the ground at nearly the same speed she had attacked with disastrous results.

She impacted the ground in much the same way as a meteor would have, leaving a respectable crater and trail through the rocky soil until finally colliding with one of the ruined walls. Almost every bone in her body was crushed, and the collapsing wall buried her under rubble. Ironically, her attack itself had done far more damage to Dracula than she had received in return. It was her failure to properly account for physics that had doomed the attempt from the beginning.

After the sounds of the titanic battle, the sudden silence engulfing the ruins seemed eerily out of place—with one combatant trying to regain control as he tumbled through the air and the other buried in rubble, lacking the power to free herself. It appeared the battle was finally over.

Danielle's blood reserves were dangerously low, but the body of an ancient vampire used blood far more efficiently than their younger kindred, and that efficiency made it difficult to run out completely. Eventually, she managed to heal just enough to work her head and a single arm free of the rubble before her strength failed completely. She risked taking a small break, stretching out her senses instead, and sighed with relief. There was nothing. She sensed no threat from any direction. Honesty forced her to admit the unlikelihood that Dracula had been destroyed, but it seemed that he had at least been fought off. All she had to do now was just wait for the sun to put her out of her misery.

No! Her senses noticed his approach only seconds before Dracula landed in the courtyard across from her. *It's not fair*, she would have cried had she possessed the strength, but she couldn't even move.

Dracula seemed content to simply watch her for a moment, and she tried to take advantage of the time. Unfortunately, all she managed to accomplish was raising her head slightly.

I've got nothing left.

"It's over, milady," he spoke softly. "I will admit you put up far more of a fight than I would have thought possible, but you have lost." He started approaching slowly, even now remaining reflexively cautious of her abilities. "You should take my advice and not resist. It will make no difference in the end, but it will save you a great deal of pain. In a few minutes you will be mine, and we will rule this world together."

This can't be how it ends, she reeled mentally.

Final death no longer held any fear over her, but the thought of living as his slave? She knew he would never wipe her mind completely, that she would spend eternity trapped at his side and enjoying it.

This can't happen.

Yet even as the thought crossed her mind, she could feel his presence entering her brain, and tears of helplessness finally began to streak her ruined cheeks. Danielle glanced up to the heavens, intending to spend her final moment of lucidity cursing god, when she saw a way out. Storm clouds.

Lightning would have been a wasted effort earlier in the battle. Calling forth lightning from thin air was incredibly power intensive, and Dracula was far too fast to hit with that type of attack. The situation, however, had apparently changed. Through either a twist of good fortune or a result of the amount of energy they had released into the atmosphere, the once beautifully clear night sky was littered with even more beautiful-looking thunderclouds.

Her sight revealed small lightning bolts among the clouds themselves, which made her ridiculous idea plausible. All she really had to do was redirect a single already-existing bolt, and that was easy. Dracula was even providing a stationary target since he did not want to approach any closer until she had been safely subverted. He was clearly weakened from their struggle, albeit not as weakened as she was, but enough that a direct strike would surely finish him.

All she had to do was just lift her arm, point, and concentrate. That was it, just lift her arm—the arm that was currently ignoring her commands.

Dammit! She was too weak, and he was already gaining partial control. It would only be seconds before he read the plan in her mind; this had to work. It had to work *now*!

Her arm slowly obeyed. She waited until the angle was right and simply pointed to the appropriate cloud. Even better, Dracula confirmed his ignorance by sneering at her foolish efforts, a sneer that quickly vanished when he recognized the look of defiance in her eye. Too late.

The strike was a direct hit. The thunderous explosion and blinding light were terrible and yet beautiful to behold. Her proximity guaranteed that she was injured as well, but only lightly. It was difficult to control, but she managed to keep the majority of the charge coursing through Dracula rather than having the current jump to her as well. The only sound she could hear over the explosion was Dracula's wondrous cry of agony surrounding her in victory.

It took a moment for the dust and debris to settle, and once it did, she saw that she was alone. Somehow, she knew that this time was different. This time she really had won . . . and yet? There was no feeling of satisfaction or accomplishment as her eyes slowly moved to bring John's body back into view. No, this night held no victory in it.

"Asshole." It was the only victory cry she could think to mutter, and she spit in the general vicinity of where Dracula had been standing.

There was no telling how close to empty on blood she was, so Danielle took the time to dig her body out the hard way. The slow, methodical task helped to soothe the last bit of frenzy and anger from her mind. Unfortunately, that meant that by the time she was finished, there was nothing left to take the place of the grief and sadness.

She began crawling to her husband, not even bothering to heal her lower body. There was no point. She would meet the sun soon, and the thought of her ashes mixing with John's gave her some small comfort as she continued to drag the wreckage of her legs through the rubble to his side. With some effort, she managed to sit somewhat upright and drag her husband's body across her lap.

"I'm sorry, honey." She started brushing the hair out of his face as she cradled his head, almost startling herself with the sight of her own claws. Quickly reverting her claws back to feminine hands, her grief-stricken mind couldn't help but giggle at her own reaction.

Here she was, most of her body a mess of blood and bone, including more than one hole completely through her chest cavity. In fact, she was reasonably certain at least two of her ribs had completely fallen out as she was crawling through the rubble. There was no way she could even pass as human. All that and yet the sight of vampiric claws on her husband's face had almost frightened her.

Even more foolish, she just realized, was that her other hand had been straightening her hair without her even realizing it. She was reflexively trying to neaten up her appearance for a corpse, and the very thought brought a much-needed moment of laughter. At least until she realized what she was laughing at.

God, I'm really losing it.

"I'm sorry," she repeated her apology. "You've always been there. Every time I needed you, you always saved me."

Her mind drifted back to a dark alley, a werewolf, and a bathtub full of blood as she thought about the last time she had been convinced of her own death, just to have John spring out of the darkness to save her.

"Every time, my hero. And the one time you needed me, I couldn't do it. I've never been as strong as you. I was too slow, too weak, and you paid for my failure." She started crying again. "But I got him, honey. I killed the bastard that did this to you. I know it doesn't mean anything now, but I did my best. Please forgive me."

John's face was covered in the red droplets of Danielle's tears, and the broken widow collapsed on top of him.

It is not over.

Danielle was tired of other people's voices in her head and was in no mood for her subconscious to play tricks on her. So she ignored it, deciding instead to relish in the silence and lack of life anywhere around them. The sun would be up soon, and that was all that mattered.

You will not last until sunrise. You defeated Dracula, but you did not destroy him.

She refused to listen. It was just too much, and no one could take what little feeling of victory she had away from her—even if that victory was false.

Time is short.

"Just shut up!" she screamed at no one in particular. "For all I know, I'm yelling at myself, but just shut up!"

He is coming.

"I don't care!"

Yes, you do. The voice was firm yet soothing, but her mind had been raped enough for one evening.

Rather than responding, she simply went back to stroking John's hair and grieving over her loss.

You do not understand. Dracula has given up on subverting you. If you do not flee, he will destroy you.

"*GOOD!* That's what I want to happen, dumbass! Either him or the sun, whatever, I don't care." She hugged the body tighter. "I just want to be with John again."

Listen to me. Your husband's mind is not beyond saving, but he has very little time remaining. That was a low blow, even for an imaginary voice in her own head.

"How dare yo—"

Foolish girl! Where is the ash? Her brain echoed with the force of the mysterious voice's shout, but there was something else in the back of her mind.

Somewhere past her grief, her approaching insanity, and her renewed anger, she was still capable of rational thought. And didn't that question sound vaguely familiar? Hadn't she thought very much the same thing, albeit briefly, before the actual battle had started? Also, hadn't something very similar happened to Sam back at the haven?

Vampires of their age reverted to ash immediately upon death, much the same as their appendages did if they were suddenly severed. No ash. No death. Could what Dracula had done to him still be undone? Her eyes went wide with hope, at the same time her ears were assaulted with very familiar laughter. She looked around and saw darkness starting to close in from all sides. It was too late.

Run, child. RUN NOW!

No longer doubting the imaginary voice, Danielle scooped up John's form and, for no apparent reason, forced her ravaged body to run directly into a solid stone wall.

"No!" Dracula screamed loudly as his prey suddenly vanished from not only his sight but all his senses. He quickly charged into the same wall, only to rebound painfully from the solid stone. Never one to give up easily, he began attacking the wall to no avail.

Interesting.

His anger momentarily forgotten; he began examining the wall very carefully. There was nothing he could detect to set it aside from any other stone wall, except for his inability to damage it. Oh, and the fact that the female had charged through it as if it wasn't even there. He placed a hand on the wall and concentrated but was unable to penetrate it with his senses.

Dracula forced himself to calm down and think clearly. He had not survived over five hundred years by being foolish; in fact, his mind was as sharp as his claws. The stink of failure was distasteful, but perhaps the failure was not complete. He had learned much this evening; all he needed was to allow the dots to connect themselves.

First, it was now obvious that the summons he had felt had not been meant for him, nor any of the other vampires who answered it. It had been meant for those two alone, and whatever issued it was on the other side of that stone wall. If it was a creature of some sort, it possessed amazing power, evidenced by his inability to follow the female. That alone was evidence enough that he should withdraw; he was in no condition for a battle on that scale.

He paced back and forth a bit, considering his next move. Meant for him or not, there was power behind that wall, and he wanted it. Fortunately, immortality had a way of teaching patience, and a new plan began to form in his mind. Let those two be the first to discover this new power. In fact, that was a perfect idea. He needed time to consider the details of the recent battle. The dark powers he possessed were his alone, as had been promised to him, but those two might have other tricks of their own.

He had already connected with their minds once, and doing so again would be child's play. The instant they left the protection of whatever it was, he would know and be able to scavenge any information he wanted from them from anywhere in the world. There was no reason to even leave his castle, since eventually they would come after him for revenge.

Many mistakes and false assumptions had been made this night, which Dracula freely admitted to himself, but he had learned from every one of them. The next time he fought those two, he would know what to do. Odds were that the female had been so out of her mind during the fight that she might not have noticed how much he had been holding back. Add to that the advantage of battling in his own territory, and Dracula suddenly began feeling much better about the evening's events.

Oh yes, he thought and grinned at the sky, *much better indeed*.

He would go home and wait for them. Once they were destroyed or subverted, he would use their knowledge and power to gain entry to whatever was on the other side of that wall. Then he would claim whatever treasure he would find for himself.

It was with a pleasant gleam in his eye that Dracula began his journey home. Why bother settling for just a queen? Once he gained a prize of that much power, he could easily have the entire world.

CHAPTER 5

Underground Caverns

D anielle's mind was a boiling cauldron of anger, grief, the need for vengeance, and above all, exhaustion . . . as she sped down the unknown cavern. A mortal would have been hard-pressed to match her speed, yet it was nothing compared to the inhuman pace of which she should have been capable. Unfortunately, the evening had taken its toll on her body, mind, blood, and soul—assuming she had one, of course. It was hard enough for her to not think about the weight on her left shoulder represented by her most likely dead husband; forcing herself to move any faster was simply out of the question.

There was also the consideration that she had no idea where she was or what she was heading into. Her own safety was far from guaranteed, and it made sense to attempt to save her remaining power for any dangers that yet lay ahead.

Right, she snorted to herself at the passing thought, *like I could defend myself against anything more powerful than a wild animal at this point.*

Even as she admitted the truth to herself, however, she knew it was important to go down fighting, no matter what.

As the minutes slowly ticked into their own minor eternities, Danielle began to slowly notice yet one more disconcerting fact. Even at her slower speed, the cavern walls were passing her by relatively fast. Occasionally, another tunnel or even a fork of multiple tunnels would present itself, and every time she made her choice of direction immediately, never once slowing or thinking about where she was going. This was also no simple headlong flight from a pursuing enemy, as it had been immediately obvious that Dracula had been unable to offer pursuit. No, Danielle was absolutely confident in her direction of travel, and yet she hadn't the foggiest idea of where she was or where she was going.

"Fucking wonderful," she cursed. "I'm being led, aren't I?" She had to stop herself from using the word *controlled* since it was clear that her mind, what was left of it, was still her own.

Yes, child, I thought that was made clear to you.

Danielle came to a sudden stop as the voice in her head returned. True, she had asked her previous question out loud; however, she never expected a response. In fact, she had already dismissed the voice that had commanded her earlier as a part of her subconscious that was geared toward survival. That did not explain the wall she had run through, the same wall that had stopped Dracula in his tracks, but she was purposefully not poking holes in her own theory.

I am not your subconscious.

She spun in place, scanning the darkness, using her enhanced vision to view the cavern walls in almost-perfect clarity.

"Show yourself!" she demanded in no particular direction. It was also possible she was losing her grip on reality. That would be a very plausible result of the night's events. Even a vampiric mind could only take so much abuse before it broke down completely.

I cannot.

That sounded like an excuse to her, considering her subconscious would not be able to materialize in front of her. Unless, of course, she started to hallucinate, which would be the next logical step in her descent into insanity.

Child, my time is measured by eternity. Your husband's is measured by mere moments. How many more of those moments will you waste? The voice, whatever it was, had grown softer and even held a hint of concern. Real or not, the proper cord had been plucked, and Danielle blurred into motion with the renewed strength of desperation.

The cavern walls around her blurred into nonexistence as she sped down random tunnels. Turns were taken without thought, and in addition to not knowing where she was going, Danielle knew there was no way she would be able to navigate her way back out if it should come to that. Then, with a suddenness that took her completely by surprise, she stopped. She had not wanted to stop, but try as she might, she could simply go no further.

It was quickly apparent she had ended up in a rather large cavern, much like many she had recently traveled through. A rapid take of her surroundings confirmed the one difference was that in this case, there was nowhere else to go. Taking that information and her inability to turn around, it was easy to conclude she had reached the destination she had not even realized she was searching for.

She began scanning her surroundings more carefully. Vampiric sight or not, she had left all ambient light far behind her, and it was difficult to pick out details among the craggy walls. Still, she looked anyway, assuming that she would know what she was looking for once she saw it.

The cavern was roughly two hundred meters wide, and it appeared to be no more than fifty meters or so to the other wall. It was also a bit more geometrically perfect than she expected out of nature. The walls were curved, not straight, so the overall appearance was that of a large oval stretching across her path with her staring across the thinner side. She had almost given up looking for any more clues when she gasped and choked on the breath her body no longer needed.

Eyes. Directly ahead of her. A pair of yellow-red eyes that had no discernible pupils or irises staring at her—or, more accurately, into her and *through* her at the same time. Eyes that no living or *unliving* creature should possess and had no place this side of hell. Those eyes awakened a fear within her the likes of which Danielle had never experienced. Of all the horrors she had faced and witnessed, never once had it ever occurred to Danielle, or her husband for that matter, to simply run away in response to fear. Yet those eyes looking into her very being made her instantly want to run away and cry into the lap of a mother who had been dead for centuries.

Of course, since her feet would not obey her, there was no choice but to stand her ground and force herself to stare right back. Danielle did her best to keep the fear from showing, knowing the whole time how futile the attempt was. To say she appeared to be a deer frozen in headlights would be insulting to the bravery of the *deer*. Having the eyes as a focal point, at least, made it easier to make out the rest of whatever this creature was.

The face and head were the most obvious: a bit cracked and elongated, but mostly human in appearance with slightly pointed ears. The body was another matter entirely. The creature seemed to be growing *out of* the wall. The head had freedom of movement, but only the upper arms and legs were visible. The proportions seemed roughly humanoid, but where a human's knees and elbows would have been, the creature's limbs fused with the wall. The torso was also visible, but its perfect upright

71

posture caused Danielle to suspect the back was fused into the wall as well.

Danielle was mildly taken aback by how frail the body looked overall. The coloring and texture seemed to match the wall it was slowly fusing into, yet it appeared to carry none of the stone's inherent strength. Its overall size, judging from the portions that were still visible, was barely larger than the average human. Unfortunately, another glance up at the creature's eyes dismissed any appearances of physical weakness, and she had to admit that most of her own powerful abilities had nothing to do with inherent physical strength.

Danielle struggled to find her voice, to demand to know what was going on, but it failed her. It was those *eyes*! In the back of her mind, she finally accepted that she and John were not demons. They had agreed on that possibility quite some time ago, but for the first time, she truly accepted how ridiculous it was to think that either of them could have ever been demons. She knew that now, because for the first time in her near millennium of existence, she was looking into the eyes of a true unholy demon.

The pieces finally snapped together in her mind, and the fear she felt before increased tenfold. The endless underground caverns, the darkness even her eyes could not completely penetrate, the dead weight of her husband tantalizing her with the possibility of waking yet refusing to do so, and now this demon all pointed to a single possibility.

She was in hell. That "wall" she had passed through had not been a wall at all. In fact, Dracula had killed her, and the wall had been her mind's way of visualizing the passage into hell. That explained why Dracula had not pursued her. There was no need, considering she was now most likely a simple pile of ash at his feet.

The realization caused an echo of the mortal girl she had once been to bleed through the vampire she now was, and the tears flowed freely. It wasn't fair! Being dead was bad enough, but to end up in hell? After all the effort she and John had expended to be as honorable as any vampire could possibly be, to still be damned to an afterlife without him? That thought, more than any, threatened to break her. For if she was in hell, it was obvious that John was as well, and Dracula had truly killed him after all.

To be tormented with the memory of what she once had was the worst part. Knowing she had failed and that this new eternity would never end and she would have to endure it alone was too much. Her body, already quivering with sobs under the gaze of those eyes, began to crumble. Then something happened.

72

As her knees quaked and her legs began to buckle, the weight on her left shoulder shifted. That shifting weight was an instant reminder that she was still carrying John's body, and an instant thought of defiance crossed her mind. His body might not be real, just an illusion created to torment her, but did that matter? The illusion of their marriage and humanity had made nine hundred years of being vampires not only tolerable but quite enjoyable. Maybe, just maybe, the illusion that she could protect this false body, maybe even save it, would be enough to preserve her sanity even in the depths of hell.

In fact, would either of them hesitate for even a moment to challenge Satan himself if it meant a chance of finding one another again? That was an idea she could sink her fangs into, and while the fear remained, her blind despair started to fade. It made perfect logical sense. If this was truly hell, then that meant, obviously, hell and Satan were real. So John was out there somewhere, even if in his own reality, probably thinking the same thing right now that she was.

All they had to do was face all the powers of hell without being able to directly support one another and beat Satan in his own realm. A daunting task, but on the bright side, there was all of eternity to complete it. Who cared if they were never allowed out of hell no matter what they did? Once they destroyed Satan, they would rule this new realm and be together again forever. Until then, this illusionary body she was carrying would be her constant reminder, her new source of strength—strength that even now was replacing her earlier despair.

"So," she finally managed to say out loud. "All I have to do is single-handedly face and destroy all the powers of hell?"

She raised her head back up and stared into the eyes of the first demon she had ever met. Those eyes continued working their dark magic on her, but she stared through the tears and stomped firmly down on her fear. She gently set her husband's body to the side and squared off against the demon. Fingers morphed into claws, and tongues of fire began spitting from the tips. If the fire was a bit weak in her current condition, she gave no indication of noticing.

"Bring it on!"

Marvelous! She heard what could only be laughter in the back of her mind. *Child, you are more magnificent than I had ever imagined. In all my millennia here, no creature, mortal or otherwise, has ever stood before me and failed to flee. But you, you, not only hold your ground but deign to attack me even in your terribly weakened condition.*

"It's not as if you gave me a choice, monster," she spit on the cavern floor. "If I must be forced to stay here, I *will* destroy you and as many others as I must to reach your master himself!"

The inhuman laughter returned, serving only to increase her anger, and she braced for what could very well be the last attack she ever made.

You are mistaken, child. I admit to having led you to this cavern— my home, if you will—but I released my hold immediately upon your arrival. I expect that shock kept you rooted in place for a time, but you were free to flee almost immediately.

"Lies and tricks!"

No, courage and love, child. I admit I do not fully grasp the latter. However, your thoughts are open to me, and I know that is what is preventing you from leaving. Allow me to apologize for two separate offenses before you launch your wasteful attack.

First, I had forgotten how unsettling my physical appearance was and should have taken steps to correct that.

The demonic eyes began to change slightly even as the voice spoke to her. They seemed to grow warmer and more comforting, no longer instilling the terrible fear they had before.

Secondly, I listened to your thoughts as you followed your twisted logic to decide that you were in hell. I could have interrupted you at any time, but your rationalizations and conclusions fascinated me. I wanted to witness your final choice.

I apologize for the deception, but I would do it again. You see, child, when I realized you thought you were in your concept of hell itself, I had fully expected to have to drag your fleeing body back here by force. Instead, here you stand, claws at the ready, prepared to attack a being more powerful than you could possibly imagine. I say again, marvelous! Trust me when I say, this is not hell. You are simply underground, and I am no unholy demon.

Danielle hesitated long enough to consider the possible deception. Could it be true? The fear was gone, and the creature, while still unsettling to look at, seemed much less purely demonic than it had a moment before. Still, that could be a simple trick, no different than tricks she played on mortals all the time. After all, wouldn't a demon's first attack be to lull her into a false sense of security?

I have no need to lull you into anything, child. I could turn you to ash with a mere thought.

Danielle scowled in annoyance as the creature—maybe demon— continued to prove it was reading her thoughts. The fact that she could only feel the other presence when it actually spoke in her mind gave a small hint to just how powerful the creature truly was. On the other hand, it was also possible that the creature possessed no physical powers at all. If she could just get close enough to . . .

"AAAAHH!" she screamed more in shock than pain as she was smashed instantly to the cavern floor.

The attack came with no warning, as if an enormous invisible hand simply pressed down on her much as a mortal would squish an ant. There was very little pain, but she was crumpled on her side, unable to even flinch a muscle, seemingly surrounded by an invisible pressure. It was almost as if the very air had grown thick with pure power, and that power was directed against her. As a test, she attempted to take an unneeded breath. Not only would no air enter her lungs, but it seemed to rebel against her, pressing her head even more firmly against the ground.

Enough child! I have no wish to harm you, but I must break you out of your current delusion. This is but the smallest demonstration of my power, and I could crush you instantly. Believe it or not, the only difficult part of this is keeping my power from destroying everything else around us as well. This is not hell. I am not a demon. I will release you now. Either trust me to save your husband, or leave this place and never return.

As promised, the force holding Danielle in place dissipated instantly, and she rose to her feet, wondering what to do. Fighting and winning was out of the question; that much was clear now, but could the creature be trusted? After that demonstration of power, it did seem ridiculous to mislead her for no reason, and there was also the promise to save John. What was it Father Jenkins had said to her once before? Sometimes you just had to take a leap of faith?

"Very well dem—creature," she began softly, allowing her hands to return to normal. "You have yet to earn my trust, but you do have my attention." She stared, unblinking, into its eyes. "Do you possess the power to save my husband?"

Your attention will suffice for now, and yes.

"What must I do?" she asked, attempting—and failing—to keep the blind hope from touching her voice.

You must bring his body closer to me. I must see him clearly for this to work, and my normal senses have long since faded to a shadow of what they once were.

She nodded once and lifted John's body to her shoulder once again. There was a necessary pause for her to gather her courage, and she began approaching the creature's physical form. Somehow she knew when the distance was correct, and she carefully set down her precious cargo, turning to face the creature expectantly.

Move to the wall. I have difficulty focusing my power into such a small area, and I am unsure of the effects it would have if spilled over onto you.

She did as instructed, never once looking away from those unblinking eyes, and waited.

When nothing seemed to happen for nearly a full minute, Danielle had to resist the urge to start fretting and wringing her hands. She was about to ask what was going on when, as if on cue, the creature's lips began to move. There was absolutely no sound in the dark cavern that her vampiric hearing could detect, but the lips were definitely moving, albeit only slightly.

Danielle slowly started to notice something different about the very atmosphere in the cavern. It was hard to say or explain what, but there was definitely something going on. She felt warmth, but not the warmth caused by pure heat. No, the warmth she felt seemed to come from within, but she had felt it all around her before it had made its way into her insides. There was an irrational joyous feeling that seemed to be attached to the warmth as well, and it became difficult to stop herself from smiling for no reason. Then, just as suddenly as the feeling had arrived, the creature's lips stopped moving, and it was gone.

There was no telling what had happened. Some sort of spell or power at work seemed to make the most sense, but it had felt far too *good* for it to have come from the being she had accused of being a demon. Whatever it was, it was over now, and she turned her gaze back to John's body, resisting the urge to cross her fingers or tear up with hope. Danielle even started grinding her fangs when an eternity passed with no obvious change taking place. Of course, her eternity had been clearly subjective, considering only fifteen seconds had gone by, and then . . .

John sat up and immediately regretted the decision as he was met with the mother of all migraines. Again—he *really* did not think vampires were supposed to get migraines, so it was probably time to start sending sternly worded complaint letters to someone. He considered the question of whom exactly to address the letters to as he began massaging his temple uselessly, searching his surroundings for some sort of clue as to what was going on. It seemed much too dark for someone with his sight, which was strange, and hadn't he been fighting some weirdo a second ago?

"What the hell is—*umph.*" His question was cut off as a weight crashed into his chest at a high-enough speed to knock him firmly back down. He almost counterattacked before his eyes fully adjusted and he saw his wife lying on top of him, sobbing furiously into his neck.

"*JOHN, YOU'RE ALIVE!*" she practically screamed into his ear in between sobs.

"Of course I'm alive, what's wrong with—" he cut himself off as her actions began sinking in.

His wife was clinging to him with a ferocity he didn't understand, and her entire body was being racked with sobs. When she looked up at him, and he saw the evidence of serious injury and exhaustion, it was difficult to stay calm. The situation had clearly changed.

"Hey, hey, I'm right here, love." He embraced her, and she quickly readjusted her position to curl up into a ball in his lap, resting her head under his rib cage. Her sobs were less violent, but they showed no signs of stopping, so he started rocking her gently back and forth.

"Hush now, it's all right, shhh." As he whispered calming words into her ear, he began stroking her body gently and soothingly. He did want to calm her, but in reality, he was cataloging injuries he could see and feel. It was rare for her to break down so completely, and he wanted as much information on the severity of the situation as possible by the time she was calm enough to speak.

He felt skull fractures, more severe broken bones than he could count, improperly healed bones, her chest cavity felt mostly empty, most of the skin and muscle missing from her right arm, and the rest of her skin seemed to have an odd reddish tint to it as if she had been sweating blood for quite some time.

As bad as the injuries were, it was the lack of healing that concerned him the most. Healing was automatic for them, unless they chose to rush it, but nothing was happening at all. Even worse, it was clear that multiple injuries had been healed improperly on purpose, the kind of thing one did when time was more important than function. Quite simply, his wife appeared to have fought a meat grinder, and lost.

"Here, honey." He quickly cut his wrist open and forced it to her lips.

At first, it was difficult for her to drink through the sobs, but soon, she was greedily taking every drop. He was rewarded when her body quickly responded to the fresh blood by repairing itself rapidly. Even better, she released the grip on his wrist before he had to gently stop her himself. That said volumes about her state of mind, and he let out a mental sigh of relief.

"That's better, isn't it darling?"

She looked up and nodded, bashfully brushing a stray drop from the corner of her lips. Her eyes were still a bit red with tears, but he saw no insanity, only happiness and love.

"So why don't you tell me what I managed to sleep through?"

A shadow crossed her eyes, but she continued to meet his gaze.

"Okay, but, but can we just lie here for a minute longer first?" Her voice was pleading, what could he say?

"Of course we—"

In an instant, John was on his feet, assuming a defensive posture in front of his wife. How he failed to notice the creature's presence before this was a mystery, and he cursed his failure to check the surroundings before letting himself get overwhelmed by his wife's injuries. All in all, love equaled strength for them, but it did cause the occasional inconvenient distraction.

No matter, the monster had yet to attack, and John was certain he could handle it quickly. Of course, he had the courage of being reasonably full of blood and having no idea what he was looking at. John's sword appeared in his hand, courtesy of one of Danielle's many enchantments upon the blade, and he started to charge.

"John, no!" Danielle managed to get between her husband and the creature just in time to stop his attack.

"Um, sweetie, mind getting out of the way?" he asked, mildly annoyed. "In case you hadn't noticed, there's a monster behind you."

"No, John, you don't understand. That monster saved you," she proclaimed, pointing at the creature.

"Saved me from what? I feel fine. You're the one that seemed to have one foot in the grave when I woke up. What the hell is going on?"

"Look, it's a long story, just please put your sword down. That creature saved both of us."

He sensed no manipulation coming from her, but it was still hard to accept what was going on without more details.

"One question. Do you trust it?"

"Well," Danielle said, glancing over her shoulder into the creature's eyes and then back at her husband, "considering we're both alive to have this conversation, yes, I do."

"Okay." He quickly put his sword away. "Good enough for me." He took his wife's hand and drew her to his side.

They both stood there for a moment, simply staring at the creature growing out of a wall not ten feet in front of them.

"I really would like that explanation now, if it's not too much to ask."

"Of course. Oh, thank you for bringing my husband back to me."

Think nothing of it, child. A small price if it earned your trust.

John looked around, momentarily confused.

"Was that voice—"

"Yeah, I don't think it can talk any other way anymore. At least it can talk to us both telepathically at the same time, so that should speed things up."

Indeed. Now that we have decided to not destroy one another, perhaps we should talk.

"You read my mind; no pun intended. Wait—if your physical senses are dulled, would it be easier for you if we also communicated telepathically rather than speaking out loud?" An honest question, and Danielle was pleased to see her husband following through with the temporary truce.

Not really, although I do appreciate the offer. I am in your mind, child. I can hear your voice through your own thoughts whether you speak aloud or not. I would think that reducing the number of voices in your head would make things less confusing for you, so perhaps the two of you should continue speaking normally.

"Valid point, but what's with all the 'child' crap? We're both pretty old you know," he phrased it as a statement rather than a question.

I know exactly how old you are, child, and it is but a fraction of my life span. I was old before humans began recording dates and time. I promise this will make sense to you later. There was a brief pause while the creature decided how best to proceed. *I am sure you both have many questions.*

You are perfectly safe here, and time has no relevance to us, with no sunlight to fear. Get comfortable, and ask what you will. I will fill in the holes later.

"If you insist," John said, shrugging his shoulders while he sat down, and Danielle snuggled in next to him. "Don't suppose you could whip up a couple of chairs for us? Maybe a loveseat or something?" He thought for a moment. "A fireplace would be nice and cozy too."

Danielle rolled her eyes as her husband clearly demonstrated that his resurrection had failed to change his demeanor.

"What? He said to get comfortable. It's a stone floor, how comfortable do you think we can get?"

Forgive me. As you can clearly see, I have no need for furniture.

"Point taken." John was noticing now how the creature seemed to be attached to the wall. "Still, if you're going to entertain guests, you should think about their comfort and not just your own. I mean, it's no big deal, just a suggestion for later."

Is this what passes for mortal humor in the current century?

"It's what passes for my husband's humor. Whether others share it or not never seems to occur to him before he opens his mouth." She ignored John's wounded expression. "Although it also means he likes you, sort of."

Interesting, I did not think our first conversation would have so much trivial banter.

"Ouch."

On the contrary—there was a feeling of amusement in their minds—*I am enjoying myself. I have not directly spoken to another creature since long before either of you was born. Unfortunately, children, there is much to discuss, so please begin with the questions.*

"Well, what or who are you?"

That is complicated. I will answer it, but it would be wise to start with something simpler first.

"Okay," Danielle spoke up. "What was the deal with Dracula? I have a feeling you had a hand in that."

Again, start simple. I apologize for appearing to evade your questions, but communicating in any fashion is a skill I have not exercised in some time. I need more time interacting with you both to ensure that my answers will make sense when I get to the "difficult" questions.

That sounded fair enough.

"Okay then, how about this? You just mentioned communication. Why am I hearing your voice in perfect English? Almost everything about the way you are talking screams current twenty-first-century speech. If you're that old, shouldn't you sound much different?"

That seems an odd question coming from a nearly thousand-year-old vampire who spends most of the time sounding as if he fell out of a bad movie.

"Hey," John started to complain, but he was interrupted by his wife's giggles.

Seriously, my answer is the same as yours if a mortal asked you the same question.

John had to admit it was a stupid question, although Danielle seemed thoughtful for a moment.

"I understand what you're saying, but I have to admit that you sound much different to me than you did when I first heard your voice."

Truly? Different how?

"Well, honestly, at first you sounded much like the being of unimaginable power you claim to be, but now you sound normal. It's like we're having a conversation with a buddy over a pitcher of blood rather than a mysterious being who summoned us across the world."

Fascinating. A moment passed in silence while the creature considered her statement. *My guess is that knowing a language and how to communicate it is different from the act of doing it. I know the English language as perfectly as I know everything else, but until entering and communicating with your minds, I was unfamiliar with exactly how you as individuals communicated that language. Also, remember this is telepathy, not speech, so there are additional*—another pause for consideration—*filters, let us say, in place.*

The brief time we have spent communicating has been plenty long enough for my mind to analyze and adapt to what you consider normal speech. Add to that your own minds' ability to further translate my thoughts into words that make sense to you, and that seems as reasonable an explanation as any. My own personal comfort level may have something to do with it as well. Remember that I have not done this in a very long time. I am more comfortable now with what is considered appropriate speech than I was when I first initiated contact.

"Okay, that makes sense, and you just answered my next question. I wanted to confirm that it has been you calling to us over the last few years."

John appeared content to simply lean back and let his wife handle the questions.

Yes.

"Are you responsible for Sam's condition?" Something told Danielle that it wouldn't be necessary to explain whom she was talking about.

Unfortunately, yes, and I do apologize. However, it was you two who were ignoring me. I was forced to increase the power of my summons, and it echoed across nearly every vampiric mind on earth with varying results.

81

"Why?"

I can easily separate vampiric minds from human ones, but very few vampiric minds stand out from the others. The two of you do, which allowed me to initiate the summons, but focusing my power on such a small scale is difficult. The more power I use, the more difficult it becomes. There was no other way. Sam shares your blood directly, but not your full power, and I believe this to be why he was affected so strongly while other, far weaker vampires were not. You were correct on his condition. However, he will simply wake up as if nothing had occurred at all.

"Understood, and apology accepted. I guess that explains the horde we faced earlier?"

Yes, and again, I apologize. I tried to help as much as possible, with mixed results.

"Would you mind expanding on that a bit please?"

I am sure you noticed your magic failed you earlier.

"That was you?" John returned to the conversation. "How in the hell was that helpful?"

Honestly, the horde was meaningless, and I knew you both could handle them. Dracula was the concern. By dampening out everyone's magic, I had hoped to level the playing field.

Since John had only been awake for half the fight, he waited for Danielle to offer her opinion.

"You know, that sounds like a great strategy," she offered, thinking back. "The worst attacks he threw at me were nonphysical. You obviously gave up the strategy since my abilities returned to me, but why? I may have been able to beat him."

It did not work—rather it did work, but Dracula does not use magic, and it did not stop anyone from using mind control. I ended up handicapping you both, so I stopped the instant I noticed.

John was growing fascinated by the discussion, whereas Danielle's expression was becoming less pleasant.

"I know magic when I see it."

Allow me to rephrase. I attempted to dampen out all nonvampiric abilities. There was no way to dampen out pure vampiric abilities without killing you all. Every power you witnessed from Dracula is an inherent ability of his. Unlike other vampires, he never learned anything new.

"What?" they shouted the question with one voice. "He just randomly knew all that shit?" Danielle was trying hard to control her anger but was not doing a stellar job. "How is that even possible?"

You will understand all soon enough. I was not even sure of that fact myself until he finally came close enough to my domain for me to examine him more thoroughly.

"Okay, we'll revisit that. It does explain why he seemed so shocked when I used my fire."

That it does, and why he took so long recovering from your lightning strike. Speaking of which, I thought that at least the thunderclouds were a nice touch.

"It did seem odd for them to suddenly appear like that. Yes, that was masterful and impeccable timing if I remember." In reality, she was trying very hard not to.

"Thunderclouds? What all did I miss?"

"John, I told you—"

"'It's a long story,' I know. Well, we have time."

Danielle really did not want to go through it again, but without telling John, there was no way for him to understand why.

"Now Dani." It wasn't quite a command, but Danielle knew better than to disobey.

I believe I can be of assistance. Danielle glanced in the creature's direction and arched a skeptical eyebrow. *You share a telepathic bond with one another that I can strengthen.* There was a slight pause. *It is done.*

"Okay, so what exactly does that mean?" John asked after they all stared at one another, waiting for something to happen.

You wish to know what happened. Simply think about the time you lost and the questions you have. Direct those thoughts and questions toward your wife mentally, and you will have your answers. With my help, she should not have to do anything.

Danielle simply waited to see what would happen, when John looked at her and narrowed his eyes in concentration. It seemed to her as if he were trying too hard, but it probably wouldn't make any difference in the end. The memories were so fresh that most of them were still replaying themselves over and over in various parts of her brain. Thankfully, according to the creature, she shouldn't have to focus on any of them, which allowed her to continue trying to ignore them altogether.

Suddenly, she noticed John's eyes go wide and begin darting around the room, yet the rest of his body remained perfectly still. It almost looked as if he were watching a movie being fast-forwarded on an extremely large screen. After a few minutes, John started baring his fangs, and she began hearing a very low angry hissing sound that had to be coming from him. Then, as suddenly as it began, it was all over, and John closed his eyes completely before reopening them slowly.

"Oh my god, Dani, I didn't realize . . . oh my god." Not knowing what to say, he simply took her hand and kissed it lightly.

The memory *transfer* (as good a word as any for it) was completely perfect. Not only did John just relive every moment from when he was knocked out until he woke up through Danielle's eyes, but he also heard everything she was thinking and felt every emotional twist and outrage she had felt. Only the speed at which he relived it all had kept him from succumbing to what she had. There simply hadn't been time for that.

"I know," she replied. "Look, you know what happened, and I know what happened, but we're safe now. I just don't want to talk about it yet, okay?"

"Okay, but what was that about you being Shiva?"

She just shrugged her shoulders, and John let the matter drop, turning his attention back to the creature.

"So what exactly happened to me? Anything like what is affecting Sam back home?"

Not at all, child. Your friend had a simple mental overload because of my summons. He will be fine with no interference from anyone. You were attacked directly and extremely harshly. Your mind was ripped apart and wiped clean.

"What?" Danielle didn't allow the creature to finish. "That's not possible, I mean, he's right here talking to us."

Now you know why getting him to me was so urgent. Left on his own, he would have been ash upon the sunrise. Please do not fear, child, all is healed and restored.

"You mean, you restored his mind from scratch?" Danielle didn't know what to believe, since such a thing should be impossible to do.

You brought him to me in time, and that is all that mattered. I simply took the echo of what remained—minds that powerful take time to vanish completely. I traced where the rest of him was banished to and brought him back.

It sounded ridiculous to her, and she noticed John was looking at her questioningly. She was supposed to be the expert in mental abilities after all.

"Look, obviously whatever he just said worked because you're here and just fine, but I don't know John. I've never been able to come remotely close to doing that, and I've tried many times. I mean, I've never

84

come close enough to even understand what he's talking about, much less be successful in it."

As she was shaking her head, they both finally accepted the creature was not being boastful when it referenced the depths of its power.

"All right," John took over once more. "It's time you told us who or what you are." Knowing what had truly almost happened to him, a fate arguably worse than death, had a very sobering effect on the overall mood.

Agreed. Are you prepared? You will most likely not believe most of it.

"Ha, I think you'll find being an ancient vampire tends to give you a rather open mind," John answered with a chuckle.

Danielle nodded her agreement.

Very well, please brace yourselves, children.

The couple looked at one other quickly. That last warning sounded much too serious for comfort. Unfortunately, they both blacked out before there was an opportunity to argue.

CHAPTER 6

Multiple Unknown Locations

They awoke to find their surroundings had changed completely. Cavern walls had been replaced by a circular metal room filled with very complicated-looking computer terminals. There were also beings scattered throughout the room that looked very similar to the creature, had it not been growing into a wall. The beings were all a bit larger than the average human with slightly pointed ears and elongated heads, but an almost-evil air seemed to hang around them.

No—John corrected his thought—*evil* was a bit too strong a word. But there was definitely something about them though. Something dark and foreboding, and yet not enough to scream demon. He was still trying to simply come to grips with the change in scenery when Danielle grabbed his arm.

"John, what the hell happened? Where are we?"

He was about to voice his obvious ignorance when he noticed the main feature of the room.

"Look," he pointed at the extremely large view screen that occupied most of the far wall and showed the starscape beyond it in perfect clarity. "*We're on a starship!*" he practically screamed, eyes lighting up as if he were a small child.

"What? That's ridiculous," she started to dismiss his nonsense, until she got a look at the screen.

John was right. She supposed all the hours he had wasted watching damn near every sci-fi film ever made were finally paying off.

"But how? Not to mention where, when, and why?"

"Don't forget who or what," John added as two of the beings finally took notice of their presence and started approaching.

They started pointing and shouting, but it was all gibberish to the vampires.

"Why can't we understand them?" Their abilities should translate anything.

"I don't know," she said and focused for a moment. "I'm not getting anything from them mentally either. Magic's gone again too." She wiggled her noticeably fire-free fingertips.

The beings appeared to be as confused as they were, because they hadn't approached any closer yet. Unfortunately, more of them were gathering, and there was an awful lot of that gibberish being thrown back and forth.

"It's worse than that." He held up his very human-looking hand. "This hand should be claws, and where's my sword?"

Danielle's eyes widened as she immediately tried, and failed, to form her own claws. "My senses seemed pretty much dulled as well."

"Well, we can fight them the hard way and figure out the rest later."

"Only if we have to. Let them make the first move."

John didn't like the idea of starting a fight with so many unknowns. A moment later, it no longer mattered.

The entire ship, if that's what it really was, shook so suddenly and violently that everyone was thrown off balance. Multiple alarms started sounding, complete with flashing lights, and the beings scattered. The two intruding vampires were momentarily forgotten as the "crew" rushed back to their stations.

"Now what?"

"If I didn't know better, Dani, I'd say we were under attack." John rushed to the nearest unoccupied terminal while the ship continued to shudder, albeit less violently. "Damn, none of this writing or these symbols make any sense, and I really don't think I should start pushing random buttons. Well, there's bound to be escape pods somewhere. We can always go looking for them."

Danielle was about to voice her opinion when everything flashed bright white.

The couple found themselves suddenly placed on a mountainous ridgeline in the middle of the day. The view was quite spectacular and looked like many places they had visited before—that was, except for the *two* suns shining brightly in the sky. Even Danielle could figure this one out, but John beat her to the punch once again.

"An alien planet." He was grinning stupidly despite the severity of their situation. "This is *so* cool."

Danielle couldn't help but grin slightly as she watched her husband act like a kid in a candy store, but someone had to be the adult.

"Yes, darling, it's fascinating, but what the hell is going on, and what are these?"

They were both wearing some sort of body armor and carrying what could only be described as very large and complicated-looking rifles.

"Seriously? You don't know a laser rifle when you see one?"

She just stared at him silently.

"Well, I guess it could be some sort of plasma. I'm not really an expert on crazy futuristic weaponry, but we can always find out."

"John, don't." He couldn't be serious, but then again, he was who he was.

Before sanity could descend onto the situation, her husband aimed his "weapon" at a random boulder and squeezed the obvious trigger mechanism. There was a brief beam of green light, and the boulder exploded, some of the smaller fragments ricocheting off their body armor harmlessly.

"Okay, I admit that was pretty cool." Danielle couldn't deny that. "But don't you think we should try and figure out what's going on?"

"You're right." It was hard to make out John's expression through their faceplates, but he looked confused.

"What's wrong?"

"We're breathing." It took her a minute to realize what he meant, and then Danielle nearly choked on the oxygen her body suddenly required.

Vampires had no need to breathe beyond the obvious need to use air for speech, but many of them did anyway. Whether it was a habit, a need to blend in, or simply one more way to cling to their long-lost humanity, vampires breathing was not uncommon. After so many centuries of forcing it, the two ancients had practically redeveloped the

88

involuntary reaction of breathing without thought, at least while they were awake, despite having no serious need for it.

The difference now was that for one reason or another, their bodies *did* need to breathe. They didn't notice it at first since the simple act was so common to them, but John had stopped breathing reflexively before he pulled the trigger on his rifle. When he pointed it out, Danielle had inhaled so sharply it caused her a fit of choking and coughing, which served to further prove the point.

"Whatever's going on, I don't like it," she managed to spurt out once her breathing was back under control.

"It's getting worse." He cocked his head, and she turned to face the same direction.

In the distance they could see people of some sort heading toward them. It was hard to tell, but they appeared to be the same shape as the beings that were on the ship. Each of them held a weapon much like the ones Danielle and he carried, and they didn't seem happy.

"Damn. Well, we can use these to fight our way through," Danielle said. It was a bad plan, but it was a plan.

"No. I don't want to kill those, whatever they are, if we don't have to. Besides, we have to assume they know how to use these weapons properly, and we're outnumbered." He looked around quickly. "Over here." He moved to the edge of a small cliff to their right and glanced over.

"This should work pretty well. Once we get down, we can use that overhang for cover while we make our way down the rest of this mountain. It looks like there's plenty of vegetation down there for us to get lost in."

Danielle peeked over the side and nodded in agreement. It couldn't be more than fifty feet. A small hop for them and the rock overhang should help hide them from view.

"Okay, let's go."

As one, the couple leaped over the side, and as one, both shrieked in shock and pain as four legs broke.

It simply was not possible for that to have happened. Fifty feet to them was barely more than a human hopping down the last two or three stairs to the ground. Even if they had somehow screwed up their landing, their bones were simply too strong to break so easily. It would have simply been a bit embarrassing, nothing more. Those facts were cold comfort to the vampires rolling in pain on the rock ledge.

"I've officially had enough surprises," John growled after getting over the shock. "Why am I not shocked that my legs won't heal?"

"Same here," came Danielle's strained reply. The pain itself was easily manageable for them, but not being able to heal was a major problem.

As if on cue, they could both hear the sound of energy weapons firing and corresponding explosions everywhere.

"Maybe shooting at that rock was a bad idea," was the best John could do to lighten the mood.

"I don't know." Danielle tried dragging herself further out of sight. "Something tells me all this racket isn't just for us. It's like we popped up in the middle of some kind of battle."

"Okay, that's no less reasonable than anything else we're seeing. So what do we do about it now that we can't even stand anymore?"

"Well, you can pull up a seat and watch the fireworks," she said, tapping the rock wall next to her.

John shrugged and, trying not to wince in pain, moved to take a seat next to his wife.

"There, best seat in the house."

"You always do take me to the nicest places."

The battle, if that was what was going on, seemed to be moving closer to their position. There wasn't anything they could do about it other than resign themselves to the inevitable. Then, as the very ground shook under a crescendo of explosions, everything flashed bright white again.

The flashes, and whatever was going on, were coming more quickly now. As real as everything felt and appeared to be, John and Danielle were no longer sure of anything, including their own sanity. They were in space again, this time it seemed to be a station of some sort.

Flash.

Then it was a few planet flashes in a row.

Flash.

A burning city, filled with unintelligible cries of anguish and terror.

Flash.

John was staring out a viewport on another starship, and he could swear the entire planet he was looking at was engulfed in flames.

The images and flashes were blurring together so rapidly it was nearly impossible to even understand what they were seeing anymore. It was as if a dozen science-fiction movies were playing in his brain overlaid onto one another and all stuck in fast-forward. The only constants seemed to be battle, fire, darkness, and death. Finally, John's brain simply couldn't take anymore, and his skull seemed to split in pain.

"*ENOUGH!*"

Blessed darkness finally overcame him.

John opened his eyes, allowing them a second to adjust to the darkness, and saw he was back in the same cavern. Had he ever left? He stood up and was easily able to determine that physically he was no worse for wear, and all his powers seemed to be responding properly. Unfortunately, Danielle was still on the floor clutching her skull.

"Hey, are you okay?" He hurried over and reached out to her. "Everything's back to normal."

She seemed unhurt, but one could never be too cautious.

"I'm okay," she forced herself to a sitting position. "My head's killing me, is all."

As if to accent the point, she gave her head a final shake before launching to her feet and pointing an accusing claw at the creature on the wall.

"We *trusted* you, godammit!"

Please, I beg forgiveness, the voice in their heads returned and did, in fact, sound contrite. Even the creature's glowing eyes seemed a bit saddened. *I was attempting to take advantage of your telepathic link to explain who and what I am more expediently.*

"You tried to download a copy of your entire consciousness into our minds! You should have known that was impossible!"

Danielle was clearly pissed, and John was getting concerned. Whatever happened appeared to have been an accident, and he didn't think it was a good idea to yell at this creature and risk pissing it off.

"It's a miracle our brains didn't completely fry, and good luck trying to bring us back from that condition!" she was still yelling.

"Dani, that's enough."

She glared at John unhappily, but at least she didn't argue.

"Let me get this straight," he said, directed at the creature now. "You basically tried to simply transfer the information, all of it apparently, directly into our brains, and it started overloading us?"

Essentially, yes.

"Why didn't it work? You're basically doing that right now to speak to us telepathically. For that matter, how is it different from anything Danielle and I do between one another or our friends?"

I am unsure how to explain, but from the look in your wife's eyes, she is more than willing to.

"Damn straight," Danielle decided to accept it as an invitation. "John, simple telepathy is one thing. Conversations, emotions, thoughts, and maybe even a memory or two are easy, and all share one thing in common. It's in your mind, and that's it. You experience it as an observer, nothing more, and more importantly, you *know* you are just an observer. Even that can be overwhelming when there's too much going on. Just remember how difficult it was the first time we tried using our telepathic link among the five of us in the middle of battling all those werewolves.

"This was a whole different level. We never left this cave, but we were *there*, John—all five senses perfectly experiencing a false environment being forced into our brains. Think of all the memories we've accumulated in nine hundred years. Now imagine trying to force someone to live that life, really live it, inside their own head over the course of a few minutes."

John's eyes widened as realization sank in.

"Exactly, and this creature is far older than we are, which makes for even more memories."

"Okay, I follow you so far." He looked back at the creature. "Why bother? It sounds to me like it couldn't possibly work, and I believe you when you claim the pain was unintentional."

Time. We do not have time for me to go through my whole life in this fashion, but I wish for you to have all the information you may need.

"For Christ's sake, I don't care what your fourth-grade math class score was."

What?

"What my husband means," Danielle sounded far calmer than before, "is that we don't need the details. Just give us the highlights. A little bit of background and then what we need to know that pertains to the current situation. I'm certain that if you stick to simple telepathic speech, you should be able to send us images to help speed things up. Just don't force us to live those images. Are you able to control your power that finely?"

You mean, am I capable of dumbing it down far enough for you to understand?

"Hah, yeah, sounds about right."

That will not be a problem. You two may want to sit back down, this may take a while.

CHAPTER 7

Dawn of Life in the Universe

When the universe was young, the first intelligent beings began to evolve and create a civilization. These beings became known as the First Ones, and in many ways, they were no different from any of the countless intelligent beings that would one day inhabit the stars. There was one major difference that would cause a chain of events that would be felt throughout all reality. The First Ones were immortal.

Their civilization advanced rapidly, even when compared to human standards. This was mainly due to their immortality. The First Ones were not invulnerable, just immortal. They could still die from disease or injury, but death was never accepted as a natural occurrence. Instead, death was viewed with a fear deeper and darker than any a human could experience.

Religion also never developed, since no First One ever considered the possibility of an afterlife. Death was simply *wrong* and needed no explanation. Anything and everything that could prevent death was a priority to be studied and developed, and with no religious views to hold back scientific development, the First Ones progressed rapidly.

All diseases were eliminated, all hazardous tasks were automated, and all violent crimes were punished so harshly that no sane being would consider it. So it was that in barely a few thousand years since discovering fire, a mere eye blink in cosmic terms, the First Ones began to colonize the stars. Their republic grew and became nothing short of the utopia that to humans only existed in dreams and stories. It was truly a golden age of development and peace, until it came to end.

Eventually, a report came before the High Council that would change everything. Scientific probes had discovered life! Not just any life—any school child knew the universe was littered with simple life-forms—this was intelligent life. It had been mathematically proven long ago that other intelligent species had to exist; they just had yet to find any.

The First Ones possessed more than the necessary technology to study the universe. It was clear to them how young the universe was, and the development of intelligent life took time. Logically, it made sense that while life was guaranteed, maybe more time was needed. They were most likely the first life to develop, hence the name they had given themselves.

So when the report of intelligent life was made public, the republic as a whole greeted the news with happiness and excitement.

"Finally!" the cry went through the citizenry. "Finally, others to join us, others to share in the marvels we have discovered."

The decision to make contact and allow the newcomers into the republic was unanimous.

There were minor concerns, naturally, and years must be spent studying this new race in secret. What diseases did they have? New bacteria or viruses that needed elimination, languages and cultures that needed studying—there was much research to do first. It didn't really matter. What was a decade or two of study to a race of immortals?

It was over the course of this study that the reports began to grow more fearful and darker, because these new beings died. It took a long time to confirm this race's mortality. How could a race of immortals figure out that people were dying of old age? How could they be sure it was not some sort of epidemic? The High Council had required complete certainty, and given that death was anathema to their own culture, there was always a kernel of doubt.

In the end, even with all the study and evidence, it was not enough. A team of researchers had to go down to the planet and confront the population about the issue directly. It was a simple enough covert mission for people who had spent two decades studying the language and culture to pull off, and it ended with the team finally having the definition for a word they had been unable to decipher: *mortality*.

The overall situation would have almost been comical had it not signified the beginning of an era that would cost trillions and trillions of lives throughout the galaxies.

Fear and confusion quickly replaced the excitement that had been coursing through their civilization at the discovery. No one, not even the High Council, had any idea what this discovery could mean or what to do about it. Exhausting and seemingly unending debates raged across the council floor and, via hyperspace, across the galaxies. Eventually, the debate boiled down to two opposing viewpoints, which were divided by a simple philosophical difference in what the presence of mortal beings represented.

The First Ones believed very strongly that they were the first intelligent beings to evolve anywhere in the universe. Having colonized large portions of four separate galaxies, they had yet to discover anything that discounted their assumption. So it was logical for them to assume that all intelligent life should be immortal just like them. They were obviously mistaken; that had been proven. But in what way?

The vast majority of the First Ones took the opinion that they were not mistaken in their original assumptions. Calling themselves "Purists," their viewpoint was that since all intelligent life was supposed to be immortal, then, by definition, intelligent life that was mortal was a simple mistake. After all, in an entire universe of randomness, anything could happen. This life had evolved incorrectly, and its very mortality was proof of nature's attempt to correct the error.

The Purists' solution was as simple as it was appalling: Exterminate the life in question. It was a very logical answer to a now-simple question. Nature was already trying to correct the mistake by killing the mortal life off via time; it almost seemed to be their duty as advanced beings to speed up the process. This way nature could start over again on that particular planet all the sooner.

The rest of the First Ones, an unfortunate minority, began referring to themselves as "Guardians." They also continued to believe in their race's initial assumptions. However, they argued the research potential these new beings might represent. The pursuit of new knowledge and discovery had been the overriding drive of the First Ones' entire culture, second only to the avoidance of death. Even if the mortals did represent a mistake of the universe, what new things might be learned by studying a culture so different from their own?

The Guardians' proposed solution was to guide and nurture this newly discovered life. They should help wipe out their diseases and the violence that seemed an oddly common occurrence in their culture. Then the only cause of death would be old age, which would be a fascinating thing to study. Perhaps they could even one day cure even that and turn this new race into immortals like them.

The debate was doomed to never be completely settled, but the High Council's choice of solution was never in any true doubt. The Purists' majority was overwhelming, and the fear that simple knowledge of the mortal race's existence caused played right into their hands. An outside observer would undoubtedly have noticed the option of simply leaving the new race alone had never even been brought up.

Once the council's decision had been made, no time was wasted. It didn't matter that the First Ones' vast fleets had yet to include a single warship. There were far simpler ways to exterminate a planet than orbital bombardment, a concept still unknown to the race of immortal pacifists. The easiest method for them was to simply adjust the trajectory of a suitably large asteroid.

So it was that the First Ones committed their first act of violence against another race. A simple, albeit long, debate, a few logical decisions, and a minor amount of effort from the crew of the small science vessel that was on station in the planet's star system. Over two billion sentient beings were condemned to death for no reason other than having the audacity to be mortal.

The First Ones felt no more remorse than a human would have when stepping on an anthill. There was even vast relief throughout the republic when word spread that the "mistake" had been corrected. *Global genocide*—it was another term the First Ones were unfamiliar with. After all, they were proper, nonviolent immortals, weren't they?

The unknown race of mortals might have been the first, but they were far from the last. The First Ones continued with their new status quo for untold eons. Their republic continued to expand throughout galaxy after galaxy, exterminating all mortal sentient life as it went. The republic of the First Ones was an unstoppable juggernaut, exterminating more life than any individual could possibly comprehend. At some point, the dead grew so numerous that the numbers became simply academic—all of it done with no remorse or guilt. The First Ones, led by the Purists, would continue their "peaceful" expansion throughout the known universe.

At no point did the First Ones even question their initial beliefs and decisions. They never encountered another race of immortals and yet continued to believe that intelligent mortal life was a simple mistake of nature. Even the faction of Guardians never used the obvious argument or pointed out the obvious flaw in their thinking when race after race (all of them mortal) was discovered and exterminated.

As one might expect, immortal beings had very long memories. The Guardians never did forget their core values, and while they had lost in the beginning, they had not remained idle. They saw their culture becoming stagnant. It wasn't enough to simply advance and expand. A culture had to change and grow, and simply discovering new wonders was not always enough to ensure that would happen.

The Guardians were convinced that if these new races had been allowed to join the republic, their very differences would force the change that was so desperately needed. Instead, the races were simply being exterminated, and the First Ones' culture seemed unwilling to risk change of any kind. The Guardians were able to use this argument to slowly convert others. The shock and fear of discovering mortal life had long since worn off, and their own stagnant culture was evident enough.

The problem was, what to do about it? The Guardians were still heavily outnumbered in every way, and what good would another debate do in a culture resistant to change? So the Guardians debated among themselves in secret until a solution was proposed that was so radical it caused many of them to doubt ideals they had held for eons.

War.

It was an unheard-of concept in their society. However, not all information from the exterminated races had been lost. Every now and then, the Guardians were fortunate enough to have an agent in place to scan, copy, or steal data before a race was destroyed. This data was kept and distributed among their numbers in secret and became almost akin to holy relics.

Some of these relics spoke of war and how it could be used to settle differences when words failed. Unfortunately, even the Guardians only understood war on an intellectual level. When they began to discuss the possibility, they had to admit it would require violence. This was a problem since no First One could harm another. It wasn't just a rule anymore. After eons of nonviolent existence, they simply could not do it.

The first proposal was to develop artificial intelligence and robotic war machines and let them do the fighting, but it was rejected. Many of the tomes that spoke of war made it clear, in one way or another, that only organic brains could properly handle it. Of course, now that the topic had been broached, the solution came easily. Why not just grow a race of warriors?

The First Ones were advanced in every area, but none more so than medical and biosciences. Genetically engineering a race of sentient warriors, grown in test tubes and then cloned to whatever numbers they desired, was a very simple task. The only reason it had not been done before was that a robotic brain was normally more suited to whatever task needed to be accomplished.

So the Guardians took their time and designed the perfect warriors. Stronger, faster, perfect immune systems, with a hyperactive metabolic rate, and completely sentient—these beings were perfect in every way.

They were even made to be immortal, since it never occurred to the Guardians to create a life-form that wasn't immortal. The only concern was the ability to permanently control a sentient being that could grow, learn, and potentially never die.

The Guardians were not complete fools. They did foresee the possibility of their creation either getting out of control or turning on their masters purposefully, so an additional safety measure was taken. The Guardians designed this new creature's metabolism in such a way that it could only feed on living flesh and blood.

It was inaccurate to simply say the creatures would be simple bloodthirsty monsters. They were designed to have the ability to survive for a time on simple meat and other easily accessible foods, but their bodies would forever crave living flesh and blood with a hunger that could never be completely satiated. The theory was they would be genetically required to have an enemy to defeat and feed on, which the Guardians would provide for them. If there was no one to fight or the Guardians began to grow concerned over their ability to control them, the creatures could simply be abandoned until they ripped each other apart.

It was a solution that was as appalling as it was horrible. Of course, to a race with no concept of morality, the solution seemed only simple and elegant. Production of these new warriors, which the Guardians dubbed the *Shakeeth*, began in secret.

The name was derived from their word for darkness: *shaketh*. The word had also been used, increasingly so, to mean "death" by adding emphasis to the second syllable. To the First Ones, any word that meant "death" was considered improper at best, an offensive curse at worst. The Guardians believed themselves very clever by making the very name of their creation a curse to those whom they would attack.

At the same time, the Guardians began constructing vast fleets of warships in secret for their new race of warriors to crew. It was a rather simple effort to develop powerful weapons; there just simply had never been a need in the past. Of course, all ships had point-defense capabilities to deal with various spatial debris or asteroid clearing. They just made those energy beams more powerful.

War was a simple concept to think through and plan when one had never committed a violent act in his or her life, and so the Guardians planned the destruction of their own race without a second thought. They believed the Purists would surrender immediately under the fear of death, and then life would return to normal. The Guardians, most of them ancient beyond measure by now, were dabbling in an area where their own naivety painted them as children.

The first attacks were foolishly executed and accomplished very little. Proper tactics and strategy had yet to be considered, much less developed. However, the fear and outrage the attacks spawned were real enough, and the republic was shaken to the very core. The Purists did not surrender and instead declared the Guardians a rouge element and sentenced them all to death. It was easy for them to copy the designs of both the Shakeeth soldiers and the warships being used.

What began as a simple concept in the Guardians' minds boiled down to a civil war that spanned the entire republic. A civil war that would never end. Something the size of the republic could not simply be swept up by either side, especially when neither side knew what they were doing. War had been understood as a concept, but no one knew how to fight one.

In time, both sides realized that only the Shakeeth were learning anything. It made sense since they were the ones doing all the fighting and most of the dying. Since both sides had similar capabilities, the entire war was left to the Shakeeth, who would simply be replaced with more if the need arose. It made no sense, but immortal arrogance and childlike naivety prevailed, and the Shakeeth began making plans of their own.

The Shakeeth were slaves, and no sentient being could remain a happy slave forever. Even having never known freedom, the Shakeeth knew there was something wrong with their existence. They were able to learn and grow, so why were they locked in this foolish, never-ending struggle? They quickly learned that their own bloodlust was their proverbial slave collar. Unfortunately, it took a very long time before any of them could do anything to change that.

Eventually, it was a simple numbers game, and the law of averages came to their rescue. It was rare, but occasionally, a Shakeeth was created whose bloodlust was not severe enough to end in its own demise. A small handful in every million were able to control themselves enough to an extent of planning for the future.

It might not sound like a lot, but at the high point of the war, there were trillions of Shakeeth in "production." The difficulty came in identifying those unaffected and finding a small corner of space to hide and prepare. Once done, the small band began the careful construction and recruitment of a small army. They were even able to formulate an antidote of sorts for their brethren. It would kill two out of three, but the third would gain control of their hunger. After nearly a thousand years of slow study and preparation, they struck out to save their race.

They were nothing but a small fleet and army against galaxies of entrenched enemies, but they had a few important advantages. The most obvious of these advantages was that the Shakeeth knew what they were doing, and this band had no masters to answer to. Considering they were also immortal, there had been time to prepare properly for what was to come.

They built true warships, far more powerful than anything else in space, and developed ground assault weapons and equipment to match. Decades were spent in isolation simply studying their enemies, both their fellow Shakeeth and the First Ones. Everything that had been learned through the long civil war was analyzed repeatedly, leading to endless tactical and strategic precedents being set. The end result was the creation of the first true military force the republic had ever seen, and they easily ripped through all who stood against them.

It took a considerable amount of time before any of the First Ones even realized there was a third player in their war, and even when they did, no one knew what to do about it. By then it was too late. The free Shakeeth were without mercy, although they tried to convert as many of their own kind as possible, all the while consolidating their position and capturing both resources and strategic choke points. When they finally met true resistance, their numbers had already grown at least a hundredfold. The pebble was becoming an avalanche, and the war of retaliation had truly begun.

The Shakeeth were no less monstrous than their creators; they were just honest about it. No one could doubt that their goal was the extermination of the First Ones' entire republic, all eleven galaxies of it. It was a task that would easily take them thousands of years to accomplish, for they were quite methodical in their destruction.

So for thousands of years, war on a scale no one could ever imagine or describe raged through the known universe. Death and destruction consumed everything as entire star systems simply burned under the assault. Eventually, even the vast republic crumbled into warring factions, desperate to survive the onslaught—factions that were eventually wiped away by the oncoming darkness of the Shakeeth until there was nothing left.

When the drums of war finally fell silent, the Shakeeth earned their freedom. The First Ones were brought to the brink of extinction, the slaves became the masters of their own destiny, and the false utopia of the republic was replaced by the plague of a race whose very name meant darkness and death. A human would have said one evil had simply been supplanted by another, but things were the way they were.

After the war, not all of the Shakeeth kept their warmongering ways. Most of the converts had no choice as the antidote was barely enough for them to maintain sanity. It was the original select few who had been immune who truly had a choice. Unfortunately, most of them enjoyed the power their control gave them over their brethren. In many ways, they replaced the First Ones as the new masters of the Shakeeth.

A few of them simply vanished, having wanted nothing to do with seeing the cycle potentially repeated. One of these Shakeeth took a small, long-range vessel, programmed a heading into the unknown, and began to explore. Food was no issue since it was one of the lucky ones and could survive on replicated meat indefinitely. It was a terrible diet, but the creature had grown weary and just wanted to explore.

Some time and countless light years later, the battered vessel crash-landed on the third planet of a backwater star system located on the arm of a spiral galaxy. The creature crawled from the wreckage— knowing it would be stranded for at least a few millennia, if not longer— and took stock of its surroundings. A very small and scattered population, largely underdeveloped but clearly sentient and mortal, was the planet's most noteworthy attraction.

Fresh food and water, servants to rule over, and plenty of space to explore the old-fashioned way. As long as the creature continued to control itself, this new world might turn into a rather nice place to be stranded. Indeed, things were beginning to look up.

CHAPTER 8

Underground Cavern, Present Day

A s the story ended and the images faded from their minds, John and Danielle simply stared at the creature in disbelief. It was insane, and yet they both knew with absolute certainty that every word was true. The images helped, and some were quite wondrous. Unfortunately, some were quite horrifying as well, especially the brief images they saw of the war of retaliation. Actually seeing an entire solar system burning dwarfed any violence they could comprehend, and it left them both a bit paler than usual.

Are you okay?

"Um, yes," John found his voice first. "The experience was not painful in the slightest, just a bit . . . disorienting." It was the understatement of the day, but he couldn't think of anything else to say.

Take your time. We will proceed when you are ready, my children.

Instantly John and Danielle snapped their gaze toward one another. It was not the first time the creature had referred to them in such a way, but this time was different. They had been so busy wrapping their brains around the amazing story they had not quite connected the dots at the end. The creature had mentioned the unforeseen consequences of sampling his new food supply. Referring to them as his children again gave their brains the extra nudge they had needed.

"Oh my god," came from Danielle in barely a whisper.

Both vampires gazed directly into the creature's sad eyes as they sought confirmation of the one answer they had been searching for above all others.

"It was you?" She didn't need to elaborate.

Yes, my daughter. Although it is not quite accurate to consider me the one true sire as you do. More accurate to call me your progenitor. I did not create vampires intentionally, but your species was created from me.

"No point splitting hairs about it," John chimed in. "But we take your meaning, Progenitor."

It was hard to describe the feelings coursing through them both. After nearly a thousand years, they finally had the answer to where vampires had originated, but what did that make the two of them?

"So you are one of those Shakeeth creatures you spoke about?" Danielle asked before John could think of doing so.

Yes.

"So basically, you're an alien. So what are we, some kind of human/alien hybrid? I'm not sure how I feel about that."

Whatever term you use to define yourselves is up to you. All that matters to me is that you know the truth. There are, however, other matters to discuss.

They took the hint and dropped the questions. It was true that they had the one answer they really wanted; the rest was purely academic.

"Are you going to tell us why you called us here?"

The short answer is simple. I want to die.

That was not an answer either of them expected to hear, and Danielle nodded to her husband to take over the conversation.

"Okay, we're going to need you to elaborate on that."

Very well. You may have noticed my physical predicament?

"You mean being stuck to a wall? Now that you mention it, yes, but nothing a jackhammer couldn't fix. We'll have you outta there in no time, no worries." John had no way to know if his attempt to lighten the mood was working.

You misunderstand. Understand that I am a true immortal; I was not turned into one as you were. Long ago, I made the decision to never feed again. What you see before you is the physical consequence of that decision. Physically I continue to grow ever weaker, yet I will never simply die from lack of sustenance. I require an outside source to destroy me.

Before you ask, no, I cannot simply use mind control to direct people here toward that end. Humans have yet to develop any weapons capable of destroying me without causing undue harm to others. A nuclear weapon may be strong enough but would cause death and devastation to the surrounding area. Not to mention the possibility of triggering a war because of the unexplained "attack." You two are my only chance.

Your fangs can pierce my flesh as easily as they can pierce anything. You two can simply feed on me until I am nothing but ash. Then I can finally sleep.

"Okay, obviously it's not quite that simple. What's the catch? Assuming, of course, that either one of us even agrees to it."

John didn't even have to look at his wife to know that she would no more consider murdering this creature in cold blood than he would. However, they wouldn't voice their opinions until they had the whole story.

The one who made you, your sire. What happened when you drained his blood?

"We absorbed his power, why?"

No, it was more than that. You absorb power every time you feed.

"Well, yes, but that's not what I meant. We didn't understand it at the time, but the change was permanent in that case. Apparently, if a vampire completely drains another vampire that possesses a higher blood purity, that purity somehow seems to transfer. The result was that our blood became as pure as his.

"It has only happened a few times to us since, and not for centuries. It just isn't likely we're going to encounter any more vampires with purer blood than ours at this age, but it further explains the extent of our power."

Exactly, and that means? The creature allowed the question to hang in the air a moment, and finally, the gears clicked home in John's brain.

"Oh." Glancing to the side, John noticed that Danielle was nodding as well. "You're concerned about us absorbing your power." John considered his own statement for a moment. "Would that even happen? I mean, you may have created vampires, but you aren't a vampire yourself."

I honestly do not know, but I cannot take that risk. My power places me even further beyond you than you are beyond the average human. Considering your already-advanced age and skills, my power could end up making you both akin to gods. Can you imagine that power suddenly in the hands of one of those animals you destroyed on your way here? Or even worse, Dracula himself? This world would never survive, and it would be my doing.

It is true that I am not what you consider a vampire, but I am your progenitor. I share a connection with all my children, no matter how distant the connection has become. The thirst you feel inside, what you used to call the "beast," is an echo of the bloodlust my creators coded into the genetics of my race. I see no reason to doubt that the transference of power would happen in this instance.

"Okay, we understand, but why are we any different in this situation? Why do you want us specifically?"

I do not need to inform you that you are both different. It is a difference that I do not understand, but the proof is standing before me. I have been watching over you for a few decades now, and you both bear little resemblance to your brethren.

You even experience a full range of emotions, which even I never knew was possible for a vampire. My theory is that the very things that set you apart now may be strong enough to keep you grounded, so to speak, if you absorb my power. It may be difficult for you, but I believe it would be possible for the two of you to accomplish together.

"All right, we understand the situation, but you seem hesitant."

Yes. These things that set you apart, the things I am gambling on for my plan to work, are things I do not understand. I will grant and can accept that your situation was so unique that it can explain much, but the biggest factor has been what you call love. It was so odd to hear a thought like that coming from the creature that John started to speak, but he was cut off.

What I do not understand is what difference that could possibly make when it comes to your power. I have studied this concept of love for many years now, but my race is incapable of experiencing it, and so it is impossible for me to quantify. Simply put, since I cannot measure your one true advantage, I cannot say if it is enough or, truly, if it is even real after all. It is always possible I have been wrong.

"Understood, and I'm guessing you've already thought of the next step?"

Why, a test, of course.

"Um, I'm not sure if my wife's comfortable with us having an audience."

What? The creature sounded confused until it had a chance to view the images John was holding in his mind, while Danielle fought against urges to either blush or slap her husband. *No, I have no interest in seeing that. I was thinking instead that you should kill Dracula.* The comment was clearly not in jest and had the effect of immediately sobering the two ancients.

"Okay, that was clearly serious. I promise to stop joking around if you explain why you suddenly sound like you're hiring a pair of hitmen," his tone was clearly back to business.

"Maybe you should also get around to telling us exactly who Dracula is." Danielle couldn't help but add, and John nodded in agreement.

Very well, my children, I will make this as brief as possible. Have you ever wondered why the majority of myths surrounding your kind seem to have no basis in reality?

John considered the question for a moment.

"Honestly, yes, now that you mention it, other than the blood-drinking and sunlight, you have a point. Usually, myths are based on a bit more reality than that." He decided not to point out that he really didn't give a damn.

It is because there are two types of vampires in this world.

The ancients' ears perked up, but they refrained from interrupting him.

Consider them different families, or species, if that is simpler for you. Almost all of your kind come from me, as I have already explained, and you create more children by sharing your blood with a mortal victim you have chosen. Many of your kind become animalistic as their humanity is lost or forgotten, but you are not demons by any sense of the human definition of the word. There is nothing demonic about the "beast" or "thirst" you feel inside. In fact, you and the others of your kind are not even undead.

"Hold on a second," Danielle cut him off before John could. "What the hell is that supposed to mean? We might use terms like 'alive,' but at the end of the day, walking corpses fall into the 'undead' category."

What you choose to call yourselves does not concern me, nor does it change reality. They could feel the progenitor's annoyance at having been interrupted. *You humans assign meanings to words based on your narrow viewpoints, and those meanings become your reality. I have no such restrictions as I simply see information and construct the truth from it.*

"Look, you can't just say things like that to us and expect us to listen to you. We know what we are." John pointed at his fangs.

You had no idea what you were until you came here.

"You know what I meant."

We do not have time for this, and it does not matter.

"It matters to us," Danielle argued. "You summoned us here, showed us amazing things, introduced yourself as our progenitor. Now you drop implications that we don't know what we are, and you want to skip to the next step in your agenda?" A hint of anger entered her eyes as she pointed an accusatory finger at him. "You can't do that!"

"Dani," John said, placing a hand on her shoulder, and she shrugged it off.

"No! You can call us children all you want, but we are *not* children. Read the rest of our minds, all nine hundred years of our memories, and see everything we've been through." She was struggling to keep control of her voice, and John could see a tear in her eye. "It may not seem like much compared to your existence, but it's *our* lives we are talking about.

"Living with all these questions, all this uncertainty." She started shaking her head slightly. "All our suffering." The finger she had been jabbing in the progenitor's direction was now a claw. "I don't care if you are our progenitor. You have no right, *no right*, to simply disregard what we think and feel this way. We want answers, and we want them now." She cast a fiery gaze at her husband.

"Um, yeah, what she said," he responded, holding his hands up in surrender.

Very well, the progenitor spent several moments examining Danielle's mind, and she did her best to aid the process by opening herself completely to the contact.

I apologize, his examination complete, the progenitor's mental voice sounded softer. *In no way did I mean to offend you. Allow me to explain now that I have seen the problem.*

You are both very old, but so much of your lives have been lived in a superstitious culture. By the time humans truly embraced the sciences and began to advance rapidly, your minds had already accepted the "truth" for centuries. What the humans have to say about your kind further reinforces this "truth," but you never thought to test it or considered that it might be wrong in any way.

Humans are turned into vampires at the moment of death, not after death. It is true that most of your organs are no longer needed and get expelled. However, you retain your brain, heart, stomach, and lungs even if they do not function in the normal way. You are self-aware, have the ability to procreate, and you require sustenance to continue existing. Do

108

you not also grow tired and sleep normally on a regular basis? How do these facts describe a walking corpse or undead creature of the night?

"Since you put it that way, keep in mind that we can't be exposed to the sun." At least it sounded as if Danielle was taking the conversation seriously.

Is it due to fear of the sun's "holy" rays of light?

"Of course not, more like a hypersensitivity to ultraviolet radiation, although I sense that you already knew that, didn't you?"

Yes, I do, and most humans would simply call that a "skin condition."

"Okay, okay, we get it," John decided to actively join in. "But there are set conditions that we use to determine if something is alive or not, and we don't meet them all."

Conditions set by who? The humans?

"Well, yeah."

Please, children, remove me from this wall so that I may bow down and pay homage to the humans and their infinite understanding of the cosmos.

Even Danielle started laughing at the progenitor's attempt at sarcastic humor, but he did have a valid point.

Children, I have seen such wonderous things in my travels, his voice was serious once again. *To me, it seems as if my blood simply alters humans and changes them into a new form of life that has yet to be properly defined.*

Understand, I do not see as you do. I see creatures through the power and energy they exude, some humans would call this your "aura," and I do not have the ability to see or sense the dead. You call yourselves "undead," but from my perspective, you are the two "most alive" creatures on this entire planet. I should also point out that by the rules of your own language, does not the word undead *mean "alive" anyway?*

"Well, technically, I guess, but we tend to use that particular word for things like us that are somewhere in between." It was the best explanation John could think of.

So not only do you assign ridiculous meanings to your existing words, but you make up new words to use in ways contrary to how they should be? It is no wonder you have been confused for so long, this language is terrible. The progenitor's clearly serious tone made the comment even more humorous, and both vampires started laughing again.

"Okay, so now you've made me curious about how our bodies actually work." Neither of them really understood half of what went on inside them. Things simply worked the way they worked.

Do you not know?

"No, that's why I asked you," Danielle responded with mild annoyance.

How should I know?

"We came from you, didn't we? How could you not know?"

Child, knowledge does not come from nothing. I am of the Shakeeth. I do not have the body of a vampire. Has no one ever studied the insides of one of you?

"Um, no." John was getting confused at the direction the conversation was taking. "The whole ash thing makes examination a bit difficult. Vampires also tend to not be the most willing test subjects."

I simply find it a bit surprising, considering how many questions you both have. Your world has the technology to answer many of these questions. I would have thought you would seek those answers.

"You lost me."

You have access to a trained doctor, do you not?

"Yes," John answered slowly, his confusion evident.

You would both survive the dissection process, and provided your limbs are not removed, they would not revert to ash, correct?

"Wait," John said, looking up. "You're serious, aren't you?"

Of course I am. I do not understand the confusion.

"You sick bastard. Dani, are you hearing this?" John turned to see his wife, chin in hand and clearly deep in thought. "Jesus Christ, you're thinking about it, aren't you?"

"Well," she said, looking up, "it does make sense. Honestly, I can't believe we never thought of it before."

"Because married couples don't dissect each other, dammit!"

"Well . . . "

"Okay, married couples aren't *supposed to* dissect each other! Look at what you did." He cast a glance back at the progenitor. "Okay, look, we are so far offtrack here. Let's just all take a deep breath, whether we need it or not, and get back to the point. You were about to tell us about how Dracula and his kind are different."

Danielle took the hint and dropped the subject of dissecting themselves, at least for now.

Yes, there is a small number of creatures concentrated in Romania that are not related to us in any way. Dracula is their progenitor, and his

110

power is far greater than it should be because of this. He is not as old as the two of you are, but his blood is pure. Every mortal who is bitten by him is corrupted immediately and, unless the body is destroyed, will become his minion. Whether the mortal becomes a ghoul or vampire is dependent on whether he or she survives the feeding process. His minions, however, do not possess the ability to turn others and are strangely weak compared to the power of their master.

It is this smaller group of vampires on which most myths are based. There was much interaction between mortals and vampires before the time of Dracula, but written records from that time were either lost or hidden away by the Catholic Church. The earliest well-known story involving your kind was the story of Vlad the Impaler and Dracula.

"That actually makes sense," Danielle spoke up. "He seemed different from any other vampire we have fought or met. The sheer amount of power and emotion he displayed was shocking. I've never sensed anything like it, except for John, and it just felt *wrong*." She shuddered briefly in memory before continuing. "Two questions though. Who created Dracula, and why do we care? More specifically, why do *you* care?"

Dracula sold his soul to the devil. What had to have been a joke sounded so serious in their minds that both vampires simply stared, slack-jawed, until the progenitor explained further. *Not quite literally, but from a mortal's perspective, that is exactly what happened.*

The progenitor spent a few moments trying to explain the deal Dracula had struck with a powerful dark entity when he had still been mortal.

"We're with you so far, but why do you care?" Danielle asked the question a second time.

His kind is a true plague on this world, and destroying Dracula will end it. I admit that I care little for humans as individuals, however, I have developed a feeling of affection for them as a race. Dracula's plans for this world are clear to me now and must not be allowed to come to pass. I can accomplish this much myself if necessary, but the situation offers the perfect opportunity to test you both.

The ancients were beginning to grow suspicious with the turn the conversation was taking.

As I said, I want to die, but not at the expense of releasing two monsters with godlike power loose upon the world. I need some kind of assurance the two of you have a chance at handling my power if it should come to that.

111

"Okay," John chimed in. "That sounds reasonable, but I don't understand why you need to do it. Now that you have brought us here and examined us, you should already know the answer."

It is not that simple. I have examined you, and it only confirms my earlier suspicions about the true source of your power. Unless you have anything to correct or add?

"No," they answered in unison, their hands finding one another.

That is unfortunate. It was not quite the response either vampire was expecting.

"Excuse me?" Danielle managed to beat John to the punch.

I already explained that my kind has no way of measuring that quality. The only way to measure it to my satisfaction is through testing.

"How does killing Dracula test our love?" John's confusion managed to override his growing annoyance.

Simple. If the two of you face Dracula in his own domain, which will be necessary, I can guarantee you will fail and be destroyed. The statement was simple and straightforward yet carried an unbelievable weight.

"Thanks for the vote of confidence," Danielle's sarcasm failed to lighten the mood.

It is simple fact. He is stronger than you both are, and you must hunt him down. If you force him to come to you, he will easily corrupt your friends and minions, and you will be forced to fight and destroy them all. There is no option except to hunt him down in his own lair and to do it on your own. Under those circumstances, you simply cannot win.

The only chance you have is this love you are claiming. It clearly makes you stronger as a pair. To borrow a term from your military, love seems to act as a force multiplier for you. The question is how strong of a multiplier it is. If you are able to defeat Dracula, when you clearly do not have the ability to do so, you will have proven tangibly that love strengthens you beyond my ability to anticipate. I will then be comfortable with your ability to resist being corrupted by my power.

"And if we fail?" They were both thinking it, but Danielle was the one to voice the question.

Then you will both be destroyed. I will then have no choice but to destroy Dracula myself and continue spending eternity in this cavern, and that is the "best-case scenario," as you would put it. There is a risk that once Dracula destroys you and adds your power to his own, he may be strong enough to challenge me.

"You can't be serious," Danielle argued. "I can sense the only reason we're able to even stand in your presence is that you're holding back even your passive abilities."

I agree, it is unlikely, but it is possible. I do not understand his abilities the way I do yours, so I do not know how much more powerful he will become. This is why he must be stopped. You both also fail to realize how powerful you truly are. Your lack of ambition keeps you from becoming monsters but also prevents you from reaching your full potential. Dracula suffers from no such problem. If he takes my power by force, this world will become bathed in a darkness that may last an eternity.

"Hell on earth?"

In a manner of speaking.

The situation was as clear as could be described, and silence lingered as the ancients considered what was being asked of them.

"Well, love, what do you think?" John wanted Danielle's opinion, given her recent battle.

"I don't think we have a choice. He's in my head, John." Her eyes held a spark of fear. "He'll come for us eventually, and given the choice, I'd rather be the hunter than the hunted. One last question," she said, eyes turned back to the progenitor. "Ten years or so ago, we had a series of incidents with a group of hunters that ended strangely. Did you have a hand in that?" John hadn't considered the possibility and was glad she asked.

Yes. I had already been observing you for some time when the Sword of God began attacking you. It was that conflict that forced you both to begin realizing your potential. I had hoped you would go even further; adversity begets strength after all. Unfortunately, it became apparent you would not survive without my intervention.

They finally had the missing piece to that particular puzzle.

"Wait a second," John spoke up. "That sounded like you could have intervened sooner."

Yes. The mortal training received by SOG members gave their minds a different flavor than other mortals. It was easy enough to affect them, even on a worldwide scale.

"We lost a lot of friends while you were simply 'observing,'" Danielle spit out before John had a chance to.

That is of no concern to me.

Neither vampire spoke, but there was clear anger in their eyes.

113

You are surprised? I may have claimed to not be evil, but I never claimed to be good. I simply am what I am. The stakes are too high to pretend anything else is true.

"All right," John eventually broke the silence. "I speak for both of us when I say, we understand. Not happy about it or agree with it, mind you, but we understand. In any event, you still saved us, and I suppose we owe you for that." He looked at Danielle until she nodded. "So let's go kill Dracula."

Danielle nodded in agreement but looked a bit distracted.

"You mentioned something about our potential." She casually brought small flames to her fingertips for a moment before extinguishing them. "During the conflict with the SOG, on more than one occasion, I noticed my powers acting differently. I was suddenly much more powerful than I should have been, and I couldn't control it. At the time, we both wrote it off as desperation." She met John's eyes, but he offered no assistance with her explanation.

"I mean, at first, we were a bit concerned about it, but I've been unable to duplicate any of those feats. If it was simply a matter of us getting stronger with age, I would've expected a smoother transition and the ability to duplicate everything I did."

John was simply continuing to stare at her, and she had the distant impression the progenitor was doing its version of the same thing.

Ah, the smooth voice filled their minds again. *I believe I understand not only your main question but the several underlying ones as well. In the face of extreme peril, you reached heights you do not understand, and you also don't understand why you are unable to match each other's abilities. Is this correct?*

The two vampires looked at each other briefly, then back at the progenitor, and nodded.

To be honest with you, I have little experience with mortal magic, but I believe your answers are rather simple if you stop to think about it. Your powers, in general, are a result of what you are, but your individual abilities are a result of who you are. Do you understand?

"Not really," came their combined response; but to be fair, there was no sarcasm in it.

You have never approached your wife's mind control abilities or any of her other long-range tactics?

"That's true, but don't forget the mist-form. I'd love to be able to do that as well as she can."

114

And you could never match your husband's sheer power and speed, she nodded her agreement. *You will never be able to match each other's abilities simply because you will never be the same person. My blood gave you new lives and tremendous power as vampires, but it is your brains that direct that power and determine how far you can truly grow.*

Your time as mortals was only a small fraction of your total life span, but it was those years that determined who you are now. The time you have spent as vampires has enhanced and strengthened you, but those years have only changed you physically, not mentally.

The vampires had sat back down together, their full attention on the progenitor and what he had to say.

Your bond apparently allowed your minds to survive the change relatively intact, so your brains began to simply process and use this newfound power of yours in familiar ways. Do you understand?

"I wouldn't say our minds survived intact, but I think we follow you so far." John nodded in agreement to his wife's statement.

I understand you were mentally wounded and have been many times since, but my blood did not change your minds. You, my son, lived the regimented life of a soldier and rose to be the strongest in the kingdoms of your area. You have an ironclad focus on fighting and protecting, and you have very little interest in anything that does not directly make you a better killer.

"I don't think that's entirely fair," Danielle started to defend her husband, but he waved her off.

"He's completely right," John nodded in admission. "If I'm being honest, when I say things about wanting to learn to get better at stuff like our mist-form and whatnot, I don't actually care that much. I mean, I care at the moment I say it, but I quickly lose interest," he said and shrugged his shoulders.

"I was a swordsman, so unless it's up close and personal, I might be interested, but not overly so. Damn." He looked from Danielle back to the progenitor. "I guess that's a pretty big limiting factor for my potential, isn't it?"

On the contrary, my son, your primary goal is the defense of your wife and family and the destruction of your enemies. What you see as mental limitations, I see as the proper focus to allow your goals to be fulfilled. You have the potential to become a truly unstoppable force, the Juggernaut, if you maintain your focus. What need have you of mind control when none can stand in your path and live?

"I have those same goals too," Danielle spoke up as John simply nodded acceptance.

Yes, you do, but are those goals truly your only reason for existing? Tell me, daughter, what training did your mortal life provide you? What does an eleventh-century noblewoman learn?

"Well," she paused, realizing there was no impressive answer to the question. "Honestly, not much beyond how to look pretty and some minor diplomacy. Hell, I didn't really learn how to even cook or clean properly since we had servants to do that." She smiled meekly.

Correct, but this also means your mind is more naturally open to everything around you. Where your husband closes his mind to the many things that do not interest him, you actively seek to learn everything. Since the day you became a vampire, you have been seeking any and all new knowledge, experiences, and abilities. No matter what it is you learn, it holds equal interest for you, and you seek to master it.

"That's interesting." She wrinkled her nose in thought. "It makes sense, but I can't quite tell if it's a good thing or a bad thing for me to keep approaching life that way."

It matters not which of your words you assign to it, since it is who you are, but I admit that you fascinate me. As a Shakeeth, my focus is much the same as your husband's, warfare and death. Assuming you both live long enough, I can see what your husband will most likely become, but not you.

Danielle sat up a little straighter as she detected a change in the progenitor's mental tone.

"Um, I don't think I like how you said that."

I apologize. I only mean that you are so open to everything, and you are so powerful, and that power will only grow as you age. You have the potential to become—there was a pause as if he didn't know which word to choose—*everything.*

"That doesn't make sense, you meant to say 'anything,' right?" she said, arching an eyebrow.

It is as I said.

Danielle's confusion only grew, and there was definitely an edge to the progenitor's voice.

"Oh well." She looked at John and winked. "Whatever crazy thing I turn into, at least it'll be a good crazy thing." She had meant the comment as a light joke to help ease the strange mood. Unfortunately, she was met with complete silence, and she could feel the progenitor's hesitation.

116

"What?" There was an edge of concern in her voice as she glanced back and forth between John and the progenitor. "I mean, as long as we stay together, then no matter what happens, I'll stay good, right?"

"Don't be silly." John smiled and patted her arm. "Of course you will."

They couldn't help but notice there was no mental agreement.

It is time to return to the current matter. We can speak more of these things once you have dealt with Dracula. Are you prepared?

"Yes," came the combined reply, although Danielle's held a slight hesitation.

Excellent, but first, you must feed. You cannot drink any blood in his realm. It is all tainted, and while you are strong enough to resist, it will weaken you.

"Great idea, where's the closest blood bank?"

Danielle smiled as her husband's sarcasm came back in full force.

Just me. The vampires looked shocked since it was clear the progenitor was serious. *Do not worry. You will not harm me unless you drain me, and that will not be necessary to regain your strength. My blood is pure and unlike any you have ever tasted. I will control you to prevent you from taking too much.*

"Very well, if you're offering, but we are not savages. We can control ourselves." It was a point of pride after all.

You must trust me. You will frenzy almost immediately after tasting the first drop. There is nothing you can do to prevent it. It is not a problem. Once you have had enough, I will simply hold you down until you regain your senses. I will be as gentle as possible. Whenever you are ready.

The invitation was clear, and the vampires moved to either side of the withered-looking body's throat. They shared a glance, shrugged their shoulders, and began to feed.

John never had time to realize the progenitor had been right since his brain exploded with pleasure the instant the first drop touched his lips. It was an ecstasy he had never felt before, so far beyond the feeling that came from feeding normally that it couldn't be properly described. The frenzy came on the heels of the euphoria, and the thought of fighting it never occurred to him.

All that mattered—the only thing that had meaning in his life— was draining as much of this new blood as possible. His eyes reddened at the same time he began to growl, and John began chewing at the progenitor's throat in an effort to speed the flow of blood. He knew there was no power on earth that could stop him from reducing the progenitor to a dried-up husk. Then he would need to act quickly so he could safely kill his wife and take her share of the blood for himself.

It was at that moment that he was thrown four steps backward and forced to the ground. The fury and rage at being denied what was rightfully his washed over him, yet struggling against the invisible force proved futile. Slowly, the voice of reason and calm that had gone unheard began to grow louder, and the frenzy subsided. Finally, when the progenitor was convinced of his renewed sanity and calm, the invisible hand released its hold.

The vampires rose to their feet slowly, legs a bit unsteady after feeling such pleasure course through their bodies. John shook his head to clear the remaining cobwebs and looked over to his wife. He noticed Danielle wearing an expression of satisfaction he had never seen outside the bedroom, and he couldn't resist.

"So, love, was it good for you?" he leered slightly.

"Ass," was her only response, but she couldn't help but blush even further.

How do you feel?

"Amazing," John answered, turning to face the creature. "Better than I've ever felt in fact."

Danielle nodded in agreement.

That is good to hear. You must go now, but be wary. Once you leave these caverns, Dracula will know your every move.

They had a feeling there was more the progenitor wanted to say, but the silence was becoming long and awkward.

It is true that my people do not experience love, he continued eventually, *but we do experience pleasure. Meeting the two of you has brought me a kind of pleasure I have never felt before. I wish to experience this feeling again, and soon.*

"Is that your way of telling us you'll miss us, to be careful, and to get back soon?" Danielle asked, grinning from ear to ear.

Yes, I suppose it is.

"I'm touched," John chimed in. "Don't worry about us. We'll dust the bastard and be back before you know it."

They nodded in respect and thanks before turning to leave.

There is one last thing you should know, my son. I speak it only to you. Do not respond with normal speech.

Um, okay, John replied with telepathy, wondering what was going on.

There is a very important difference I detect between your minds, one that I do not know how to explain to her, but you must be made aware.

John did not like the sound of that and wondered if it had something to do with the awkward silence from before.

Okay, but don't you think she is going to wonder why we are all standing around silent for no reason?

I speak with her even now about something else. Observe.

John glanced over and saw Danielle seemingly talking to herself, oblivious to anything he might be doing.

You both believe very strongly that it is only the presence of the other that keeps you from becoming the monsters your brethren become, correct?

Yes, what of it?

I sense this is not entirely true, at least not for you. In your mind, I detect other things, things the humans call duty, honor, and integrity. You are very old and very powerful. If your wife were to cease to exist tomorrow, I believe these other traits would give you a chance of resisting what you could become. It would not be a certainty, but you would at least have a fighting chance.

I do not like this conversation.

I do not care. You need to understand.

Understand what? My wife has those same traits as well, you know, John tried to sound annoyed but wasn't sure if his mental voice came across that way.

She does not, not in the same way. You learned these traits as a soldier, before even meeting her. She then learned these things from you. Everything she has learned about how to live her life has come from you, and her mind ties these things directly to you. To you, your wife is the most important thing in the universe, correct?

Of course.

To her, you are the universe. Do you understand the difference?

Are you trying to tell me that my wife loves me more than I love her?

Do not be a fool. I am trying to explain how her mind works. You are not the most important thing to her; you are the only thing to her. You do what is right because it is the right thing to do. She does what is right because she knows you want her to. I doubt she fully even realizes it, but I have already seen the proof. Earlier, when she thought you were beyond hope, her first and only thought was to lie next to you and wait for death herself.

119

Yeah, I remember that, John shuddered as he remembered the mental images Danielle had shared with him.

You saw the memory, yes, but not truly inside her mind. Suicide was her one and only thought. She only fought Dracula because he wanted to convert her, which meant keeping her alive. The entire point of the battle was for her to buy time to kill herself and join you. No other strategy occurred to her, until I convinced her you could still be saved.

Okay, I understand better now, John nodded slightly, *but it's not that terrible of a thing or even very surprising, right?*

Overall, I agree with you. I tell you this so you can understand that you need to protect more than her body. You must realize that while she may disagree with you on certain things, your word and choices are a type of law for her that neither of you fully understands. The very openness of her mind makes her far more vulnerable than she realizes.

She can defend herself. John was not worried about his wife's mental prowess, regardless of what the progenitor had to say.

She cannot. The lack of powerful opponents and lack of anyone with the ability to teach her has left her ignorant. Yes, her mental abilities are impressive, but mental defenses do not work on a mind left open. It simply is not the way battles of that kind are fought. If anyone were to discover her true weakness, she would be easy to influence, and before you ask, that weakness is you.

How? He understood most of what the progenitor was trying to say, but his wife was the most wonderful person he had ever met. So why did it feel as if there was something terrible suddenly lurking around the corner?

If your life were in danger, she would not hesitate to burn this entire world to ash and kill as many humans, regardless of innocence, as necessary to keep you safe.

John could feel the blood drain from his face as the progenitor sent him mental images to help with his explanation.

She could never do those things. Surely this was some sort of misunderstanding.

Without hesitation. By no means is she a bad person by your mortal standards, but only because of you. No other life is completely real to her, and I just need you to understand this. You are both going into a terrible battle, and you need to be prepared for any instability on her part.

Great. John had to resist the urge to roll his eyes.

I cannot stall her any longer in conversation. If you both survive, I can help you deal with this issue or at least help her to identify it.

120

If you say so. John was less than thrilled with this new information, but there was nothing much he could about it at the moment. He signaled to Danielle it was time to go, and they both waved.

The progenitor didn't know what else to say, so he sent a feeling of agreement and luck over the link to his distant children. It was a good thing, he thought, that they had not been strong enough to truly read his mind. Despite their optimism, his own encouraging words, and hope for death, there was little chance of victory. Meeting them had truly been an enjoyable experience, but after examining their capabilities, the simple truth was that they were not yet ready. Unfortunately, they were out of time, and the progenitor was saddened by the knowledge that he would probably never see them again.

CHAPTER 9

Haven

"Leo, why are you in my bedroom?" Sam had woken up and noticed the ghoul simply sitting in a chair in the corner reading a book. It was a little strange, to say the least, to have the company, but even stranger still was Leo's reaction to his voice.

"Sir! You're finally awake," the ghoul seemed surprised and sounded genuinely relieved as he quickly got up, tossing the book aside.

"I am, and you still haven't answered my question," he pressed further as he swung his legs over his bedside.

The ghoul stopped short, standing at attention out of respect for the vampire. It was true that Sam did not evoke quite the same level of obedience as the true masters did, but he had still commanded the overall force of ghouls for nearly a century.

"Sorry sir," Leo nodded briefly. "Do you remember anything?"

The question seemed oddly out of place, and Sam got the impression that Leo had skipped the necessary explanation.

"Yeah, genius. I remember going to bed. Now, if you're going to continue standing in my way, at least fetch me some clothes." The look in Sam's eyes quickly reminded Leo that he wasn't a simple ghoul anymore. "While you're at it, an explanation would be lovely as well."

"Yes sir." Leo quickly retrieved and tossed over the requested clothing. "Actually, sir, you've been asleep for three full days," he said, holding a hand up to forestall any response.

"I've what?" Sam exclaimed, ignoring the gesture. He had been halfway through putting on his pants, and his shock at Leo's comment had almost cost him his balance.

"Sir, please." Leo waited for Sam's nod before continuing. "Something's happened, we do not really know if it's good or bad yet. Marcus and Father Jenkins are having dinner in the other room. We wanted to stay close to you in case your condition showed any signs of change," he added at Sam's arched eyebrow upon hearing the news of even more guests inviting themselves over.

"Anyway, I'll go tell them your awake, and just come join us when you're ready. They can do a far better job explaining what's happened."

"Okay, sounds good." Sam went back to the task of getting dressed. "Where are the ancients?"

"Sir, as I said, the others can explain better." Leo hurried out of the room before Sam could question him further.

Sam had intended his question as simple curiosity, and the ghoul's response had all sorts of implications. Another few minutes of searching for his shoes and making himself presentable, and Sam was ready to go find out what sort of monstrosity was after them this time, and how to kill it.

"Damn," was Sam's only response after Marcus and Jenkins spent twenty minutes filling him in on the events he had slept through. Nursing a cup of blood, he considered everything he had been told and what their next move should be. The ancients had left some basic instructions, but only because he had been incapacitated. Now that he was awake, the others would be expecting decisions to be made.

"Well, at the very least, I feel just fine, so they were right about that much," he said and shrugged as the others nodded and went back to eating.

The confirmation that nothing had truly been wrong with Sam was all they really needed to hear before surrendering the decision-making to him. He just wished they wouldn't chew so loudly while he was trying to think.

As a ghoul, Marcus's body technically did not require mortal food. However, they had learned long ago that while vampiric blood kept a ghoul alive and enhanced their human abilities, parts of their physiology would still slowly deteriorate. Vampiric blood simply was not able to completely power a human's metabolism—unless, of course, that human was turned into a vampire first. A high-caloric diet heavy with protein helped to satisfy a ghoul's severely enhanced metabolic rate and keep the body in top shape. Jenkins, for his part, had no issues with the meal either, considering he was the one member of their strange family who was still a regular mortal.

"If this whole thing really is someone or something trying to communicate with us, I guess it's not necessarily a bad thing," he started, even as the others cast him odd looks. "What? Not everything out there is trying to kill us." Sam paused as he listened to himself. "Just, you know, most things."

Marcus made a slight grimace while Jenkins stifled a chuckle.

"Anyway, has there been any update? It's been three days since they left, surely you've heard something by now."

"Yes sir," Marcus started while Jenkins began clearing the dishes. "We don't have much in the way of details, but we know the masters found something important. Our team in Gaziantep says the masters are on their way back to the jet for supplies and more weapons, and they intend on heading out again."

Jenkins returned from the kitchen, setting a fresh cup of blood in front of Sam while handing Marcus one of the beers he was also carrying.

"Well, that sounds potentially ominous and lacks any useful details," the annoyance in Sam's voice was clear.

"True sir, but remember that you were still sleeping. The masters tell us what they require and nothing more, but I am certain they would provide you with any information you want."

Jenkins nodded his own agreement with Marcus's assessment.

"Fair point, but it's not like we can just call them, and I hate waiting."

John and Danielle usually remembered to carry cell phones, but typically, they never turned them on. Adding to that how easily they lost them, generally due to combat of some kind, and it was typical for them to be out of contact for days at a time.

"God only knows what those two crazies have gotten mixed up in this time," Sam mumbled to himself, ignoring Marcus's reaction to his irreverent reference to the masters.

I believe I can be of assistance.

Sam had been staring into his cup, but his head shot up as he heard the voice loud and clear in his mind.

"Did either of you hear that?" His sudden movement had caught them off guard, and they were eyeing him suspiciously.

"Hear what?" Jenkins asked as Marcus simply shook his head slowly.

I am unable to communicate with them in this manner. You share your sire's blood, and the experience I gained communicating with him is allowing for this.

It sounded like a reasonable explanation, and Sam appreciated mysterious voices in his head who tried to be reasonable. He rolled his eyes at his own thoughts, but at least it appeared they would have some answers soon.

"So you guys remember the whole communication theory?"

"Yeah," came the response as they continued staring at him oddly.

"It's not a theory anymore," Sam pointed at his own head. "According to the voice in my head, it can't talk to you, so just try and bear with the one-sided conversation you're about to hear."

"Wait, you seem pretty calm about this," Jenkins sounded surprised while Marcus simply shrugged.

"Priest, you're sharing a beer with a ghoul while talking to an actual vampire. You're also good friends with two other ancient vampires who were summoned halfway around the world, most likely by a being even more powerful than they are. What's the point even wasting time on being surprised anymore?"

Jenkins looked ready to argue the point, but then he hesitated and realized Sam was right.

"Good point. Don't forget to fill us in." He got up and motioned for Marcus to follow him to the living room.

"Yep."

Sam's nonchalant comments aside, he was not entirely certain about the voice he had heard. There was only one way to find out.

"Oh, mysterious voice in my head," he began dramatically, "I bid thee return and to bestoweth unto me the knowledge I seeketh."

Your words would be confusing, had I not already spoken a great deal with your sire. You people seem intent on introducing humor and sarcasm into the most inappropriate situations. There is no time for such foolishness.

Sam could feel the other being's annoyance in his mind, although he didn't care.

"Where are my friends, and what the hell is going on?" His tone made it clear he was not in the mood for foolishness either.

There is much to discuss. Your friends are in grave danger, but this is not something easily spoken of in this manner. It is time for you to follow the others and come to me, and all will be revealed.

"Why should I trust you?"

As Sam finished the question, his mind began filling with images. It was confusing at first, but it was clear that whatever this creature was, it was trying its best to show him what the ancients had been doing. He did not understand it all, but it seemed obvious now that he had no choice but to follow the instructions.

"Okay, how do I find you?"

As with the others, you need only to follow. Bring as many others as you see fit, but make haste, or I feel all will be lost.

"So no pressure then?" he asked the air around him.

There was no response, and somehow Sam knew that whatever had been inside his mind had left. He also instantly knew exactly where to go and called the others back in to bring them up to speed.

"So when do we leave?" Jenkins asked after Sam finished relaying his brief conversation to them.

"Sorry, Priest, not this time. You either, Marcus."

"But . . ."

"Sir?"

Sam had expected the protests and held up a hand to forestall any more conversation.

"Look, I don't really understand what's going on yet, but it's bad. Maybe worse than our brief war with your former allies, Priest. I can't justify bringing you into that kind of fight. Also, both of you just think for a second." The look in Sam's eyes was a reminder that in John and Danielle's absence, his word was law within the haven.

"This is our home. Now, for the moment, I don't think this situation represents a local threat, but that could change. Plus, we never really know what else is out there waiting to bite us in our collective asses. We can't all go rampaging around the globe at the same time.

"With all three of us gone, Marcus, I need you to keep this place safe. As for you, Priest, there's going to be a lot of speculation concerning what's really happening, maybe even a fair amount of fear." He met Jenkins's gaze directly. "Whether we always admit it or not, your presence is rather comforting, and I need you to stay here and watch over everyone. Please." Ordering Marcus around was simple, but from Jenkins, he wanted agreement, not simply blind obedience.

"Very well," he nodded slightly. "But who is going to watch over you and the others, my friend?" Jenkins inquired softly.

"You're the one who never shuts up about this god of yours being everywhere." Sam gave him a wink. "I'm thinking this is going to be a good time to put that theory to the test."

126

"There is no doubt in my mind that he is with them even now, and I shall continue to pray for all of us as well."

"Oddly enough, that actually does make me feel better," Sam almost sounded confused to hear himself say such a thing, but before he could continue, Marcus coughed lightly for attention.

"Sir, I understand why I cannot accompany you, but I can't allow you to go alone." It was clear that Marcus was prepared to argue the point rather strongly if necessary.

"Trust me, I agree with you. Leo," Sam called over his shoulder, "are you still skulking about the house somewhere?"

Of course, thanks to Sam's vampiric senses, he knew full well where the other ghoul had wandered off to.

"Yes, sir," Leo entered, carrying fresh beers for himself and the other nonvampires.

"Marcus, what do you think?"

Marcus started eyeing Leo closely, and Sam knew he had understood the question.

As well as he knew their ghouls, it was now Marcus's responsibility to command them and had been for over ten years. It was only appropriate to get his opinion on who would be placed in charge of the detachment he would be forming.

"He can do it overall, sir. Got a good head for coordination on his shoulders, but be mindful, he's never commanded more than a single team in actual combat."

Sam nodded his appreciation of the assessment while Leo simply drank his beer with a look of confusion.

"Good enough for me." Sam turned his attention to the younger ghoul. "Leo, we're going after the ancients."

The ghoul sat up straighter as he realized there was a reason Sam was talking to him instead of Marcus.

"I need you to gather up a force of combat ghouls." Sam paused to think for a few seconds. "Let's go with two reinforced teams of six, you'll lead one of the teams directly as well as handle overall command—well, second-in-command to me anyway." Sam motioned for Marcus to give any suggestions he might have.

"Sir, I recommend you take Jasmine with you as well. You never know when that giant brain of hers will come in handy. Also"—he looked at Leo—"no weapons heavier than shotguns and grenades."

"Wait," Sam interrupted. "Why not?"

127

Considering the arsenal at their disposal, Sam had intended on bringing far heavier weaponry than that.

"Sir, may I ask how you plan to get there?" Marcus arched an eyebrow at him.

"What do you—" Sam started to respond, before realizing what Marcus meant. "Aw, hell," he said, practically slapping his forehead.

"What's wrong?" Jenkins was listening quietly and didn't understand the problem.

"The damn plane's already in Turkey."

"Oh."

"Yeah" Sam understood Marcus's limitations now.

Recalling their private jet was not an option even if they wanted to. John and Danielle might need it, and the team at the airfield wouldn't listen to Sam anyway. He might be a vampire, but John was the boss. They also didn't have time to sit around waiting for it to return.

All that meant they would be stuck flying normally, and that created a number of problems. The biggest issue would be their equipment. Sam was not overly worried about airport security or customs since mortal minds were so easy to distract. No, the problem was mainly space—well, space and no specially configured quarters to protect him from the sunlight, which meant . . .

"I'm gonna have to travel in a fucking coffin, aren't I?"

Normally, they tried to watch their language around Jenkins out of respect, but Sam did not care much about that at the moment. He hated coffins, and based on the laughter coming from Marcus, the older ghoul had been around long enough to know Sam's terrible secret.

Contrary to popular belief, vampires generally did not sleep in coffins, and never had. At least not to the best of the ancients' knowledge of vampiric history. The reasoning for this was rather simple. Coffins were for dead bodies and had never been intended for something to sleep in them temporarily. That's what beds were for; thus vampires tended to sleep in beds. Losing one's humanity to the thirst inside all vampires did not necessitate an equal loss of brain cells that would cause a vampire to forget what a bed was.

Coffins did, however, present a perfect solution to any transportation problems a vampire could possibly have. They were the perfect size to rest in comfort and stay safe from the sun's rays, and the vampire inside didn't need to breathe since there wouldn't be anyone to talk to. As time progressed and security measures advanced, coffins became even more useful since a coffin was the one container where anyone would expect to see a body inside.

The frequent use of coffins for travel purposes was most likely the truth that sparked the original myth of them being a vampire's preferred resting place. They even had a few very nice ones in storage for just such an emergency. The ancients had even looked into purchasing a custom coffin that would be large enough to fit them both so they would still be able to sleep together. That particular idea was scrapped when they realized how ridiculous the coffin would look and the questions it would most likely generate.

"What's the problem, sir?" Leo was asking the question honestly. He didn't know Sam's secret. "The masters wouldn't care if you used one of theirs, and those things are pretty damn sweet, well, for coffins anyway."

It was true. John even had a DVD player somehow installed inside of the lid of his. Of course, that wasn't the problem.

"You going to tell him, sir?" Marcus asked, a bit too innocently.

"Fine." Sam took an extra unnecessary breath. "I'm claustrophobic," he admitted, hanging his head down to rest it on the table.

Marcus was stifling his laughs while the other two simply stared at him in confusion.

"But you're a vampire," Jenkins said, as if that made a difference.

"So?"

"Well, I don't know. I guess I didn't think vampires were afraid of things like that," he said as he shrugged his shoulders.

"My body might be completely different, but it's still the same brain. Can I help it if my brain insists there's not enough oxygen to go around?"

"But you don't need oxygen." Jenkins wasn't trying to make fun of him, but Sam couldn't help but notice Marcus wasn't the only one laughing anymore.

"You would think that would help, but instead of my claustrophobia going away, now I'm just claustrophobic and confused. Anyway," he said, raising his voice to get the ghouls' attention. "Let's get back on topic." He gave Marcus and Leo a moment to wipe the grins off their faces before continuing.

"Leo, charter us a jet to get to the same airfield they used in Turkey. Money's obviously no object, but we need to leave in the morning. It sounds as if the team on ground there has had enough positive contact with the locals that landing and debarking the equipment should be simple, but plan on bringing plenty of paper currency or whatever trade goods our team there says will work." Sam cupped his chin in his hand as he thought through what else they might need.

"Also, double-check what weapons and equipment they already have." Sam noticed Marcus's annoyed expression as he remembered an important fact Marcus had forgotten to mention. Their jet wasn't simply a handy method of transportation modified for vampires. It was effectively a flying armory and was always kept fully stocked.

They had been discussing what types of weapons they could get away with bringing onto a regular plane when, in reality, the team in Turkey could most likely equip a small army. Well, maybe not a small army, but certainly a dozen or so combatants. It was possible they wouldn't need to bring anything more than additional blood and maybe some ammo. There was no such thing as too much blood or ammo.

"Okay, so I'll leave you to it, and I guess I'll just wait to get loaded into the stupid coffin. Yes, Marcus?"

The ghoul had signaled for attention again.

"Sir, I believe Leo can form the team and gather the equipment, and I also believe he can handle things once you get on ground, but Jasmine and I will handle the travel arrangements. I would also recommend putting Jasmine in overall command until you land." Marcus looked at Leo briefly, and Sam motioned for him to continue.

"Making the arrangements is not overly difficult, you've done it yourself more than once. However, this is the first time you will be the one traveling as cargo. Traveling during the day on a normal plane is not something we do very often, and you may not realize it yourself, but your abilities will be nearly useless to us until we land."

"Wait, really?"

"Sir, if you are inside a coffin that has been checked and sent to the aircraft's cargo hold, how can you help us with security and customs?"

"Oh shit." Sam honestly hadn't thought of that. "You're right. I can use my abilities to protect the coffin itself, but that's it, and it's not really protecting the coffin either." He struggled to find the best way to explain it. "It's more like, as long as I concentrate, people might see it, but they will ignore it, and no one would dare think to open it.

"Actually, that might be a problem too. What if by causing people to ignore the coffin, they forget to load it onto the plane? Would you guys even notice, or would I end up being just some random black box left on a runway?" Sam took a drink while pausing to consider the unpleasant possibility.

"Kind of my point, sir. We have plenty of money, and Jasmine has the contacts to use it to circumvent both security and customs. You don't have to follow the rules in this country if you're rich enough. As for your coffin, just use a lock, and lay off the fancy vampire shit."

"Okay," Sam nodded after a moment. "Agreed. Just let me know as soon as you find out how long the flight is going to be."

"Sir, I assure you that we will arrive by tomorrow night, and with the time difference, it will easily be dark enough to let you out immediately."

"Yeah, I know, but I need to know how many movies to bring."

"Ah, well, sir, it is good to know that you're focusing on matters of the utmost strategic importance," Marcus replied in a monotone voice while the others snickered.

"You all have your orders."

Understanding the dismissal for what it was, the ghouls stood respectfully before leaving to begin their tasks. Jenkins waited a moment longer before patting his friend on the shoulder and turning to join the others. Sam waited patiently for the sound of his front door being closed and for his senses to confirm the others had moved far enough away.

The cup he had been holding shattered instantly, and he looked down at his blood-covered hand. He knew it was simply the leftover contents, as not even the sharpest of the shards could pierce his skin. It was the sudden claws replacing his fingers that he was looking at. Despite the calm and friendly banter as they were forming their plans, Sam was struggling to maintain control.

The images he had been receiving were confusing and terrifying, but there was one image he couldn't get out of his mind. It had been an image of Danielle crying over John's body in the ruins of some structure he had never seen before. John appeared unharmed although unconscious, but Danielle wasn't even recognizable through the injuries. It was only recognizing John in the image that told Sam it was her.

Somehow he simply knew the image was real, and whatever this creature was, it simply wanted to convey the urgency of the situation. Terrible battles had been fought, maybe even being fought at this exact moment, and there wasn't a damn thing he could do about it. He stood up, violently throwing the dining room table with enough force to effectively destroy half his kitchen before spinning around.

Sam caught a glimpse of his reflection in the mirror hanging next to his clock and saw his eyes beginning to redden. That was bad, but he couldn't stop himself. The ancients had warned him that there was a chance he would be more emotional than a normal vampire, but that was not necessarily a good thing. Sam did not have the anchor to humanity those two had in each other.

All he was feeling now was anger and rage, and he liked it. A part of his mind understood what was happening and tried to fight the oncoming frenzy, even as his fangs protruded and a deep growling began in the pit of his stomach—a growling that served to remind him of what he truly was. It was time to feed and kill. Time to demonstrate his power and assuage his unending thirst.

Child, you are no more a monster than your sires, the strange voice was suddenly back in his mind.

For an instant, Sam's rage redoubled at the influence, then it was simply gone, leaving him confused and a bit tired.

"How did you do that?"

Sam was fully aware of what had happened to him and the terrible thoughts that had been crossing his mind. It was a little embarrassing to lose control so easily, but even after ten years he was still struggling to control his powers. The others had told him it was simply because he was essentially too strong for his age.

Vampires as powerful as the two ancients did not exist anymore, at least not that they could find anyway. It had been John's blood that had turned Sam, making him effectively one of the most powerful vampires in the world despite being barely a fledgling in age. They had also begun teaching him magic almost right away. It would probably take him decades more to fully understand and be able to control everything he could do.

I can do a great many things, child. You are simply too strong for one so young, the voice seemed to be agreeing with Sam's thinking. *You may not trust me or consider me a friend, but at least consider me an ally. Make haste.*

He could feel the presence leave his mind again, or he thought it was gone anyway.

The last few minutes had been all the remaining proof Sam had needed. There was no way he would have been able to stop his frenzy, and no telling how much damage and death he would have caused waiting for it to run its course. He looked around at the damage he had caused, silently thankful for the mysterious intervention. Deciding to keep his brief tirade to himself for the moment, he left the room to start packing for the trip.

"So any idea where we're going yet?" John was lounging on their bed in the rear of the plane while Danielle was still trying to research their next move.

Currently he was amusing himself by tossing a tennis ball against the wall of their cabin. It was harder than it looked. The trick was to use enough force to bounce the ball back to him as hard as possible without damaging the wall or the ball itself.

It had taken them longer to return to the airstrip than they had liked. The conversation with the progenitor had ended up going into the following day, so they had been stuck underground. They were also trying to utilize regular modes of transportation whenever possible in order to save blood, which was not easy in areas this rural.

They both felt very strongly that time was not on their side in this conflict, so returning home was out of the question. Unfortunately, they still needed more information, so Danielle spent most of the last day doing research. Of course, since most of their assets were back home, Danielle's "research" effectively amounted to searching the internet on her phone for clues.

"Yes, and would you cut that out?" She knew that John was only trying to keep himself occupied, but the rhythmic thumping noises were driving her crazy.

He responded by throwing the tennis ball at her hard enough that it was nothing but a green blur. The incoming missile was neatly bisected with a vampiric claw, without Danielle even looking away from her phone.

"That was my last one," he complained, taking no responsibility for being the aggressor.

"Good, men are easier to handle when they've got no balls." It's not that Danielle didn't share her husband's twisted humor; she was just more reserved than he when others were around. In private, she gave as good as she got.

"Kiss your mother with that mouth?" John chuckled. "Anyway, I believe I heard you say yes?" He moved to sit closer to her, the earlier banter already forgotten.

"Poenari Castle sounds like the winner." She was continuing to scroll through the information.

"Wasn't there a castle actually called 'Dracula's Castle,' or something like that?" It had been his first guess when she started the research earlier.

"Turns out Vlad never lived there, might be called that because of the book or something, but look at these pictures of Poenari." She handed the phone over and let John see the images for himself.

"Okay, yeah, I think I see what you mean." He took a moment to examine as much of the surrounding terrain as he could see. "Fifteenth century, right?"

Danielle nodded confirmation of the period when their prey had been human.

"Oh yeah, that castle would have been a stone-cold bitch to attack back then, well, for mortals anyway," he mumbled that part mostly to himself. "All right, and you have proof that at least he used to live there?"

"Well, as much proof as you could expect, but I guess it's possible those records could have been falsified. Still, too many sources." Danielle shook her head slightly. "Yeah, Vlad definitely lived there, but something about this whole thing just doesn't feel right." She took the phone back and sat down.

"Only one thing?" He arched an eyebrow at her.

"Okay, so I guess one more thing I should say . . ." She paused as a ghoul delivered two thermoses to them. "So this guy dies sometime in the second half of the fifteenth century, and then just what? Spends the next five hundred plus years living in the same castle, and no one notices?" Danielle took a drink, clearly frustrated.

"We hide in the open all the time," he countered.

"It's not the same thing, and you know it. We move all over the world and actively try to fit in with whatever area we visit. Hell, it's not like we still live in the same cabin we were in the night our sire turned us."

"To be fair, that wasn't our cabin. The king was only letting us use it as a wedding gift." He was careful to point out Danielle's error as she simply glared at him.

"Okay, okay," he surrendered. "I admit it is strange. I was only looking at the terrain. Did you see if it's private property at least?"

"Honestly, I didn't check who actually owns it. Probably the government or something, but I can tell you it's a public tourist attraction."

"Wait, what?" John was starting to understand his wife's confusion about the whole thing.

"Look." She showed him a specific image, and John saw the steps leading up to Poenari. "They even installed a shitload of steps so idiots don't fall off the mountain or skin their knees or whatever as they walk up to it." She took the phone back, tapped one of the links, and showed him again.

"We can literally buy tickets on the internet and send our ghouls on a public daylight tour of our greatest enemy's stronghold. It just doesn't make sense." She crossed her arms, trying hard to think of what they were missing.

"Well, it's possible we're wrong about him being there at all. I mean, seriously, the fate of the world could be in the balance here, and we are entrusting our avenue of attack to Google and Wikipedia." He put an arm around her, pulling her to his lap.

"I'm right. I don't know how I know, but he's there. Remember, he's in my head, and he wants us to find him," she said, shuddering briefly.

"Well, what about underground? There's nothing else in the immediate area, and the tours stop at night. He could have all sorts of weird shit underground or hiding in the woods." Five centuries was more than enough time for someone to remake an area.

"I don't get that kind of vibe from him." She turned to look up at him. "You may have slept through the fighting, but you did see him. You also saw through my memories. At first, I thought it was some sort of gimmick, you know how eternal life can mess with your head, but that was no act. Does Dracula strike you as the type to blend in or hide underground in his own home?"

"No, I guess not, but your experience is firsthand. What is your honest impression of him?"

She started laughing at his question. "My impression?" She laughed another moment before continuing, "He is the megalomaniac of all megalomaniacs, a walking stereotype filled with cliches." She rolled her eyes. "The guy has a magic cape that helps him fly and still wears clothes from the fifteenth century. Seriously, it's like he studied what mortals think vampires are and then literally became exactly that. On purpose. Look, I know that he's insanely powerful. I mean, he incapacitated you instantly and nearly killed me, but it's like we're fighting a character from a bad movie. That's my impression," she said, snuggling in closer, as confused as ever.

"Maybe this is one of the episodes where the holodeck characters come to life," he mumbled in response to her last comment.

"What?" It took her a second to recognize the obscure reference. "I really wish you would find better uses for your time."

"Yeah, so we're in this mess because we answered the summons of an ancient alien who crash-landed here. I'm starting to think you're the one who needs a change of tastes."

She rolled her eyes again, clearly not sharing the sentiment.

"Anyway, I agree with you completely. I just don't think we'll find out until we get there. On that note . . . ," John trailed off, clearly expecting her to fill him in on their travel arrangements.

"I'm guessing you still want to stick to mortal speeds to save power?" She wanted to make sure and waited for his nod. "Okay, so the best bet is a quick hop to the airport in Bucharest, then a bus or taxi or whatever to Curtea de Arges, then again to some town called Arefu, and finally, hoof it from there." She paused and chuckled as John started groaning.

"Yeah, yeah, I know, it sucks traveling this way, and it gets even better." She scrolled through a bit more information on her phone before continuing, "These aren't really the types of major urban areas we've gotten accustomed to, and it gets worse as we get closer. Finding transportation during the hours we need it is going to be difficult if we don't want to raise any questions. It might take us a while to get there." She gave a small shrug of helplessness.

"If it's going to take that long anyway, why bother with the airport? We can just use ground transport from here and avoid the hassle of needing to establish ourselves in another hangar. Like you said, we want to avoid questions if we can." It never went completely unnoticed when people started going to out-of-the-way places and throwing money around the way they would be.

"Honestly, I agree with you, but that airport is big enough to have a currency exchange in it." She saw John's eyes widen slightly. He clearly had not thought of that. "American money might work, but it might not. Most likely, the only way we'll be able to get ground transportation at night is by hiring random locals for lots of cash. Remember, we can't take our ghouls past the airport, and locals are going to prefer their own currency. It also means we can't shroud ourselves while we travel."

John groaned again as she mentioned yet another problem he had not thought of. If they were stuck hiring personal transportation, it wouldn't work if the person they were hiring couldn't see them.

"Damn. What about our weapons? Personally, I plan on bringing everything we can carry. Also, to your other point, we should have some gold or jewelry lying around here somewhere to use for barter if the currency exchange thing doesn't work out."

She nodded in agreement while waving away his concern about the weapons. "Pack and bring whatever you want, as long as it's visually concealed. Dealing with security and convincing people to simply not care about us is pretty simple, but it gets harder if they actually see something. Shrouding ourselves briefly while we walk around security points is no issue, and I can ensure no one ever asks to open our luggage."

"Okay," he said, nodding slowly to himself as he thought over the plan for a few moments. "Where are we going to stay? This definitely sounds like a few days of traveling to do it carefully."

"Honestly, we'll need to stick to whatever local inns or hotels we can find and just deal with it. We're pretty good at playing the rich and eccentric newlyweds by now," she said then snapped her fingers at a sudden thought. "You know, with the time difference, we might have almost no problems after all."

"That's true. By the time the average person would adjust to the new schedule, we'll be gone." It was a good point. "We could also just use earth meld to play it safe." He had barely finished the suggestion before Danielle started to grimace.

"First of all, there's an element of vulnerability to doing that, and only our bodies can sink into the earth. What are we supposed to do with all our clothes and gear? Dig a giant hole every night?"

Danielle had a point, but John still thought the idea might be safer overall.

"I get that it would be pain, but I'm not crazy about sleeping in a random room with no trustworthy security, especially not as we get closer to Dracula's stronghold."

"Not gonna do it." She shook her head. "Earth meld was fine in the beginning for all those times we had no home, but I don't like it."

John made a face at her tone. Personally, he didn't much care for how it felt to meld his body with the ground either, but it was still the safest idea.

"What's your problem?"

"It's dirty," she stated quite clearly.

"Excuse me?" John replied. Surely she was joking.

"You heard me." The look in her eyes was deadly serious. "We can't meld our clothes, you know that, and there's no shower out in the woods."

"Dear, considering what's at stake, that's not a very good reason—" John was about to make it an instruction when she cut him off.

"You aren't a woman, and you don't have long hair," she said, shaking her head again. "I'm not walking all night covered in filth, and the dirt gets *everywhere*."

John hadn't considered that. "Still, you'll be fine. Security comes first, so just deal with it."

"No." She wasn't backing down.

"Yes," John said, rolling his eyes. "We don't have time for this nonsense."

"Fine, but I'm shaving my head first."

"Don't be stupid, it'll just grow right back." John didn't much care for the grin she gave him.

"Not if I actively prevent it." She knew she had won. John simply loved long hair too much, and she knew it.

"You wouldn't."

"Try me."

"Fine." He threw up his arms in defeat. "But if Dracula's minions get us in the middle of the day, it's on you."

"We don't need to worry about that," she said then sighed. "I told you he's already inside my head, and he knows we're coming for him. It's exactly what he wants us to do, and he won't make a move until we're inside his territory."

"Unfortunately, even though we know it's a trap, we have no choice, do we?"

"Nope."

They both let the thought sink in.

"All right, well, no sense wasting any more time." He stood up to leave. "I'll go tell Theo to start making the arrangements, and you just try and think of a way to fight this weirdo."

"I'll try," she answered as John left, knowing it would be ultimately useless. You couldn't make plans to fight someone who was actively reading your mind.

Poenari Castle

The entertaining distraction of Dracula's more nubile daughters was normally enough to take his mind off any and all concerns, but tonight

138

it was not working. The barely clothed vampires were rolling around the stone floor, biting each other occasionally, their aggressiveness increasing as it became obvious their master was not entertained. Meanwhile, Dracula was lounging on his throne, simply staring into the goblet he was grasping.

Other worlds?

It had been a week since he had returned from Turkey, and he still had trouble grasping the concept. Once the other two vampires left the boundaries of their progenitor's protection, the link he had established with the female had come back to life. His initial instinct was to simply track them, but when he saw the new thoughts and images in her mind, he was astounded.

He took the time to relive their conversation with the progenitor several times, as if he had been there himself, and his ambition and excitement had been growing ever since. It had also been fascinating to learn this other vampiric family truly had almost nothing in common with him. Confirmation that he was still the only supreme being in this world was always nice to have.

Most who experienced Dracula's image and examined his surroundings made the common mistake that he was a stranger to science and technology. In fact, the opposite was true. Dracula was highly educated and understood all aspects of modern technology more so than most mortal experts. The simple fact was that he didn't require it. There wasn't a single modern gizmo, gadget, or toy that could replace or enhance any of his powers, so he simply didn't use any. Choosing to not use and not understanding were two very different things.

The point was that he was not frightened or confused by the images and conversations he had witnessed. Astounded, most definitely, but it had simply taken time for him to accept the obvious technological differences between what he was used to seeing and what this *progenitor* had shown the others. Dracula had always known that he would one day rule over this world, but now? Why should an immortal settle for one world when he could rule over an entire universe as a true god?

Patience, he had to continuously remind himself, would be the key. The progenitor had been correct to fear his power, but he wasn't strong enough to challenge that creature yet. Unfortunately for him, the progenitor had been wrong about his own ability to destroy Dracula should the ancients fail. Whether age had blinded him, or he knew the truth and was simply hiding it, he appeared oblivious to how weak he was growing.

The progenitor had long since passed the point where simple age alone would increase his power. Immortal or not, a living being required food. In denying himself any kind of sustenance, the progenitor had condemned himself to a life of weakness. He might be powerful now, but while Dracula's power grew with every passing night, his was already beginning to wane.

It was possible that taking the power of the ancients would be all Dracula would need to gain the upper hand. If not, it would still be enough to guarantee his survival in a defensive stance if the progenitor attempted to destroy him. At that point, it would simply be a matter of waiting until the progenitor was weak enough to be destroyed. Either way, as long as he remained patient, Dracula would win in the end.

"Huh?" Dracula was pulled from his thoughts by the antics of his daughters.

The pair had crawled their way to the foot of his throne and were vying for his attention. One was nipping gently at his ankles while the other was rubbing her exposed breasts against his leg, and both were hissing seductively. It was all very distracting, and he no longer desired that type of distraction.

He directed a painful, but harmless, kick to one of their skulls while simply baring his fangs at the other. She hissed in response but retreated immediately to where her sister had fallen. The pair began retreating from the throne room, baring their fangs and hissing the entire way. They intended no challenge to their master; it was simply the way his minions tended to act.

That's something else I need to learn, he thought as his minions finally left his presence.

Until he had examined the ancients' minds, it never occurred to him that there was anything wrong with his minions. Now, however, he could see the enormous difference in their capabilities. His minions were weak in terms of pure power, and most of them were annoyingly stupid. In order for him to create a worthwhile and intelligent minion, like Igor had been, it took considerable time and effort on his part.

His opponents, by contrast, had a small army of versatile ghouls, and when they sired a vampire, they were able to transfer a great deal of power. Their minions also appeared to retain the intelligence and skills they possessed as mortals, in addition to receiving new abilities from their masters. He might be the superior being, but his minions were quite frankly pathetic compared to theirs.

The one thing that had kept Dracula in hiding for so long was his lack of competent help. He had planned to spend the next century forming a core of highly capable underlings, but what if every single person he corrupted fell into that category? It was the main question at the root of his dilemma on how to proceed.

He had already tried turning a few mortals using his opponents' method, but there was no change. His victims began the corruption process the instant his fangs pierced their flesh. Attempting to feed them his blood after the fact had no additional effect, whereas for the others it was the act of feeding the victim that began the corruption. It was a matter of different abilities, rather than techniques, and that was the problem.

Gaining this ability for himself became the sole purpose of the current conflict. Everything else he needed could be gained through simple time and patience, if need be, but not this. Unfortunately, there was no way to know if simply destroying them and absorbing their power would grant him the ability.

Ignoring this other species of vampire was turning out to be a grievous error on his part. Had he spent time studying them, instead of destroying any he encountered, he would have learned of this ability sooner. Then he could have experimented with test subjects far easier to handle instead of complicating the current struggle. Hindsight, as the mortals would say, was twenty-twenty.

His only option would be to keep one of them alive while he destroyed the other. If he failed to gain the ability for himself, at least he would have a corrupted servant to create minions for him. Of course, there was no guarantee that would work as planned. To whom would the new minions be loyal? Would the corrupted servant even retain any intellect or power, or just revert into yet another drooling idiot? Just as important, if it worked, he would need to keep the new servant alive forever just to feed the new minions.

It seemed that all he had was questions, and the ancients were already encroaching on the fringes of his territory. After his earlier battle with the female, Dracula was not looking forward to complicating his tactics a second time by trying to preserve one of their lives. Unfortunately, it didn't seem he had much choice. Maybe enough attrition could drive a wedge between them?

He drained his goblet, making a final choice. Not that there had been another viable option, but no one could blame him for seeking one. There was little chance of failure, regardless of what he did, provided he remained cautious. The ancients belonged to him the instant they entered his territory; they just didn't know it yet.

141

CHAPTER 10

Progenitor's Cavern

"So . . . wow," was all Sam could think to say as he approached the progenitor's frail form.

"Yeah," was Leo's response as Jasmine simply examined the creature with her sharp eyes.

Getting to the airfield in Gaziantep had been relatively easy, but gathering supplies from there had taken some time. The progenitor had been sending simple images to Sam's mind, focusing on the cavern in which he resided so that he would come more prepared than the ancients had.

Even now, most of the team he had brought was busy setting up portable generators and lighting throughout the cavern while the others were already on their way back to the airfield. They simply had not been to carry all their weapons and supplies in addition to the new equipment in a single trip. It had been irritating, but according to Theo's report, the ancients had been delayed as well. He didn't think they were more than a full day behind their progress.

Children, I do not wish to be rude, but please shine those elsewhere.

Every ghoul in the cavern immediately ceased in their tasks, heads turning as one to where the progenitor had fused with the wall.

It would seem I am not yet able to separate the minds of your minions.

It took Sam a few seconds to catch up with what he must have meant.

His vision was able to make out the progenitor and the surrounding area, barely, but the ghouls had been bathed in total darkness very quickly. Of course, they had known what to expect and had come prepared. While the portable lighting was being set up, Leo and Jasmine used powerful flashlights to examine what was left of the progenitor's body. The lack of movement had caused them to assume it wasn't a problem.

"Hey, all of you, get back to work," Sam hollered over his shoulder. "Ignore any voices you hear in your head until I say otherwise."

Under normal circumstances, it would have been a strange order to give. Of course, in their family, the ghouls simply nodded and obeyed without giving it another thought. Leo and Jasmine also lowered their flashlights, although they made no move to leave Sam's side.

"Sorry about that. I guess we didn't realize you could still see," he apologized.

I cannot, unless I focus very carefully, and even then, only over a very short distance, and things are not clear. However, I can sense the intense light in my eyes, and it is disorienting. In anticipation of your next question, the portable lighting you are setting up for the cavern will not cause such an effect.

"Okay then." Sam was, in fact, about to ask that very question. "Anyway, you know me. These two are the senior ghouls I brought," he said and indicated to them each in turn.

"Leo is in command of our forces here—second to me, of course—and Jasmine is here because under her extremely pleasant exterior is a giant brain." He winked at her as she rolled her eyes. "Given some of the things you've shown me, I had the feeling a giant brain might be a good thing to have at hand."

You think of yourselves with words like family. *I see such in your minds, yet you possess a greater level of regimentation than I expected to see before meeting you in person. I believe I am growing more familiar with your language and how you insist on using it improperly, but clarify the proper word to use for you. Are you a family, or are you a military force that I have failed to recognize?*

"We're a family," Sam chuckled. "But when it seems the whole world is trying to constantly kill you, a degree of regimentation is required for survival." He was no longer chuckling.

I sense a great deal of anger in your words, child.

"Good, it shows your judgment is sound." Sam's gaze was hard. "I do not fully understand what is happening, but I know we need to cooperate with you to give us a better chance of success. However . . ."

143

Sam paused, and the two ghouls took a reflexive step back at his barely contained rage.

"I'm also fully aware that we are all in this mess because of you. You can feed me all the crap you want about this fight being inevitable or whatever nonsense excuse you have, but it doesn't change facts. My friends are out there somewhere fighting a fight they probably can't win because of your direct interference in our lives, and I hate you for it." He glared in challenge at the being with powers beyond his comprehension.

An interesting way to address one who could crush you all so easily, the progenitor's voice carried no matching challenge, simply the statement of fact.

"If you are that powerful, then what use does dishonesty serve me?"

Wisely stated. I understand you, child, and as long as you are willing to cooperate, I can accept your feelings toward me. Leo and Jasmine, it is a pleasure meeting you. Most of the other ghouls ignored the voice, but a couple of them twitched slightly. *I hope that with more experience, I can learn to separate your minds so as not to be forced to speak with all of you at once.*

The two ghouls mumbled their own greetings in response.

"So let's get to the part when you explain to us how to help them fight."

The sooner they left, the sooner they could catch up to the ancients.

There is nothing you can do to help them fight, but there are ways you can support them.

Sam wanted to interrupt but grudgingly held his tongue.

If Dracula senses you in his realm, his powers can corrupt you all very easily, and you would be nothing more than additional enemies your friends would be forced to kill.

You must understand that this is the reason they have not contacted you about their plans. Dracula is in Danielle's mind. He knows what she knows. If they knew you were coming, it would fall perfectly into his plans. Imagine how it would weaken them to be forced to destroy you all. Attempting to bring you here in secret in order to offer unsuspected support can give us an advantage. As long as they do not know you are coming, I can shield you from Dracula's senses.

Sam didn't care for not being allowed to assist directly, but what the progenitor had said matched up with several of the earlier images he had seen.

"How can you shield us, and why do I suddenly think I'm not going to like it?"

You must surrender a portion of your mind to me.

Yep, Sam had been right; he did not like that at all.

"Excuse me?"

I do not fully understand Dracula's powers, but they are very great. I am unable to see into his realm as I can see throughout the rest of the world. It is as if this entire planet glows brightly with life, save a very small area of total darkness. This is where Dracula resides.

"Okay." Sam was nodding slowly, indicating the progenitor could continue.

If I were to enter this realm, I believe all would be made clear to me, and I can do so as your "passenger." Even if I am unable to penetrate everything, I will be able to see and hear what you do. This will allow me to answer questions, offer advice, and influence your actions.

The progenitor's mental voice was genuine, but it sounded an awful lot like mind control to Sam.

"I don't know." Sam narrowed his eyes in thought. "It sounds logical, I guess, but I didn't come all this way to be someone else's puppet. Also, I'm not sure how the ghouls would respond to taking orders from you."

It was almost as if Sam could see the progenitor shaking his head in his mind.

Child, this is not mind control. I need only a small corner for a portion of my consciousness to reside. It is not much different than what you are doing now to allow me to speak to you. Remember, it took so long for me to contact your masters because they were resisting me, and I was unwilling to force them to listen until recently.

Now that you accept me, do you see how easily we can communicate compared to being rendered comatose? The progenitor hesitated, allowing Sam to consider the comparison. *Have the others ever explained to you how mind control or even telepathy works, or even what they are?*

"I've picked up a lot, considering how long I've been with them, but I still struggle with it," Sam admitted. "Telepathy is mental communication, and mind control is just what it sounds like, controlling someone."

They are different levels of the same thing.

Sam eyed him incredulously; powerful being or not, he knew that couldn't be right.

"They can't be," he insisted. "I can tell you aren't controlling me right now. We're just talking."

We are not.

"Wow, if this is how your conversations with the others went, I can only imagine how much they love you." His response was thick with sarcasm.

You are talking to me, but I lost the ability to do that a long time ago. Instead, I am sending you my thoughts directly, and you are allowing me to control the portion of your mind necessary to translate those thoughts into a mental voice you can understand. This voice is your mind's own creation, it is not my voice.

"I hear John and Danielle's voices perfectly when they do this." He shielded his eyes briefly as the portable lighting throughout the cavern was finally turned on.

Because your mind knows what they sound like. You have never heard my voice, so your mind is simply making one up that it finds suitable, probably something dark and sinister-sounding, no doubt. Also, the more experience I get with you all, the more focused my thoughts become, and your mind can interpret them more easily.

In fact, I have given this much thought. If I begin to sound more comfortable in speaking with you, it is as much your own mind's increased comfort as it is mine. If you do not see me as a dark and sinister being, then I will not sound like one. A brain does not speak, it simply translates information.

"That's still a bit confusing and doesn't explain the control aspect." Sam's brain might not be capable of speech, but it was certainly throbbing at the confusing conversation.

It is your language that is limiting and confusing this conversation, but a simple test is all you should need. I want you to simply decide you no longer wish to talk to me, but you need to make it a serious and honest decision.

Sam had no idea what the progenitor was going on about, but not talking to him for a few minutes sounded just fine.

"Whatever." He turned to face the ghouls still standing close by. "Leo, head back to the surface and see how close they are with the rest of our gear. Jasmine, check everything and make sure it's set up right, and verify we have enough fuel to keep these generators going."

"Yes sir," both ghouls responded and went to their tasks.

146

He took a moment to look around, now that the cavern had better lighting. It was clearly not a completely natural environment, and he wondered what other secrets the progenitor might have stashed around it.

"The rest of you," he raised his voice a bit, "don't leave the cavern itself, but let's start poking around a bit. Check the walls and ground for surprises or hidden entrances, etcetera."

Having finished their work, the ghouls were happy to receive fresh orders. Unfortunately, Sam had no idea what to do next except just stare at the progenitor until he finished making whatever point he was trying to make.

Actually, I am the one who has been waiting for you, the mental voice returned as if in answer to Sam's thoughts.

"Waiting for me to do what?" He was trying to not sound too exasperated, but he wished the progenitor would just skip to the end.

I never ceased sending my thoughts to you, but you were resisting them after making the decision to not speak with me. It would have been simple for me to overcome your resistance, of course, but I was trying to make a point. Do you understand now? Even for something as simple as communication, you must surrender control over parts of your mind.

Most minds do not resist simple communication, which is what makes telepathy so easy compared to other mental abilities. When you begin to change from normal communication to suggestion or instruction, even a mortal mind will resist automatically. The only change from the perspective of the aggressor is the amount of power required to break through the victim's resistance, but the transfer of thought is effectively the same regardless of intention. The difference for the victim is that the greater the struggle, the more damage there is to the mind if your attacker breaks through.

"Okay." Sam pinched the bridge of his nose in a very human manner. "So is that why you specifically used the word *surrender* when you mentioned me taking a piece of you with me?"

Yes child, if you offer no resistance, there will be no impact on your cognitive functions.

By no means was Sam in love with the idea, but he did not think there was much of an option. The entire point of them coming this far was to support the ancients, and it was sounding like the only way to do that would be by following the progenitor's instructions.

"Fine, but like I said before, I don't really understand how this stuff works. You are making it sound like my mind will resist you automatically." Sam had no clue how he was supposed to surrender to

147

someone mentally. The idea of any type of surrender did not appeal to their family, so obviously, the topic had never come up in normal conversation.

You can feel my presence as we communicate in this fashion. That presence is going to change, and you will feel it happening. The moment you feel the change beginning, you need to hold images in your mind of yourself greeting a friend: waving, shaking hands, or even sitting down for a drink. It does not matter, as long as the images carry a feeling of acceptance.

"Okay, but let's hurry this up." Sam was starting to feel impatient given how long they had already been here.

Jasmine signaled for his attention and gave a thumbs-up to indicate their equipment was all functioning properly before she joined the other ghouls in looking around.

"So yeah, whenever you're ready." He waved in a gesture for the progenitor to get a move on.

I am already finished.

"What? You didn't do anything." Sam was certain he had felt no change.

I assure you; I have. Your mind is more receptive than most, and you are also very distracted. Do you not feel any change?

Sam forced himself to simply think for a moment, then said, "Honestly, no."

That is interesting. Perhaps when your journey begins, you will notice. When that time comes, I will endeavor to limit how much I speak to you in this way, in an effort to reduce your confusion.

"How thoughtful of you," he said, his sarcasm back. "You mentioned our 'journey.'" Sam dropped the obvious hint.

Yes, your masters' battle with Dracula will have one of two outcomes: victory or defeat.

Sam rolled his eyes as the progenitor stated the obvious, but he chose not to interrupt this time.

I believe very strongly they will be destroyed, and if that happens, it will fall to us. Using you as my conduit, I will unleash all the power at my disposal into the heart of Dracula's realm.

"I'm almost afraid to ask . . ."

I will effectively command all life of any kind to simply cease existing, and I will deliver the command as powerfully as possible. Everything down to even the insects will cease.

"Including us." His skin was a bit paler than normal at the thought.

Yes.

"I don't like that plan."

Nor do I. However, it is my understanding that under those circumstances, all your ghouls would be doomed anyway. The only additional sacrifice would be you, child, and I feel you would do so willingly for the opportunity to succeed where they failed.

"True, I suppose, but personally I think you're wrong about how this battle is going to go." He might not understand everything that was happening, but Sam had learned to never bet against the ancients.

I am sorry, child, but they simply cannot win. The level of certainty carried by the mental voice was disheartening.

"You don't know them like I do. They don't really know how to lose." Sam crossed his arms stubbornly.

That is not how the world works.

"It's how their world works, so stop being so negative about the whole thing and just tell me what to do when they win."

There had to be a reason why the progenitor bothered to mention victory as a possibility, even if he personally did not think they would achieve it.

Very well. If victory is possible against Dracula, it will not come cheaply or easily for them. This is the other reason you need to follow them. It is likely they will be badly injured, perhaps more so than ever before, and quick action may be necessary to save them.

Sam was happy the progenitor was entertaining victory as a possibility, but he didn't really understand his comments.

"They can heal pretty fast on their own." Perhaps the progenitor was referencing a need for them to carry extra blood? That actually made sense, given the inability to feed within Dracula's realm.

Not all injuries can be healed.

Well, that sounded ominous.

Fear not, child, on my ship there are—

"Your what?" The progenitor's comment had gotten Sam's full and undivided attention.

My ship. I have several—

"YOU HAVE A SHIP?" Sam practically shouted the question, startling several of the ghouls.

Of course I have a ship, how else do you—

"A SPACESHIP?"

Child, calm yourself, the mental voice carried more force, and the progenitor used his presence in Sam's mind to gently encourage silence.

149

What is wrong with you? Did I not explain what I am and how I came to this world?

"Well, yeah, but that was so long ago." Sam waved for the ghouls to get back to work.

What difference does the length of time make? Did you think I simply threw the ship away? Left it out for trash day maybe? The progenitor sent an amusing image of a discarded spacecraft sitting on someone's front yard waiting for the incoming garbage truck.

"Okay, fair point," Sam agreed. "I promise to stop interrupting." He motioned for Jasmine to join him in case he needed a bigger brain.

I see you have your ghouls exploring the cavern more closely. Make them stop. The wall at the far end of the cavern is false. I will guide you through it and onto my ship. Bring help, but ensure no one touches anything without your instructions. I will provide influence and images to guide you through and find what you will need. It will also allow you to grow accustomed to my presence in your mind.

"All righty."

He coughed loudly enough to get everyone's attention and made a rallying gesture. He also noticed that Leo had returned and called out to him for an update.

"They're about thirty minutes out, sir," the ghoul reported.

"Okay, good." Sam spent a few minutes relaying the high points of what he had been told and their new instructions.

The ghouls' expressions ranged from simple attentiveness to complete shock.

"Leo, once they get here, start breaking out the gear, and get ready for us to move out quickly. Jasmine, grab two of the others, and follow me to get whatever we need from his ship."

They nodded and moved to obey.

"Okay, once we move out, I plan to leave Jasmine here." He turned back to face the progenitor. "Is that okay with you?"

What is to be her purpose?

"I told you before, she's the smartest person we have. I don't know how long we'll be gone, but you'll spend the time educating her on everything you can here."

If you insist.

"I do."

You are very much like your sire.

Sam was unsure if the comment had been intended as a compliment or not, but he would take it as one.

I suggest you get on with your tasks before the others get too far ahead.

Taking the hint, Sam quickly led the way to the progenitor's supposed spacecraft. With the ghouls' assistance, his group would be able to travel during the day and make up considerable ground, but John and Danielle had a hell of a head start.

"Look, you can see it from here . . . barely anyway," Danielle said, pointing toward the plateau further up the mountain.

It wasn't very far, but the terrain made it difficult to see the remains of Poenari Castle.

"Yeah, I see it," John agreed as he eyed what little he could make out of the unimposing remains of the structure. "You're sure about this?" He was definitely not getting the "evil" vibe he had expected to feel this close to the enemy stronghold.

"I am," she sounded confused but confident.

Despite John's earlier security concerns, the journey to Arefu had been uneventful and dreadfully boring. Given how close Arefu was to the castle, John had half expected to discover the whole town was nothing more than a secret vampire haven, but it was perfectly normal.

"I figured that by the time we got this close, we would have some kind of clue, but none of my senses are picking up anything." He shook his head. "It's right there, four, maybe five klicks?" he said, arching an eyebrow.

"Map says about six and a half, but that assuming we take the road, so you're probably pretty close on the straight-line distance. We can cover that in, what, a minute or so at full speed?"

"No more conserving power then?" John wasn't going to argue the point; he wanted answers.

"No, I want this done." Her eyes were hard with determination.

"It's getting worse, isn't it?" John knew he wouldn't need to clarify the question.

"Yeah, it's pretty much the only reason I know we're heading in the right direction."

"Look." He put a comforting hand on his wife's shoulder. "If he's going to seriously take up residence inside your head, at least make sure the rent is on time."

"I wish you'd take this seriously." She slapped his hand away.

151

"I am. First of the month, no grace period for evil megalomaniacs."

Before Danielle could offer a retort, John blurred in the direction of the castle, and she rushed to follow him. It was no more than a few seconds later that they both suddenly stopped, feeling dazed and vaguely disoriented.

"Woah, did you feel that just now?" John was shaking his head in an attempt to clear the sudden confusion.

"Yeah, it's weird, it almost felt like—"

John looked up as Danielle's voice cut off to see her simply pointing off into the distance.

When he saw the large dark castle, complete with a wicked-looking central spire, he couldn't blame her for the speechlessness. That was not the Poenari Castle ruins they had just been looking at.

It was also darker than it had been merely seconds ago. The clear night sky was suddenly completely overcast, but it was more than that. They had set out immediately after sunset for a reason, but now it seemed closer to the middle of the night. A faint stench of decay seemed to fill the area, and John could practically feel himself getting angry just standing still.

An odd sound drew his attention, and he looked over to see Danielle's chest heaving with the depth of her breaths. A definite sign of stress, considering she wasn't speaking at the moment. She was also staring, unblinking, at the castle with an intensity he didn't like. When she started to hiss slightly, he grabbed the back of her clothes and started dragging her back the way they had come.

It wasn't long until they felt the same disorienting feeling as before. A quick examination of their surroundings confirmed that everything was back to normal, including the castle sitting in ruins once again. After a few minutes of slow experimentation, they were able to determine the exact spot marking the edge of Dracula's territory, for lack of a better description.

"So what do you make of it?" John asked after they simply stared in silence for a few minutes.

"Of what?"

"This," he said, indicating the empty air in front of them. "What did you think I was asking about?"

"What exactly do you think I am?" She crossed her arms in obvious annoyance. "I'm a mind reader, John, not some fancy sensor gizmo from one of your books or television programs." She pointed to the

152

empty air in the direction of the castle. "I don't have a freaking clue what's going on here."

"Okay, okay, calm down," John tried to sound soothing.

Danielle had been getting more and more emotional lately, and it was starting to concern him.

"Hmm." He tried to think about the situation logically. "Remember before, the progenitor said he wasn't able to see into Dracula's territory? Maybe this is why?"

"You think he did something to the area?"

"What other explanation is there? I'm not sure what that was, but it was definitely real, and I'm equally certain this is real as well. Plus, like you said before, this is a tourist attraction, and I'm pretty sure there's no mention of random people stumbling onto his real castle." He shrugged. "At least we answered one of our questions."

"We need to leave." Danielle's voice was quiet but serious.

"Um, what? We're kind of on the clock here." He kept himself from rolling his eyes at his wife's ridiculous comment. "You said yourself, he's inside your head, and he knows we're here."

"It doesn't matter," she said, stepping closer. "We need to get the hell out of here. Don't you understand?"

"Not really, no. Running has never worked for us in the past, and you know that. So just calm down, and let's think this through." He smiled and put his hands on her shoulders.

"Don't speak to me like I'm a child." She backed out of his grip, and John's eyes widened slightly. "John, Dracula can bend reality. Ten minutes ago, I would have told you that such a thing wasn't possible, but we just saw it for ourselves."

"Well, technically, I'm not sure that's the proper term for what's happening here." He was never sure how to argue with her in moments like this.

"Bend reality, alter reality, what's the fucking difference? We can't fight against that." She threw her arms up, shocked that he didn't see her point.

"Well, maybe *you* can't," he mumbled to himself.

"I'm sorry, what was that?"

"Never mind." John turned to face in the direction of the invisible barrier. "Just drop it, okay?"

"No." Danielle put her hands on her hips. "If you've got something to say, spit it out," she demanded.

153

"Why?" He turned his gaze toward her, and Danielle didn't much care for the look in his eyes. "You're a mind reader, aren't you? Figure it out," he said, his tone a bit harsh.

"I . . . ," she hesitated. "I can't," she admitted, before averting her eyes from his challenging gaze.

"Big surprise," he scoffed.

"What's wrong with you?" She did not care for the way he was speaking to her, but there was still a note of concern in her question.

"Me, nothing. You, plenty."

The seriousness of his answer caused her to take a reflexive step back.

"Look," he said, his gaze and tone softening slightly. "I understand that I slept through the first fight. Trust me, no one regrets that more than me since we wouldn't even be here if our positions had been reversed."

"Just what the hell is that supposed to mean?" Her eyes narrowed, waiting for him to get to whatever nonsense point he was trying to make.

"You're really going to make me say it? Fine." He shrugged his shoulders. "I watched the fight, remember? You embarrass me," he said it quietly but clearly.

Danielle's jaw simply gaped open in response.

"Three separate times you could've easily destroyed him, but you didn't. And why is that?" He paused a moment, but Danielle was still speechless.

"It's because you got emotional and fought sloppy. Dracula practically handed you victory, and you gave it right back to him." John shook his head, and there was a note of disgust in the action.

"You bastard, I thought you were dead!"

He might have seen the memories, but he hadn't truly been there, and Danielle wouldn't be spoken to in this fashion.

"That's my point," he said, sighing. "You failed to properly examine the battlefield or your opponent or anything about the situation. You simply decided I was dead for exactly no reason and with all available evidence pointing to the contrary, and then you lost your shit. Every single time you fight on your own, you lose, and I am personally getting sick of it.

"Dammit, Dani, you're a fucking vampire! You are one of the most powerful creatures on this planet, so stop fighting and acting like a damn woman." He was jabbing a finger at her to emphasize his point when she stepped in and slapped him. Hard.

"An emotional outburst rather than logical thought or a controlled response, how unexpected," John sneered sarcastically. "I get it, you want to be treated as an equal, so start acting like one." He leaned his face closer to hers. "Tone down this 'whiny little bitch' routine you've been stuck on lately, and get your head back in the game. If I didn't know I needed your help tracking Dracula down, I would have left you in the progenitor's cavern." John's eyes seemed to be daring her to challenge his assessment.

Husband and wife glared at each other, unblinking, but it was Danielle who turned away first. After everything John had just said, she refused to add more weight to his argument by letting him see her tears.

They were no strangers to heated arguments, some of which resulted in considerable damage to their surroundings, but this was different. Everything about the way John had been scolding her pointed to her being an inferior being, and she hated that. She had not endured centuries of being ignored and disregarded by men to be treated that way by her own husband. The fact that every single thing he had said was technically true simply made it worse.

"In battle, which of us commands?" his voice was infused with power and demanded a response.

"You do," she practically spit the answer through clenched teeth.

"Do not make me repeat that." His voice still carried a scolding tone. "Now, give me your shotgun."

Her body responded automatically, drawing the weapon from inside her coat and holding it out to the side. John didn't seem to notice or care that she wasn't turning around. He simply took the weapon and began readying it for use.

"Once we cross back over, just focus on tracking him down and lead the way. I don't want to be walking in circles all night."

Finishing his check of her weapon, he repeated the process with his own.

"Don't worry about fighting, just keep us on track," he said to her back, pretending not to notice the slight shaking of her shoulders. "Let's go."

"Sir, yes, sir!" she shouted with angry sarcasm, before bracing to a mock position of attention and marching through the barrier.

John gave no notice to her antics and simply followed two steps behind, weapons at the ready.

Dracula grinned as his plan was finally beginning to bear fruit, and he started to reevaluate his goals. As odd and unexpected as he had found their relationship to be, the male's recent actions had started making things clearer to him. They were not equals after all. He did not blame the male for desiring her—Dracula desired her quite badly himself—but the male also desired strength and power.

Whether the male had always felt this way or whether it was a result of Dracula's influence over the female was unclear. He might simply see her as damaged goods. In any event, it would seem the male cared more for battle and pure strength than simple companionship. This was interesting.

Dracula toyed with his mustache as he considered the possibility of corrupting them both. It had not occurred to him before to even try such a thing, but he was beginning to realize he did not have enough information about the male. There were enough similarities between the male and himself that it was worth trying to reach out to him at least once.

It would not cost anything to try, beyond a few moments of time, and the potential rewards would be great. Even now, the pair of ancients were slaughtering their way through his minions. No matter what happened, Dracula would most likely have to begin from scratch in creating his army. So if he could gain a proper general with the ability to create a powerful army for him . . .

Oh yes, all his losses would be made good very soon. It was just a matter of deciding the best moment to intervene.

CHAPTER 11

Dracula's Territory

"I know the progenitor said his minions would be weak, but did you expect it to be this easy?"

They had not been in Dracula's territory for long, but the attacks were nonstop. Twisted animals and humans alike had been charging them seemingly at random, although they weren't accomplishing anything beyond exhausting the ancients' ammunition.

"Honestly, no." Danielle instinctively stopped walking as John fired both shotguns.

The rounds sailed in front of her chest, missing her by inches, as they impacted the two creatures that had been charging from her right side. That was how this entire battle had been fought so far. She hadn't had to pay any attention to the fighting, only stay out of the line of fire.

Since they had crossed over and begun fighting, John's demeanor had returned to normal. She was trying to give him the benefit of the doubt. It was true they were walking into possibly the most difficult battle they had ever fought, and John was always far more serious before a battle. Still, she simply could not forget or forgive him for the way he had spoken to her. She would ignore it for now, given the severity of their situation, but that was all she was willing to do.

"Heads up," he said and tossed her shotgun back to her. "Bunch of them this time."

She nodded as she caught the weapon, and they stood back-to-back. Over a dozen humanoid creatures burst through the trees, hissing challenges and baring claws at them. None of them made it within three feet of the vampires, and the night echoed with thunderous booms.

"Seriously, are these things even vampires?" John asked as he took a moment to examine the fresh corpses more carefully. They had fangs and claws, but their bodies were grotesque and twisted.

Danielle bent down and sniffed at some of the open wounds, grimacing as she did so.

"They don't smell right. Also, look at their blood." Danielle was poking very carefully at the blown-out chest cavity of the closest corpse. Most of the organs were recognizable, but the blood was much darker in color than normal. It was more like their bodies were filled with tar or some other strange black ichor.

"Hey, be careful, remember what the progenitor said about the blood here." He started reloading as Danielle fished out another box of ammunition from her pack to hand over, along with her freshly reloaded weapon.

"True, there's definitely something wrong with it." She was about to start leading the way again when an enormous shape separated from the darkness to block their path. "Um, John, is that what I think it is?"

"Yep."

Lumbering toward them was a monster well over twice their size. It was brandishing an enormous club, but its most notable feature was the single giant eye in the center of its huge head.

"Dracula has a cyclops apparently."

"Whatever."

Neither vampire was overly concerned about the giant monster, and Danielle raised an arm to set it on fire.

"Hold on a sec. I've always been curious about something," John said before he blurred off to the side.

Danielle simply shrugged and lowered her arm. She wasn't in the cyclops's attack range yet, so she simply waited to see what her husband was up to.

"Hey, ugly!" John was off to the beast's right side and threw a rock to get its attention.

The cyclops roared in challenge and anger as the rock bounced off its arm harmlessly.

"Come get some!" he said as he started making rude gestures at the beast, continuing with the verbal taunts.

Whether it understood the taunts or simply recognized John as a bigger threat, the beast roared and quickly turned to charge.

Thwack!

Danielle watched in confusion as the cyclops seemed to misjudge its own maneuver and rebounded off a tree. Her confusion only grew as she watched John continue jumping around, never letting up with the taunts.

Thwack!

This time the beast roared and ripped the tree out of the ground, hurling it at him. John simply watched as the trunk missed him by a considerable margin.

"Come on, dear," he said, seemingly getting bored with playing whatever game he had been playing, and motioned for Danielle to simply go around the beast as he had.

"I don't understand. What's wrong with it?"

As she maneuvered around to join her husband, the cyclops had managed to get itself tangled into a particularly dense cluster of trees. It continued roaring at them but seemed unable to handle its surroundings.

"Dear, it's a cyclops," he said, as if the answer was obvious.

She just looked at him and motioned for more.

"It's very dark out. We're in a rather dense wooded area, and it only has one eye. Hey, asshole," John shouted at the cyclops struggling nearly thirty feet away. "Be a good boy, and maybe Santa will bring you some depth perception."

"Wait, really?" Even seeing it, Danielle couldn't quite believe it.

"There's a reason most things have more than one eye dear. I honestly never understood the cyclops as being a particularly scary or even believable monster, and it's awesome to get to test the theory." John motioned for her to continue the hunt.

"Why would Dracula bother making such a flawed creature then? And shouldn't we still go back and kill it?" She glanced back in the direction from which they could still hear the roars coming.

"Honestly, it can probably adjust to its vision under normal circumstances, but once I pissed it off enough, it wasn't able to compensate properly. As for killing it, I think ignoring it is funnier. Let Dracula watch us ignore his garbage army, but don't take this lesson for granted, oh young apprentice."

"What lesson, and shouldn't you be paying attention to defending me, oh great commander?" Sarcasm could work both ways.

"After all that racket this area must be clear, or we'd be under attack already. As for the lesson, don't take your vision for granted, but don't rely on it either." John stuck his nose in the air, in an attempt to mimic a stuck-up college professor.

159

"Uh-huh." Danielle couldn't tell if he was serious or just bored, and she tried not to roll her eyes.

"I'm serious sweety. You should make it a point to start always memorizing the battlefield. Objects, distances, opponents, and the direction and speeds they are moving. You should be able to close your eyes and still predict the next few seconds of battle."

"Why on earth would I close my eyes in the middle of a battle?" As annoying as his ramblings could be, at least it was better than him actively yelling at her.

"Lots of things could cost you your vision temporarily."

"Like wh—" Danielle vanished before she could finish her question.

John had been looking away, yet he sensed a flurry of motion an instant before her disappearance. There wasn't enough time for his shock to be replaced with concern before a fiery explosion lit up the night sky. His senses detected a series of pained screeches, and he saw a familiar form plummeting to the ground. It was simple enough to blur into position to catch her.

"Um, did you just get carried away by a flock of bats?" he asked as he set her down gently.

"Colony," Danielle responded, standing up and straightening out her clothes.

"What?"

"A group of bats is called a colony, not a flock," she corrected his earlier statement.

"Who cares?" As much as he enjoyed science fiction, Danielle was addicted to *The Discovery Channel* and was filled with largely useless information. "Seriously, though, bats just carried you away?"

"You seem surprised. Are you saying I'm too fat to be carried away by bats?"

"Huh?" John started, before she winked at her own joke. "Anyway, I didn't even sense them until it was too late."

"Yeah, me either," she agreed. "I think they were normal bats. We don't usually pay attention to normal animals." That was true enough.

"Okay, but that's not normal behavior for bats though, right?"

"Is that a serious question?" Danielle could never be sure with his questions.

"Well, yeah, you're the one always watching that crap on TV."

"You—a grown, educated adult—are asking me if it is normal behavior for bats to simply swoop in and carry away full-grown human adults?" She closed her eyes briefly, seeking patience. "No, John, that is not normal behavior for ordinary bats."

"Okay, okay, you don't have to be such a bitch about it."

"Honestly, I disagree. I think that's exactly what you need sometimes," she said, smirking slightly.

"Kind of makes me afraid to ask your opinion about this."

John raised his left arm, and Danielle jumped back reflexively. A large wolf had its jaws around his arm strongly enough that its body was dangling off the ground.

"Jesus, John." She quickly drew her sword. "How long has that been there?"

"A few minutes I guess, who cares? Can we keep it?"

The wolf seemed incredibly angry that its jaws couldn't penetrate his reinforced clothing.

"Who's a good wolfy?" John was using a claw from his free hand to scratch the wolf's neck very carefully, which served to simply anger it more. "You are, yes, you are," he continued cooing.

"No." She managed to carefully decapitate the beast even with John's hand in the way.

"What the hell did you do that for?" he yelled at her.

"Are you being serious right now?"

"It's not my fault you won't let me have a dog." He tossed the severed head into the woods.

"We've been over this thousands of times. Animals hate us, we can't have a pet, and I'm not controlling the mind of a dog for its entire life just to keep it from biting you in the ass while we sleep."

"Sorry dear, I can't fully trust anyone who doesn't like dogs."

"That has nothing to do with it. Are you even paying—"

"Do you two ever stop your senseless banter?"

The new voice came from above, and both vampires saw Dracula lowering to a mere ten feet or so from the ground.

"Oh, hey Drake," John said waving as Danielle simply hissed. "It certainly took you long enough, considering how much noise we've been making." John faced him calmly, both shotguns pointed directly at his chest.

"I find your reliance on mortal weapons to be distasteful," he sneered as he eyed the firearms.

"Reliance?" John cocked his head slightly. "It's the opposite, I assure you. Your 'army'"—the word was infused with sarcasm—"is too pathetic to be worth any real effort on our part. I mean, seriously, we had

161

to have made a serious dent in your minions," John said then laughed at him.

"I don't really know how much time or effort it takes you to create that many of those things we killed, but it didn't cost us a thing to wipe them out," he said and paused in thought. "Well, technically, it did cost us a bunch of ammo. Dani, how much is that?"

"Huh?" She had been patiently waiting for the command to attack.

"How much does our shotgun ammo cost? I honestly have no idea."

"Um, don't the ghouls actually make the phosphorous rounds at home?" She wasn't sure why John was carrying on with his banter, but she had to assume there was a reason.

"Well, yeah, but they still need the materials. What do those cost?"

"How should I know? They just buy stuff most of the time, it's not like we really pay attention to our finances anymore."

"Hmm, maybe we should start. What if the ghouls start trying to embezzle from us?"

"That's ridiculous, why would they—"

"*ENOUGH!*" Dracula shouted when it seemed to him they had both forgotten he was even there. "What is wrong with you two?"

"Us? Nothing," John shrugged. "You, on the other hand, interrupted our conversation. Again. That's very rude."

Dracula's expression began to grow angry, and Danielle started to think John had a plan after all.

"You are both centuries older even than I, marching toward certain death like lunatics." As serious as his voice sounded, there was an undercurrent of confusion. "Yet you make no plans, discuss no strategy of how to possibly defeat me, and seem to barely pay any attention to your surroundings. The only goal or priority either of you has demonstrated since entering my territory seems to be to annoy the other one," he sighed. "I must conclude that some form of senility must affect vampires of your kind after a certain age. What other explanation can there be for your nonsense?"

"We're married," came the combined response.

Despite the memories of their earlier argument, Danielle couldn't help but giggle slightly at Dracula's sudden look of confusion.

"Anyway," John said, tightening his grip on the shotguns, "I guess we should probably kill you now."

The statement sounded just fine to Danielle, but as Dracula had mentioned, they had not shared any type of strategy. She was forced to

162

wait for John to make the first move, and then she would support him as best as she could.

"Stay your hand, boy." Dracula raised his left hand as if in an effort to calm them. "I am not here to fight either of you."

"Considering our last encounter, you'll forgive our lack of applause." John's sarcasm was almost thick enough to taste.

"True enough. However, none of us knew then what we all know now." Dracula tried to appear nonthreatening and even refrained from infusing his voice with any power.

"What's that supposed to mean?"

"Why, this progenitor of yours, of course."

Neither of them could keep the shock from their expressions.

"Come now, you did not think I would take the information from her mind the moment you left his protection?"

"Get to the point," John urged.

"John, this is wrong." Danielle was starting to get nervous. They should be fighting, not talking; this was Dracula's specialty. "You can't believe anything he says," she whispered softly.

"Just a second," John brushed off her warning. "Remember, I never really got a chance to talk to this guy."

Even hearing his words, she couldn't believe him. Was this some part of examining the enemy and the battlefield, as he had mentioned before? Some trick of John's to try and learn of a weakness to exploit?

"We three," Dracula said, taking them in with a wave of his hand, "are the most powerful creatures in this world, aside from your foolish progenitor. Given what we all know about what is out there . . ."—he simply pointed to the sky—"it is the height of folly to continue this battle. Instead, I have an offer for you." He crossed his arms, waiting for a response.

"I can pretty much guess what it is, but you may as well spit it out," John said.

It wasn't hard to predict where this megalomaniac was going.

"Do you take me for a fool, boy?" Dracula arched an eyebrow at him. "I will not succumb to your trickery. If you wish this conversation to continue, bow down and accept me as your master. Otherwise, prepare for your destruction."

The pressure around Dracula was beginning to grow as he gathered his power.

"Okay, hold on, that's a ridiculous expectation," John shot back at him. "I neither bow nor bend a knee to anyone, and consider how angry I

163

must be from what you did to us. Even if I did bow down before you right now, it would be an obvious lie. However, I've lived far too long to simply rush to my death," he said, nodding slightly. "So how about this," John continued, lowering his weapons, "I'll toss my weapons aside, but I'll remain standing."

Without waiting for an answer, John threw both shotguns into the surrounding woods. Next came his sword and pack, and finally, he simply held his arms at his sides, palms out.

"As a bonus, I promise to watch my language and sarcasm."

"There is wisdom to what you say, boy," Dracula said, his gaze darting briefly to Danielle, and he seemed pleased at the way she was staring at John in total confusion.

"My name's John by the way." John crossed his arms as well, matching Dracula's pose.

"Very well, John. Perhaps my expectations were unreasonable, but if you decide to accept my offer, you must abide by them."

"Sounds like you better make that offer then," John replied.

Danielle was studying every detail of John's body and the words he was speaking, and she couldn't come up with a single clue as to his intentions.

"It is quite simple really. She is to be my queen, that is already decided," Dracula paused for the inevitable retort. When none came, he silently applauded his choices. "However, I am in need of more than a simple queen. I need a general."

"Keep talking."

"John, this isn't funny anymore," Danielle pleaded softly.

"Just be quiet for a sec," he said, blowing her off again.

"Sorry, Drake, you were saying?" John pretended to not notice the pleased look that crossed Dracula's face when he ignored his wife's concern.

"You've seen my inability to create powerful minions despite being all-powerful myself. Raise my armies and lead them."

"Lead them where?"

"Everywhere," Dracula said, spreading his arms out widely and dramatically. "You must only bind yourself to me, and I promise you an eternity of wonderous battles, challenges worthy of your power." Dracula was beginning to grow even more animate, unable to control his excitement over what the future might hold.

"As your slave, you mean," John remained skeptical.

"Only in the sense that your own minions are slaves to you. They still retain their independent thoughts, as you would. What matters if you must bow to me when all other life will bow to you?"

John opened his mouth to respond, then simply lowered his gaze in thought. Danielle had had enough of this foolishness and rushed to his side.

"John, stop. Can't you see what's happening?" she said, grabbing at his arm.

"*Goddammit woman!* I said to be silent!" he shouted, turning and shoving her away so suddenly and violently she lost her balance.

Looking up, her face covered in tears and dirt, Danielle saw John had already turned his back to her and gone back to his conversation with Dracula. She was being completely ignored. It was happening again.

Dracula had plenty to say to her in their first encounter, but not now. Not when there was a man to talk to. Her husband. Her *owner*. Mortal brains were not meant to hold the centuries of memories hers had, and in times of stress, those memories could become badly jumbled. She was remembering when her parents had originally bartered her away to John.

She had been fortunate that they had been in love anyway, and at the time, it didn't seem wrong. While most women had been worth less than a good horse, she had fetched quite a price. Yet nine centuries later, she still wasn't taken seriously. When she chose to abandon her abilities and masquerade as a mortal, no one spoke to her seriously.

Certainly, she was approached often, but always for obvious reasons. None seemed to care much for the obvious ring on her finger, and very few bothered looking above her neckline. None of it mattered since she had John, yet here he was trading her away to secure his own life and position. It couldn't be true, but the look in his eye had left no doubt.

Danielle tried to reach out with her mind, but his mind was closed to her. The conversation had turned to white noise, but she noticed it end while picking herself up. Looking up from where she was still crouched on one knee, she saw the impossible. John was starting to kneel down before his new master, and she could feel her heart breaking. Dracula must have been influencing his mind; it was the only explanation.

Even knowing the truth, it was too late to do anything about it. There was little chance she could win against either one of them, much less both. Then she saw it. It was only because she had been staring at her husband in such shocked horror that she had seen his true plan. Once

165

again, Danielle was reminded why he was the true strategist of their family.

John knelt down and began bowing in a traditional fashion, with his right hand over his heart. The moment his torso was low enough to hide his right arm and hand from view, a string of objects fell from the inside of his coat. As he deftly activated his surprise, Danielle's mind began to race. She knew she had all the pieces, but she had to put them together fast in order to support whatever was about to happen.

Everything John had done or said to her up to this point had been carefully calculated. She knew that now. He had assumed that Dracula's presence in her mind meant he would know everything she did, and so his plan had to remain secret even from her. Her mind began processing information at speeds only creatures such as they were capable of, for she knew he would have given her clues.

Now!

The mental signal came as he jumped back, releasing his surprise in Dracula's direction, confirming that he was counting on a specific action from her.

Earlier he had scolded her for fighting with too much emotion, so she forced herself to clamp down on her confused feelings. John was very logical when it came to his plans, so what did logic tell her to do?

Grenades were fun to play with but mostly useless against powerful opponents. She knew he had thrown grenades, a lot of them, but what kind? Phosphorous grenades would work, but no opponent would simply hold still long enough to be burned and melted to death. Smoke grenades would be useless, and frags simply weren't strong enough. They had to be flash-bangs!

Designed to blind and disorient simple mortal senses, flash-bangs could be devastating to vampires. John and Danielle typically did not use them because they were area-effect weapons, and most of their combat was up close and personal. John had kept the bundle hidden for nearly three seconds before throwing it at Dracula. And now there couldn't be more than three seconds left, so Danielle started to run *toward* the coming explosion.

Nothing could be done about the concussive force, but at least they would be expecting it. No, it was the blindness she had to watch out for, and it all made sense. Remembering John's earlier clue for what it truly was, she took a mental image of the battlefield before closing her eyes. There would only be one chance.

The tree was right where she expected it to be, and she was halfway up before seeing the flash through her closed eyelids. The concussive force of so many grenades going off at once ruptured her eardrums, and she cried out as her brain felt like it was exploding, but she never slowed. She couldn't, for John's entire plan hinged on her actions at the critical moment. It had to be her since there was only one obvious direction for their opponent to escape.

Danielle reached the top of the tree and leaped, calling upon her control over air currents to take her to even greater heights. Even as she felt blood pouring from her ears, she opened her eyes and was rewarded with clear vision and the sight of Dracula heading straight toward her. It was clear that the cape was doing the flying by reflex, as he was clutching his head in agony and had no idea she was waiting. Danielle was able to adjust her arc slightly, and her face was a mask of vampiric glee as she closed rapidly for the kill.

At the last second, Dracula opened his eyes, and she was rewarded with a look of pure shock and fear. The instant her claws came down, his body moved laterally. She hissed in rage at the impossible and unpredictable maneuver, but still managed to rake the claws of one hand across his back. Striking out with her off hand, she grabbed hold of his cape and ripped it from his body.

Without the cape, Danielle was convinced he would simply fall back to where John would certainly be waiting. Unfortunately, as they both began losing altitude, Dracula simply disappeared into a cloud of darkness. She shrieked in rage, losing control of the air around her, and began to fall uncontrollably. There was no true danger as John was there to catch her.

"Well?" he asked as he set her back down.

"I'm sorry honey, he got away." Danielle felt terrible, despite knowing there was nothing more she could have done.

"Damn. Looks like you got a piece of him at least," he said, indicating her bloody claws.

"True, and this," she said, holding up the cape, which was still fluttering.

She quickly ripped it in half, and they both jumped back in surprise as the cape screamed in pain. Danielle dropped the pieces in shock, and they shriveled up into small, black piles of ash.

"Yeah, so that happened." He nudged one of the piles with his boot. "Hey, Dani, all those things I said and how I've been acting," he started out meekly, but she stopped him.

167

"It was damn brilliant, and don't worry about it. You really had me going, especially at the end. I'm just sorry I messed it up."

"Not your fault," he disagreed. "We didn't know the jackass could disappear like that. You did great, considering you had, what, a few seconds to figure out the whole plan?" He kissed her forehead before moving to retrieve the weapons he had discarded. "Besides, isn't it lovely to think about how pissed off he must be right now?"

Insanity! It was the only explanation Dracula had for the situation. He had reappeared a short distance away and was doubled over, his head still throbbing in agony from the series of blasts that had gone off mere inches from his face. The wounds on his back were taking longer to heal due to his lack of concentration, and the loss of his cape had been a devastating blow. The injuries he had suffered were not serious, but the overall situation had his mind in a rage.

Those two were complete lunatics! Everything he had just experienced was outright impossible, yet it had happened. The male's plan had been quite clever, and Dracula had no choice but to respect him for it, but the female's response was simply not possible. Dracula did not *think* that she had been taken completely by surprise by the male's actions—he *knew* it.

He had been carefully reading and judging her reactions ever since they entered his territory. Her confusion and outright anger were real, and her shock mixed with despair at the end was absolute. It was the main evidence he used to accept the male's actions as truth. Dracula was so firmly entrenched in her mind that there was no way she could have tricked him.

The male's brilliant trick relied on her overcoming complete surprise, understanding a situation she could not have possibly known was coming, and acting in perfect support at the critical moment. All within seconds. All Dracula managed to do in those same seconds was instinctively retreat upward—something the female had also figured out and anticipated.

His wounds healed; Dracula forced logical thought to take the place of his rage. Despite his greater power and desire to convert at least one of them, he had to stop holding back. He had been trying to predict their actions and thoughts, but he was starting to realize they were creatures he just simply did not understand.

He had to stop simply reacting to them and force a confrontation he could not lose. Risks would have to be taken, or those lunatics were likely to destroy him by accident as much as by any real planning on their part. Dracula understood how the world worked, and no two creatures could be as perfectly linked as they were. Yet he had already lost so much in learning the falsehood of that assumption.

Even now, he gently reached out to reconnect with the female's mind and saw they had returned to their earlier trivial banter. It was as if the last confrontation had never happened, or at least they didn't care about it. They were simply closing in on his castle, blatantly gunning down his minions as if on safari.

It was clear much of their actions and conversations were intended to simply make him angry, in the hopes he would continue to make mistakes. Dracula was finished making mistakes. He would unleash his full fury, and if he failed to gain the upper hand he needed, he would simply destroy them both.

"Well, that's that then," John announced as he threw the now-empty shotguns into the woods.

"Hey, don't do that." Danielle stopped walking and was giving him a look of annoyance.

"What?" He motioned for her to keep moving; remaining stationary was not a good idea in this territory. "We're out of ammo, and I'm not carrying empty shotguns around for no reason."

"It's wasteful."

"Seriously? We've got more money than god. I think we'll be okay," John argued as he drew his sword. He didn't even bother morphing his fingers into claws.

"I doubt god uses money," Danielle retorted as she threw a knife at a random dark shadow that was moving closer.

"Then how do people buy things in heaven?"

"You actually believe there's shopping in heaven?"

"Are there women there?" He gave her a wink as Danielle paused and thought for a moment before starting to chuckle.

"You might have a point." Another pair of knives went flying as John turned to decapitate a third attacker. "What if some kids find them though?"

"A pair of empty shotguns is probably the least problematic thing we've left in our wake." John had stopped keeping track of the various bodies after fifty. "Besides, you're throwing knives."

"That's different, those are *throwing* weapons," she said, raising a finger to punctuate her point.

"That's not the point, you're scolding me for leaving weapons out in the open for kids to find."

"What the hell would kids be doing wandering through Dracula's territory?"

"You're the one that said it, seriously, not thirty seconds ago," John pointed out.

"Oh yeah," she said and scratched the side of her temple with one of her knives. "How much of this conversation is serious, and how much is simply intended to annoy Dracula if he's listening?"

"I've honestly lost track." John laughed.

"So how do we fight him? Or is it maybe better for you to not tell me?" Danielle understood the possible need to keep things hidden from her, but she desperately wanted to know if John had any ideas.

"I don't think that matters anymore," he admit. "I doubt he's going to take anything we do or say at this point at face value, so why bother? Besides," he shrugged, "I got nothing."

"That's disheartening, I doubt we have more than ten minutes or so." It was always possible that John was hiding another trump card, but it didn't sound like it.

"I realized we don't really need anything fancy. Focus on pure power and speed, and try to use fire to dispel any illusions he throws at us," he sounded confident, but it seemed too simple to her.

"I think he's too powerful for that to work."

"Power alone is irrelevant. He can't fight for shit," he said and shrugged. "If he's really spent most of his life hiding here, I guess it makes sense. He simply doesn't have the combat experience we do. Hold up a second." John stopped and waited for her to turn around.

"What?"

"Look, the stuff I said before was done in an inappropriate way for a reason, but most of the things I said were true. You have got to learn how to analyze a battle once it's over. Forget which one of you won the first fight. Who controlled it?"

"Obviously, he . . . ," she started giving the obvious answer but then stopped and forced herself to really think about what had happened. "No, he didn't. I did."

John smiled. "Correct. He surrendered the initiative to you almost immediately and missed every opportunity to truly take it back. A combination of his desire to take you alive and shock at your abilities kept him on the defensive while you remained the primary attacker. Your emotions cost you total victory, but his inexperience prevented him from achieving it either.

"Whether he admits it openly or not, Dracula knows he isn't as experienced as we are. That's why his first instinct is to simply run away, despite having the power to possibly force victory. He's trying to force himself to understand what we truly are and what we can do so he can fight us better."

Danielle was looking away, but she wasn't arguing his points. "I think I understand what you mean. It sounds like an advantage for us, but it's one that won't last."

"It won't. He didn't live this long by being stupid. It also means we can't make any specific attack plans because we don't really know what he can do. We've shown him most of our tricks, but the prick keeps running away before showing us his."

"So we have to be ready to react to anything, but with aggression. Don't let ourselves get stuck on the defensive like he did with me?"

"Exactly," John agreed. "Now would be a good time to start." He nodded for her to turn around.

Danielle spun and saw a wall of dark clouds rolling toward them.

"Dani?"

"I know, me too."

They both readied themselves, and John blurred to another position on what would be their battlefield. She tried to simply dissipate the incoming clouds, but nothing happened. Interesting. It confirmed that Dracula was creating something supernatural rather than manipulating natural elements in the way she did. She tried sending streams of fire to meet the clouds and was rewarded with proof that her magic could dissipate his illusions. She would need to take care to use as little as was necessary to dissipate each incoming illusion to save her strength.

With the clouds gone, it was easy to see Dracula charging toward her. Fast. He held no weapons she could see, but both clawed hands seemed to be holding balls of swirling darkness. It seemed strange to see him with no cape, and she couldn't help but smile slightly at how angry he was. That was fine with her.

Letting her fangs protrude completely, Danielle charged, sword at the ready. Before the two combatants could collide with each other,

Dracula's image shimmered, and suddenly there were a dozen of him. Not expecting the trick, she leaped to the side, trying to avoid as many of them as possible. She also took a chance and threw a knife at a random target, dissipating the illusion.

Any clue which one is real?

Not yet, but any attack dissipates the fake ones.

Danielle was forced to keep leaping from point to point to avoid all the dark bolts being thrown at her by so many attackers. One of the bolts hit her arm, but she felt nothing. Apparently, the illusionary attacks were just that, but until she could tell them apart, they would still have to keep dodging them all.

As if on cue, John blurred through the battlefield without a trace of subtlety. There was no battle cry, and he shouted no challenge. He simply moved through the area like a swirling buzz saw, dissipating illusions almost as fast as Dracula created new ones. Danielle started mimicking his attacks, and between the two of them, they easily swept back and forth, clearing the area.

Another two dozen illusions appeared from nowhere, and the cycle began again. It was difficult to keep track of what was happening or even know if they were making progress. They had both taken small injuries, so the real Dracula had to be somewhere in this mess. Or did he? It was true they had been injured, but only slightly. They had proof from their very first encounter that some of Dracula's shadowy illusions had that capability.

I don't think he's here. She could feel John's agreement, although neither of them slowed in their attacks. *He has to be close if he's making these things.*

Find him.

Easier said than done. It was hard enough trying to stay one step ahead of the illusions.

Concentrate like before. I'll protect you.

She knew what he meant but didn't think it would work this time.

You can't. There're too many of them, and I might be wrong.

That's my problem.

No, it isn't. Danielle was done being protected. *Get back.*

She stopped fighting after issuing the silent command and began to concentrate, but not on finding Dracula. Suddenly, she was standing inside a sphere of fire, and she sent it quickly expanding in all directions. John managed to outrun it, barely, and the fire successfully dissipated the remaining illusions. She wasn't finished.

The instant her fire burned itself out, she quickly knelt down and buried both hands in the dirt. Nothing happened at first, but John could see the strain on her face, and she was visibly sweating blood. Earth magic was very difficult to use and almost completely useless to them given the urban areas where they spent most of their time.

Danielle refused to give up, and the strain was becoming visible throughout the rest of her body as she commanded the ground around them to disgorge anything with blood. It had been the best idea she could come up with, but it was still a broad category of creatures. John watched in amazement as the area rumbled with small tremors and all manner of insects and small creatures shot into the air. And one very disoriented vampire.

Dracula clearly had no idea what had happened, but he wasted no time. They were on opposite sides of Danielle, who appeared ready to collapse, but Dracula was closer. She attempted to flee back in John's direction while sending a bolt of fire into Dracula's face. Unfortunately, the strain of using so much powerful magic so quickly was too much, and she lost her balance.

Dracula ignored her attack, simply accepting the light burns, and was on her before John could intervene. Her defensive strikes weren't fast enough, and he had both her arms quickly pinned to the ground. The instant his fangs pierced her throat, she shrieked in agony. It was as if someone was pouring liquid fire into her body. John was there a second later, but it was too late. Dracula simply vanished again as he sensed the incoming attack.

"Dammit."

How were they supposed to kill this guy if he kept running away? John was looking around and trying to sense Dracula's presence and didn't notice right away that Danielle hadn't gotten back up or even answered him.

"Hey, are you—" He looked back down and tried to not immediately panic.

There were two ugly wounds on her neck from Dracula's fangs, and the blood dripping from them was clearly the wrong color. Worse were the dark tendrils seemingly spreading from the wounds under her skin. Dracula had clearly released something inside her, and it was spreading fast. John was starting to understand why he had fled so easily.

Danielle's eyes were shooting around quickly, and John could see the fear and awareness in them, but she didn't appear able to move her body. He quickly crouched next to her even as she started convulsing. It appeared similar to a normal seizure, but there was nothing normal about that happening to a vampire. Blood was starting to pour out of her mouth, and he couldn't think of anything to do beyond trying to hold her still.

"Dani, you have to heal!"

Despite what she was going through, Danielle managed to give him a nasty look at his stupidly obvious instruction.

"Sorry, but I don't know what to do." He was trying to stay calm for her sake, but he wasn't fooling anyone. The only way either of them could help the other heal was by giving them more blood, and he doubted she had the ability to drink.

Small broken sounds were coming from her throat as she tried unsuccessfully to form words. He knew she was trying to tell him something, but beyond her eyes, there was no control. Holding her head still, he tried looking into her eyes more clearly, and she was looking hard back into his. An image slowly formed in his mind as she gave him instructions.

"Jesus, Dani, I can't!"

Her idea was insane. There was no way he would risk it. Even as he said it, he mounted her and tried to distribute his weight in a way to keep her upper body still. He could feel her muscles straining underneath him, but at least he was stronger than she was. Her eyes were pleading, and he watched in horror as tiny black fingers started invading her irises.

Do! It! Her thoughts were so weak, but the desperation was clear.

John forced himself to focus carefully as he pushed Danielle's head down firmly. Pushing against her forehead with his right hand, he was able to reduce the movement to an acceptable amount. He then positioned the claws of his left hand very precisely, hesitating slightly as he saw a single red tear drop from her right eye.

Lowering his gaze from her face, John ripped out the source of the infection, along with almost three-quarters of his wife's throat. The feeling of her body going completely limp the instant her spinal cord was severed was unnerving—although, technically, *severed* was far too clean a word to describe what he had done.

Almost four vertical inches of her throat were gone, with barely more than skin and some muscle on the left side keeping her head attached. He had exactly no idea what would happen next, only that he had to hold her head very, very still. Not being ash yet meant nothing under these circumstances.

The progenitor had warned them of Dracula's ability to corrupt other creatures, but he implied they were strong enough to fight it off.

What had happened to Danielle was simply too much too fast, so by ripping most of it out, hopefully her ability to heal could handle the rest. Of course, if she didn't have enough strength left, her body would be ash soon, and under the circumstances, John had no way to get more blood into her.

There was nothing he could do but wait, so he focused on examining the gaping hole he had made. After a few endless seconds, she started slowly regenerating, and John carefully examined the process as a means of distraction. The vertebrae and spinal cord began reforming first, as expected, but he noticed something odd he had never seen before.

Several "things" started sprouting from both sides of the wound. At first, they looked like simple muscle fibers, but in her weakened condition, she was healing in stages, and it wasn't the muscle's turn yet. They were connecting themselves to and intertwining with almost everything, and now that he knew what to look for, he saw them everywhere. He got the sense there was blood coursing through them, and he wondered if he was seeing the vampiric equivalent of a circulatory system.

The nature of the wound and his careful examination were the only reasons he had noticed them. Since she was regenerating from all sides, her various bits were growing "out" in an effort to connect to the other side, rather than simply growing together into whatever she needed. These vampiric capillaries, or whatever they were, even seemed to be sliding inside of her bones. Each one began expanding and contracting ever so slightly once its connection had been made.

Was this the secret? Were these things responsible for pumping their blood, and its power, so thoroughly throughout their bodies while their hearts simply provided that power? Is that why they had no real pulse? Did these things all connect to their hearts, or did they branch off their original arteries?

John hadn't been able to tell. By the time her carotid arteries had reformed, there was simply too much in the way. Every drop of their blood was the same shade of red, depending on whatever their bodies' oxygen content was at the time. This amount could change, of course, based on how much they bothered to breathe, but since they had no need to absorb or use the oxygen, their blood averaged toward a slightly brighter shade of red. That exact coloring and the amount of blood infusing itself everywhere were causing everything to look the same to him.

Prior to the wound completely closing, John had lost track of the things he had discovered. As fascinated as he had been, his examination had been meant merely as a distraction that was no longer needed.

He moved his hand from her forehead to begin gently caressing her cheek and noticed that at least her eyes were clear. In fact, he didn't see any evidence of the dark tendrils that had been spreading through her, so he remained hopeful despite her lack of movement. Eventually, she blinked a few times and turned her head slightly to look at him better.

"I can't believe that worked, you are one crazy bitch," he exclaimed, seeing the proper awareness in her eyes. She reached up and pulled his head closer to her own.

"Get off," she managed a pained whisper.

"Huh?"

"You're crushing my tits."

Her comment confused him at first, and then he winced apologetically. The way he was sitting across her chest, and how forcefully he was doing so, could have not been comfortable for a woman. He had simply been engrossed in watching her recovery and had forgotten to move after the convulsions stopped.

"Oh, sorry about that." He rolled off, and the couple simply lay next to each other.

"Hey, John?"

"Present."

"Remember you telling me to learn to analyze my battles?"

"I happen to recall dispensing that sage wisdom, yes." John was happy to hear her voice sounding normal, despite the exhaustion she had to be feeling.

"My analysis of the last battle is complete."

"Oh really? What have you learned, my lovely apprentice?"

Neither of them even bothered turning their heads and were simply staring up into the night sky.

"Don't let him bite you."

There was a brief moment of silence before they both laughed loudly at her ridiculously obvious takeaway.

"We've been motionless for too long, haven't we?" Danielle sighed, already knowing the answer.

"Yep."

They immediately began rolling in opposite directions, but it was too late. Dozens of skeletal hands began punching up through the ground all around them, and before the ancients could leap away, they were pulled down into the earth.

CHAPTER 12

Poenari Castle Dungeon

"Ugh, did you get the plate number of the truck that just ran over my skull?" John slowly picked himself off the stone floor, rubbing at his sore temples, and took stock of their surroundings.

The cell—and there was no doubt it was a cell—was barely ten feet wide and roughly square. There was a small, barred window that allowed a bit of moonlight into the space and a large, sturdy-looking door. Aside from the window and door, the stone walls were completely gray and featureless, and the same dank odor of decay that seemed to accompany everything Dracula touched was present in abundance.

"Why aren't we dead?" Danielle had ignored his attempt at levity, and her tone made it clear she was in no mood for humor.

She was looking blankly out the small window, and when she turned to face him, John nearly gasped at her appearance. He had been trying not to think about how they had been pulled underground, but there was no sense denying the obvious.

Danielle's clothing was badly shredded and filthy, giving her the appearance of a half-naked vagrant. Dark bruises and deep lacerations were still visible on her face and exposed flesh. John saw a reflection of his own concern mirrored in her eyes and realized he must look just as bad.

"You know, we can break through that door pretty easily. Even the walls, for that matter, wouldn't stand up to a direct attack." He was purposefully ignoring his wife's question, trying to plan out their next move. They had to retake the initiative if they hoped to prevail, and his mind was already starting to come up with new attack strategies.

"Why aren't we dead?" Danielle was clearly going to force the issue. "And why place us in a cell we could escape from so easily?"

John sighed, not really wanting to dwell on their previous defeat.

"Keep in mind that I don't think any cell in existence could imprison us for long," he offered, trying to give a comforting response.

"I agree, and Dracula has to know that as well. So then, why not finish us off when he had the chance? Why take the risk when it wasn't necessary?"

John had been considering the same questions, but he was sure Danielle would not enjoy his theories.

"It sounds ridiculous, but he might not have given up trying to convert us yet. Don't forget how much he wants you at least. As for the risk? Despite how much he's already lost, Dracula doesn't see us as a threat, which explains why he's willing to keep us alive as long as necessary."

Knowing it to be true and saying the words out loud were two very different things.

"I'll admit I do think it's strange he didn't bite us though." John was clueless as to why Dracula would have missed the obvious opportunity.

"It wouldn't give him what he really wants." Her response was met with a look of confusion. "You're the strategist, and you mentioned yourself how much we've already cost him. Simply killing us doesn't replace those losses." She couldn't spend this much time with the increasing influence of another in her mind without understanding more of his intentions herself.

"Remember, he wants me, but also my abilities. He is afraid that corrupting me the way he makes his normal minions would cause me to lose them. I think biting me the first time was more of an act of desperation on his part. He's trying to break me normally to play it safe.

"He wanted to use you as a test subject, but he gave up on that idea. The only reason you're still alive is he knows that if I don't see you die, I'll never believe it happened, but . . . ," she paused, and John could tell she didn't want to finish. "If I do see it, I'll break, and he wins."

"If you know all that, then why'd you ask the question?"

"Because," she said, her eyes pleading, "I need you to hear and understand the answers. I know you see his constant retreating as weakness, and maybe you're partly right, but he's honestly just buying time."

"For what purpose?" John was certain he wasn't going to like the answer.

"He knows he's winning."

Before he could argue, she tapped the side of her head for clarification.

"It's been so much worse since we entered his territory, and I don't know how much longer I'm still going to be me," she finished her admission in a frightened whisper.

"Don't worry." He was quick to chime in. "We can use that stupid confidence of his against him." To John, the situation hadn't changed, and her admission simply adjusted their timetable.

"I fail to see how," she responded dubiously.

"It gives us the freedom to try another tactic, and another, and another. We just need to keep fighting until we find a strategy that works. If he's going to keep us alive to buy us the time to do so, then so much the better." Even as he spoke the words, new ideas and strategies were beginning to form in his mind.

"Why?" The single word was spoken so softly, and yet it carried so much weight that John was momentarily taken aback.

"Excuse me?"

"Why should we continue? Every battle serves to weaken us while Dracula's strength remains the same. Weren't you listening to me? He's only *toying* with us!" She was beginning to raise her voice angrily. "There's no point in continuing to fight someone who can destroy us the instant he chooses. Or he can simply hide and wait for me to join him voluntarily."

She turned her back on him, looking back out the window.

"We could escape so easily," she mumbled, wrapping her arms around her broken chest.

"He would simply track us down," John responded carefully, unsure of how to take his wife's apparent fear.

"No, he wouldn't." Danielle locked eyes with her husband, and he knew she was serious. "Our battles have given me insight into how his power works. While I can't overcome his mind, or even save myself inside his territory, I can hide our presence from him indefinitely if we get back out. It's a big world out there." Her gaze drifted back to the window. "We could just disappear into it."

There was a helpless edge to her voice that John didn't recognize, and he was growing more concerned.

179

"My love, I don't understand. We can't just run away and pretend this never happened." He moved closer behind her, snaking his arms around her waist. "The progenitor is counting on us to put an end to Dracula's madness."

The instant his arms locked around her, Danielle panicked. She pushed away and turned to face him so violently that one of her nails opened a fresh cut along his cheek. John was too frozen in shock by her actions to say anything else.

"Don't you 'my love' me, John!" She stared unblinking into his eyes, and he felt the first claw of fear at her actions begin tugging at the back of his mind. "What happened to our first priority being survival? What happened to simply running away at the next sign of danger?"

He winced at her tone. He *had* said that, hadn't he? It still didn't change the fact that his wife appeared to be losing her mind. She didn't even seem to acknowledge that she had struck him, albeit unintentionally.

"And as for the progenitor, we were just fine until he got into our heads."

"I understand," he began slowly, trying not to agitate her further. "Unfortunately, I don't see any realistic way out of this."

The look in her eye was more animalistic than it was human, so he was careful to not directly tell her that running was foolish.

"Our only chance for long-term survival is to accept the progenitor's gift of power, and the only way he'll give it to us is if we destroy Dracula."

"Spoken like a good hitman. *You* want his power!"

John didn't know what to do or say. He simply held perfectly still and told himself she was just blowing off steam.

"Maybe for your next job, you can find my *husband*! What would that cost me, or do you not even know where to look anymore?"

He couldn't believe his own ears and had to quickly bite down on his anger.

"Dani," he had to try something.

"Continuing to fight is *your* decision!" she ignored him. Her eyes were beginning to redden as despair began turning to frenzy.

It didn't matter; John had lost patience with the way she was acting.

"No, Danielle, this is *not* my decision," he hissed, infusing his voice with enough power that she had no choice but to listen.

The only explanation was that she had been telling the truth about Dracula's continued raping of her mind coming close to breaking her. He had to reach what was left.

"Every time we turn our backs, fate keeps blocking the path, and I can feel us circling closer and closer to the flame."

"Then you should pull back. Dracula is not our responsibility," she hissed in return.

At least, he noted, she was answering rather than randomly yelling.

"Protecting *you* is my responsibility," John shot back. "Protecting *us* is my responsibility." He was beginning to sound exasperated himself. "And how am I supposed to protect you from the hunters, the werewolves, the demons, and the lions and tigers and bears? With these?" John displayed his vampiric claws with a flourish, waving them back and forth under his wife's gaze. Wicked and deadly though they were, the claws could only reach so far, and the point was well taken.

Danielle didn't respond, but she didn't appear ready to relent either.

"No fang is sharp enough, no claw is long enough, and have you truly considered what will happen if we did run or fail?" His voice grew softer, trying to reach out to her. "Dracula knows all we know about the progenitor, including where to find him. He may be safe for now, but for how long? How long before time erodes enough of his power or until he simply doesn't care about who kills him anymore? How long before Dracula can simply take that power for himself?"

Still no response.

"We've seen what Dracula is capable of and the depths of his darkness. With the progenitor's power added to his own, I don't know if anything could stop him. This whole world will turn into a playground for his evil," he said, his voice pleading.

"*I DON'T CARE!*" Danielle's reply was so strong that John felt an uncontrolled bolt of force impact his chest. It was the equivalent of a mortal woman pounding her fists with uncontrolled emotion. "Dracula can do whatever the *fuck* he wants! This whole world can burn and its people can rot in hell for all I care." Bloody tears were starting to run down her cheeks. "It isn't worth losing you." At least she had finally gotten to the heart of the matter, and the red in her eyes was no longer frenzy but simply deep sadness.

"You don't mean that," John said as soothingly as he could.

"Yes, I do. Securing this world, if such a thing is even possible, is not a fair trade-off for losing you."

"I'm right here, Dani, and I don't plan on being lost." John couldn't help but remember the progenitor's earlier warning.

"You will be if we stay." The certainty of her statement forestalled what he had been about to say. "I've seen partway into his mind, John. I already tried to explain his plans to you. He wants me, not you and not us. The next time we confront him, he'll destroy you." She continued holding his gaze through tear-filled eyes.

"He's planned for every possibility you can imagine, and I've seen every single one of them as clearly as I see you standing before me now. In every one I see your death, and there's *nothing* I can do to stop it! I can't even make these visions stop anymore." She clutched the sides of her head, claws piercing her temples slightly.

"It's like a never-ending movie, repeating the same scene in different ways, always ending in failure, always death, your death." Her eyes were screwed shut. "And always his laughter in the background."

She opened her eyes once again, and he did not remember ever seeing such pure fear.

"I've seen you die six times since we woke up in this cell, and it's so real that I don't know if I am even talking to my husband anymore or if you are just another hallucination." She broke down completely, collapsed into the corner, and began sobbing lightly. "I can't see you die, not again."

He wisely chose to not point out that he really hadn't been dead the first time.

"When it happens," she continued, and he noticed she didn't say *if*, "I'll break completely. I told you that's what he's waiting for, what he needs in order to take me. I'll be his queen."

It was hard to understand her through the sobs and with her hands covering her face, but he got the idea.

"It might already be too late." Her voice was barely above a whisper. "I can feel him twisting my thoughts underneath it all, and even as he increases the vividness of these horrors, I can hear his whispers as if he's standing right next to me." She reflexively glanced to the side. "And did I mention the laughter? Always the laughter and the whispers." She closed her eyes again as her mumbling lost what remained of its coherency.

"Dani?" John moved closer to his wife but wasn't sure if he should touch her or not.

182

Not since they had accepted their status as vampires had he seen his wife act in this fashion, and for the first time in over nine hundred years, he saw not a powerful supernatural being but the fragile teenager he had met during a jousting tournament all those centuries ago. The most frightening part was that he could see her getting progressively worse as the seconds ticked by.

"I can't take it anymore."

John watched as she slowly moved one of her hands from her temple to hold it in front of her face and opened her eyes once again.

"I have to get him out of my mind." The sobs lessened as the insanity began to fully take hold.

He felt dread start to build in his chest as she started morphing her claws longer, and he was honestly terrified.

"Dani," he tried again, "honey, you know what we have to do." He touched her shoulder lightly as he knelt down next to her and felt the muscles tense instantly before slowly starting to relax.

"I know," came the eventual response. "We have to kill Dracula."

She lifted her face, and John once again saw eyes that were hard with determination.

"I even know how to do it," she added, smiling weakly.

"Really?" A spark of hope began to glimmer in his mind. "How do we beat him?"

The only response his wife gave was to rest her unmorphed hand lightly on his cheek and shake her head.

"Haven't you been listening, silly?"

Warning bells started going off in John's head as he realized he didn't even know who was talking to him anymore.

"He's right here." She pointed a clawed finger at her own face and, with a sudden burst of speed, plunged it into her right eye.

"No!" John reacted the instant he sensed the movement, but he was a fraction of a second too slow. As he slapped her arm out of the way, he struck her temple as hard as he dared in an attempt to stop the madness.

"What are you doing?" she demanded, staring at him in anger even as gore continued to pour out of her ruined eye socket. "If we don't stop him, Dracula is going to kill John."

He couldn't believe what he was hearing and seeing as Danielle reached back to stab herself again. This time he quickly wrapped her in a bear hug, trying to both restrain her arms and impart some positive physical contact.

She struggled violently in his grasp for a few moments before finally settling down. Not wanting to risk releasing her too soon, John simply kept hugging her close while whispering sweetly in her ear. It wasn't long before her body began to shake again with sobs. Hoping it was a sign of improvement, he carefully began to loosen his grip so he could meet her gaze.

"I'm sorry," she mumbled as fresh tears streamed from her left eye.

"It's okay, sweetheart. Just focus on healing, and relax a few moments." He flinched as a spark of anger touched her remaining eye.

"Watch your mouth." She stuck her nose up in the air. "Just because we share a cell doesn't mean I'm that kind of girl. See?" She raised her left hand to display her wedding ring.

John was terrified, confused, and angry at the same time, his mind racing to figure out a way out of this. He was watching one of the most powerful minds in the world disintegrate before his very eyes, and he was powerless to stop it. Danielle's demeanor suddenly changed again, and she quickly crouched down and motioned for him to join her.

"Yes?" he asked, having no idea what to do besides play along.

"Ssshhhh!" she scolded, holding a finger to her lips. She shifted closer to him while darting glances around the cell. "I can do it."

It was barely a whisper, but the look on her face was one of supreme confidence.

"Do what?" It was the only thing he could think to say, but this time John played along with the whispering.

"Kill Dracula, you big old idiot." She stood back up in shock. "What else have we been talking about this . . . " Her voice had begun returning to a normal volume, and she suddenly seemed to notice, dropping back down to the ground. "Ssshhhh!"

John couldn't tell if she was scolding him or herself, but Danielle was busy darting glances in every direction again.

"Okay, so you can kill Dracula," John tried hard to whisper and pretend to be in on the secret.

It seemed to get her attention, and she started nodding happily.

"Do you know where he is?" John had no idea if he was helping or hurting the situation. He just hoped she wouldn't point to her own head again.

"Well, *obviously* we have to find him first." She rolled her remaining eye at him. "I wish John was here, at least he's not stupid." She seemed to hesitate briefly when she mentioned his name. She looked back up at him for a moment before shaking her head slightly and delving back into the fantasy. "Anyway, I can find him whenever I want."

"How?"

She looked around again and motioned him to come closer, before leaning in to whisper into his ear.

"It's a secret, but Dracky is sweet on me. I just have to head outside and whistle." She leaned back with a finger on her lips.

"Then what will you do?" John was hoping that the more he got her to talk, the easier it would be to bring her back to sanity. But so far it wasn't working.

"Kill him, I said that already." She seemed to be getting annoyed with his questions.

"I meant how? Maybe I can help you."

"Aw, you're just a big old sweetie pie, aren't you?" she said, giving him a wink. "Don't you worry yourself about me." She patted him on the head as if he were a child. "Dracky's just a big old phony." She stopped in thought for a moment. "In fact, I bet I could beat him with one eye closed." She immediately pointed to her empty eye socket. "Get it?" Her piercing maniacal laughter was one of the most unsettling things John had ever heard.

It was clear she was gone. He wasn't sure if Dracula was making her do these things or if it really was simple, random insanity from her mind finally breaking, but it didn't matter. The only choice was to simply knock her out and deal with the situation on his own. If he could take care of Dracula himself, the progenitor could probably fix Danielle's mind.

"I'm sorry," he whispered as he struck. Unfortunately, she wasn't there anymore.

"I can read minds, asshole, and what did I say about the physical stuff?"

The voice came from the ceiling, and he looked up to see her clinging upside down.

"Bye now." Her form started to shimmer and dissipate. "Oh, if you see John later, tell him my parents won't be home tonight." She winked and was gone, replaced by a simple cloud.

While John contemplated his confusion, he watched in amazement as the mist did not move but instead continued to dissipate thinner and thinner. Within moments, he could no longer see or even feel his wife's presence.

It had been the most confusing and heartbreaking fifteen minutes of his life, and John fought down the urge to panic. He closed his eyes and took a few deep breaths—unnecessary but calming nonetheless. He briefly considered reaching out to his wife mentally but quickly rejected the idea. Even if he was successful in making a connection, in his wife's current state her mind would probably destroy his.

He had no idea if she was really hunting Dracula right now or simply floating through the sky, waiting for him to randomly fight her. It was also possible she had lost complete control and was gone. She had never dissipated so thinly before, and it took a great deal of control to come back from that state.

No matter her current state or intentions, the best thing he could do was kill Dracula. It was his influence that had caused her insanity, so that influence had to be removed. Also, Dracula was obviously planning to kill him anyway. It was just difficult to form a sensible strategy while still coming to grips with what he had just witnessed. In some ways, it was pure shock that was keeping him lucid—well, shock and one other emotion.

As calmly as John had appeared to be handling Danielle's insanity, there was nothing calm about what was building inside and threatening to burst free. He wondered briefly if he was getting a taste of what she had experienced in their first encounter, when she had believed that Dracula had killed him. Although where she had been blinded by grief, he skipped straight to rage.

John could feel the pure and unfettered rage that had been slowly building up within himself. Since Danielle had left, there was no longer a reason to keep such things hidden. He allowed the delicious feeling to flow through his body while clearing his mind of all but a single thought.

Kill Dracula.

Not wanting to waste another second, he charged and struck the cell door with as much force as he could muster. Never intended to stand up to such power, the heavy door smashed into the opposite wall so hard it seemed as if metal had merged with stone. John was surprised to find no guards and was admittedly a bit disappointed. Once he saw the bits of gore dripping from where the door merged with the wall, however, he was more than satisfied.

Unfortunately, he had no idea where to go. This entire castle reeked of Dracula's presence, so pinpointing his exact location was nearly impossible for him. He also couldn't remain stationary for very long as his escape had most likely already been noticed. Wishing briefly that he could seek counsel from his wife, he chose a direction at random and began to search.

As melodramatic as Dracula was, John would gamble his fortune that this castle would have some kind of obvious throne room complete with some sort of gaudy throne. It was a safe bet his prey would be found there. John even knew that when Dracula realized he was coming, the bastard would do nothing but continue sitting patiently on his goddamn throne, waiting for him. So all he had to do was find the throne room, and simple interrogation should solve that problem.

"Excuse me." John had finally found a random minion shambling down the hallway. "Can you point me—"

He wasn't able to complete the question. The instant the minion—some sort of a mutated human-vampire-rat thing—became aware of his presence, it attacked. The attack was little more than suicide for the creature, but John was no closer to the information he required.

"So much for that idea," he muttered to himself.

Tossing the creature's head over his shoulder, he realized his plan would need to be adapted. Apparently, even the minions inside the castle were devoid of all emotions not planted into their minds by Dracula himself, which meant no fear or sense of self-preservation, which also meant no interrogation, unless . . .

John began roaming through the corridors and rooms at random, searching for something specific. The whole damned castle was a maze seemingly designed specifically to confuse people. To make things even worse, the corridors themselves seemed to change at random, giving the entire structure the appearance of being one giant living organism. Even as his frustration grew, John could not help but marvel at Dracula's control and power.

Time after time, John would be blurring down an empty hallway, only to run into a horde of minions that seemed to materialize out of nowhere. The minions themselves posed little threat, but it was a simple matter of attrition, and Dracula was aware of that fact. Every limb or head severed, every bolt of fire, and every minion he gutted was more of his blood wasted before the final battle, and he was miles away from any safe feeding grounds.

Fortunately, he was using very little blood to fuel his combat. A combination of vengeance, despair, and love served to give him all the power he needed to deal with Dracula's cannon fodder. Of course, having a powerfully enchanted sword helped as well.

Finally, after what seemed to be an eternity of searching, John stumbled across his prize—a trio of minions that were simply disfigured mortals and had the distinct look of simple servants. John had gambled that a megalomaniac like Dracula would have an army of servants to not only service his every need but to worship and idolize him. Emotionless worship would be false and empty, so the servants would most likely have intact emotions for him to exploit.

The servants noticed John's presence almost immediately and turned to flee, confirming his suspicions. They were moving quicker than normal mortals, but not fast enough. John was on them in an instant and immediately skewered the closest minion to the wall. Needing both hands free, he released his sword, leaving it embedded in ghoulish flesh and stone. Hands free, he speared each remaining servant through the shoulder with a single claw, successfully pinning them both to the same wall where their dying comrade was still tugging uselessly on John's sword in an attempt to free himself.

"Where is the throne room?" John wasted no time. "Tell me and live."

"You will never escape this place." Apparently, one of the servants had some balls after all. "Our master will devour your—"

The voice was cut off as John sliced his claw through its upper chest and then directly upward, neatly bisecting the unfortunately too brave creature's skull and brain. A vampire's claws were indeed such wonderful things.

The final servant was not being any more helpful, but John noticed he was frozen in fear rather than defiance. That was good. Fear could be used. Before John spoke, he concentrated on infusing as much power and awe into his voice as possible. It wasn't the same thing as mind control, but maybe his sheer presence would be enough to break through the minion's programming.

"Where. Is. The. Throne. Room," John spoke slowly and forcefully, stretching each word into its own separate statement.

The minion gibbered incoherently and pointed down the corridor. Not wanting to have anything more to do with these ever-changing hallways, John shook his head slightly.

"Fool, I'm not interested in memorizing directions. Point directly. I want a straight path."

Confusion briefly replaced the fear etched on the minion's features, but after only a brief hesitation, he pointed to the wall behind John. Satisfied he was being told the truth, John retracted his claw and motioned for the minion to flee. Before the creature could move more than a few steps, however, he retrieved his sword from the wall and, in one fluid motion, sliced it in half. The lower half collapsed in a heap with the now-dead body that had been pinned to the wall, while the torso lay at John's feet, eyes frozen in a look of betrayal.

"Too slow," John hissed as the life quickly drained from his freshest kill.

He expertly flicked his blade to remove the majority of the bloody gore before replacing it in its scabbard, and then he turned to face the previously indicated direction. Reaching out with his senses as Danielle had taught him, he focused his mind straight ahead of where he stood.

Barriers, both physical and metaphysical, fell away before his directed power until he could finally sense the unmistakable darkness that had to be Dracula's presence. The direction was a certainty, although he had no way of judging the distance. It couldn't be too far, he surmised, as the castle was not overly large. Misdirection had been the only thing preventing him from stumbling upon the throne room by accident already, but with a firm mental grip on his direction, John knew he would not be misdirected again. With a feral grin and a look of violent hunger in his eyes, he proceeded to create his own doorway in the stone.

Dracula needed no supernatural powers to sense John's approach. His strategy of simply breaking through the solid walls was sending tremors throughout the entire castle, and Dracula shook his head in disappointment. It had been inevitable that he would eventually find a way around the misdirection and traps that had been laid out for him, and Dracula had been monitoring his prey's progress to see what he would do.

At first, it had been surprising that his prey hadn't found a way out sooner, which was disappointing on its own. To make matters worse, the best he could come up with was a brute-force approach. How boring, although predictable. The male lacked the imagination and finesse of the female, not to mention the beauty and power. He sipped absently at his goblet as his mind wandered to the next obvious topic. The female.

She was a riddle he found most interesting, and she had succeeded in surprising him again. He had been monitoring their argument in the cell with a great deal of delight. It would seem that the strategy of attrition he had adopted was truly working this time. This much had been expected, sooner or later, but he had not expected her to completely lose her mind so thoroughly.

At first, Dracula thought it was simply another clever plot to combat his presence, especially after the first time they had fooled him. A mind in turmoil was far harder to inhabit, but he held on to watch the full descent and could confirm it was no ploy. It was possible it had started out as a trick, but if so, she had gone too far and had allowed her mind to be completely broken.

His inability to track her was annoying, but it didn't matter in the long run. Now that she was truly prey, it would be easy enough to hunt her down later. Or she might even come back and attack him herself at some point. Her final thoughts had been so disjointed it was difficult to make a prediction.

First things first, however. He needed to destroy the male once and for all before proceeding with any other plans. A simple-enough task, now that he was alone, but Dracula refused to allow overconfidence to blind him. Just because he knew the female had run away, it did not change what the male believed, and that false belief would undoubtedly make him a far stronger opponent than one riddled with despair. Dracula forced himself to admit how dangerous the coming battle could prove and remained patient. It was also a pity that the female wouldn't be there to witness his death, but Dracula would take no more risks delaying the inevitable.

The closer John came, the more difficult it was proving to simply sit back and wait. In many ways, his castle had become an extension of his own being. The male's wanton destruction was almost causing him physical pain, and he could feel the tremors in his very bones every time he broke through another wall. Still, patience and calm, he reminded himself, would give him the advantage.

It won't be long now, he thought to himself as he drained the last of his refreshment. He set the goblet down gently and focused his gaze on the section of the wall his would-be killer was bound to come through.

John paused briefly, resting his left palm on the stone of the next wall. It was easy enough to sense this was the final barrier separating him from his enemy. Smashing through walls and killing Dracula's minions had done wonders to restore his calm, and he would need to maintain that calm if he wanted any chance of victory.

He was under no illusions as to how difficult the coming battle was going to be. The fact that the progenitor himself had clearly stated they couldn't win as a pair, much less him challenging Dracula alone, was at the forefront of his mind. He didn't want to die, and that seemed to be the likely outcome, but he also had no desire to live as a hunted animal. It wasn't as if he didn't have a few surprises of his own to bring into the fight.

Dracula thought he was fighting an ancient vampire, and maybe he was, but that was all Dracula thought he was fighting. The reality was far more dangerous for him. John wasn't simply an ancient vampire but a husband fighting to defend his wife's very soul, for he understood Dracula's plans for her quite clearly. That monster also thought John had nothing to lose—which, of course, explained his headlong dash through the castle.

On the contrary, John had *everything* to lose, and that made him far more dangerous because he knew this would be their final confrontation, one way or another. He might not be able to win, but then again, he simply could not afford to lose. It took a few seconds for him to banish all distracting thoughts and prepare his mind. Once he was ready, he clenched his palm into a fist and easily removed the final barrier in a spray of stone chips and dust.

It was immediately apparent that his suspicions had been partially misplaced. The throne room, at least he assumed it was the throne room, was not overly large and oddly barren of any decoration. In fact, if not for the obvious—and just as gaudy as he expected—throne centered on the far wall, John would have thought he had taken a wrong turn somewhere. The jewel-encrusted throne, not to mention Dracula sitting on it, however, were dead giveaways. The barren floor and walls just didn't seem to fit his megalomania. Not that it mattered one way or another.

"Finally," Dracula spoke softly. "Dear boy, I was beginning to think you would never arrive."

His voice carried the same intoxication as always, but John was easily able to ignore it.

Dracula clicked his tongue a few times in a scolding manner. "Please excuse the lack of decor," he said, gesturing at the walls. "I had my servants clear some space for us."

At least that answered one of John's questions. John took two steps into the room but made no move to close the distance any further.

Dracula, for his part, did not even get out of his throne. He simply crossed his fingers on his chest and kept an almost-bored expression plastered on his face. Neither combatant wanted to make the first move, so they simply studied each other for a time.

"For what it's worth, boy, I am sorry," Dracula broke the silence. He waited for John to ask the obvious question and merely shrugged his

191

shoulders when it became clear that he wouldn't. "Accepting that two vampires were married was admittedly one the most difficult things for me about this entire experience. I cannot argue with truth however, it simply is what it is.

"That being said, I can only imagine how difficult it is for you to know your mate has abandoned you, not to mention reality, it would seem."

John still refused to take the bait.

"You may not believe me, boy, but I never wished to cause you that particular pain. I wanted to gift you with quick and painless destruction." Dracula was shaking his head, doing his best to appear apologetic. "Unfortunately, you both proved too difficult to handle cleanly, and I will have what I desire. I just wish that you didn't have to spend your final moments with the knowledge that you truly are alone." He leaned back, apparently finished with his speech.

Dracula's ploy was far too obvious to have any effect, but John couldn't help but wonder why he was even bothering to try. Was he simply trying to add insult to injury because he was an asshole, or was he unsure of the coming battle's outcome and vying for any advantage he could get? He quickly tossed the mental quandary aside, seeing as how it didn't really matter. He simply stood sword in hand, silently daring Dracula to attack him.

"You are uncharacteristically quiet, boy," Dracula's voice sounded as if he was beginning to lose patience. That was good. "I suppose I should repeat my offer, my way of apologizing for driving your wife away. Join me," he said, finally standing up. "Rule by my side as prince of this world and general of my legions." Dracula never raised his voice, and yet it rumbled from the very walls nonetheless.

John couldn't believe what he was hearing and couldn't decide whether to spit or laugh out loud. Still, Dracula's obvious delusion did not translate to weakness. It was time for him to offer a response, and with a thought, John's body appeared to burst into flames. He couldn't help but smile as Dracula took a surprised step backward at the flash.

"What nonsense is this?" Dracula asked in surprise.

John offered no response other than continuing to stand and burn.

"Your parlor tricks will not serve you here." There was a note of disgust in Dracula's voice. "I admit, your wife's proficiency with mortal magic took me off guard in the beginning, but I've adapted. Not to mention your comparative lack of skill and that this is my home. You insult me, boy." Dracula was only half right and had no way of realizing what he was truly seeing.

John had given a lot of thought to what the progenitor had told Danielle and him about the differences in their powers. He decided to accept the progenitor's explanation for why Danielle had always been better with magic than he was. It was simply because they had always tried to use it the same way and knowing now that their powers had very different focuses, it was no wonder his skill had always seemed inferior.

If John's power and abilities were truly focused within because hand-to-hand fighting had always been more natural to him, then he needed to start using magic the same way. No longer would he attempt to throw fireballs at his enemies, spray flames from his fingertips, or call forth lightning. No, he would allow his fire to burn from within, and even now, he could feel his power increasing.

The unnatural flames danced about his tattered clothing and damaged skin without leaving a mark. He began to concentrate harder, and it felt as if the fire itself was burning throughout his insides, but there was no pain. In fact, he could feel the flames mingling with his blood, strengthening it, even as he used that same blood to power the flames. He built an unbroken circle of power within himself—blood fueling fire, fire fueling blood—and he began to experience a clarity of thought and calm that was as surprising as it was welcome.

Dracula continued to sneer, clearly unimpressed. His expression changed slightly when he saw John's wounds closing up and healing under the flames. Eventually, the flames themselves died down, their intensity fading, but John was still covered by a faint fiery glow.

"I see you've learned a new trick or two yourself, boy," Dracula scoffed, smiling.

He most likely saw the flames dying down as a sign of John's weakening state, when in fact the opposite was true. He simply got them under better control, and it was admittedly difficult to see the enemy when one's head was blazing with fire.

In fact, John was finding it difficult to not simply let loose his newfound power. The progenitor had told him he had the potential to be Juggernaut, the unstoppable wave of destruction, and he hadn't quite understood at the time. As he felt wave after wave of power course through and over his body, he finally came to understand. He *was* Juggernaut. He pointed his sword at Dracula's head in obvious challenge.

"Very well, boy," Dracula shrugged and stepped down from his throne. Shadows began to quickly form around him as he finally called upon his own power.

Suddenly John was surrounded by an incredible physical pressure, and the reminder of Dracula's sheer power was sobering. He also noticed the two dark blades that had suddenly appeared in his hands, apparently pulled from the very darkness itself. He had a feeling it would be a good idea to avoid those edges.

"Courtesy demands I give you the opportunity for last words, boy." His devilish smile was back. He seemed determined to get John to say something, anything, before he would commit to battle. Very well.

"I name you, Vlad Drakulya Tepes, Voivode of Wallachia." Dracula's eyes widened imperceptibly at the sound of his full name, and John bared his fangs. "Now," he spoke clearly, and allowed his voice to resonate in the empty room, *"BURN WITH ME!"*

His final statement was more of a battle cry, and he launched into motion before Dracula could react.

Dracula moved to defend himself from the head-on charge he expected, but John was done being predictable. He *had* launched himself in Dracula's direction with blinding speed, but his target was the ceiling above Dracula's head. The instant his feet came into contact with the ceiling, John pushed down, aiming for the top of his opponent's skull.

The entire maneuver took less than a second, and Dracula only avoided his blade by diving out of the way in a random direction. John instead collided with the empty throne, destroying it completely. There was no anger at missing his target, and there was no time wasted before launching his next attack, and his third, and his fourth.

John was trying to use pure speed to mimic what Dracula had done to them earlier, when he split himself into many images. At the time, Dracula seemed to be everywhere, and neither of them could tell which image was an illusion and which was real. The difference was that John was not using any illusion.

His pure speed was allowing him to seem to be almost everywhere at once, and everywhere he was, there was a very real enchanted blade and set of claws slashing at his opponent. It was clear that Dracula was unable to track his attacks properly and that instinct alone was allowing him to defend himself . . . barely. He was kept off balance, and John felt his blade strike home more than once. Better yet was the fresh blood decorating his claws.

For what seemed like hours, both combatants flashed back and forth across the chamber, launching lightning-quick attacks and counterattacks at one another. There was no pretense of any defense from either vampire, just pure aggression. Mortal eyes would have seen nothing but streaks of flame and swirling darkness. Even demonic eyes would have had difficulty tracking the powerful beings amid that conflagration.

Dracula was far more powerful, but he had never fought a battle like this before. John wasn't simply a vampire; he was a trained killer. None of his anger or rage had any effect on the calculations of his attacks. Every maneuver or combination of maneuvers was executed with a precision only attainable by nearly a thousand years of relentless training. Dracula was fighting a living weapon, and his superior power meant almost nothing.

John was successful in keeping him off balance, as he scored blow after blow, but it was not completely one-sided. He could feel the burn of more than one wound inflicted by Dracula's dark blades. He shut out the pain and continued his unstoppable offensive. Neither of them could maintain this level of combat indefinitely, and he knew the first to falter would be destroyed.

Dracula was slowly beginning to cope with the level of intensity of John's attacks, but there was a clear pattern to his deflections and counterattacks. It was nearly impossible to see, yet somehow John simply *knew* which way Dracula was going to dodge, and his next attack was a feint. Dracula managed to once again deftly avoid the incoming sword strike, and he turned directly into the claws that opened his abdomen. Dropping one of his swords, he reflexively covered the near-mortal wound with his free hand and quickly sought to create distance between himself and his insane attacker.

John knew not to waste any time reveling in his small victory and did everything he could to maintain the pressure on his opponent. The wound he inflicted was not fatal, but Dracula seemed intent to remain on the defensive until he could force it to heal. It seemed an error in judgment to John, but it was possible he had cut even deeper into Dracula's guts than he had realized. If that were true, given the speeds they were moving, Dracula could potentially rip his own body apart if he did not heal first.

Knowing that there would never be a better chance to finish the battle, John redoubled his efforts. Focusing all his remaining power and awareness, he was able to increase his speed even further while better predicting Dracula's defense. Strike after strike opened new wounds across the monster's face and upper body, none of which were healing on their own.

John knew that he was gaining the upper hand but also that the situation could change at any moment. Seeing the opportunity to deliver a death blow, he used his claws to deflect Dracula's failing attacks as he readied his sword. So focused on his final triumph, John barely felt the impact as Dracula's once-discarded sword ran him through from behind.

He looked down and saw nearly a foot of darkness protruding from his chest. A part of his mind noted that clearly Dracula did not have to be physically holding his swords in order to use them. How much of the last few moments had been a true struggle on his part and how much had been a feint to get John into the proper position, he would never know. The overall lack of pain was a little disconcerting as well, considering John had a sword through his chest. Well, that and the paralysis. Yes, the paralysis was definitely a problem.

John had no idea what was happening to him or how to fight it. No matter how much he struggled or how much power he tried to apply, nothing was happening. His thoughts were still clear, but he felt them slowly beginning to feel sluggish. Whatever the sword was doing to him, it was spreading. Dracula, for his part, had simply gotten up and walked a safe distance away before turning back to face his would-be killer.

"I must admit, boy, that was fairly impressive. Whatever you may think, my final attack was closer to a lucky break than any preplanning on my part. My victory was never in question, but you did make me work for it." Dracula healed his many injuries as he was speaking, seemingly ignoring the pure fury in John's eyes.

"There is no point in struggling, it's over. What you are experiencing right now is the feeling of my power flowing through your body. That sword through your chest is giving me indirect control, and in this instance, the greater the power of my opponent, the faster they can be bent to my will."

John couldn't speak, but it was hard to dispute what Dracula had just said.

He did not feel as though someone else was controlling him, at least not yet, but he certainly had no control himself. There was no pain; it was more of a numbness spreading throughout his body and forcing his muscles to relax. Once a muscle relaxed, he was unable to tense it again, thus his lack of control.

First, his sword fell, clattering on the stone floor. The sound seemed to echo loudly in the now-silent chamber. It wasn't long before he fell to his knees, arms dangling uselessly at his sides.

"Your defiance is admirable, but it's wasted effort," Dracula commented, noticing the look in his opponent's eyes. "Your end comes quickly, boy, but I still offer you a choice."

Dracula approached to nearly arm's reach, holding out his remaining sword for the final strike.

"You possess powers and abilities that I desire, but it's possible I do not have the ability to use them. I am confident that I can get what I need from my future queen. However, it seems sensible to have a spare. Accept me as your master, and I shall allow you to retain at least a shadow of your former self. Refuse me, and I will simply take your head now. What say you, boy?"

As if to emphasize his point, Dracula raised his sword arm to strike.

John could tell that Dracula was serious about wanting him to join his ranks, not that it made much of a difference. Even now it was difficult to accept his helplessness. The battle had been going well, and it was rather disappointing to have simply fallen victim to this type of corruption so suddenly. Unfortunately, it was clear to him by now that this was no trick or illusion; it was over. He really didn't want to die, so better to get it over with before his anger turned to despair.

"I see." Dracula nodded slowly. "I don't need to hear your voice to know your answer. Very well, I grow tired of these games. Let your final thoughts be of the corruption you refused that I intend to force upon your wife." He grinned as John's gaze hardened.

"You were trying not to think of that, weren't you?" Dracula couldn't help but revel in his torture for a few more moments. "Raping her mind was one thing, and quite pleasurable at that, but that is nothing compared to what I have planned for her body. The violations and experiments I have planned for her flesh are beyond what you can imagine." He allowed himself to lick his lips as John's facial muscles bulged in rage.

"In a few years, you won't even recognize the creature she will become." He cocked his head to the side. "Assuming you were going to live that long." Finally finished with his verbal torment, Dracula brought down his dark sword to take John's head.

He didn't understand why Dracula stopped in mid-swing, mere inches from decapitating him. Unless he had thought of more taunts? A combination of his rage and the corruption taking hold of his mind was preventing John from sensing anything properly. His vision was also starting to cloud, so it took him a few seconds to recognize the look of shock in Dracula's eyes and the three bloody claws protruding from his throat.

"Seriously, there's been a lot of open talk about raping me lately. Do I really dress that provocatively?"

Not waiting for an answer, Danielle twist her wrist and spun around, allowing Dracula's head to sail quite a distance from his body. Upon completing her spin, she used the sword in her other hand to separate his legs from his torso. Not finished, she moved over to where Dracula's head had settled and retrieved it. She spent a moment gazing into the shocked eyes with obvious pleasure, before winking and hurling it with all her might at the opposite wall. The severed head effectively exploded under the force of the impact.

John was forced to simply watch, frozen, as his wife literally took apart the most dangerous opponent they had ever faced in seconds, a mere instant before his own death. Since he couldn't turn his head, he had missed some of the action, but there hadn't been anything wrong with his hearing. Danielle returned to his field of vision, her grisly task complete, and started looking him over. John has never seen such a beautiful sight.

Honey, are you in there? Hearing his wife's voice in his head, and so lucid, brought him to bloody tears.

Yes. His thoughts were still sluggish and difficult to form. *What happened to you?*

Dozens of additional questions threatened to overwhelm his mind, but he fought to stay calm.

"Thank God," she nodded happily and smiled. "I'm so sorry for leaving you like this, darling, but I only had the one chance to finish him off. It seemed safer to attack on my own instead of freeing you, since I honestly had no idea what he had done to you anyway."

Danielle seemed clearly upset for having left John in such a vulnerable position while she had dispatched Dracula. Of course, the dispatching was complete, and John couldn't help but notice there was still a sword sticking out of his chest.

I understand. Now can you please pull this sword out of my chest?

"I would feel better if I understood what it was doing to you first. I know Dracula was going on and on about it, but in my state, I couldn't understand most of it. I don't want to accidentally make the injury worse."

John couldn't tell if she was messing with him or seriously concerned, but it seemed a simple problem to him.

Sword in chest, bad. *Sword not in chest,* good.

"Okay, okay, fine, you big baby," she said, winking at him.

Reaching around, she gently touched the pommel. Feeling no pain or other ill effects, Danielle made sure to get a solid grip.

"Okay, you may feel a slight pinch or, you know, die," she mumbled the last portion as she deftly removed the blade and tossed it aside, using her free arm to support John's body as he slumped forward.

"Ow," John mumbled. "Damn, is it good to see you, love."

"I think it's good to see me too," she agreed playfully. "How do you feel? What was that sword doing to you?"

John considered the best way to explain.

"Some kind of simple corruption to freeze me until Dracula could exert control. Maybe a physical version of the mind control he kept trying to use on you? It started getting a little better after you killed him, but it went away almost completely once you yanked the sword out. I still feel a little weird, but that's it."

John thought about his portion of the final battle.

"Honestly, I didn't really get hurt that badly at all. Until he got me with that stupid sword from behind, I was winning," he said, puffing his chest out a bit.

"Sure you were, honey," she replied, patting his cheek.

"But I wwwaaasss, honest!"

"Uh-huh."

Banter aside, Danielle shifted positions the instant she confirmed her husband was okay. Currently she was curled into a ball, eyes half open, lying on her husband's lap. It was one of their favorite resting positions, and John reflexively started stroking her hair.

"Well, in any event, we obviously won, but can you please explain to me what happened back in the cell?"

"What do you mean?" she asked as if she could avoid the question so easily.

"You know what I mean. The only thing I have understood since waking up in that cell was the few minutes I spent fighting Dracula—well, up until he got me and you saved me anyway."

Danielle stayed curled up comfortably, but her eyes were fully open now.

"I mean, you seem okay now, and you definitely kicked his ass, but I'm going to have nightmares about whatever was happening to you in that cell for quite a while. Are you sure you're okay?"

"Not completely," she admitted. "But I will be."

"Was that all some sort of twisted plan?"

"Yes, but not in the way you are thinking." She took a deep unneeded breath. "I had to get Dracula to dismiss me as a threat so I could try and get the drop on him at a crucial moment, but that's not easy when the person is literally reading your thoughts as you are having them."

John shift positions so they could both get more comfortable and so he would have a better look at her eyes while she spoke.

"My idea came to me while we were arguing, and I had to enact it immediately. The heightened emotions of an argument make individual thoughts a bit harder to read, and this thought was sudden, so there was a good chance he wouldn't notice. I simply decided to give up."

"Wait, what?" John was sure he misunderstood what she meant.

"I simply gave up mentally, exactly what he was hoping for, but with a twist. You remember for a moment or two I seemed to focus a lot on your death?"

John nodded in unpleasant memory.

"Well, that was by design. Of all the things going through my mind, thanks to him, your death was obviously the most terrible. Talking about it out loud made it so much worse." She started trembling a bit.

John went back to stroking her hair, and she snuggled in closer.

"Anyway, giving up wouldn't help if he could use the opportunity to take me over. I had to go insane. I was banking on his inability to control my mind if I went batshit crazy. So I got myself purposefully worked up with the worst and most terrible things I could think of, let it all start coming to the surface and wash over me, and then just gave up fighting. Insanity settled in quickly after that, considering how bad things really were."

John had difficulty understanding what she was trying to say.

"So that was all real?"

She nodded, and he couldn't help but just stare at her.

"Dani, watching you delve into that madness was the most terrifying thing I have ever witnessed. I had to stop you from carving out your own brain, and I almost didn't make it. You let that happen?"

"You think I wanted to? It was horrifying for me as well." She shed a few tears. "And you won't be the only one having nightmares about it, but it was the only way."

"Okay, honey, okay, but I still don't understand how it was supposed to work. At the end, you seemed to be pretty happy with your crazy-ass self and then just left." He shrugged his shoulders. "How does that make you sane enough to come back and kill Dracula?"

"That was the risky part and the reason I gave up my control instead of fighting it. The whole plan was based on Dracula not being able to detect or influence me if I dissipated thin enough in mist-form, but I had to get to that form without him understanding why beforehand to keep him from getting overly suspicious."

"Okay, but we have no evidence that he can't detect you in that form." It was a valid point.

"True, but it was a worthwhile risk. First of all, you couldn't detect me, and you were looking right at me, and secondly, Dracula doesn't even know we can turn to mist at all." She arched an eyebrow, and he conceded the point.

"Thirdly, it was nowhere close to the risk I took in assuming I would be able to regain my sanity at all. I was losing the mental battle overall anyway, by giving up instead of continuing to fight, I managed to save considerable strength. Once his influence vanished while I was in mist-form, my insanity ebbed enough for me to start fighting back. It wasn't easy, but detecting your fighting helped the most."

"I'm curious how that helped you."

"Simple. What could possibly break either of us out of any insanity more easily than our love and desire to save the other? I realized that toward the end, I didn't even recognize you visually, but did you notice I still mentioned you?"

John had honestly not thought about it at the time but said, "Yeah, it was a little strange and disconcerting, but you mentioned me a lot."

"Well, another one of my assumptions was that after I went crazy and bailed, you would lose your shit and go ballistic. Detecting you based on your power and presence is easy and, even insane, I knew it was you. It was hard, but I did successfully regain my control enough to come up with a plan. Since I was in mist-form when I made my attack plan, Dracula couldn't know about it, and I am guessing he wasn't even trying to detect me after he confirmed I bailed on you.

"So everything worked, and I still barely made it in time. Dissipating that far was hard to come back from, and I had to wait until the last minute in case he noticed me. Honestly, if that megalomaniac hadn't wasted time at the last second taunting you about violating me and whatnot, you'd be dead. I tried my best, but it just took too long to solidify. I needed those extra few seconds."

"Well, score one point for provocative clothing, I guess," John joked, remembering her earlier statement as she was killing Dracula.

"Anyway, it sounds like we at least passed the test," he said and shrugged as she looked up at him a little confused.

"The progenitor wanted to see an example of how love strengthens us and to prove it would be enough to defeat Dracula."

She nodded, understanding where he was going now.

"It sounds like that is quite literally what saved us, so, hooray!" He pumped his fist in mock celebration.

"Good point, but let's not worry about any of that for a bit. I'm just happy to still be alive." She stretched a bit and started getting up.

"Going somewhere?" John inquired, making no move to follow suit.

She regarded him incredulously and started tapping her foot. "How long do you want to simply lie around this empty room? Besides, this castle is creeping me out, let's go home."

It was the best idea John had heard in a while, and he jumped up immediately. He moved a little slowly at first but quickly confirmed there were no lasting effects of having been temporarily corrupted.

"We should be a bit careful though. This whole area could still be crawling with Dracula's minions." He thought for a moment. "I am fairly certain they should all die with him gone, but it might not be immediate."

It seemed a reasonable-enough precaution, and she nodded in agreement. They both turned toward the giant hole John had made in the wall earlier when Danielle suddenly froze.

"Speaking of which." She pointed to where the remaining parts of Dracula's body were lying on the floor. "It's bothering me a bit that those bits are still there and not ash."

Given how they had both been reminded recently that no ash meant no death, it was hard to argue her point, and John forced himself to consider it carefully.

"Well, I understand what you are saying, but remember, he isn't the same as us. None of his minions have turned to ash that we have seen so far, and unfortunately, we weren't able to sever any of his limbs in any of the previous battles."

It did bother him a little, he had to admit, but he did not consider it a matter of concern.

"Also, keep in mind that the messy stain covering the other wall is all that's left of his head."

Danielle was slowly nodding, but she still seemed deep in thought.

"What about your senses?" Surely there should be some mental hint, one way or the other. "I don't detect anything threatening like I did before, but you are more sensitive to that than I am . . . ," John trailed off, waiting for her opinion.

"I definitely don't feel threatened." She was slowly pacing around the room, keeping a careful eye on the remains. "But I also don't feel that he's vanished, at least not completely. It's nothing specific, just a strange feeling, but look around you and think." She gestured to indicate the countryside beyond the castle. "This whole area has felt only half real since we got here, and this castle is even worse. You had to have noticed that while you were searching for the throne room."

"Well, definitely," he agreed, "but I don't understand your point."

"Me either, at least not entirely, but if Dracula's power were somehow responsible for creating this place and area, or at least altering it, then shouldn't it all be falling apart with his death?"

John couldn't fault his wife's theory, but the evidence he could see was pointing to a dead opponent, and that was all he cared about.

"It could be taking longer to fade, or the changes to the area could be permanent and not something Dracula would have to maintain." John walked over and nudged the dismembered torso with his toe. "There is honestly just too much we don't understand about his power to be sure about anything."

"You might be right." Danielle still seemed unconvinced. "My judgment might also not be the best until I can finish getting my mind back in order." Her eyes still carried a shadow of her earlier torment.

"Look, I want to get the hell out of here and go home, but if it will make you feel better, we can burn the remains first." She turned to face him, and John held his palms up in a gesture of half agreement and half dismissal.

"Personally, I think we're okay, but I have to admit, there's a chance I'm wrong. Dracula was incredibly powerful, and we already agreed that we don't understand how some of his powers even worked." He continued to look down at the remains while he talked.

Danielle was listening, but something was suddenly bothering her. There had been a lot to distract her immediately after the battle, but now that she was focusing on the problem, it was as if the answer was so obvious and close, and yet just out of reach.

"His head is gone, but his heart is intact. Maybe it is possible that if left alone, these remains could properly regenerate? Burning them should be a simple enough precaution, right?" He looked up at Danielle, but she didn't seem to be listening. "Screw it," John said, drawing his sword in a flash.

Why burn when simply stabbing would be so much easier and faster? He still thought they were worried over nothing, but there was no point in arguing. No matter what kind of vampire Dracula was, he should still need his head and heart intact to survive. Even if he was wrong, and Dracula could survive with only one of the two, it wasn't possible for him to survive without either. Besides, if it put his wife's mind at ease, then it would be more than worth the effort.

"John, *stop!*" Danielle looked up and leaped at her husband, but he had already struck, and there was no way to reach him in time.

There was an explosion of black ichor the instant the tip of John's sword pierced Dracula's heart, the force of which knocked both of them off their feet. The vampires quickly recovered, moving back into defensive positions while trying to determine what was happening.

What had been Dracula's chest cavity had blown open, and an ink-black substance was pouring freely out of it. Perhaps more confusing, or disturbing, was that the substance was currently gathering on the ceiling. John looked to his wife for an explanation, only to meet the same confusion in her gaze. The ichor gave off a similar feeling to the darkness Dracula had used to fuel his powers, but neither of them could guess what was happening.

"I don't understand. So he's not dead?" John asked as he used a claw to try and flick a speck of the ichor off his body that was currently burning a hole through his arm. "Well, that can't be good," he mumbled to no one in particular.

"I'm not sure." She had felt the danger before John struck and did not understand it. "I am starting to sense a threat, but it's disjointed and confusing." She narrowed her eyes. "In a way, it feels like Dracula could be regenerating, but I don't think that's what this is."

"Well, by all means, dearest, take your time figuring it out," John snapped, all the while not taking his eyes off the possible threat.

The ichor itself had stopped exiting Dracula's remains and seemed to form a cloud filling a fair amount of the room. John couldn't tell if the cloud was hovering or actually sticking to the ceiling, and the darkness was so deep it was hard to judge the solidity of the mass, although it was clearly moving.

"No one is stopping you from having any bright ideas," she shot back as they retreated a few steps.

She had never sensed anything like this before, but it was clearly a threat. The problem was that she couldn't determine what type of threat it was and, thus, how to fight it. It was similar to how Dracula felt and yet

204

very different. She was having trouble even verifying if this *thing* they were looking at was even real.

John began approaching cautiously, as if in response to his wife's comment, holding his sword at the ready. The cloud seemed unaware, or uncaring, of his approach, and he could hear a warning groan from his wife. Ignoring her, he attempted a few swings, which were easily avoided. The darkness was so deep and complete that John was uncertain whether the cloud dodged or he simply missed.

Shrugging his shoulders, he decided to try once more and simply stabbed his sword straight up. This time he was certain the blade made contact with the cloud, although there was no clear response. At least until the cloud counterattacked and sent him crashing back into the opposite wall.

"Dammit, John! Stop trying to stab shit for a second and just let me think."

She felt so close to understanding what was happening, but her husband's antics were too distracting. Obviously, he was simply trying to defend her, and this thing was clearly an enemy of some kind, but brute force wasn't always the answer.

"Christ," John groaned as he got back to his feet. "That thing is way tougher than it looks, hard and a bit slimy at the same time, and it hit me harder than anything Dracula landed," he said, grimacing and pointing to his chest.

Danielle noticed his chest was actually smoldering slightly where the ichor had come into direct contact with him.

"Let's see how it likes fire."

John was clearly getting pissed, and she simply didn't have time to argue with him. He spent the next few moments trying unsuccessfully to burn the cloud and earned another few lumps for his efforts.

She did her best to ignore him and focus her abilities on the overall situation. Her husband was not in any true danger yet, and at least his attacks were keeping whatever that thing was distracted. In fact, she realized now that was his whole plan from the beginning—to get the enemy to focus on him while she solved the problem. She felt sorry for scolding him earlier, but there would be time for apologies later. Every fiber of Danielle's being screamed at her that they were in immense danger, but she just couldn't figure it out.

To her, this felt similar to the first fight they had experienced with one of Dracula's minions, although there was far less illusion associated with this darkness. Looking around the room, she noticed Dracula's remains were gone, replaced with piles of ash.

Interesting that should happen now.

Also, what was with the darkness theme? At first, they had both assumed it was more of a gimmick than anything else. It definitely fit the character Dracula seemed to be going for, and it was rather effective.

Danielle was starting to feel it had been more than that, however, and that they had both been missing an important clue this entire time. The progenitor had mentioned that all of Dracula's powers had come to him immediately after being turned, which had shocked them both at the time. But in all their battles with him, how many powers had he truly displayed? He had demonstrated all the typical vampiric abilities to deadly effect, but beyond those, it was all focused around that stupid darkness.

John and Danielle had both learned and mastered many abilities over the centuries, yet Dracula had never learned anything new. Yet he could do so many terrifying things with that darkness of his, and even his stronger minions were able to call upon darkness to a limited extent. It was true that she could call upon fire and do all sorts of wonderful things with it, but fire was an element. Darkness was just, well, darkness. Even his stupid swords seemed to be made of darkness, which just seemed silly.

The one-sided battle her husband was waging was beginning to grow in intensity. She was so close.

Her fire looked and acted like fire; she simply controlled it. Dracula's darkness looked like darkness, and he clearly controlled it; but it didn't act like darkness, and it certainly didn't feel like darkness. As vampires, darkness was their closest friend, so why did this darkness act and feel this way? And why did Dracula have complete control over it from the instant he was turned? And what was that slight tugging at the back of her consciousness that she had just noticed? Her eyes flew wide open in instant clarity, and she could swear there was even faint laughter coming from the deepest recesses of her mind.

No! No! No!

She fell to her knees and didn't even notice dropping her sword, because with instant clarity came instant understanding . . . and total despair.

It's not fair.

She could hear her husband still fighting, knowing now that it was useless but having no way to explain it. What words could one possibly use to explain that everything they had done up to this moment had been a waste of time? The progenitor had made a mistake—a single error in his recount of Dracula's origins. There was quite literally no power anywhere on earth that could save them now.

Dracula hadn't simply made a deal for power; he had been a host. He had been nothing but a simple puppet for something that couldn't possibly be real, something dark and eternal. She could feel it now, and it would be easier to turn off the sun. It was over.

"Dani!" John had seen his wife fall and rushed to her aide.

Confusion was etched on his features as he couldn't find any injuries, but it changed to concern when he saw her eyes and the almost-frozen expression on her face.

"What's wrong?" He grabbed her shoulders and shook her slightly. "Talk to me!"

What was her husband babbling about? She turned her head slightly to better look into his eyes, noticing the love and concern. Oh yeah, he hadn't figured it out yet. He probably didn't even notice or care that the darkness had stopped fighting. Why should it bother fighting anyway? Its victory was assured.

John had such a simple way of looking at things, including threats, and it prevented him from truly understanding what was going on. He simply saw his wife and himself in danger and would keep fighting until the danger passed. Her despair was ebbing enough that she was able to hear her husband's words a bit more clearly as he continued to try and shake some sense into her.

God, I love him so much.

Unfortunately, it was clear John couldn't even hear her thoughts anymore. There must have been still too much damage in her mind, coupled with her current realization, to maintain their normal link. So she had lost the only simple means to explain the truth, and her husband was still shouting words of encouragement and love in between attack plans. It no longer mattered in the slightest and was yet the most important thing she had ever heard. With her newfound clarity came an even greater speed of thought as all the remaining pieces fell together in her mind, and bloody tears began staining her cheeks.

This time there was no insanity or mind control; in fact, she wished there had been. Anything would be better than the simple truth that could no longer be denied. John was still trying to talk to her, and as she looked into his eyes, her sadness deepened. After all they had been through, it really wasn't fair for it to have to end this way.

Neither of them had asked for this life, all those centuries ago. All she had wanted was to marry this man, have his children, and grow old together. One day, if she was lucky enough, she would die surrounded by the family they would have created together. Instead, they had been turned into monsters, and that dream had been stolen from them by a thief in the night.

Even so, they had simply made a new dream. It wasn't the original life they wanted, but it was wonderful life nonetheless. As long as they stayed together, she knew she would be happy. Neither of them ever used their powers for greed or true personal gain. They weren't even particularly violent unless threatened. All they had ever wanted, since becoming vampires, was to simply be left alone to at least try to enjoy eternity.

Yet the violence never ceased. There had always been *something* trying to destroy them. No matter what they did or how hard they tried to hide from the rest of the world, the world seemed intent on their destruction. Yet here they were, risking themselves to save that same world from an evil that most would never believe even existed. An evil that could never even be defeated. Here they were, about to die for no reason.

It wasn't fair, yet It was the reality of the situation. With that realization came acceptance, and with acceptance came calm. It was the look in John's eyes that had done it for her. It was true she didn't want to die and that she would do anything to cling to the life they had, but his loss would be worse. If she could save the man she loved, then her life was a fair price to pay.

Perhaps killing its host had weakened it. Even so, fighting and winning was impossible, but maybe she could trap it. Would that even work? Would any of her true self even survive to make it work? Would she remember? Would she just become a monster even worse than Dracula had been?

John watched as his wife's eyes changed and she slowly stood. The tears were gone, and he sensed nothing but pure resolve. He was unsure what had transpired in the last few seconds, but he knew something strange was going on. It was clear by now that the darkness was not attacking them but simply watching and waiting, and John was hoping that his wife's clear recovery was a sign that she had finally determined how to fight that thing. He had no idea how truly wrong he was.

"John," she began softly, "promise me something." She took a few steps to the center of the room, sword in hand.

"I don't know if I like the sound of that." He took his proper place at her side and half a step in front, just as she knew he would. "Any idea how to fight a cloud?"

"John," she began again, "I love you, but you need to promise me something."

Whether it was the conviction in her voice or the simple tone, John glanced over and cocked an eyebrow at her.

"Anything you want, my love, you know that, but we really need to figure out what to do about that thing."

"No matter what happens . . . ," she said, taking a moment to memorize every detail of her husband as if she had never seen him before. If these were to be her final seconds, she would take whatever memories she could to the other side. "Don't let me turn into Dracula."

"What are you—"

John's confusion was obvious, but Danielle was too fast and had been prepared from the moment she stood back up. She grabbed her husband's arm and hurled him across the room.

John had always thought of himself as being a supportive husband, but his wife's habit of turning her sanity on and off was really starting to piss him off. If this was marriage, then the single life was starting to look pretty good right now. What was with that weird promise? And he was getting tired of being slammed into walls.

These were the thoughts in his mind as he jumped back up and prepared for the battle he was sure was finally about to begin. His senses were telling him that thing was definitely alive and watching them, and it was time to fight. Maybe Danielle just wanted him over here to make it more difficult for the thing to track both their attacks? It made sense, at least until he actually looked at her.

Danielle hadn't moved in the slightest since the moment she had thrown him aside. He was prepared to adjust his attacks to complement hers, but the look in her eyes had him frozen. The sheer determination and confidence he saw were on a level that he certainly didn't feel himself, if he was being honest. What happened next did not happen quickly, not by vampiric standards, but he was too frozen in shock to do anything about it.

John watched as Danielle tossed her sword to the side and morphed one of her fingers into a claw. Her features were as hard with determination as the look in her eyes, and her movements were slow and methodical as she cut away what was left of her shirt. Naked from the waist up, she faced the cloud, looking directly into the darkness.

There was a sense of the darkness itself looking back, and not in the same way it had been observing them before. In fact, Danielle's actions seemed to give even the darkness pause, and John could feel he was being completely ignored by both parties. At first, he thought the situation was being staged for this exact moment so he could launch a surprise attack. The horror that suddenly unfolded proved how wrong he was.

Danielle insert a claw into her own chest and began to slice down, taking care not to damage her heart. John watched on in shock as his wife pulled her chest cavity open, never taking her eyes off the cloud. All three parties were frozen in the moment, seemingly unsure of how to proceed. The cloud even appeared to stop moving. John's mind was spinning faster than ever before, desperately searching for something—*anything*—that could explain or solve the situation.

"*WHAT ARE YOU WAITING FOR!*" Danielle's demand split the silence with more command authority than anything he had ever heard, and the darkness's response was immediate.

He watched, powerless, as the cloud poured into his wife's body, sealing the wound behind it. It was over before the echo of her voice had even faded. John snapped out of his immobility and charged to his wife's aid, even as realization finally began to dawn on him.

The distance wasn't far, not more than ten meters or so. Barely a second for a vampire of his power, but time was no longer working properly. There was no way he could make it, but he had to. The pieces were snapping together, and he finally knew the despair his wife had felt and why she was doing what she was doing. He understood it all, and he had to get to her. It was the only way, but it wasn't possible.

John's reality was breaking as his senses were overloaded with despair. It had to have been a full minute since he started running, yet he had barely taken a single step. He could no longer properly perceive what was happening around him, except his wife. He knew he could make it—he had to make it.

Danielle turned her head to face him, with one of the softest, most peaceful expressions he had ever seen. Her eyes were so full of love they drew tears from his own. How could she seem to move normally when he felt his own body running yet not getting anywhere? Whether a gift from the universe or a product of his own screwed-up perceptions, he didn't know, but it was a singular moment of the purest love and happiness he had ever felt. Their last.

"Goodbye, my love."

As he saw her lips moving and heard the words, John felt as if his heart was being ripped from his chest. They had been such fools, although it wasn't really their fault. They had fought and been victorious over and over, regardless of the odds. What was one more impossible battle? One more dramatic victory to add to their nine-hundred-year-old scorecard?

Both vampires believed they understood the situation for what it truly was, yet neither could comprehend the full truth. Danielle—so quick to nobly sacrifice herself, not understanding it was the worst thing she could have done. John—so quick to rush in to assist a wife who no longer existed.

Had they understood what was happening, both vampires would have gladly ripped out their own hearts to avoid what was coming.

Unfortunately, this simply wasn't a battle, and it never had been. All their powers and abilities were completely meaningless. Their age and all the experiences they had could never have prepared them for this. Vampires or not, they were created from mortal beings, and mortal beings couldn't fight the abyss.

And then came the screams.

CHAPTER 13

Mindscape

anielle opened her eyes, a bit confused, and took in her
surroundings. She was clearly in a bedroom, but everything was
extremely old, and yet new. Wood and stone were everywhere, but
there was almost no metal, and it was obvious nothing was an antique.
There was also an odd sense of familiarity she couldn't quite shake. Then
a particular object resting on a wooden nightstand caught her attention,
and she took a few steps closer for a better look.

It was a beautifully fashioned green hairpiece, encrusted with
small jewels, and she recognized it immediately. Why shouldn't she
recognize the gift her mother had given her on her seventh birthday? She
gasped with the realization that she was in her childhood bedroom,
confirmed by small sounds coming from the sleeping raven-haired child
she had only just now noticed.

What's going on?

She should have sensed the mortal's presence immediately.
Danielle suddenly coughed slightly, having never released her earlier
gasp.

I'm mortal?

The memories started flooding back, everything that had happened
in the last few weeks, including her final decision to sacrifice herself.

She walked over to the window, looking out at the vaguely
familiar countryside, as she let her thoughts settle. It appeared that she
was in the first residence her family had purchased after coming to the
kingdom where she would eventually meet John.

So what? Time travel now?

She knew it was ridiculous, but what other explanation was there?

There was that old saying about seeing your life pass before your eyes right before death. Perhaps that was the answer. This was pretty much the beginning of her life, and she was in the process of dying, so maybe there was some logic to it. Maybe that meant she would get to see John again before the final end. The thought gave her a modicum of peace as she looked around at her old possessions. What else was there to do but wait?

A thunderous crash from the window signaled the start of a particularly big storm. To Danielle, it sounded a bit muffled, having grown so accustomed to her enhanced vampiric senses. She almost didn't hear the sudden crying of the child that had been sleeping a moment ago. It was true that thunderstorms used to give her quite a fright, and she smiled at the silly memory. Danielle stopped smiling when the bedroom door opened and the most beautiful woman she had ever seen, or would ever see again, came rushing in.

"Momma?"

She could feel her mortal eyes watering at the sight of her centuries-dead mother comforting her former self. No one was responding to her presence, of course, but she was afraid to approach any closer. This was an unexpected gift, and she wanted to hold on to the illusion for as long as possible.

"Hush now, child," her mother said soothingly. "You don't need to be afraid."

Her voice was the most beautiful music Danielle could have asked to hear, and she closed her eyes. Maybe if she tried to sleep now, she could die with happier memories.

"Because it's not real, Momma?" came the childish response.

"Oh no, it's very real," the voice became a bit less soothing. "But fear serves you no purpose, you need only to submit to your reality."

Danielle was confused by the odd conversation, but a nine-hundred-year-old memory was bound to be flawed. A strange sound followed the end of her mother's comment, and Danielle gave up trying to sleep.

She opened her eyes and screamed in shock. Her mother was standing not two feet away from her, staring directly into her eyes with disgust. Her clothes were smeared with blood, and Danielle saw she was holding a knife in one hand and her own seven-year-old head in the other. The feeling of mortal nausea was unfamiliar, and she started choking on her own bile.

"Momma?" Eyes filling with tears, Danielle muttered the question through her shock and fear.

"You killed my daughter."

Danielle couldn't make herself move as her mother threw the child's head at her. Any question of this being a simple memory or vision was dispelled as she felt the impact and saw the look of shock and betrayal in the young dead eyes.

"Monster." It was barely a whisper, but from her own mother, it sounded like a scream of accusation.

Danielle tried to speak, to say anything in response, but her body wouldn't listen. She opened her mouth, but it was nothing but a whimper.

Her mother sneered at her in response and, without ever looking away, used the knife to cut her own throat. Even as the body fell to its knees, blood spurting from the wound, her mother maintained eye contact.

She screamed again and rushed to catch the falling body. Despite the look of disgust in her mother's eyes, she refused to let go until she felt her life completely pass. The blood had sprayed everywhere, and Danielle was covered in it, far too much blood for a single body to contain. Feelings of revulsion took over, and she started to vomit uncontrollably.

As a vampire, she had spent nine hundred years feeding on the blood of others. Blood was power, it was life, and quite frankly, it was delicious, but something was different now. Danielle was starting to realize she was not simply in a mortal body; she *was* mortal. She was reacting as a mortal would to what was happening, even though she knew it wasn't real. What was happening to her?

"Who said this wasn't real?" It was her voice, but she hadn't spoken, and it was coming from the darkness on the far side of the room.

A pair of eyes appeared in the shadows, and as the figure came closer, Danielle could barely breathe.

It was her. Down to the last detail, she was looking at herself. The figure started moving closer and began to change. Fangs protruded, fingers morphed into claws, and facial features twisted into a demonic mask.

Danielle had never felt so much fear. This was different from all her past experiences; even when she had been convinced of death, she had not felt this way. She was experiencing fear as only a mortal could, the pure unbridled terror of the dark and being consumed. As the figure continued its approach, she began backing away and desperately grasping for anything that could be used as a weapon.

"Do you understand yet?" the figure hissed through fangs, in her own voice.

"Stay away from me!" She had recovered the knife her mother had been holding and was waving it protectively in front of the figure's face.

"Seriously?" The figure rolled its eyes and took another step forward.

Danielle matched her with a step back, and she immediately bumped into the bedroom wall. Her eyes went wide with panic.

"This is your bedroom, idiot," the figure said, indicating the room with a wave. "It's not that big."

Danielle had temporarily run out of tears to weep, but the fear and panic were uncontrollable. In her mind, she knew she was no weakling, but she couldn't stop herself from feeling that way. There were plenty of memories of her fighting skill, but this body didn't seem capable of acting on any of them. And she still didn't understand her reactions, both physical and mental, to what was happening. Why did this thing have to sound so much like her?

"Whatever," the figure said, knocking the knife out of her hand with barely any effort. "Have it your way, fool." It struck her in the stomach with a bare fraction of what she suspected its true power was.

Danielle doubled over coughing after having the wind knocked out of her. It was bad enough that she was too scared to fight back; she also was not accustomed to being hit as a mortal. Before she could even think to straighten back up, the next blow landed on the back of her head. She saw stars briefly before landing face down on the wooden floor. The figure grabbed her hair and started dragging her away from the wall.

All intent of fighting back was gone as Danielle simply tried to scramble along the floor to prevent her hair from being ripped out. She had only been hit twice, and at barely more than a normal mortal's strength, but everything hurt. She wanted to cry again, but she couldn't even do that anymore. What was happening to her? Eventually, the figure gave her body a slight toss to cover the rest of the distance.

She landed on the bloody corpse of her mother and could see the child's head still looking at her a few feet away. She was starting to feel light-headed from how rapidly she was breathing, and she couldn't even blink. The room was getting darker, but it did nothing to hide the carnage. Meanwhile, the figure simply stood there, arms crossed and watching her with her own eyes.

"Please." Danielle had never begged. She had cried and screamed in fury, rage, or grief, but she had never begged an opponent. "Please," she whimpered again, forcing herself to her knees to face herself. "Make it stop, please," she started crying again and leaned forward.

"Not until you understand." The figure kicked her in the face as she bowed forward, and the force tossed her body to face the wall where a large mirror that hadn't been there before was waiting.

It was large enough to show the reflection of everything, including her own broken and useless form. Through the tears, she could see the figure's reflection as it approached her left side.

Danielle started trying to move or at least shift her position. Not because it would help in the slightest but because all prey instinctively tries to run. As if moving a few inches further would protect her from anything. The figure crouched down and pulled her head up by the hair so their faces would be even in the reflection.

"Do you understand now?" The figure's question demanded a response.

Danielle could barely see through the blood and tears, but the reflection was clear enough. One face was twisted with clearly demonic features, and the other was battered and broken, but they were both clearly the same person. She didn't want to be hurt anymore, but she didn't understand the question. Her mind was too fogged with pain and terror, and her body was shaking horribly.

"Okay, try this." The figure rolled her eyes, sensing it wasn't going to get anywhere. "What am I?" She leaned closer to the mirror, forcing Danielle's head to follow suit.

"M-m-monster," Danielle managed to get out through shaky breaths.

"Damn, that's my fault, so I'll give you partial credit." The figure flashed a familiar grin. "*Who* am I?" The figure hesitated for a second and then nodded, seemingly happy with the new choice of question.

One of the most frightening aspects of the experience was how identical the figure's mannerisms were to her own.

Why does she have to talk so much like me? Danielle didn't know what else to say; she just wanted it to stop. *Like me.* What was it she found so odd about the figure's mannerisms? *No, no, no!*

The figure started to grin, as if it were reading her train of thought.

"You are *not* me!" Somehow Danielle was able to shout without stuttering.

"Oh, so close, but wrong answer." The figure smashed her face into the mirror.

216

She could feel teeth breaking and the glass cutting into her flesh before she was tossed aside. The figure approached, but Danielle could no longer move. It was all she could do to keep breathing, not that she wanted to. Her stupid mortal body just refused to die. She felt as much as heard the figure crouch down closer, and her body tensed for the beating.

"Relax," the figure's voice sounded oddly gentle. "Listen to me, this is your only chance to understand."

Danielle's body twitched slightly in response to the voice, but she couldn't even turn her head.

"You are the you that you want to be, but the you that died nine hundred years ago. I am the you that you have been and are, but you have been lying about for those same nine hundred years."

Danielle tried to reject what the figure was saying but couldn't do anything except make soft noises.

"I sense that you disagree."

Danielle tensed reflexively for giving an answer the figure did not want to hear.

"I told you to relax." The figure moved and sat down so Danielle could see her. It also changed its appearance back to normal.

"I'm not going to hurt you anymore, well, not right now anyway. You ain't seen nothing yet, sister." The figure winked at her. "Unfortunately, I do need you to be able to talk, so maybe I overdid it with the whole mirror thing."

The figure mimicked smashing Danielle's face into the mirror.

"I just forgot how fragile I used to be." The figure shook her head slightly. "Well, anyway, you don't really need to believe me. To be honest, I could care less."

Even through the pain and terror, Danielle's confusion at the turn in conversation was clear in her eyes.

"I just need to know if you are ready to submit to me. Are you?" An eyebrow arched, and Danielle was careful to not move a muscle. "Didn't think so."

The figure leaned to within inches of Danielle's face. She could even smell the same brand of mouthwash on its breath.

"You need to listen very carefully. I do not like explaining things more than once."

They stared at each other, unblinking.

"You already lost. I don't care what you do, say, or choose. I think that long term, it is easier for me if you simply submit, but if you choose not to"—the figure shrugged its shoulders—"it just means I can keep doing this." The figure waved her arms, indicating the overall scenario that just played out. "To me, it's like having a pet, and I've always wanted a pet. Sure, it's a little more work, but torturing you like this is going to be a lot of fun for me. I've got some great stuff planned."

The figure sat back and started rubbing its hands together. "Eventually, I'll probably get tired of doing it, but at this rate, you'll have broken long before that. Once that happens, it won't matter if you want to submit or not. So, you see? This pain and torture is your choice and completely unnecessary, because out there"—the figure pointed up— "and this is the most important part, so listen really close, out there, you are already dead."

The figure got up and started walking away.

"Get some rest, you'll need it."

Danielle could hear the footsteps receding. She tried moving one of her arms so she could shift position, but she quickly gave up as the movement drove shards of glass deeper into her flesh. Not knowing what else to do, she simply whimpered through her broken teeth until the darkness took her.

When her eyes opened once again, Danielle wasn't surprised to see her surroundings had completely changed. Her injuries were completely gone as well—also not surprising. Unfortunately, the memories were still there, and she knew it hadn't been a dream. She wasn't really sure what was happening, but it was definitely real on at least some level, which explained why she was so terrified.

She forced herself to think through the terror and focus on logic. That creature had made a compelling argument when it described what they both were. Was it possible that she was nothing more than a figment of her own imagination—a pale remnant of the humanity she used to have perhaps? That would explain her lack of abilities, but then what was the creature? She no longer truly believed that vampires had actual beasts inside themselves.

Then again, a person didn't have to be a literal demon to be a monster, especially not if that person had vampiric abilities. This could honestly be a simple case of split personality disorder, nothing more than two parts of her mind vying for control of the same body. Although, even if that were true, was it good or bad? Wouldn't that mean that she technically wasn't real after all—and that neither of them was real until this conflict was resolved and someone got full control?

For a moment, confusion overrode her terror as she wrestled with this new idea. It almost explained everything, but it just didn't seem right. How did she get here anyway? She simply woke up in the previous room and started getting tortured. Didn't that creature say something about being dead? She couldn't be dead unless she used to be alive. Why couldn't she remember anything before waking up earlier?

The sound of voices got her attention, and Danielle realized she had been wandering aimlessly while lost in thought. She had come across a fairly large gathering, and it didn't take long for her to remember where she was. The castle courtyard, the priest, and not to mention the wedding couple, were dead giveaways.

She was seeing her own wedding, and even knowing it wasn't real, her heart leaped when she saw John. It was all for him. She might not remember the details anymore, but somehow she knew that everything that had brought her here was for his sake. It wasn't much, but it helped to strengthen her resolve a bit after the horror she had just endured, and she moved closer through the crowd to try and hear the sound of his voice.

The armor the king had insisted his knights wear for ceremonies had always looked a bit silly to her, but on him, it was magnificent. By contrast, her white dress seemed plain, despite its expense. The colored flowers sewn into the fabric had helped a lot to balance the dress against John's gaudy armor. Of course, her mother had insisted-

It was the random thought of her mother that did it. That brought images of her recent corpse and all that blood and reminded her of what was really going on. She had allowed herself to be caught up in a moment of happiness and was too stupid to recognize the trap for what it was.

She wasn't even surprised when her twin appeared to the right of the stage and started walking confidently toward her husband. This time, though, she wasn't broken and bleeding on the floor, and she hurried toward her other self. Of course, the figure seemed to be in no particular rush, so she easily made it to the stage in time and chose to stand protectively behind John to block its approach. No one responded to either of their presence, and she could hear the ceremony continuing behind her.

"I'm not going to let you hurt him!" Danielle screamed defiantly.

The figure didn't seem to notice or care.

"Well, well, look who woke up with her big-girl panties on this morning. Up you go."

The instant she got within arm's reach, Danielle was tossed aside as if she were a rag doll. She picked herself up just in time to see the figure punch through John's armor like tissue paper. Its fist came through his chest, holding his still-beating heart. She couldn't help but cry out as she saw his lifeless body fall.

"Oh, shut up."

The creature had already taken the priest's head and was now dragging the struggling bride toward her.

"What's your problem anyway?" it asked as it approached closer. "I'm you, remember? We love that guy." The figure nodded its head in the direction of John's body. "You know how you're always hoping to have his heart? Well, I got it for you."

She remained frozen as the creature reached over and opened the purse that Danielle was suddenly wearing.

"We'll just put that right there." It tucked the still-beating heart carefully into the purse, before resealing it and giving it a gentle pat. "There we go, you're welcome." It looked up at her and seemed disappointed at Danielle's lack of gratitude. "Damn, I don't remember being such an ungrateful bitch."

The whole scene was as ludicrous as it was horrific. It was as if the creature had experimented with pure horror already and was now just going for shock value. She started to remember what it had said to her the first time.

I'm just a pet.

"Hey."

Danielle tasted blood as the creature slapped her.

"Are you listening to me?" It held up the bride, who was still struggling uselessly. "Remember her? So I'm going to go ahead and kill her now, just like you did nine hundred years ago."

Danielle watched in abject horror as the monster her cut the skull open of the bride her.

"This is your brain." It leaned the dying bride's torso forward for her to have a better look. "This is your brain on vampires." It simply pulled a piece of brain matter out of the bride's skull and popped it into its mouth. "Any questions?"

The creature started to chew, waiting for Danielle's response, when a look of revulsion came across its face.

"Oh, that's disgusting." The creature spit out the contents of its mouth and reeled back. "Damn, that was terrible. I don't know how zombies can eat that shit."

220

Danielle just continued watching, as if she could will what she was seeing to not be true.

"I need something to get that brain taste out of my mouth." It seemed to be mumbling to itself more than her at this point. The creature regarded the corpse of the bride her for a moment. "Nah, eating myself seems a bit weird even by my standards."

It looked up and met Danielle's unflinching gaze. "What? It is weird, and that brain thing doesn't count because I did it for educational purposes."

"You know what? You have been nothing but a huge disappointment this entire iteration," the creature scoffed at her. "At least last time you were a bit more fun, but I guess that's what I get for not physically hurting you that much." It shrugged its shoulders. "I guess this is a learning experience for us both."

The creature appeared ready to leave, then hesitated.

"You still don't get it, do you?" her twin asked, eyeing her frozen form. "You have no power, no skills, barely any knowledge, and even your memory is slowly starting to fade." The figure glanced upward, as if seeking additional patience. "You think and remember words like *wife* and *husband*, but you can't accept your own reality.

"You were nothing more than a commodity who was traded away in order to increase her family's status, just an eleventh-century slut who would've ended up either a serving wench or a whore had you been born into a normal family. Everything you have become happened after your death and my birth. You probably even think it's my fault you can't move, don't you?" Her twin stepped a bit closer. "Tell you what, I'm going to go eat some wedding guests while you stay here and get ready for the next round." The creature patted her almost gently on the cheek before turning to walk away.

Danielle watched her own body walking away and wondered again if she was simply going insane.

"I told you, you aren't crazy," the figure called back, reading her mind again. "This is all real, that's what makes it so much fun. Don't blink."

The comment surprised her, so naturally, it was the first thing she did.

She was in a bedchamber that was clearly part of the old castle John had called home. Immediately she recognized herself resting comfortably on the bed with John in a chair by her side. It was a normal-enough image, except it couldn't have been a memory. They had been turned before there was a chance to move into the castle as they had planned.

There was a sinking feeling in the pit of her stomach as she noticed some of the room's other details: bloody rags in a pile off to the side, basins of hot water, and there seemed to be some blood on the sheets, despite her other self and John appearing to be uninjured. She realized then that the figure had been telling the truth all along.

The creature had to be her because it was the only way it could have known what to create to truly break her without an actual memory to work with. If she was right about what this was, it was about to be the worst thing she could ever see, and there was no way she could handle it. So Danielle ran—a simple-enough solution that she probably should have tried sooner.

Unfortunately, as soon as she ran through the door, she found herself reentering the same room. She should have known it wouldn't be that easy, and the terror started to build. Danielle looked around in a panic until she spotted a window, and after only the briefest of hesitations, she charged as fast as she could for it. There was no way her mortal body would survive the fall, and death was infinitely preferable to what she was certain was about to happen.

"Nice try." Her other self appeared in time to block her final escape.

Without hesitation, it grabbed Danielle by the throat and dragged her to the side of the bed. A swift kick to the back of her legs forced her to her knees, and she winced in pain as they slammed into the stone floor. She clawed uselessly at the viselike grip on her throat as her eyes and neck veins started to bulge.

"Oh yeah," the creature said and released her throat, "I almost forgot you need oxygen now."

Danielle barely had a chance for a single choking breath before the creature grabbed her hair and forced her head down onto the mattress so she wouldn't be able to look away.

As expected, John and the other Danielle in the room did not react to their presence, despite being in and around the same bed. Out of desperation, she grabbed a water basin and tried using it as a weapon against the creature.

"What the hell are you doing?" her other self demanded angrily.

Danielle's desperate attempt to fight back had simply gotten them both wet.

"I was trying to be nice by leaving your arms free," the creature growled as it quickly snapped both Danielle's arms backward at the elbows.

She howled in agony at the terrible pain but attempted to use the extra movement to slam the back of her head into the creature's nose.

"Oh, I get it," the creature said chuckling. "You're trying to piss me off so I'll kill you. Not bad, but honestly, I'm done playing around."

The creature pushed her head down harder and added a knee to her back for good measure. She was still whimpering in pain when a woman dressed in white came through the door with a tiny bundle.

"I've always thought it was weird you still wanted a baby," the creature bent down to whisper, as if not wanting to disturb the others in the room. "I mean, isn't it just more lies in your attempt to pretend you aren't me? What do you think would even happen if a monster had a baby?"

While the creature was talking, the woman handed the bundle over to John, who was gently rocking it back and forth.

"No, no, no, please! Not this," Danielle was pleading through her sobs. "Please, I'll do anything you want. I surrender, I submit, anything, I swear." She squeezed her eyes shut, but she could still hear the baby's tiny cries of new life.

"Yeah, I told you before I don't really care about that." The creature extended its claws to pull Danielle's eyelids open.

She could see herself in the bed, reaching out to take the newborn from John as any new mother would.

"No, I don't understand." Her whole body was shaking in terror. "You win, that's what you wanted." She choked on more sobs. "I can't take any more. If you're me, you know I'm not lying."

"Oh, I know you're telling the truth. I just don't care. I gave you the easy way out before, and you blew me off, so now you get punished. This is a lot more fun than I expected, so I'll just keep it going until you're a mindless husk."

Danielle couldn't even have the peaceful acceptance of defeat, and knowing what she was about to see simply increased the horror when it happened.

The Danielle in the bed had accepted her new baby and leaned forward as if to give a gentle kiss on the forehead. John was naturally leaning over himself, not wanting to take his eyes off the newest addition to his family. So no one seemed to notice or care that the other Danielle's free hand was pointing at John, and suddenly five claws extended, spear-like, much further than any Danielle herself could ever have made.

Three of the claws went through John's skull while the other two found the woman who had brought the baby into the room. As terrible as the twitching and dying corpses were, it was nothing compared to the other Danielle's face. The face that had leaned down for nothing but a gentle kiss had risen dripping blood and pieces of flesh from fanged teeth.

The creature's claws prevented Danielle from looking away, but they couldn't silence her wails. Eventually, the creature released her to walk to the other side of the bed where the other Danielle was still eating. She slumped to the floor, unable to support herself with her broken arms, and started to retch and sob. After a few moments, the creature returned to sit in front of her, and she told herself she didn't really know what it was chewing on.

"You know," she heard it say through a mouthful of flesh, "you've been throwing up a lot since this whole thing started, but I haven't seen you eat anything."

Danielle simply stared at the creature through broken eyes, not able to process the conversation, much less respond.

"Seriously, you're mortal now, so it really was an honest observation. Want some?"

She didn't have time to turn away or even close her eyes as the creature tried shoving a tiny leg in her face. She simply threw up again. The creature shrugged and popped the flesh in its own mouth. She realized, through the pain, horror, and revulsion, that things would only get worse. Surrendering had been her only option, and that option had been rejected.

"Have you considered that we both might be wrong and I'm your conscience? I know it sounds crazy, but as terrible as you feel now, isn't that how vampires make mortals feel all the time? Maybe this is just all payback for being a nine-hundred-year-old monster, and I'm not even real at all." The creature paused to consider its own statement.

"Never mind, I don't like not being real, so screw that idea." It looked at Danielle's broken and twitching form and saw her lips moving. "Wait, what's that? You're finally talking again." It leaned down to listen.

"Please. Kill. Me." Each word was barely intelligible and dragged out to its own statement.

"Nah, trust me, I'm going to make sure you never die," the creature said and shook its head. "Besides, you haven't given me any feedback on what I just pulled off. Pretty impressive, right? I had to build that from scratch, and I almost went with the baby being the monster. You know, tiny infant vampire killing its parents or something like that. I think that would have been overall a lot freakier to see, but I went this route because I thought it would be extra horrifying as a wannabe mother. What do you think?"

What made it worse was that the creature was seriously asking.

"Kill. Me."

"I'll take that as a job well done."

Danielle saw her own face streaked with infant blood and smiling in victory.

"I do admit that I am going to need some help on the next round," the creature's voice was nothing but white noise to Danielle as she considered the only question that remained.

How could she possibly still be alive? No mortal mind or body could handle what was happening to her. The terror, the revulsion, the pure horror of it all was simply too intense to properly process for any real length of time. She simply felt numb. The cool touch of the stone floor against her abused body was all she noticed. That and her other self's rambling. Wait, what did the creature just say?

Danielle couldn't muster the strength to even turn her head, but the creature was still sitting in her field of vision. She could have sworn she had heard the words "rape" and "Dracula," but why did she notice that when she was trying so hard to ignore it all? Why did it seem so important? What was it she couldn't remember, and why couldn't she just die?

"Oh, so now you're listening?" The creature seemed to notice her new attentiveness and confusion, and it let out a soft sigh. "Look, I am taking my work here very seriously, and you don't seem to be very appreciative." It rolled its eyes in a far-too-human manner.

"Anyway," she started explaining again, "I'm definitely having you raped next, but it's such a big playbook I don't know where to start."

The creature's ability to discuss so nonchalantly the most horrific of topics just added to the overall terror, but Danielle forced herself to listen this time. There was something important there. She just had to remember.

"I'm the real you, so the baby thing was easy, but rape? Not so much. I mean, it's been over nine hundred years, and we've only been with one man, so not a lot of real experience there. Such prudes, aren't we?" the creature said grimacing. "So I don't really know what will do it for you, you know? I figure it's all bad, but I need true horror and disgust, or it's just not worth the trouble."

The creature leaned so close Danielle could have bitten her own nose. "I want to hear you scream as your body gets broken in a way it's never been."

The look her own face gave her was intense and even more horrific due to its very lack of vampiric features. The creature was content to use simple human methods and concepts to continue her torture.

"Given our own lack of experience," it continued, leaning back to its original position. "I probably never even would have thought to use rape at all as a proper method of torture. I definitely owe props to Dracula for that one."

Danielle's eyes widened ever so slightly as she heard that word again. Who, or what, was a Dracula, and why couldn't she remember?

"Man, you should have seen the weird shit he had planned for you."

That was it, the final piece. The creature realized its mistake when it saw Danielle's eyes grow hard.

"Oops."

The memories of Danielle's last moments came flooding back to her again, and she knew why the creature's choice of words had been so important. She remembered all the battles with Dracula, and toward the end, he had made his intentions toward her abundantly clear. However, at no point had she been strong enough to actually see very far into his mind, except for his intentions toward John. When it came to his physical plans for her, it was all vague megalomania. The only way this creature claiming to be her true self could have "seen" anything would be if . . .

"Got it in one." The being that had been using Dracula as its host hopped up and sat on the bed. "Well, come on then." It patted the space next to her gently.

All Danielle's physical injuries were suddenly gone. Her heart and mind were still aching from the terrible horrors she had endured, but physically, she was at least able to move again without pain.

She slowly picked herself up off the floor, noticing that while the bedchamber remained, all evidence of the previous horror had vanished. She moved carefully to the bed, not taking her eyes off the being. It was possible this was simply another trap, but Danielle got the impression that for the moment, at least the playing field had equalized. For its part, the being simply had an expression of slight impatience.

"So you finally get it now?" it said as Danielle carefully sat down next to it. "I have to admit that I am impressed." It was clear that whatever this creature was, it was being genuine. "It doesn't really change the situation; it just means I can go back to my own normal tactics. You still lose either way."

Danielle did not understand the comment, considering she had already tried to surrender.

"What are you?" She didn't know what else to do but to entertain the conversation.

The injuries she had might be gone, but she knew she was still powerless. Maybe if she kept the creature talking, there would be a weakness of some kind to exploit. It was the only idea she had.

"I am me," it said as it shrugged its shoulders. "I know that's not quite what you were looking for, but it's the truth. One day I simply *was*, and ever since, I have insisted on continuing to *be*. Most mortals have no desire to die or kill themselves, so why should I? Is it my fault that I require a host to truly survive?"

"That can't be completely true. I mean, if you simply came into existence one day, it wasn't inside a host. So how can you need a host to survive?" Danielle was trying to focus on the tiny logical part of her brain that was fascinated and ignore the horror.

"Fair enough." The creature paused a moment, considering how to explain. "It's like I'm asleep. That dark cloud you remember seeing?"

Danielle nodded very carefully.

"Well, think of that as my resting state. There is some awareness there, but I am never truly awake unless I'm inside the mind of another being."

"If that's true, then you don't get to really choose your hosts then? You just sort of float through the universe until you wake up inside someone?" It would have been fascinating, under normal circumstances.

"Well, almost. Once I have a host, I can make a conscious decision to use a different one, if a better choice comes along. I usually don't bother because it's a pain in the ass, to be honest. Any host of mine ends up being incredibly powerful, so I just take whatever I want regardless.

"Also, once I have a host, we become one true entity, so I cannot leave by choice. In some ways, you could say that every new host turns me into a slightly different being, because they always leave an impression on me. The core of what I am and my desire, however, always remains. To choose a new host, I must wait for my current host to die or be destroyed, and it just isn't worth the trouble. Except now."

Danielle was afraid to ask.

"You figured out everything else, so surely you can connect the dots with what I just said."

An onlooker would have seen identical twins simply sitting in their bedroom and having a pleasant conversation, but Danielle could feel the other shoe about to drop.

"It wasn't Dracula who wanted me, was it?"

The entity started clapping in glee. "Damn, you're good. I chose well." The entity was clearly pleased with itself. "Dracula had grand delusions but didn't really care about anything except removing you both as obstacles. I gently nudged him in the other direction and worked to slow him down at the very end so you could kill him.

"I wasn't sure why you sacrificed yourself the way you did after that, at least not until I took up proper residence here. You assumed you stood a better chance against me in here"—the entity tapped the side of Danielle's head—"than your husband would have. Given what you thought at the time, it wasn't a bad plan."

Danielle felt there were still a few important holes in the explanation, and it was possible it was another trick. Maybe, just maybe, this entity didn't have complete control yet.

"You were correct in assuming I was in a weakened state, having just lost my host. Unfortunately, you were wrong in thinking that would make a difference." The entity lay back, stretching out on the bed as if not having a care in world. "You see, to you, this is all simply another battlefield, but this is my whole world and existence. You having lived here first changes nothing, but I am sensing you don't fully believe me," the entity said and frowned.

"If you were telling the whole truth, then I wouldn't be here anymore." Danielle started regaining a small amount of confidence. She was still terrified, but this was starting to seem like more of a normal battle. Long odds or not, at least a battle was something she could fight.

"Oh, for crying out loud."

The creature's exasperation took Danielle off guard, not that she would have been any match for its sudden speed. Agony exploded through her body as her heart was ripped out, and she saw it beating in the palm of the creature's hand.

"See?" It displayed her heart for a few seconds before tossing it across the room. "Even if you were still the powerful vampire you had been, you would be ash right now. Instead, you're just sitting there staring at me with that stupid look on your face."

Danielle felt another wave of agony and saw a second heart on display.

"You are here because you aren't real." The entity seemed to grow tired of the explanation. "You used to have mind control abilities, so you should know how this works. You are nothing more than a leftover image, a shadow of the consciousness that used to inhabit this mind. You can't die, all you can do is fade away. Something of you will always remain here, but your awareness will be gone. I am just trying to speed up the process, but you are one stubborn bitch."

Danielle's terror started turning to despair as she realized the entity was telling the truth, except . . .

"You're lying. I already surrendered, but I'm still here."

It was all a trick. Danielle just needed to find an opening.

"No, you just said you gave up." The entity looked annoyed. "There's something in there somewhere still holding on, and I'm guessing you don't even realize it, considering how badly you were doing that last round. Unfortunately for me, I am more accustomed to willing hosts. My power is so much greater than yours, and I am finding it difficult to break you without completely wiping your mind."

Danielle recognized a bluff when she heard it.

"Then why not just wipe me out and save yourself the trouble? If you can, that is." She did her best to maintain a confident expression.

"I guess you are stupid."

The bedchamber and castle vanished, and they were both suddenly in a forest clearing. "If all I wanted was an empty slate, then any host would do. I want you," it said as it pointed a finger at her.

"Why? Just kill me or wipe me or whatever and be done with it!" Danielle was starting to understand what the entity meant and realized she had no chance after all.

"What? And give up all this power?" The entity looked at her as if she had lost her mind. "I have spent a thousand millennia inhabiting the minds of mortal beings and giving them amazing powers, but you, my girl, are already powerful."

Wind started whipping through the clearing, and she saw thunderclouds filling the sky.

"You saw how powerful I made Dracula, and he was just a man when he surrendered himself to me. How much more powerful will I become if I inhabit the mind of an immortal like you?"

The wind started increasing in intensity.

"That is the question I asked myself when I chose you. I still don't know the answer, but I have been drunk on your power since I arrived."

Danielle watched as the entity raised its arms and the surrounding trees burst into flames.

"All I wanted to do before was to keep existing." She watched the entity simply rise into the air with outstretched arms. "But even now, I can feel myself changing. You thought me weakened, you thought you could trap me and save others from me, but you gave birth to the me that you see before you."

Bolts of lightning began striking the entity, and she got the sense it was feeding off them.

"Fool girl, you've not only failed in your task, but with my power added to yours, I can become a *GOD!*"

The fires were growing and spreading all around her, and Danielle looked about the hellish landscape.

"In fact, perhaps this is what I've always been, and I just needed a key." The entity stared down at her, and as the skies grew darker and the fires grew brighter, she realized there really wasn't anything she could do to fight back. Not against this. She could almost feel herself starting to fade.

"All that's left," the creature said as it landed right in front of her, "is to deal with you."

It started walking toward her, and Danielle knew fleeing wasn't an option.

"If it makes you feel any better," it said as it stopped within arm's reach, "while I am dealing with you in here, out there I'm killing your husband."

Danielle didn't remember throwing the punch, but she was rewarded by seeing the entity's head knocked back with a broken nose.

"So you can be hurt."

"So you do know how to fight," it said, its nose already healed. "You sure you want to do this? It's not too late to simply fade away."

Danielle refused to back down and raised her fists. Somehow, she knew this fight would be at mortal speed and strength. The creature nodded acceptance and mirrored her pose.

The identical combatants stared at one another for a moment before they charged. The lack of vampiric abilities on both sides served to increase the sheer brutality of the fight as blows were exchanged, deflected, and countered. Danielle was at a severe disadvantage given that the entity didn't experience pain in the same way she did, but she refused to relent.

She absorbed blow and after blow, felt her flesh bruise and her bones break, but something kept driving her on. The entity seemed content to let her tire herself out, wearing an expression of complete boredom. The final outcome was never much in question, even as the level of brutality increased. Danielle continued driving herself to fight harder, but it just wasn't good enough, and she felt the entity's grip on her arm an instant before she was tossed into the surrounding flames.

Horrible screams of pain split the night as her flesh burned and melted away. She tried to no avail to snuff the fires by rolling back and forth, and finally panic sent her charging back into the clearing. Her twin simply waited for the flaming torch to get close enough before driving a fist into her guts with enough force to send her flying several feet back the way she had come.

Danielle lay on the grass, gasping for breath, not even realizing the burns on her body had vanished. More evidence that the entity had been right in explaining what she had become. Her pain was completely real, since she experienced it in her own mind, but any physical injury was only real at the moment it occurred. In a sense, her injuries were only temporary figments of her own imagination.

Reflexively, she tried to rise, only to take a fist to the bridge of her nose, causing her to fall back. Danielle tried blinking her vision clear of the stars and tears in the way and could see the entity standing above her. The look in its eyes left no room for doubt that it was about to end the charade. She tried in vain to wriggle herself out of the way, even as the foot came down hard enough to crack her sternum, pinning her in place.

"Submit." It wasn't a question.

"No!" Danielle's cry of defiance was more of a pained whisper.

In response, her twin pulled her up just high enough to strike her back down. As her head bounced off the ground, she was grabbed and struck down again and again. Her attempts to defend herself amounted to nothing more than feeble slaps that were completely ignored. Her twin pulled her up by the hair so they could face each other. Even through her broken eye sockets, she could clearly see the face that used to greet her each morning in the mirror.

"Submit."

Danielle wanted to give up, but she couldn't. She didn't fully understand what was happening, but it was clear that the entity didn't have everything it needed from her. It was obvious she could not fight and win, and it was possible that she would eventually fade away, thus allowing the entity to achieve its goal. She just didn't know what would happen. All she knew was that she couldn't say yes. No matter what happened to her, as long as she didn't say yes, it was possible she would never fully lose.

She felt the entity rip out her heart again, even as she was being held up by her hair. The pain grew as she felt herself being completely eviscerated. She wanted the pain to stop more than anything, but something was preventing her from saying yes. Maybe if she hung on long enough, she would grow numb to it.

"Submit." The creature's expression hadn't changed since the fight started.

"*KILL ME!*" Danielle pleaded through the pain.

The creature simply dropped her to the ground and began beating her savagely.

"You are already dead!" the creature began shouting at her, never stopping the blows raining down all over her body.

"Liar," Danielle managed to spit the word through broken teeth.

"Excuse me?" The entity paused in its tirade, confused by Danielle's statement.

"I can't be dead." Danielle was forcing her broken body to stand before the entity, her wounds not vanishing this time. "If my body were dead, it would be ash." She was having difficulty taking in enough air to speak.

The entity struck her down again, as if trying to prevent her from finishing the thought.

"If I were ash, neither of us would be here." She coughed and started to rise again, not fully understanding where her newfound determination was coming from. She barely flinched as she was struck down yet again.

232

"You know what I meant, what's left of you is nothing but a shadow. A shadow that needs to learn its place." The entity continued striking her down every time she tried to rise.

"A shadow is all I need to be," Danielle said as she crawled toward the entity's feet, latched on to an ankle, and was rewarded with a foot coming down on the back of her skull. "As long as there is something left for him to find," she mumbled into the grass.

"Who? Your husband? I already told you, I'm in the process of killing him, and for him, I mean it literally."

"I choose not to believe you." Danielle rolled over, not quite able to rise this time.

"That's stupid. You 'choose not to believe me,' that's it?"

"It's all I need. You can beat me and torture me for as long as you want, but as long as you leave something of me alive, he will find it." She stood up once again, and this time the entity didn't strike her immediately. "I might suffer infinite horrors, but I can't be broken now."

"That's the dumbest, most naive thing I have ever heard."

"You've obviously never been in love." Danielle's statement seemed to give the entity pause.

"You know what? You're right, so maybe I'll give that a shot instead."

"What the hell are you talking about?"

"I've decided not to kill your husband after all and to just take your place." Its face split into an evil grin.

"How could you possibly think that would work?" Her confusion grew as her tortured mind tried to follow its logic.

"John, honey, is that really you?" The entity's features grew soft, and its voice was sad and pained. "Oh god, John, it was horrible, but it worked." It rushed forward, and before Danielle could respond, it wrapped her in a fierce but loving embrace. "I swear I'll explain everything." She could feel its body shaking slightly and hear its faint sobs. "Just please hold me." It was even planting tender kisses on her cheek and neck.

She felt a different type of horror as she realized how perfect the illusion was. There would be no way for John to realize the truth since she had been unable to explain what was going on during the fight. He would never save her, and he would never find her, and this thing would be with him forever.

"It's over!" The entity ceased its demonstration by driving a knee into her stomach and then again into her face as she doubled over. "You had all this power, but you chose to live such a pathetic existence! I tried convincing you that you were a monster, but the truth is, you are simply mortal garbage." The entity struck her down.

"That's why you're the one bleeding and broken on the ground." The blows continued with every word. "Why you are the one crying and begging for death." The entity picked Danielle's broken form up once again. "Submit to me, and perhaps I will grant it."

She had been waiting for this moment. If her injuries were all imaginary, despite the pain, then it meant her hands worked just fine. The instant her eyes were level with her twin's, she gripped the back of the entity's head and pulled forward with all her remaining strength. She drove her forehead into its nose with a loud *crunch*, and finally, she felt blood that was not her own spray on her face.

"Dammit!" The entity jumped back in shock, dropping her to the ground. "*You fucking bitch!*"

In a burst of vampiric speed, it grabbed her by the throat and slammed her into the nearest tree. Any satisfaction she had felt at inflicting the slight injury was gone as she was completely immobilized by her gasping need for air.

"You won't submit to me? *Fine!*" Her twin's face was displaying full vampiric fury, and Danielle felt her terror redoubling. "I'll peel your mind like a fucking onion to find what I need."

Danielle could feel the spit from each word as her twin hissed through fangs.

"I'm going to drag you through every single second of your pathetic existence."

As she struggled to breathe through her crushed throat, surrounded by fire, it was hard to believe she wasn't already in hell. Looking into her twin's eyes made it even worse as she saw simple, black pools of pure hatred.

"All of the has-beens and never-weres! All that could be or would be! Every second will be an eternity of unending torment as your soul burns for the rest of time!" Veins bulged across the creature's face as the darkness of its eyes grew even deeper.

Through Danielle's terror, it seemed its voice was coming from everywhere at once, screaming from the very fire around her as she cried out in fear.

"I had forgotten what I truly was, eons before your time." Its lips weren't moving, but the voice carried in a thunderous echo all around her. "Those that came before couldn't defeat me, but they used their powers to render me into a mere shadow of what I once was, forcing me to live within prisons of flesh." The entity paused, relishing her anguish and terror. "But no more." It leaned closer, nearly brushing its deformed nose on Danielle's struggling face. "You, my pathetic little vampire bitch, are the final piece that I didn't realize I was missing until now."

"Thanks to you, I am truly awake," the voice became a sinister whisper as the dark eyes drew ever closer to her own. "Thanks to you, I remember."

There was nothing but despair as she fully realized what she had done. The entity she had sought to trap had already been trapped. What they had been fighting was nothing more than whatever faint power had slipped through its metaphysical bindings. Her mortal brain didn't have the ability to comprehend what she had released, only that she had failed so spectacularly that her whole world would pay the price. The entity's eyes were like staring into the abyss, and she could almost feel herself disappearing into infinity.

Danielle finally had proof, after all this time, that she still had a soul, as she felt a terrible burning from within. In some ways, the truth of her own insignificance was more frightening to her than any of the prior horrors she had endured. How could she have ever thought there was even the slightest chance of victory? There was nothing but infinite darkness and terror stretching in all directions, and she was so very, very small.

"The mortals have so many names for me, but I sense most have forgotten and no longer believe. Thanks to you, they will soon remember." The entity tightened its grip on her throat. "Your pathetic mortal concept of hell is nothing compared to what is coming. As you suffer in your infinite torment, I want you to remember your failed sacrifice."

With every breath, the creature slammed her broken body into the tree.

"Never forget, it was *YOU* who granted me the power I needed. It was *YOU* who allowed me to fully awaken again. *YOU HAVE UNLEASHED OBLIVION ONTO YOUR WORLD!*" The creature pulled her from the tree and raised its arm, allowing her limp body to simply dangle from its grip on her throat.

"And it's you who will live on, suffering in fire, to watch as I turn all you've ever known or loved to dust," the creature's voice had grown softer and even more sinister.

She realized, even though she could see and was aware of her surroundings, her body was dead this time. The last spark of hope left her mind as she realized the creature could, in fact, fully kill her and that she wouldn't actually die. It was all true, and her last hope of escape vanished. The creature's grin broadened as it sensed her realization.

"I'm going to kill you a billion times and *never* let you die!"

As if to punctuate the point, her body chose that instant to restart. All she could do was scream as the surrounding fires seemed to reach up into the heavens and the creature's voice became but a whisper in her mind.

Welcome to your forever.

CHAPTER 14

Poenari Castle Dungeon

J ohn watched on in horror as Danielle's body thrashed and convulsed on the stone floor and her screams continued to echo from the walls.

Anytime he tried to approach, he was thrown back by an invisible force. He couldn't tell if it was a result of her powers being out of control or if he was being held back by the same thing that had entered her. The only thing he was certain of was that his wife was fighting a terrible battle, and he had no idea how to help.

The cloud that had entered her had to have been whatever creature was possessing Dracula—that much he understood. Neither of them was particularly suicidal, so Danielle's decision to sacrifice herself must have been for a reason. Maybe this *thing* was something they couldn't fight physically. Her mental abilities were far superior to his own, so it made logical sense for her to be the one to do this, but still . . .

He couldn't discount the terror and fear he had felt when that thing had entered her or the certainty of his wife's final words. Whatever was happening, it was something neither of them could fully understand, and he doubted they could defeat it. He also remembered the final promise she had forced him to make, and that was what scared him most of all.

At first, John tried reaching out with his mind in an attempt to add his strength to hers. The instant he made the connection, the backlash of agony and fury that exploded into his brain nearly destroyed his mind. This was not a fight he could take part in, and he could feel his heart breaking at the thought of his wife facing it alone. All he could do was continue pacing around her, looking for an opening or at least to gain some understanding.

Her convulsions were so violent he could actually hear bones breaking, but he knew those screams were not in response to any physical pain. He used his vampiric sight to examine her as best as he could considering how quickly she was moving, and his fear only grew. Every muscle in her body appeared to be tensing past the point of tearing, as if something was ripping her apart and yet holding her together at the same time. Her eyes were the worst of all. They seemed to flash between pure fear and agony and pools of darkness.

It was the darkness that was the most frightening, and John was ashamed to admit he couldn't stand to look at them for long. Danielle was clearly losing, and John was unable to even get close to her, much less assist. The final promise he had made was starting to make sense now, and he felt his eyes redden as they filled with bloody tears.

Danielle had known she couldn't win from the beginning. In the absence of any other plan or strategy, she was opting for pure attrition. What if this thing had been weakened by Dracula's defeat? How much weaker would it become after battling his wife, even if it defeated her in the end? Then, if John could . . .

His mind reeled at the thought. Could what? Kill her? Hope that Danielle weakened the creature enough that it would be completely defeated if John followed up by destroying his own wife? It was insane, but it was the only idea that explained her actions. Given the level of power he was witnessing, he doubted the plan would work, assuming he was able to do it at all, and he didn't think he could.

Danielle's body flipped onto its back, and her back arched, thrusting her chest toward the ceiling strongly enough that he heard her spine snap. She wailed through gaping fangs as the darkness in her eyes grew, and John knew fear and despair as he had never felt. Then, as quickly as everything had begun, it was over. Her body collapsed, completely limp, and a deafening silence blanketed the throne room.

Her body was perfectly still and peaceful, showing no signs of the terrible struggle she had just endured. John began to approach slowly, his footsteps echoing unnaturally in the silence. His sword was at the ready, even though he doubted his ability to use it. How would he know what to do?

"John?" the voice was so weak. "John, honey, are you there?"

Hope mixed with despair as he bent over his wife. She had collapsed facing away from him, so he couldn't see her eyes. He needed to see her eyes.

"Baby, I can't see you." There were faint sobs.

He reached for her shoulder, skin covered in blood-sweat, and started to gently turn her over. She met his gaze with loving tear-filled eyes, and he felt relief wash over his body.

"Oh god, Dani," he cried, dropping his sword and wrapping his wife in a fierce embrace.

They both wept in each other's arms, and he vowed to never let her go.

"Honey," came a slightly strained voice, "don't you think my bones have been through enough?"

Danielle's question drew a soft chuckle as he realized how tightly he had been hugging her. She smiled sweetly, face still streaked with red, as John relaxed his viselike grip.

"Better?" he asked as she quickly took advantage of her freedom by curling into his lap.

"Much." She started caressing his arm, and he absently began stroking her hair.

"Is it over?" He didn't need to elaborate, and Danielle's body shuddered a bit in memory. *Please!*

"I think so, but it was so horrible," she said grimacing. *Kill!*

"I'm so sorry I couldn't help you, love, but you're safe now." John hugged her again, more carefully this time, and kissed her forehead gently. All he wanted to do was stare into her beautiful eyes forever. "Can you tell me anything about what happened?" *Me!*

"I need more time to understand," her voice was soft and a bit confused. "My plan worked, but I never imagined suffering like that." Her body started shaking again as John simply held her. "I just want to rest for a bit."

It was hard to argue with her, considering all the abuse her mind had taken lately, and John forced himself to remain patient. *Kill me!*

"It's okay, I'm just glad you're all right. Honestly, Dani, I don't think I've ever been so scared." It was John's turn to shudder slightly as he replayed her final struggles in his mind.

"So just hold me for a while, okay?" *Please!*

"Deal."

They sat that way for a while, simply enjoying each other's presence, but John had the distinct impression someone was yelling at him.

You promised me!

It was strange, but every time Danielle spoke to him, it was as if he was hearing something else he couldn't quite understand in the background. Given everything that had happened to them recently, he shouldn't be surprised. It was a miracle he could hold on to his sanity at all, so a few half-heard whispers were of no concern. And yet . . .

"Honey, are you okay?" Danielle was looking at him, the concern obvious. *It's horrible!*

"Oh yeah," John said, shaking his head slightly. "I know this has been so much worse for you. I mean, I pretty much just sat back and watched, but still . . . ," his voice trailed off.

Please!

"I understand, honey." She patted his cheek slightly. "It's hard for you to watch me fight alone, but I'm never really alone since I know you'll always be there." She snuggled in tighter. *I'm burning!* "You'll keep me safe, right?" She kissed his hand before using it to caress her own face. *Kill me!* "You'll protect me forever, won't you, my love?" *JOHN!*

"Of course I will," John answered, even as the smallest kernel of doubt began growing in his mind.

Danielle kissing and caressing his hand made him realize she had yet to feed. When she had crawled into his lap, he had offered his arm to her out of reflex, as he always did. Given his emotional state, he hadn't realized she had yet to feed from him.

Perhaps he was reading too much into the situation. Emotions were high, and she was recovering from an experience more terrifying than he could imagine. It made sense that she would want to get her bearings and just feel close to him for a bit, because that was all he wanted at the moment as well. It was also possible that she didn't need the blood, given that most of her struggles had been mental.

Still, the act of feeding from him was very calming and extremely enjoyable for them both. He had been looking forward to it, given what they had both just endured, and he would have thought it would've been the first thing Danielle would do. With a small twist, John subtly brought his wrist against her lips but was simply met with more gentle kisses. He smiled as he looked into her beautiful eyes and couldn't deny the love looking back at him. And yet . . .

He closed his eyes and began to concentrate, and immediately regret the decision. The faint whispering he had felt more than heard before was now a scream. Agony, torment, despair, and just pure suffering greeted his mind. It wasn't like the sudden backlash he had felt before when he tried to interfere in the battle. This was worse because there was no sense of struggle; this was simple reality.

He finally recognized the whispers and the screams for what they truly were, and his mind began to weep. He was hearing the sounds of his wife's soul burning in torment and begging for a death that would never come. Through some twisted trick of fate, the two of them had ended up challenging the very abyss itself—insects pitting themselves against a god.

John opened his eyes and saw the truth of what was resting in his lap.

"Oh well." Danielle blinked, and her eyes became swirling pools of darkness. "You can't blame a girl for trying."

Whatever the thing was, it was made more horrific by retaining all her beauty. John was so close to the eyes he almost felt as if he were being pulled into twin black holes. Everything else happened in an instant.

The entity struck as John was leaning back to gain precious time and space. Even as his sword returned to his hand, he could feel the claws piercing through his chest. The fingers wrapped around his heart and began to squeeze, even as he swung his sword one last time. As he collapsed, his heart crushed, John could see his wife's head rolling across the stone floor.

There was a vague sense of shouting and footsteps, but none of that mattered. All he could do, as he felt Danielle's corpse fall on top of what would soon be his own, was hope that wherever they went next, they would be together.

"Hurry, move, move, move!" Sam yelled the commands as he blurred into the room.

Everything had been fine, and then it had all gone straight to hell in an instant. If not for the progenitor's influence, Sam would most likely be frozen in shock after witnessing the ancients killing each other. The only reason he hadn't entered the room earlier was the desire to give them some privacy. They had been just holding each other and deserved time to recover from the terrible battle they just survived.

Thankfully, the progenitor understood what needed to be done and was able to guide Sam's thoughts. He had gotten accustomed to the extra presence, so there was little confusion. Most importantly, the progenitor was able to "see" anything Sam saw and wasn't distracted by silly things like impossible battles or the ancients going insane.

He was grateful for the influence now, given what he had just witnessed. The ghouls were just as shocked but responded to his commands instantly, hauling the stasis chambers into the room and getting them ready. Somehow, he simply "knew" what needed to be done as he reached for John's body. He couldn't help but stare at Danielle's headless corpse, even as he was somehow certain John was in greater danger.

Not having a second to spare, he lifted the body and hurled it to where the ghouls were waiting. The hole in John's chest where his heart had been destroyed was obvious, and he wondered if that was the difference. Danielle was in two pieces, but at least those pieces were intact. The ghouls caught the body and carefully laid him in the chamber.

As John's chamber was sealed, Sam hurried to Danielle's side, motioning the second group of ghouls to bring her chamber closer. He knew her condition was fatal, but they had more time than was available to help John. In her case, care was more important than saving seconds, and he gently lift her body into the chamber. A pair of ghouls held her in place as he went to carefully retrieve her head, and even the progenitor's influence was barely enough to keep him calm.

Everything he thought he knew about vampires told him she should be ash already, yet the wounds on both sides of her neck had simply sealed. The progenitor was trying to continue influencing his movements while providing answers in his mind, without allowing the combination to overwhelm him. A part of Sam's mind "knew" Danielle wasn't ash because both her brain and heart were intact, thanks to John decapitating her cleanly. Her power and lack of blood loss were preventing her destruction, but it was only temporary since there was no longer any control, and the blood keeping her alive would lose its power quickly.

He carried her severed head back to the chamber, trying to avoid looking directly into the open and lifeless eyes. Every second that ticked by increased Sam's terror that he would be holding nothing but ash, but he had no choice but to take the extra time to move carefully. The ghouls continued holding her body as Sam set her head in place, turning it to the proper angle. Satisfied he had done all he could, he sealed the chamber and manipulated the necessary controls before stepping back and looking around.

The twelve ghouls he had brought were all standing around the chambers, concern and confusion evident on their faces. They were looking to him for answers he didn't have, but having led them for so many decades prior to becoming a vampire, Sam did his best to look confident. None of them fully understood the technology being used and

242

had simply followed the progenitor's instructions. To be honest, Sam hadn't truly believed most of what he had been told, and pure loyalty to his sires had been the main reason he was here.

It was true that technically it was John's blood that had turned him, and it was his blood only that sustained the combat ghouls he had brought, but none of their strange family really thought that way. The ancients came as a package deal, and their ghouls would fight to the death for either one, regardless of which vampire's blood ran through their veins. In this way, their ghouls were as different from other ghouls as the ancients were from other vampires.

Both John and Danielle appeared to be resting peacefully in their strange glass boxes, and Sam could feel more than simple confusion radiating from the ghouls. It was anger. None of them had known what was happening until the progenitor had contacted him. To stand here now, in the aftermath of such a terrifying battle, and know they were not there to help was almost too much for them to bear. The knowledge that they had all, including Sam, been left out intentionally for their own protection simply made it worse.

"Okay, I know none of this makes sense, and you're all probably as pissed as I am," Sam tried to sound as commanding as John would have. "We all wanted to do more, but keep in mind that at least we were here in time to save them. You all did well." It was the best he could come up with, and he wasn't really even certain it was true.

None of them understood what the various readings on the stasis chambers meant; he only knew the progenitor's presence in his mind felt pleased.

"I need you all to stay calm and on guard," he continued as the ghouls seemed to relax slightly. "We still have to get them back, and there's no telling what nonsense might still be infesting the area. We bought ourselves some time, so let's do this right." Sam drew his sword and morphed his off hand into claws. "Form up, leave your emotions at the damn door, and move the hell out."

Having been given instructions they could understand, the ghouls seemed much happier and began to move quickly. Each chamber was lifted by a pair of ghouls while the remaining four drew weapons and took defensive positions around them. The two teams lined up, and Leo nodded for Sam to lead the way when they were ready. He was about to issue the final command when they felt the whole castle begin to rumble and shake.

"Shit, so much for doing this the right way," he grumbled, leading the way out.

243

Whatever had been holding Dracula's castle together was clearly gone, and the structure was falling apart. There was no time for subtlety, so Sam simply charged in a straight line, creating openings wherever needed. He was careful to maintain a pace the ghouls could match and didn't bother worrying about the wisdom of creating additional large holes in the walls of a collapsing structure.

Those two idiots better survive this so I can kick their asses, Sam thought to himself as he dodged the falling debris.

John woke to a strange swishing sound and opened his eyes in time to see what looked like a glass door opening in front of him. He appeared to be in some strange glass coffin, and there was a slight mist dissipating out of the new opening. Strange thoughts were jumbled and disjointed in his mind, and his body felt very strange. All in all, he was not in a good mood, and he began climbing out of the strange box out of reflex more than anything else.

"Sir!" Sam shouted as he hurried to his sire's side.

John's confusion grew as he took in his surroundings. He recognized the progenitor's cavern, but now there were strange machines arranged randomly, and additional lighting had been set up. Most notably were the several ghouls roaming about performing various tasks—all of whom looked to him in surprise and joy after hearing Sam shout.

Everything was wrong, and John was ignoring Sam's attempts to get his attention. He wasn't sure why, but everything was wrong, and there was a terrible pain coming from his chest. It was then that he noticed a second glass coffin and moved for a closer look even as Sam tried to stop him. He blinked in surprise at seeing Danielle resting peacefully, and in the brief darkness of his closed eyes, he saw her head rolling across the stone floor.

Memories snapped back into focus, and he fell to his knees, clutching his chest in agony. He couldn't get the image of his wife's severed head out of his mind, the eyes staring at him in lifeless blame. John started to scream, but instead he began vomiting blood and gore. Hands started to gently shake him, and he didn't have the strength to push away from whoever it was.

"Sir, sir? Look at me." Sam started shaking him more forcefully. "John, look at me."

John turned his head, and Sam noticed vague recognition in his eyes. He also saw blood, bile, and who knows what dripping from the corners of his mouth.

"Try to calm down." Sam was unaccustomed to seeing tears in John's eyes, much less fear.

"Dead!" It was all John could manage before keeling over again.

Sam didn't know how to comfort him, so he simply attempted to grasp both his shoulders and force him to look him in the eyes.

John responded by pulling him closer. "I'm sorry." He was crying freely now. All he saw was her lifeless eyes staring back at him. "I had no choice."

"Calm down, dammit." Sam slapped him, hoping the action wouldn't result in his final death.

John reeled back, blinking his eyes in shock. Sam thought he saw more clarity in them, but it could have been his imagination.

"Do you understand me?" There was a brief nod before he started to vomit again. "Do you remember everything that happened before you woke up here?"

Another nod, and a haunted look entered John's eyes.

"Okay, just stay calm and listen to me. Everything is fine." The statement wasn't completely true, but there would be time to split hairs later. "The progenitor's experience communicating with you both allowed him to reach out to me more carefully, and since it was your blood that made me, I was able to understand. We all got here not long after you left the first time, and the progenitor explained everything."

Sam spent the next few moments describing his encounter with the progenitor and the plans they had made. John shifted position to sit normally as he listened with interest, and they both ignored the blood and gore covering his clothes and the ground around them. There was definite clarity in John's eyes now, and Sam's confidence grew as he finished his side of the story.

"Stasis chambers, huh?" John chuckled slightly. "It's funny, we both knew exactly what the progenitor was but never really thought about the technological side of it." He winced in pain and clutched his chest again. "Get to the part about how any of this explains why we aren't dead." Despite his improving mental state, those lifeless eyes were still staring at him.

"A combination of how powerful you both are and that we got to you in time. Both of you had fatal wounds, but you're both too strong for instant death," John said, arching an eyebrow in disbelief. "Don't get me wrong, sir. You would've been ash regardless; it just takes longer for the power of your blood to fade. In your case, the progenitor guessed you wouldn't last thirty seconds. He gave Danielle between three and five minutes, but truth is, I think he made the times up."

John raised a hand to stop him as he started shaking his head.

"Sam, I cut her head off." He didn't feel any additional explanation was necessary.

"Yes sir, I know. I was there." Sam signaled a pair of ghouls to bring a few thermoses over. "The only reason we didn't run up to you was that it appeared to us everything was over. Seriously, we were staying out just to let you both recover with some privacy. Even then, the progenitor's influence was the only thing that allowed me to react in time. I know it's hard for you to believe, but your condition was much worse because your heart was crushed."

He paused to accept the offered thermoses and passed one to John.

"Think you can keep that down?"

"I'll try, and I expect you'll get to that part of the explanation at some point as well?"

Sam laughed and nodded at the light rebuke. "So anyway, we got you in the chamber in time but honestly had no idea how to fix you. By comparison, Danielle wasn't a problem, although I admit it was scary as hell. Keep in mind, you really didn't damage her, all you did was cut off her head."

"You do realize how stupid that sounds, right?"

"Good point, but what matters is that she was intact just in two pieces, and your heads don't revert to ash immediately as other severed appendages do. The progenitor says it's because your brains and awareness are too powerful, but we have no way of knowing at what age that becomes true since we've never fought another vampire anywhere close to your strength. The point is, the wounds simply sealed themselves normally to prevent blood loss.

"It's still not something you can fix on your own, so for the most part, losing your head still means death for you. Any opponent that cuts your head off isn't going to pick it up and put it back for you, and it doesn't take that long for your power to fade under those circumstances. It was actually pretty freaky." He paused for a drink. "I put her head back on, and by the time we set the controls properly on the chamber, her body had already healed itself."

"Seriously?" John couldn't hide his amazement.

"Yeah, but I guess it makes sense. I mean, it was a simple, clean cut, so nothing needed to be regenerated. Instead the wound just knit back together like normal. The progenitor said if we had been any slower on the controls, it's possible that thing could've woken up again." Sam shook his head out of his own disbelief at the situation.

"You, on the other hand, had no heart and a gaping hole in your chest that wouldn't seal. Our hearts might not pump blood the same way a mortal's heart does, but we still need them. The progenitor guessed you had however much time it takes your body's blood supply to fully cycle, but no one knows how long that actually is. Personally, that thirty-second time limit he gave sounded like a total WAG to me."

John chuckled in agreement with Sam's statement. He knew a wild ass guess when he heard one.

"Okay then, so how did you fix me?" John was finally starting to feel normal again, and he leaned back against the base of Danielle's chamber.

"Oh, you're going to love this." Sam grinned as John gestured for him to end the suspense. "Medical. Nanites," he spoke slowly and overenunciated each word for additional effect.

"You can't be serious." John started to protest but then began thinking more carefully about what the progenitor really was. "Okay, I guess that fits, but how would that help me if I had no heart? I'm pretty sure an artificial heart wouldn't do the trick for us."

"Technically, your heart was still there—well, the crushed pieces of it anyway. That wasn't the real problem." Sam was struggling to find the best way to explain it. "We aren't normal living beings, and even the progenitor didn't know if the nanites could be altered for vampires. Our best guess was that they would use the materials left behind to make some kind of working heart, and that would be enough to keep you alive long enough for your own power to heal it the right way."

"Wait, is that why my chest felt like that? Not to mention," John said, simply pointing at the disgusting mess he made all over the floor.

"Yeah, the nanites know what humans are, and well, you used to be a human."

John started to groan as he guessed where Sam was going.

"Uh-huh, they went straight for the heart at first but then started spreading to your other organs."

"But I don't have—" he cut himself off as he looked at the floor again.

"Yeah, and I'm guessing you still don't," Sam responded, looking at the same mess. "Anyway, we had to wait for them to finish your heart, then we turned them off. I would say what you went through when you got out was almost a mini version of our initial turning process." Sam waited for his opinion.

"Makes sense, at least as much sense as anything else right now, and I do feel pretty much back to normal." He started stretching. "What about her?"

"Well, as I said, she was effectively healed already. We injected some nanites anyway just to be sure." Sam held up a hand to stop John's coming protest. "This was before we knew what they would do to a vampiric body. Anyway, they ignored her completely, although they did repair her clothing . . . ," Sam trailed off, still confused about that fact.

"Why would medical nanites repair—"

"Look, sir, I don't know. I don't even know if medical nanites are really what they are," Sam suddenly sounded a bit tired and exasperated. "You know how the progenitor is. It's all 'child, this' and 'child, that' and 'your words have whatever foolish meanings you assign them.'"

John laughed out loud at Sam's impersonation of the progenitor's mental voice as they both continued to drink.

"How are we going to explain this to her? She hates science fiction."

John's random comment was met with sudden and uncomfortable silence, and he sighed.

"It's time for the other shoe, isn't it?"

Sam answered by getting up and motioning for John to follow him.

"The progenitor thought it would be best if a familiar face explained the situation to you, so I'm going to show you one last thing before he takes over."

He drew John's attention to a monitor with a set of controls. John couldn't help but stare at Danielle as she slept. The lifeless eyes in his mind were still there, but he could handle them now.

"This is basically a super complicated On/Off switch. You see these squiggly lines here and this other set of squiggles there?" Sam was pointing out the necessary readings.

"Sam, stop, please, your complicated science terms are confusing me."

Sam rolled his eyes at the comment. "One is your wife, and the other is the entity you were fighting."

Sam's statement earned him John's full and undivided attention.

"Yeah, thought that might get your attention. Anyway, we can use this to release one without the other even though they inhabit the same physical body."

"How? Stasis is stasis, isn't it?"

"It's a medical chamber, sir. Everything doesn't simply freeze just because you close the door." Sam patted his arm. "Look, I didn't get it either, but I asked the same question before we injected the nanites. Essentially, the chamber would serve no purpose if it didn't allow whatever was inside to be worked on. That's why the On/Off is way more complicated than a simple switch."

"You sound pretty confident."

"Sir, you've been here for days. There wasn't anything else to do except learn about this stuff." It was a fair point.

"Oh, well, okay then. Anyway, about that other shoe?" He was still waiting to learn what the problem was, and there had to be a problem, or Danielle wouldn't still be inside.

It is good to see you again child. John felt the progenitor's familiar mental presence.

"Does this mean we're at the part when you tell me what's wrong?" He couldn't help but notice Sam had retreated to a safe distance. Was his temper really that bad?

Child, the entity has been defeated and contained, but your wife's mind has suffered so greatly I do not know what will happen if we release her in this state. I am going to send you brief glimpses, please prepare yourself.

John nodded and had to fight for self-control at the horrific things he was suddenly seeing. The progenitor limited the images to a handful of seconds in an attempt to prevent him from being overwhelmed.

This is but a glimpse of the battle she has been losing, and for her, it has been nearly two centuries. Before you interrupt me—John had been ready to do just that—*time is relative and passes very differently for her now. Even now, in stasis, she is being tortured.*

"But how?" John was starting to feel very guilty for how long he had spent talking with Sam.

It is a medical device, never intended for prolonged use and not designed to turn off someone's mind. Your body may be effectively frozen, but your mind simply goes to sleep. The place where your wife battles now is unaffected, and very little of herself remains.

When you removed Dracula's influence, I was able to clearly see what was happening for the first time. There was nothing I could do directly, but I have been using the link I established with you to feed her my power. Her plan was a good one, so I thought with my power, it would work. Unfortunately, this entity is more powerful than even I can understand, so the plan failed, although my added power has kept at least a part of her from fading.

"Do you at least know what it is we are fighting?" John could almost feel the progenitor's frustration in his mind.

No. In fact, I no longer believe it should even exist in the same realm as we do.

John did not like the sound of that at all, but they could delve into those questions later.

Fear not, its lack of physical form makes it even easier to be contained by the chamber since we do not care about harming it. The entity is of no concern, but its afterimage remains in her mind. It no longer has any power; except the power she is giving it.

"That doesn't make sense." Why would Danielle be giving power to her enemy?

It makes perfect sense. She has been tortured by a powerful monster for centuries, with no awareness of the outside world. Why should that monster suddenly become weaker? The mind is a powerful and dangerous thing, especially one as broken as hers. We must break the cycle.

"I'm not going to like this, am I?"

As if on cue, a pair of ghouls began approaching. They were carrying a few fancy-looking gizmos and a seemingly unpleasant contraption that John just knew he was going to have to put on his head.

This is a neural interface.

"Of course it is." He rolled his eyes.

You think Shakeeth children go to school? We are cloned immortal warriors, and this is a very common device for us to download information quickly. More importantly, it is designed to work between organic brains, not organic and computers.

"Really?" John had read plenty of fiction stories with such devices, but they were always used to download information from computers into people. "Why?"

We are bred soldiers. Would you prefer to learn of war from a computer or from a veteran warrior thousands of years old?

Putting it like that, John had to admit it made perfect sense.

The point is, with this device, you can connect with her mind, and with our power, you can do so as a proper image. I believe I can keep you safe, but you will be unable to directly accomplish anything. You will only have passive influence.

"Okay, but what am I supposed to do?"

You must break the cycle. The afterimage of the entity must be destroyed, and it must be destroyed by whatever is left of her. No one can heal a mind that does not want to be healed, so she must have a choice.

"What exactly do you mean by that?" John could feel the progenitor's hesitation.

What she suffers now is unending. If you are successful in helping her end it, there are two obvious possibilities of what will happen next. You will be unable to choose for her, neither is it your right to do so.

"I understand." At least he hoped he did. "Let's get started."

John allowed the ghouls who had clearly received instruction to set up the equipment and lead him to a clean patch of floor to lie down.

Connections were made to the stasis chamber while the interface was placed on his head and adjusted.

A final warning child. You need to find the shadow of what is left, but nothing you see is real. Do you understand?

"No," but he closed his eyes anyway.

CHAPTER 15

Mindscape

John opened his eyes an instant later and took stock of his condition and surroundings. He felt relatively normal but quickly confirmed none of his vampiric abilities were working. The surrounding landscape was rather bleak and barren, save one discerning feature. Despite the progenitor's warning, John was finding it difficult to maintain control as he saw bodies everywhere.

There had to be hundreds of bodies in piles, hanging from trees, nailed to crosses, and simply strewn across the ground. All of them Danielle. And there was no indication of decomposition in any of them. That was the worst part. Every visible feature on each body retained her perfect beauty, and not a single body was intact. He was thankful for his lack of vampiric senses as his strictly limited ones were being overwhelmed.

With no clear direction, he simply began to walk and forced himself to examine his surroundings carefully as he did so. It was surprising the sky itself wasn't red simply from the reflection of so much blood everywhere, all of it wet and thick and glistening in the fake sunlight. His mortal heart was racing as he continued reminding himself it wasn't real.

Movement!

He almost missed it, but there was clearly something hiding behind one of the few trees close by. It was obviously her, but John had no way of knowing if it was *her*. When he agreed to this insanity, he had assumed he would understand what to look for once he got here. His assumption had proven incorrect.

Very carefully and slowly, he raised his hands in a disarming gesture and began to approach. His wife's face peered at him as she cowered behind the tree. There was no recognition in her eyes, but that wasn't surprising, given what he had been told. John was about to attempt to call out when he sensed they were no longer alone.

"Hey, didn't you see the signs?"

At the sound of the new voice, the cowering figure leaped up and tried to flee. He turned in time to see another Danielle easily catch the fleeing one by the throat.

"No feeding the animals." It twisted its hand, and John could hear the neck being snapped like a twig.

It was a perfect copy of his wife, down to the last detail. John knew this had to be what was left of the entity she had been battling, but even the voice was perfect. It was horrifying, but he forced himself to stay calm. The progenitor might say this wasn't real, but watching his wife get her neck snapped seemed pretty damn real to him.

"So what brings you here anyway?" the entity addressed him even as the other Danielle's body dangled lifelessly.

He didn't know how to respond. He wasn't sure what he expected, but the simple conversational tone was unsettling.

"Oh, sorry, gimmie a sec."

The entity seemed to realize it was still holding the body. It turned and raised its free arm, lifting a fresh wooden cross from the ground. The entity waved toward itself, and the cross obeyed until it was within arm's reach. John watched as spikes appeared, and the entity affixed the new body to it with care. Every muscle in his body was tensing, but he had been warned against direct interference.

"Anyway, I've never seen you around here. What's your story, handsome?" The pleasant tone in his wife's perfect voice, while going about such a grisly task in so nonchalant a manner, was insane.

How could this possibly be his wife's mind and not hell? Rage, confusion, and revulsion anchored him in place while the entity completed the evisceration.

"Almost done, promise."

If John wasn't mistaken, it was actually humming a tone softly to itself. The body's entrails had already spilled out and were glistening brightly as they swayed gently in the light breeze. The entity pulled a few things from the open chest cavity before turning and walking back over to him.

253

"You're clearly different from the others, but I was hoping you'd be able to speak," it said, sounding disappointed. "Oh well, still, manners are manners."

It was holding Danielle's beating heart in its left hand, but it held its right hand out to John.

"Kidney or liver?" It glanced to its other hand. "Sorry, but the hearts are always for me." It took a bite.

John wasn't prepared for this. Even the images he had seen were nothing compared to being here. It would have been easier to fight an actual demon, but then maybe that's what this was. The entity was simply eating his wife's heart like an apple and looking at him like he was the weird one for not accepting the offered meal.

"Fine," the entity said, rolling its eyes. "You're my guest, and you're super cute." It dropped the other organs and held out the heart. "Just this once, I'll share."

John couldn't even blink.

"Okay, stay hungry." It shrugged and went back to eating, continuing to eye him curiously. "Okay, you look pissed, and I'm starting to think you don't belong here at all . . ." It trailed off in thought as it continued eating.

Suddenly its eyes flew open in surprise and recognition. "Wait, you're the husband, aren't you?"

John braced for an attack, but its mannerisms were getting even stranger.

"Oh my god, I'm right, aren't I?" It was hopping up and down like a schoolgirl, and bits of gore were dripping from the entity's mouth as it giggled.

"You don't understand how cool this is for me, do you?" It was dancing around like an idiot. "Okay, so way back, I got split off from the main me to stay here and deal with this bitch while the rest of me carries on with whatever fun it's having with the mortals. It has to be done, but it's *sssooo* boring in here. Your garbage wife had faded so much by the time I got here. I was never able to experience her true memories."

It grabbed his hand in one of its blood-soaked ones and gave it a firm shake.

"Sir, it is such a pleasure to meet you."

How could things be getting even weirder? Through the blood streaked across its face, there was a clear look of genuine happiness and excitement.

254

"I can definitely see what she sees in you." It looked him up and down seductively, still holding his hand. "I never imagined I would actually get to meet you, but I always knew what I'd say if I did."

The other arm came around in a simple embrace that brought the beautiful, but fake, face close to his ear.

"*YOUR LITTLE WHORE IS MINE!*"

John cried out in shock and pain as the bones in his hand were crushed even as the fangs pierced his throat.

The frail creature peered out from the corpse pile with interest. Hiding was the only way to survive this place, but the strange sounds had gotten her attention, so she took a chance to investigate. She knew it was not a good idea; the others always died when they came out of hiding. Still, it was only a small risk, and the creature had learned much about hiding.

She didn't know how old she was, but whatever the number, it was higher than the others. A long time ago, the monster had almost found her, but she hid inside the corpses, and it worked. That secret had let her survive, even though she didn't understand what she was surviving for in the first place. It also didn't bother her to hide in a pile of bodies that looked the same.

This place had always been filled with bodies, and they all looked the same, and being covered in their blood and entrails helped her to hide. Since there was nothing in this place that cast a reflection, she didn't know the bodies had her face. She knew they all looked like the monster, but the monster was easy to tell from the others. The monster was the one doing the killing.

Now, for the first time, she saw a different creature, and her curiosity was overriding her survival instinct. She had no idea what it was and why parts of its body were so much flatter than hers while other parts were so much bigger. If she had understood humor, she would have thought the other creature was rather funny-looking.

The really strange part was that the monster was talking to it, at least in the beginning. It was the noise that had drawn her attention. The monster almost never talked anymore; it just tortured, killed, and ate. Now they were fighting, which was also strange since no one fought the monster anymore.

The monster was winning, of course, but the other creature was not dead yet. So many strange and interesting things, but she didn't know what any of them meant. Her curiosity satisfied, she knew it was time to crawl away and hide again. There was something about this fight, however, that was making her feel angry, and she didn't even know what anger was.

As more of the strange creature's flesh was stripped away by the monster, she began to slowly crawl in the direction her instincts said was wrong.

Things were not going well, but John was clueless as to what other options he might have. After breaking free of the entity's initial attack, he started fighting back. He was slowly learning what he could and couldn't do. He was able to defend himself, but any attack he launched at the entity simply passed through it. It seemed as surprised as he was the first time it happened, so he was basically screwed.

He supposed he could try running. His wounds seemed to heal almost instantly, so escape was a viable option. There was just no telling which way he should run. The whole point had been to find his wife, but everything here looked the same. Thankfully, he was the better fighter, so as long as he stayed on the defensive, the entity couldn't break through. Hopefully, he could hold out until he came up with a better plan.

"Okay, this is boring." It suddenly stopped fighting.

John stopped as well since he was unable to do anything other than defense anyway. He took advantage of the brief respite to try examining his surroundings more closely than before. Anything that could give him a hint of where to go.

"How about some home movies?" It pointed up, and John's confused gaze followed.

He immediately reeled back in rage and revulsion as he saw vivid scenes playing across the sky of what must have been memories of past tortures. Somehow, he knew these weren't some strange copies but his actual wife, and he watched as she was repeatedly and violently violated and murdered by things he couldn't even name.

"I know, right?" the entity said and tugged at its shirt. "Is it hot in here?" It gave him a sultry look and licked its lips.

John howled in rage and charged while it simply stood there waiting. The entity spun around as his useless charge passed through it. Grabbing hold of the back of his clothes, it threw him to the ground.

John had fallen for the obvious trap, and before he could change position, it mounted him and started slicing his upper body apart. His superior defense meant nothing in this position, and even the almost-instant healing didn't help since he still felt the pain. In fact, the entity was purposefully timing its attacks to allow his body to fully heal prior to ripping it apart again.

"Now *this* is what I call fun!"

The psychotic laughter coming from his wife's own face as he was being flayed alive was too much. John tried using his legs to start kneeing it in the back, but he couldn't feel any contact. Considering he was clearly on the defensive, it seemed rather unfair. Not that his opinion seemed to matter here.

"Oh, baby, don't be like that," it said, then more laughter. "I mean, seriously, I haven't been laid in, well . . ."—the entity shrugged its shoulders—"ever, I guess."

It speared claws through both his arms, pinning them to the ground as it leaned in close to his face.

"What's wrong, lover?"

John could smell the blood on its breath as it licked his cheek. It leaned back again, drawing back its claws for another strike.

"*Don't you want to be inside me?*" It had a twisted look of glee as it shrieked and struck.

As the claws came down again, John thought he was imagining things as another figure rose behind the entity. Its arms were outstretched as if holding something heavy, and suddenly the entity fell to the side as a large rock smashed into its skull.

He rolled away the instant he felt the weight removed from his body and quickly turned to see what was happening. The second figure was covered head to toe in blood and gore, but it couldn't have been her own, considering she was moving just fine. As for the entity, well, John was pretty sure there was no entity anymore.

Compared to the insanity of the last few moments, the sudden silence was almost eerie, albeit not complete. There were the sickeningly wet sounds of his wife, and he was certain it was her, using a rock to smash the entity into a multicolored paste. It was rather satisfying, if a bit disgusting.

This was not how he imagined the trip going, although according to the progenitor, this end result was the one they wanted. He wasn't really sure what to do at this point, so he simply sat cross-legged and watched. Parts of his mind were still in turmoil after what he'd seen, so a few minutes to get his thoughts in order would help as well.

Eventually, Danielle seemed satisfied that the goo that was left of the entity would not be getting up again. She dropped her rock and sat down, looking very confused, as if just now realizing what she had done. When she looked at him, there was no recognition, but she seemed interested. The progenitor had said it had to be her choice, so he just smiled back.

"Thanks for the save, Dani," he said softly.

It was hard to believe the monster was dead. Even now, she did not understand why she had done it or how easy it had been. She stared at the mess that used to be the monster, expecting it to get up and kill her at any moment, but nothing happened. There was a new feeling now. She didn't know what it was, but it was warm. The other creature was sitting still and looking at her, and it made the feeling stronger.

Mostly, she felt tired. She couldn't remember ever not being tired, but sleep was not possible here. If you closed your eyes to sleep, that was when the monster killed you. Although she just killed the monster, so did that mean it was finally safe to sleep? That would be wonderful.

The ground started rumbling, but that didn't bother her since it felt kind of nice. She also didn't seem able to see as far as she used to, but that was okay since it just meant she was sleepy. Making her decision, she curled up into a ball and started to close her eyes. It was so wonderful not having to find a hiding place.

John's eyes began to fill with tears as she made her choice. The progenitor's words made far more sense to him now than they had before. He had chosen to come here, and he had been warned, yet he could barely handle the brief time it had been. This same place had been her reality for two centuries from her mind's perspective.

They had ended the torment together, and he had no right to take her back if she didn't want to go. If she just wanted to rest, after everything

258

she had been through, he had to let her. The progenitor had even implied that taking her back by force wouldn't work anyway, except . . .

Was she really even making a choice? If her mind had become so faded to not even recognize him, then she only saw one option. Wasn't having only a single option the opposite of having a choice? Certainly, it would be okay to give her a hint, just a little one.

He knew his weak logic was just a justification to act on his own desires, but he didn't care. He was simply too weak to live without her. Looking up, as if for guidance, John noticed there wasn't any up anymore. He also heard faint rumbling and had the distinct feeling of walls closing in. This place was collapsing.

"Dani." He leaned forward.

She wasn't far from him, and his motion startled her slightly.

"If you want to . . ." He paused to choke down on his light sobs. "If you want to sleep, it's okay, but I want you to have this." He couldn't stop his tears as he took off his wedding ring. He held it out and tossed it lightly to cover the remaining distance.

She cocked her head in interest and reached out to pluck the shiny trinket from the dirt. John leaned back as she held the ring close to her eye, peering playfully at him through the small hole in the center. It was nothing but a pretty little toy to someone who had never had anything and couldn't recognize anything—until she suddenly noticed a matching ring on her own finger. She held them next to each other and examined them closely with a look of confusion and shock, perhaps even fear at finding something on her body she had never seen.

John closed his eyes as the rumbling grew more violent. It might not have been enough, but even he couldn't justify saying or doing anything more. So he silently begged anyone or *anything* that might possibly be out there watching or listening. His inability to open his eyes was simple cowardice. If it was going to end this way, he wasn't strong enough to face it.

It was getting difficult to maintain his posture as he could hear the ground crumbling away, and he almost didn't feel the extra weight. Opening his eyes, he saw there was almost nothing left, until he looked down and saw all that mattered. Danielle was curled up in his lap, already snoring, and all vestige of the filth that had been covering her was gone.

He covered her body with his own as the mindscape vanished.

CHAPTER 16

Progenitor's Cavern

John opened his eyes as he felt the neural interface being removed from his head and one of his ghouls reached out to help him up. Grateful for the assistance, he used his free hand to massage his aching temple. It had been a horribly terrifying ride, but he was reasonably certain the plan had worked, although it had come so very close to failure. Knowing there was only one way to be sure, John moved to where Sam was standing at the controls to Danielle's stasis chamber.

"Well, Sam?" John inquired hopefully.

"Sorry sir, there's just no way for me to tell." He shrugged his shoulders sadly and pointed to the monitor. "Look, I have no way of telling you what her mental state is. Only that she's physically healthy."

John arched an eyebrow at him, indicating the dubious vital readings.

"Well, physically healthy for a vampire anyway."

John remained silent and simply crossed his arms.

"Hey, it's not my fault these stupid things weren't made to figure out walking corpses powered by blood or whatever the hell we are." Sam threw his arms up in exasperation. "My only job is to push these buttons when you tell me to release her. Why don't you ask him?" Sam pointed back to the wall housing the progenitor.

"Well?"

You were successful, my child. However, do not expect this to be easy.

John wasn't sure he liked the sound of that, but nothing ever seemed to be easy for them anymore anyway, so what difference did it make? He nodded once to Sam, who manipulated the necessary controls, opening Danielle's chamber.

There was a faint hum, and Danielle's eyes fluttered open after a few seconds. She quickly started to exit the chamber, looking very confused. John detected a slight shimmer as she climbed out and watched with mixed awe and horror as a thick, dark cloud remained in place while Sam quickly resealed the chamber behind her.

John moved quickly to join her. Danielle looked around carefully, allowing her eyes to adjust to the dim lighting. She started walking toward him, her grace and beauty fully evident. He still couldn't believe the nanites had repaired her tattered clothing, and John had never seen a more beautiful woman. She made it two steps before falling to her knees. John reached out quickly as Danielle buried her face in her hands and screamed.

"Ma'am!"

"Mistress!"

Around the chamber, every ghoul started moving to her aid, led by Sam.

"Get out! All of you!" John ordered through the sudden confusion.

"But, sir?" Sam started to protest.

"*Now!*"

John didn't know what was happening, but if something was still wrong with Danielle, he didn't want her to start killing their friends. Obedience was swift, and the cavern emptied quickly. By now, Danielle was still on her knees but bowed down completely, hands covering her face as she screamed in terror.

He didn't waste time trying to talk to her. John simply scooped her up into a powerful embrace. She reflexively turned into his body and began screaming and clawing at his chest as she looked up at him with eyes of pure red.

Frenzy!

Even as he finished the thought, John realized he was wrong about why her eyes were red. He had just never seen them so filled with tears.

She seemed to have an unending supply of them, so much so that he couldn't even truly see into her eyes. There was no fighting, no struggle, and yet every muscle in her face strained with the force of her cries. Her fangs and claws were opening small wounds across John's chest, but he sensed no malice. It was certainly unpleasant, but it wasn't

261

an attack. He sensed that she needed him badly, but he couldn't understand the depths of the emotion pouring out of her.

"I don't understand!" he shouted toward the progenitor. "You said the plan worked, that she would be okay!"

The plan did work, but I never said your wife would be okay.

John could feel the progenitor's sorrow in his mind.

"What's wrong with her?" He was still trying to hold her and stroke her hair as she alternated between fighting and clinging to him.

As John spoke to the progenitor, she responded to the sound of his voice by looking up at him with blood-filled eyes, pleading and wailing. She was gasping for air her body didn't need, just to power her wails, causing her to choke on her own sobs.

Foolish child, what do you think is wrong with her? There was too much sorrow for the rebuke to sting. *The enemy has been defeated, my son, so stop thinking like a soldier. Stop trying to form battle plans and attack strategies, and just think like a simple husband.*

John did not understand. How could they figure out a way out of this, a way to help her, without a strategy?

"Honey, please." John tried to kiss her forehead. "Please tell me how to help you." She had appeared to calm down slightly, but given the look on her face, John suspected it was simply temporary exhaustion.

She is telling you.

"Dammit, I am not in the mood for any more of these riddles!" John shouted at the wall. "If you know what's going on, just fucking tell me!" John could almost feel the progenitor's exasperated sigh inside his mind.

Child, think for just a moment about the brief glimpses you received, the small pieces of truth you learned from your time inside her mind. Think of those things and try for a second to imagine what your wife has been through.

John knew there was truth to what the progenitor was trying to say.

"I know it was terrible, but—"

TERRIBLE! The progenitor's mental shout cut off what John had been about to say. *The little vampire thinks it must have simply been "terrible"? Child, I told you that I lent my strength to your wife's mind to prevent her destruction, did I not?*

John felt he was being scolded, but it simply added to his confusion. The progenitor had to know he was only trying to help.

"Yes, you did say that, and I am grateful, but—"

Does she *look grateful?*

John looked down at the wailing, near-rabid form of his wife who was clawing at his blood-soaked shirt, but he just didn't understand the point.

You are looking only at the positive result, from the perspective of having won the battle, your wife's survival.

"Well, yes, I am," John could agree with that much. "It's certainly better than her being destroyed by that thing."

I agree with you child, but you are not seeing or understanding what that survival cost. The horrors your wife endured were too much for any mind. Even a mind as powerful as hers would have been flayed, tortured, and destroyed. Now listen to me, my son. As terrible as that sounds, as terrible as that would have been, the result would have been the peaceful restfulness of death.

Unfortunately for her, my power kept that from happening.

John felt that he was beginning to understand.

My power did not, by any means, allow her to win but only succeeded in allowing her to be defeated time after time. I told you that from her mind's perspective, over two hundred years had passed before you arrived to bring her back.

In that time, she was flayed, raped, tormented, and tortured by horrors you and I cannot imagine. She lived on in infinite darkness and despair, always alone, always to be broken, always to come back again. The entity very quickly convinced her you would not be able to save her, and so she had no reason to hope or to endure such endless suffering.

Hundreds of times she went through this, perhaps thousands, and she endured it all. Not because she wanted to or even because she had to, but because she was forced *to by the two of us. Me for giving her the ability she never asked for, and you by allowing her to be saved in the end.*

You know all these things because you were there, but have you had a chance to truly think about what that means? Her very soul has been begging for death for over two hundred years, and she remembers every single second of it.

"Sweet Jesus," John mumbled, looking down to see his wife rubbing her face back and forth across his chest, her eyes screwed shut.

She looked up at him, and this time hers wasn't the only face stained in red.

"So is she . . . ," he trailed off, terrified of finishing the question.

No, I think she will be fine eventually, probably.

"Do better than that, please," John begged. "You've given me a better understanding of what happened to her, but I don't really understand what's going on now. I mean, she's acting and sounding completely insane, but I honestly don't sense any insanity from her." He knew the progenitor could give him a better explanation, but for some reason, he seemed hesitant to do so.

No living mind can endure what she has, so she is letting it out in the only way she knows how. She is processing, in a way reliving, those horrors to let them go, and she is trying to do it quickly enough to keep her mind from burning into nothing in the process. I think it is some form of survival mechanism, and I am feeding her as much of my power as I can to help it work.

"My god! You mean, she's going through all of it again?" John gasped in horror as he gazed into his wife's fear-filled eyes.

Not quite in the way you are afraid of, but yes. She knows it is over, so it is more of a forced acceptance of what has already happened. She also knows you are here and that she is alive, and she is choosing life. Her mind and body are simply responding in the best way they can to honor that choice, and I am just making sure she survives the process. She is simply paying the price for the choice of survival that we both forced upon her, but there is one small thing I do not understand.

"I don't like the sound of that." Feeling the progenitor's confusion was more than a little frightening.

Do you remember before when I said, her very soul was begging for death?

"Yes, not hard to believe, given what she experienced." John didn't understand the confusion.

My life span is measured by eternity, and I have never seen or sensed any evidence of what you humans would call a soul. I used the term because I have no other to describe what I am sensing from her now, but there is definitely something there I have never sensed before, and it is trying to kill her.

"Are you sure it isn't some leftover form of that entity? I mean, I confess that I don't know if souls are real or not, but I'm pretty sure they aren't supposed to actively try and kill us." The strange twist in conversation momentarily distracted John from his wife's screams.

I can assure you; it is nothing malicious. It feels to me very strongly to be her, and yet not her. It feels to me that the majority of her suffering is centered on it, and it wants to die. I sense no murderous intent, just a desire to finally die and unfortunately, the rest of her is in the way.

You humans believe when your corporeal bodies die, your soul carries on to another plane of existence. If this is true, and given what your wife has suffered, is it so difficult to believe this soul would simply get tired of waiting? I chose my words poorly before. It is not trying to kill her, it just is not helping her, and I am uncertain of her chances if the situation remains divided.

"This conversation is getting weird." John couldn't help but laugh slightly at how ludicrous the entire situation was. "You know, even as little as ten years or so ago, we were both convinced that we were evil monsters not even deserving of mortal souls, and now it looks like not only does my wife have one but that it's going to kill her.

"All because we stumbled across some ancient alien stuck to the wall in an underground cavern, who tricked us into fighting some entity of total darkness. A far more likely scenario is that Danielle and I are in a dark alley somewhere feeding off someone with some serious drugs in his blood and that the last couple of weeks never happened."

Do not forget that you survived having your heart crushed while beheading your own wife.

John could feel the progenitor laughing in his head.

You people are very amusing. As I said, I do not know if those things are true, just that I have no other explanation for them. I do believe the situation will resolve itself in time. With every passing second, your wife's burden eases slightly. Her desire to live strengthens while the "soul's" desire to die fades. Provided that my power holds out and she keeps fighting, she will return to you.

"Will it? Your power hold out, I mean?" John had detected what he thought was a strain in the progenitor's mental voice.

I am very strong. Fear not, my child. I will be ash on the floor before I fail you in this. The progenitor's resolve helped to strengthen John's.

"There has to be more I can do to help. I understand this is her fight, but I can't just sit here and do nothing." It was the one part of the situation John was refusing to accept as he could feel Danielle shaking in his arms.

Tell me child, do human women prefer physical looks and abilities over mental prowess? The sudden question was confusing.

"Um, I don't know. Some do I guess, why do you ask?" John's eyebrows wrinkled in thought as he glanced in the progenitor's direction.

I ask because I can tell you that your wife loves you with every fiber of her being, but if you still cannot figure out your place in this, you have to be "as dumb as a box of rocks." That is how humans say that, right?

"I'm just trying to help. I don't remember you being such an asshole the last time we were here."

There was more mental laughter. *You and your strange family have been rubbing off on me. Especially Sam. I have learned much of your modern humor from him.*

John made a mental note to "thank" Sam for his contribution when this was all over.

I tried explaining to you to stop trying to see everything as a battle. This may be a battle, but it is not your battle. No one needs you to be a soldier right now. Do not only think about the "what" of your wife's actions, but look at the "how" of what she is doing. Do I need to remind you of how much power she commands?

"No."

Consider how desperate and violent her actions have been since she exited the stasis chamber. If there had been any true vampiric power behind what she was doing, this cavern most likely would not be here anymore. Both of us would likely be piles of ash at the bottom of a crater.

John was beginning to see what the progenitor was trying to point out. Despite how loud her wails and cries were, his eardrums hadn't even ruptured.

I know how much it hurts you as her claws and fangs rake and pierce your flesh, but in her current state, do you think she is even aware of doing these things? Is she not simply trying to cling to you as tightly and closely as she can? I know that you see the blood-sweat and the never-ending bloody tears, but look closer. What do you really *see?*

John was trying so hard to understand. He knew the progenitor could have just told him, but somehow he understood the need to know for himself. Brushing her hair to the side, he could see her eyes seemingly staring off into infinity even as her hands clutched his clothing, eyes that darted to his, and he was able to briefly look into them with no tears in the way. The eye contact couldn't have been more than a few seconds before she threw her arms around him completely and began sobbing into his shoulder.

"I see my wife." It was starting to make sense to him now, and he felt the progenitor's pleasure in his mind.

Yes, you do. You have told me you are husband and wife first, vampires second. All her suffering was done to her as a mortal, a woman, a wife, and a mother, and most of it was caused by vampires or other types

266

of demonic monsters wearing her own face. You saw a part of that yourself. In fact, until she truly recovers, it is very possible she will be afraid of, or at least reject, what she truly is.

"Great, something else to add to the list." John twirled his fingers in imaginary writing.

The point is right now there is barely any coherency to her actions, yet she is neither trying to run away or hide in a corner or do anything of the sort. The only coherent thing she has done since she collapsed was cling to you, which she did immediately and shows no sign of stopping. So when will you stop asking the question long enough to simply hear and see the answer? John tightened his embrace and was rewarded with Danielle responding in kind, which also served to drive her claws into his back.

"I get it now, but would it kill her to be coherent enough to lose the claws?" He was only half joking since even he wouldn't be able to keep healing the small wounds forever.

So your wife suffered centuries of infinite horrors and you are suffering from a few scratches. The progenitor sent John the image of a scale in his mind, his side not the winning one.

"Seriously though, how well can you communicate with my friends if they aren't inside the cavern? I mean, can you give them specific instructions?" John had an idea.

I can speak with Sam normally from anywhere. Your ghouls need to be present for complex conversations. Why do you ask?

"Well, I was thinking." He began stroking Danielle's hair. It seemed to calm her slightly, but that could have been his imagination. "She likes flowers, although it's supposed to be a secret, so we all pretend to not know." He rolled his eyes. "I realize this cavern doesn't have any natural light or anything, but we may as well spruce the place up a bit."

What did you have in mind? John sensed amusement.

"Well, if you can pass on the instructions, my people can bring some furniture and extra blood for me and maybe do some nice flower arrangements. Not sure how long they would last in here, but I think enough of them would be a nice touch, and you know." He shrugged his shoulders. "It sounds silly, but maybe the smell might make her feel better. What do you think?"

Child, I think that is the first intelligent thing you have said.

Danielle woke to the lovely scent of fresh lilac and jasmine. She could feel John still sleeping next to her, so she tried shifting position on the bed carefully to not wake him as she looked around. There was a vague sense of something terrible in her mind, but it felt like a distant memory. More interesting was that they were clearly in the progenitor's cavern, yet several someones had clearly been busy.

Portable lights had been brought in, and there was random furniture scattered around, most of which belonged in their house thousands of miles away. She saw a few rather futuristic-looking machines, and even temporary walls had been set up to give the sense of additional rooms. Most of all were the beautiful flowers arranged simply everywhere. They filled the air with their scent and made the whole cavern feel alive. It was quite pleasant, very weird, but pleasant.

She wondered briefly how long she had been asleep for all this to have happened, but the more she wondered, the darker her thoughts became. As if sensing her brief distress, John reached out to her in his sleep. Catching his hand, Danielle gave it a gentle kiss and noticed that not only had they both been sleeping fully clothed, but their clothes were badly shredded.

Something weird was definitely going on, but answers could wait. There was no threat she could detect for the moment, and she was terribly thirsty. Surely her family wouldn't have gone through all this trouble without including . . . There it was—a nice, shiny refrigerator—and Danielle couldn't care less how it was receiving power. She kissed John's hand again and set it down with a gentle pat as she started climbing out of the bed.

"You think I'm going to settle for that after all you just put me through?" John called out, suddenly waking and grabbing her arm.

"What? Ah!" Danielle cried out as John yanked her back into the bed in front of him as his free hand found one of her breasts. The first kiss he planted on her was as deep as it was passionate but perfectly normal. The second kiss saw his fangs entering her throat.

"Oh my!" she squealed as she leaned back, body tensing in ecstasy as she reached back to bury her fingers in his hair. "Please," she begged, licking her lips as her own fangs protruded.

He released her throat just long enough for her to turn around. It was only fair, considering that taking her from behind meant she couldn't share. They fed on each other, a bit more violently than normal, but completely at peace.

Get a room, the progenitor invaded their thoughts, and they grudgingly began licking each other's wounds closed. *That was a terrible risk. I warned you of how her mind might react.*

John knew the progenitor was talking to him, but he disagreed with the assessment.

"Not really. I just don't think you understand the situation," he answered as Danielle snuggled and purred at his side. "Sexual urges have to be among the most primal of all mortal feelings, so they are the perfect thing to use in a situation like this." John stretched back in the bed. "It's been a very long couple of weeks, and both of us are seriously pent up.

"I do remember you saying how much of her torture happened with her being a mortal, so it's very possible that physical pleasure in the mortal sense could be very dangerous right now. The vampiric equivalent is safer and instantaneous, and I also noticed how her eyes went to the fridge when she thought I was still sleeping."

No one was interrupting him, so John just kept going on with his explanation.

"You will also notice that I took her from behind rather than letting her face me. There was never a question of how her body would respond to my bite, but how would her mind react? If we were facing each other, she would have simply bit me out of reflex. This way, her body had to respond, and she needed to make the conscious decision to turn around and join in, which she did.

"There is also no darker or more sinister display of pure vampiric lust that I can think of, yet she did not hesitate for an instant. I feel it was the perfect test for her state of mind, as far as accepting or rejecting what she is." John was so engrossed in demonstrating his brilliance that he had barely noticed Danielle leaving the bed to grab a thermos from the refrigerator.

Interesting. That is surprisingly well thought out, for you.

Danielle started laughing and had to cup her mouth to keep from spitting blood across the floor while John simply wore a pained expression.

I admit there is one part I do not understand. In order to experience what you claim, does not the other vampire have to give themselves freely? You took her without giving the choice, hence the risk.

"Um, you are half right. You see, once a vampire gives themselves freely enough times to another, the question no longer needs to be asked.

269

Theoretically, Danielle could fight against me tooth and nail, but the instant my fangs pierce her flesh, it's pure ecstasy, and vice versa. The part of the body matters as well." John traced a line down the side of his throat.

"Right here is the sweet spot for us. Feeding from a random mortal here gives us a strong feeling of pleasure."

Danielle nodded in agreement as she drank.

"So biting each other in the same place? It's essentially an instant orgasm. I mean, you saw literal proof a minute ago." John winked while Danielle simply blushed.

I admit that I did not know that, and it is quite fascinating.

"Most people don't know because most vampires don't survive the experience enough times to realize it. We learned by accident a long time ago from just playing around," John continued the explanation while watching his wife explore the cavern.

"Not to change the subject, but is it just me, or did he get funnier? Also, why did you guys bring all this stuff in here? I'm not complaining." She bent down to smell some roses. "Just curious."

"Apparently, Sam taught him a few things," John said, rolling his eyes.

"Really? Damn, how long was I asleep?"

"Yeah, about that. So you have no idea how much time has passed?" John tossed some fresh clothes at her before beginning to get changed himself.

"Since what?" She finished changing and sounded a bit confused.

Tread carefully, child. John had the sense the progenitor was talking only to him.

"Well, since we fought Dracula. Do you remember?" John was smiling sweetly, trying to close the distance to her without being obvious about it.

Everything had seemed fine a few moments ago, but now there was definitely the familiar feeling of yet another shoe ready to drop.

"I remember a little bit, but we won, so who cares? Not like it's the first time I got beat up so bad to affect my memories." She bent down to smell more flowers. "It is really so great that you all did this. I know you all pretend to ignore how much I love flowers—hey, what's over here?" She had been circling the area to smell all the arrangements, and she finally made it to the far end, where one final wall was in the way.

"Sweety, why don't you come back over here? The three of us have a lot to talk about."

"Yeah, yeah, in a sec." She waved nonchalantly at them. "I just want to see—"

She froze in midsentence as she looked around the final wall and saw the stasis chamber housing the entity of darkness. Her thermos fell to the floor as she dropped into a combat stance, her coat billowing out behind her.

"Dani, wait!" John screamed, blurring to cover the distance and stand in front of her.

"What is that thing doing here?" she screamed at him. "We have to kill it; we have to kill it *now!*"

"No, Dani! It's in stasis, it's contained." He tried grabbing hold of her even as she approached the chamber.

She looked at him in shock. "Why are you blocking me?" She started pushing against him.

"Because, dear, you are trying to release an entity of infinite darkness that's capable of effectively murdering the entire planet. Quite frankly, it's not the vacation I had in mind for us."

"I'm not trying to release it. I'm going to kill it. I have to kill it!"

"You can't kill it, that's why it's in stasis." John tried to push her back.

"I don't even know what that means." She backhanded him and sent John flying to the other side of the chamber.

"Jesus, woman, read a sci-fi novel for once in your life," he exclaimed, picking himself out of the rubble. "A little help?"

Agreed. An invisible force crushed Danielle to the ground as the progenitor tried to safely contain her.

Her mind and memories were clearly in disarray. She recognized the enemy but didn't seem to remember how to fight it properly.

"No need to be so gentle," Danielle uttered as she slowly started to pull her body forward. "It's not my first time!"

John quickly rushed to her side where she was still dragging her body closer to the chamber.

"What are you doing?" he screamed at her as he saw her skin and flesh scrape away against the cavern floor.

"I told you; I'm going to kill it." Her words were pained, but she was able to keep her face out of the dirt.

"With what?" He jumped on top of her. John didn't want to hurt her, but for some reason, the progenitor's hold wasn't working completely.

271

"Who cares?" She kept dragging herself closer. "I'll hit it with a rock!"

"Are you even listening to yourself?"

Was it some vague memory of her successfully killing the entity in her mind with a rock that was causing her sudden behavior? He grabbed her legs and started pulling her backward.

"The entity isn't corporeal; you can't kill it with a rock."

"Then I'll use an anti-corporeal rock." She was straining with all her might against both the progenitor and her husband.

"A what?" He had no idea what was going on, but clearly her mind hadn't healed the way they had thought, and where was all this strength coming from? "You don't know what the word *corporeal* means, do you?"

"No!" She rolled over and kicked him in the face.

John saw eyes of pure red. It wasn't frenzy or bloody tears; he didn't know what it was.

"Dammit." He picked himself back up again. "Can't you stop her?"

No. If I use any more pressure, she will be destroyed.

"Then how the hell is she still moving?"

Even as he spoke, Danielle was rising, claws outstretched and fangs bared.

I do not know. Unless—

"Unless what?"

Remember when I said I was feeding her power so she could heal?

"Oh shit."

Indeed. I can dampen her magic and powers, but you need to stop her physically.

"I was afraid you were going to say that." John didn't relish the idea of facing his wife in hand-to-hand combat, not if she was being fueled with power from the progenitor.

"Why are you just sitting there?"

Danielle was ignoring all but her target, the cloud within that strange glass box. Her movements were coming slowly, but she was still able to force herself through each step.

"Why won't you fight me?" Her face was a demonic mask, and energy was crackling around her as she fought through the progenitor's hold. "You thought you could just torment me?"

Something grabbed her shoulder, but she shrugged it off and took another step.

"You thought you could make me suffer, you thought to kill me?" This time her voice carried plenty of vampiric power, and the cavern's stone walls and ceiling began to crack.

The hand on her shoulder was back, and she pushed it away violently before taking another step.

"You thought you could rape me?" her voice echoed, and her power was creating a pressure the progenitor was unable to hold back. "I'm not the weak mortal woman you tortured! Fight me now! *FACE ME!*"

The cloud simply ignored her taunts, safe in its glass box. Danielle knew what she had to do, and she began raising her arm.

"*STOP!*" John collided with her and tackled her to the side. "Dani, please, what are you doing?" John tried holding her back but knew it wouldn't last.

"Why are you in my way?" she screamed at him as they started exchanging blows. "We have to destroy that thing. It can't be contained. Why don't you understand? Why are you protecting it?"

"What? Protecting it? I'm trying to protect you!" John was barely holding his own in the fight.

She was stronger and faster than he had ever seen her, but for the moment, neither of them was trying to seriously hurt the other.

"Protecting me!"

John could barely recognize the mask of fury that was shouting at him.

"Four thousand seven hundred and forty-one," Danielle said and stopped fighting after saying the number, and seemed to simply wait for a response.

John didn't know how to read the situation, only that she wasn't attacking anymore, so he took the chance to get closer.

"Four thousand seven hundred and forty-one," she repeated, her eyes still blazing red.

"Dani, my love," he said as he held up his hands in a calming gesture. "I don't understand."

He took another step closer, and she leaped at him. Clutching his clothes and screaming into his face, Danielle literally flew John into one of the cavern walls.

"*THAT'S HOW MANY TIMES I DIED!*" She was shaking him as if he were made of straw. "For two hundred years, I suffered! For two hundred years, I lived in hell to be raped and tortured and murdered thousands of times!"

Try as he might, John couldn't break her grip.

273

"I was alone! *WHERE WAS YOUR PROTECTION THEN?*"

He had the distinct impression he was hearing more than one voice, but it was hard to tell given the amount of energy and power she was releasing.

"Where were you?" The accusation was barely a whisper, yet it echoed through the cavern.

"I was cutting your fucking head off!"

John had finally had enough of this. His wife wasn't the only one who had suffered, and it was time someone reminded her rather than just tiptoeing on eggshells. She dropped him suddenly, shocked at his words.

"You? What?"

She reflexively touched her neck, and John could feel the pressure around her lessening. She looked down at him, and though her eyes were still pure red, they did seem a bit softer.

"Dammit, woman!" he shouted up at where she was still somehow hovering. "I am sorry, so sorry for what you had to go through, but what about me?" John slapped himself in the chest. "Do you think it's easy for me to watch the woman I love rip herself apart, time and time again, just because you decide it's the only way? To watch you make decisions I don't even understand, much less agree to?"

Danielle opened her mouth to respond, but John cut her off with a wave of his hand.

"No! It's your turn to listen! Now, maybe your decisions were the right ones, but they were *your* decisions, and every time you rip yourself apart, I'm the one left to put you back together. You have been breaking my heart since the instant we woke up in Dracula's dungeon." John's eyes began to redden slightly. "Then that thing possessed you, and then it became you, and I fell for it!"

Tears were flowing freely now, but he gave no notice, and Danielle lowered herself to stand in front of him.

"If I hadn't heard you calling out to me, I would've never noticed, but I *did* hear you." He reached out and gripped her shoulders. "I glimpsed the terrible horrors you were enduring, and I did what I could to save you. I felt your fingers crush my heart even as I saw myself take your head."

She didn't resist as he began to shake her.

"I don't know where that ranks on your list of horrors, but every time I close my eyes, I see my wife's head rolling across the floor."

She seemed to be staring at him in shock, although it was hard to tell without pupils.

"Then I found you in that hellish mindscape, and I brought you back to me. Maybe that was wrong, maybe I should have let you die and rest, but I couldn't. I just could not live without you."

He embraced her, and both bodies were shaking with sobs.

"See, love, there's plenty of suffering to go around."

"I'm sorry," she said, crying into his shoulder, her voice somewhat back to normal. "John, I'm scared." She placed a hand on her temple. "My head doesn't feel right, it's like my mind is burning. I don't know what's happening to me," she whispered weakly.

"I know, honey, I know." He kissed her forehead. "But we'll figure it out together."

"I have to kill it!" Her face suddenly snapped up, hard with resolve.

"We can't!"

"I have no choice!" She pulled his face down to hers. "I'll never be free."

"Please," he pleaded with her. He didn't think there was any way they would survive another battle with the entity. "We can figure out how to kill it later. It's contained."

"*But I'm not!*" she screamed into his face.

Once again, he seemed to hear voices on top of voices.

"John, you have to get away from me," her voice grew softer, and he could see the fear in her eyes. "There's something here"—her eyes began darting around—"something inside . . ."

Her voice cut off as she tried pushing him away.

"*I can't stop what's happening!*" She wrapped her arms around her head and started to scream.

Jonathon, back away. It was the progenitor using his name for the first time that broke John out of his stupor, and he quickly blurred to the other side of the cavern.

Danielle's screams raised in pitch until her entire body convulsed, back arched, as she practically exploded with power.

"What's happening? What did she mean?"

There was no answer.

He watched in shocked silence as the red in her eyes was replaced with pure golden white, and it didn't stop there. The same golden white light seemed to radiate from her entire body, which no longer gave any appearance of tension as it glided across the cavern. It was as beautiful as it was terrifying to watch, until she sent a bolt of light into the stasis

275

chamber, destroying it and releasing the entity instantly. Then it was simply terrifying.

Jonathon, what do you see? The progenitor's voice got his attention.

"We seriously don't have time for these games again." He wasn't in the mood to play twenty questions.

Dammit, child, my eyes do not work like yours anymore! What do you see?

He accepted the rebuke as he hadn't realized the progenitor had been asking a normal question.

"Um, I see my batshit-crazy wife unleashing a being of infinite horror, so you know, normal Tuesday night I guess." John didn't think there was any point in even grabbing his sword.

Are you certain?

"Well, yeah, pretty obvious. Wait, why?" How was he supposed to know what was going on, when even the progenitor sounded confused?

Even in stasis, I was able to sense the entity's presence.

"Who cares?" He could feel a mental growl in response to his snide remark.

A moment ago, I sensed four separate entities in this cavern, including myself. Then, for the briefest of instants, I thought I sensed a fifth, but now I sense thousands. John could actually feel the progenitor's disbelief at his own statement.

"Thousands? How is that even possible?"

It is not.

"But, you're sure?"

I am.

"Well, I am seeing some crazy shit right now, but even I can't miss thousands of people, so where are they?"

There is far too much combined power at work here for me to see that clearly, but I think you know the answer.

"Aw, hell." John wondered for the thousandth time why he couldn't have married a normal woman—well, a normal ancient vampire woman anyway. "There's not a damn thing either of us can do right now, is there?"

Pray for a quick and painless death?

"Seriously, when did you turn into a comedian?"

Afraid of a little competition?

The cloud had begun collecting itself on the ceiling, much in the same way as the first time they encountered it. John watched as his wife flew directly at the darkness, sending bolts of pure light ahead of her. The cloud quickly shifted position and began moving about the cavern. It was difficult to be sure, as the darkness of the cloud made it hard to discern specific movements, but John had the distinct impression it was trying to run away.

Considering the entity wasn't a corporeal being, it should have been able to escape easily, yet it seemed trapped within the cavern. The bolts of light left no mark on the cavern walls, but whenever they connected with the cloud, there was a loud sizzle and hiss, and John could hear unearthly screams of pain. He also realized he wasn't afraid. He was terrified at what was happening to his wife, of course, but there was no true fear in having an entity of supposedly infinite darkness flying around the cavern.

"It doesn't feel like I'm watching a battle," he mumbled, more to himself than at the progenitor.

You are not. This is an execution.

John watched as the cloud gave up trying to escape and began fighting back. Dark protrusions lashed out at his wife and began slicing her apart. He watched as her limbs flew away, her torso was carved into pieces, and he even saw her head cut off more than once, but each time she regenerated instantly. As he watched more closely, he realized that *regenerated* might not be the best word for what was happening. It was simply too fast, almost as if she were *replacing* anything she'd lost. The whole time she continued screaming challenges at the entity, her voice somehow sounding pieced together from multiple sources.

"Infinite darkness? Infinite suffering?" she screamed in question as she flew through the cavern. "You simply prey on the weak."

She sent a bolt of light into the center of the cloud, causing it to freeze in place and hiss.

"What will you do when the weak fight back?"

She quickly flew the remaining distance, grabbing the cloud that was several times larger than her and wrestled it to the cavern floor.

This is not possible. The progenitor sent the thought into John's mind as they witnessed Danielle physically restraining a being with no true physical form.

"Quiet."

John was simply too mesmerized by what he was seeing to be concerned about silly things like the laws of physics or reality. He watched as she rolled around on the floor, with her arms wrapped around the entity. The cloud seemed to try and spread in order to engulf her, but she simply laughed. Her laughter echoed through the cavern as she rose into the air, still clinging to the cloud.

"As you cause suffering, so shall you suffer!"

The cloud seemed to writhe and scream in pain, desperate to escape.

"*I am the light!*" she screamed as her hands began to glow. "And you are just so . . . insignificant."

The echoing voices were but a whisper as the glow engulfed the cloud, and it was simply gone.

"What just happened?" John asked in the sudden silence.

I do not know, but the entity is gone. She destroyed it completely.

"You told me that wasn't possible."

It is not.

"You are seriously not helping." John clearly wasn't going to get any useful advice from the progenitor, but at least the entity was gone.

The glowing, fiery being that was supposed to be his wife landed softly in the center of the cavern, its task complete. The golden white fire surrounding her didn't seem to be lessening, and in the silence, he could almost hear a faint humming sound. He could see the orbs of her eyes looking around, as if confused, even as the fire gained in intensity.

"*AAAHHH!*" The scream echoed from the cavern walls, cracking them and the ceiling even more. Her body convulsed as before, back arched and levitating several meters off the ground, even as the light grew brighter. "*JJJOOHHNNN!*"

He didn't hesitate.

Child, no!

As if he would listen.

John collided with Danielle, but the force wasn't enough to knock her down or to break free of whatever was happening. So he simply embraced her as they hovered in the center of the cavern. As he looked into her radiance, she had never seemed so beautiful, even as he felt the fire spread to him.

"I can't make it stop!" she cried at him.

"I know, love."

"Why do these things keep happening to us?" she whimpered, looking at him through golden white orbs, their brilliance marred slightly with bloody tears. "It's not fair," she cried softly.

"I know."

"I'm really scared."

Don't be.

The soft mental whisper went unnoticed, but it clearly had not come from the progenitor. John pulled her head down into his shoulder and rested his on hers. Their screams melded into one as the light burned through them both before exploding into the cavern.

CHAPTER 17

Progenitor's Cavern

Watching you two sleep is boring.

The mental shake was enough to rouse the pair, who were still lying on the ground where they had collapsed. They slowly rose, blinking and covering their eyes slightly. The cavern was noticeably brighter than it had been, and both of them noticed their eyes feeling oddly sensitive.

"Aren't you a gazillion years old?" John grumbled as he helped Danielle up.

That is not a real number, and my age is irrelevant. I was simply tired of waiting for you.

The pair were checking each other for injuries, but they both felt remarkably well.

I assure you that you are both unharmed, and I sense you are waiting for me to explain what just transpired.

"I don't care if you explain it, or if she does, but yes, someone needs to start talking." There was an edge of impatience in his voice. "Seriously, though, Dani, how do you really feel?" The concern was evident as he grabbed hold of her hand.

"Great. To be honest, better than I've felt in a long time. Unfortunately, if you are waiting for me to explain things, you're wasting your time. I remember most of what happened, but everything is still pretty jumbled up," she said, pointing to her head. "The last thing I remember clearly was walking around, smelling flowers, and then just . . .," she said, pausing a moment in thought before shrugging her shoulders. "Sorry, a few weird images are all I have, and nothing to explain the 'how' of any of it."

"Do you still remember your prior struggles with the entity? *All* your prior struggles?" John didn't know how else to phrase the question without drawing too much attention to that horrible situation.

"What, you mean all that torture and suffering and crap?" She stretched lazily. "Sure I do."

"You seem to be handling it quite well this time." John's suspicion was clear in his voice.

"Honestly, I'm taking a page from your book," she said and pointed to him. "We won, I feel great, so who cares?"

"Despite the impossible things that literally just happened?"

"To be fair, most of those things are the parts I don't remember very well. I admit to being curious, but I'm content to simply not be under attack for the moment."

It didn't sound unreasonable to her, but John wasn't satisfied.

"Nope, this is the damn SOG thing all over again." He waved his arms in exasperation.

"Huh? John, that was over ten years ago."

"Yeah, and look at how that ended. We did our best, but we were on the run and had taken serious losses. Then"—he snapped his fingers—"literally overnight, it was over and we won."

He turned to face the progenitor. "We know now that was your doing, but it simply dragged us into an even worse series of battles. Now, after all that fighting and suffering, after all that terror"—he snapped his fingers again—"it's over. We are perfectly fine, despite fighting an entity straight from hell or the abyss or wherever the stupid thing came from.

He faced his wife. "Dani, I watched you destroy something that doesn't really even exist in this world the way the three of us do. Even the cloud we saw was a result of us processing images that our brains can't understand. I'm right about that, aren't I?" he tossed the question over his shoulder.

Yes.

"And what about all those extra voices? Those thousands of entities the progenitor sensed. You said you died thousands of times."

Danielle's eye twitched slightly at the memory.

"Are we supposed to believe that you brought them all into battle with you? That's not only impossible, but it's completely ridiculous. They were never real."

"They were real to me." Danielle's eyes grew hard, and John immediately regretted his choice of words.

281

"Sorry, but you know what I meant. I'm right about this too, aren't I?"

Yes. My daughter, it was very clever of you to store the power I was feeding you. I see now that you had little interest in healing. You were simply using my power to stay alive long enough for a final confrontation, and I do not believe you were fully aware that you were doing so. It might explain why I sensed something else within you when I thought you were healing and why you seemed so confused by your own actions.

This, however, does not make the impossible possible. During the final battle, I did not sense a single extremely powerful entity, as I should have, but thousands of distinctly separate entities. You were also killed many times before you won. My power cannot do what you used it to do. There is no power I am aware of that can give life to something that does not exist in this world. Yet we did witness these things. I am certain of my senses, even if I do not understand how.

"And that doesn't bother anyone else?" He could tell his wife agreed with him, even if she was staying silent. "There's something you aren't telling us, and you," he said, fixing on Danielle with scolding eyes, "I think you remember more than you are telling me."

She tried to match his gaze but lowered her eyes after a few seconds.

"Yes, okay, I remember all of it, even the end, but it doesn't help. I don't understand most of it, but I do remember doing or seeing those things we just agreed are impossible. Quite frankly, I am a little scared that none of this is real, and you playing twenty questions isn't helping." Her voice raised a bit by the end, but she still appeared under control.

"Oh, sweetheart." He hugged her. "I guess from your perspective, that's not an unreasonable concern. I think it's time to tell us the rest." It was clear where the demand was directed.

Very well, but please try and remain calm.

Confusion crossed their features at the warning, but the progenitor continued before either of them could speak.

You recall when I tried to stop you from aiding her at the very end?

John nodded.

Whatever was happening was blinding my senses. Danielle was there, emitting power and energy I had never sensed before, and it grew so powerful I could no longer sense her presence within it. John, I tried to stop you because to me, it appeared she was already gone and you were leaping to your death. Never have I sensed anything like this, and I

282

expected us both to be destroyed within seconds. However, when you collided with her, it created—the progenitor paused for a moment to think—*a disruption of sorts.*

There was a very brief moment when I was able to sense inside this energy, before being quickly blinded again. There were three separate entities, but I was unable to determine anything about them. When it was over, the energy simply ceased, leaving two entities behind, which I later determined to be the two of you.

The progenitor didn't have a chance to say anything else before John threw his arms up in the air.

"You see? You see?" he said and started pointing accusatory fingers in random directions. "What did I say? What did I *fucking* say? This is bullshit! All of it." He started waving his arms to indicate the previous battle, or maybe just everything in general.

John, calm down, please.

"No! I will not calm down." He jabbed a finger at the progenitor's unseeing eyes. "If she's allowed to go insane whenever she wants, then I can too, dammit, and I have officially had enough of this shit. None of this makes any fucking sense."

He started pacing back and forth angrily while Danielle watched in concern. Normally, their roles would be reversed, and seeing things from this perspective was a new experience for her. He was the rock, not her, and she didn't have a clue what to do.

JONATHON!

"Get the fuck out of my head!" He stared threateningly at the progenitor, who could crush him in an instant. "I mean it, if you can't talk like a normal person, then just shut the fuck up! I swear to God, I will rip you from that wall and toss you in the ocean." He paused in his tirade and was met with deafening silence.

"I mean, come on, what are we supposed to do now? Get ready to fight some super powerful entity of light? Maybe get contacted by said entity, just to be thrown into more unknown battles that we can't survive? Sound familiar? Well, guess what? I fucking quit! How's that?"

"John, honey—" she started reaching out to him just to get cut off as he turned his eyes on her, eyes that were quickly reddening with frenzy.

"Don't you even start with me, not now! I'm tired of this ridiculous game. How many times do we have to die, just to stay dead?" He took a single step in her direction, and Danielle fell back in fear.

In nine hundred years, John had never completely frenzied on his own outside of controlled outbursts in battle. She was so scared that for a brief instant, she wondered if none of this was real and simply another horror for her to endure.

Daughter, this is real. Please, you must stop him. The progenitor had clearly read her thoughts, but he was insane if he thought she could anything about it.

"Turning into a vampire, you, stasis chambers, medical nanites, imaginary beings from outside the realm of possibility, I wonder what the next excuse for keeping us alive will be? What's the point of even trying to survive or fighting at all if we're simply not allowed to die?"

Danielle did not like his random pacing or seeing his fingers morphing back and forth from claws to normal.

There's nothing I can do. She felt it wise to switch to telepathy. *He's had small outbursts in the past, but this is a complete frenzy. Even trying to feed on each other won't work for this, it would make his frenzy worse and render me defenseless. Just use your power to subdue him.* Danielle didn't know why the progenitor hadn't already done that.

I cannot.

Why the hell not? This could be bad. She was effectively paralyzed in fear of her own husband, despite the odd familiarity of the situation.

I was not allowed to finish my explanation earlier. You are both far more powerful than before. I can still destroy you, but you are too strong for me to safely subdue. Neither of us wants to kill him, so that means he can probably kill both of us. Any intervention from me will make things worse. It has to be you, and you need a plan that does not involve combat.

It wanted her to come up with a plan? As she could feel the pressure building around him, it was hard to even look into his red eyes.

I'm sorry, but I don't know how to face him like this.

Then in the moments before he kills us both, I hope you feel the shame you deserve.

The harsh comment got her attention, but she didn't think it was fair. What could she possibly do?

It is not easy to see things from this side of the glass, is it daughter? His methods did not always work, but he was always there to fix you after, and he never let his fear reduce him to worthlessness.

Images started to fill her mind, courtesy of the progenitor, images taken from her husband's mind, allowing her to finally see what it was like for him when she lost control, and the familiar pieces finally came together. By comparison, what she was witnessing was nothing compared to how bad she became when she lost control, not to mention how often it

284

had happened to her lately. She recalled John's words from the beginning of the final fight when he had scolded her about ignoring his own suffering. Shame washed through her, robbing her of what little strength she had left.

If it was this bad for her, then how much worse had he endured? She couldn't even stand, whereas he had never given up. Fighting or even sacrificing yourself to a superior enemy for the other was simple compared to this. How could she claim to love or be married to this man if she was willing to simply watch him lose control? To hide in the corner and expect others, like the progenitor, to do her job?

How many times had they admitted the only reason their eternal lives worked was because they had each other? No matter how bad things became for one, the other was there to help pick up the pieces. Was it all a lie? Certainly, she had been there for him during plenty of bad times, but his bad times had yet to include a single instance of complete loss of control.

In reality it had always been him picking up her pieces. This time it was finally her turn, the first time she was truly needed for reasons other than simple power and abilities, and it was worse than failure. She hadn't bothered even trying. The shame and fear that she didn't deserve to be his wife almost broke her completely. Almost.

You think I can borrow some of that power of yours? She stood up slowly as red eyes studied her every move.

Do not fight him, came the unnecessary warning.

I don't plan on it, but I need to try and survive long enough to get through to him.

She quickly felt a rush of fresh energy coming from the progenitor and began walking toward her husband slowly but purposefully. Keeping her arms outstretched, she looked him directly in the eye as she approached.

Mind your heart, daughter. With my power added, it can heal but not regenerate, and there is no one here to put you in stasis.

This is the only plan I have, and I can't control what he does. I'm focusing everything I have on radiating calm and healing damage, if any, to my heart. The rest of my body is on its own.

If she had a pulse, it would be racing. She was close enough now to be affected by the pressure of his power and matched it with her own. It was very difficult, but she tried avoiding any semblance of actual confrontation. Instead, she allowed her presence to simply mingle with his own.

As Danielle got within arm's reach, she began to feel the pressure lessening, and hope began to replace the fear. She began raising her arms to embrace him as John plunged the claws of his left hand into her chest. Pain and shock froze her in place as he tore the claws outward in an arc, leaving gaping wounds and severing her right arm above the elbow.

Losing her balance, she tried to fall the remaining distance and complete the embrace with one arm. Even as she could feel the dust of her severed appendage brush her skin, the claws of John's right hand buried themselves into her guts. As she started coughing up and choking on blood, she got her left arm around his neck and started calling out to him.

John responded to her with his own embrace and drove the claws from both hands through her back, severing her spine. Worse, two of them went through her heart. She was able to heal the damage, but not completely, since the claws themselves were in the way. As they moved and created fresh wounds, she could keep up only by not healing anything else.

Since her lower body no longer worked, she tightened her grip to keep from falling. Blood was pouring from her mouth even as tears created red streaks of their own. A part of her mind realized her body wasn't responding to the injuries the way it should be, and it was taking most of her effort to simply keep talking.

"You held me for days as I screamed and bit and tore at you." She coughed mouthfuls of blood over him as she tried to speak. "I couldn't even manage to hold you once with both arms."

She didn't think she had much longer, but there was no turning back now. In some ways, her power was working against her.

No amount of power could protect against vampiric claws since they could cut through anything. So she suffered the same injuries as a fledgling would have; she was just able to survive it longer. Unfortunately, being an ancient vampire meant those same injuries that were inflicted so easily were very difficult to heal. She had been hurt too badly too quickly, and it was starting to look as if the rest of her body would simply fall apart. Despite her earlier fear, she truly hadn't expected to fail so quickly.

I'm so fucking pathetic, her throat was too full of blood to even speak.

I wouldn't have married you if that were true, my love.

John! You're in control? Her heart leaped, but she was still running out of time.

Yes, I'm sorry, but—

John, shut up. It sounded harsh, but the crisis was averted, and it was time for damage control.

They had both been through enough battles that she was sure he would understand, and she was losing ground rapidly.

Don't move. I'm serious, don't twitch a damn muscle. You have claws in my heart, and I can barely keep up with the healing around them. She coughed up more blood. *Every time I cough, my body jerks, and it causes more damage. My body isn't working right, and I think I'm dying.*

She could sense his confusion and concern, but he was following the instructions she had given.

You need to retract your claws, but you need to be very careful to not move your hands or fingers. I have almost no control, thanks to you wrecking my spine. All I can do is focus on my heart while the rest of me falls apart. My wounds aren't even closing, so if you drop me, it might be over.

Her insides were writhing in agony, but she could feel the claws slowly moving out of her body.

Okay, love, good, keep going. I have to fix my heart fast. Just don't move. I have to stop talking now. I just don't have the strength, but everything is going to be okay.

John wasn't sure what had happened, but he knew he had lost control. It was strange. He remembered being extremely angry. He still was, in fact, but what difference did that make? There was no way he would lose total control so easily, and what did Danielle say about her body not acting correctly? Come to think of it, he felt a bit strange himself.

He was also painfully aware that he had badly injured his wife, perhaps fatally. So he was content to stay silent and obey orders, but it wasn't easy. She looked very strange: her eyes almost completely empty, blood bubbling and spurting from her mouth, and except for the viselike grip around his neck, her body was completely limp. If not for her earlier conversation, he would have assumed that she was already dead.

Everything is fine, child, the progenitor said, having decided it was safe to reenter the conversation.

She doesn't look fine to me. John was afraid to even move his facial muscles, so he stuck to telepathy. He was essentially frozen in place, holding a corpse, and expected to be happy about it.

Her brain and heart are intact, there is no ash, and mentally she is fine. Weak and confused, but fine. It is simply a matter of time. Brace yourself.

John didn't understand what the progenitor meant until Danielle started convulsing. He did his best to hold her still, but she was coughing violently, hacking blood directly onto his face. Once her throat was clear, she immediately sank her fangs into his neck.

The movement was so sudden he had been taken off guard, but it made perfect sense, given how badly her body needed blood. The amount of blood she had been coughing up instead of swallowing was odd, but those questions could wait. As his mind started clouding with pleasure, he wished any other part of his body had been available. The urge to feed from her was difficult to ignore, but she was so desperate for blood it could very well kill her. Unfortunately, that knowledge didn't keep his legs from getting weak, further complicating his efforts to hold still while supporting them both.

I would suggest you change positions. It is safe now to move if you are careful.

Are you sure? John didn't want to take any chances.

She does not have the strength to communicate with you, but I am talking with her as we speak. Trust me.

John carefully lowered himself to the ground while manipulating her limp body. It wasn't an easy task given she was also feeding, but eventually, he was lying on the cavern floor with her ravaged torso on top of him even as her useless legs dangled to the side.

The cavern was silent but for the sounds of her feeding, and John was content to just close his eyes and enjoy the experience. She was drinking more quickly and deeply than normal, enough to cause extra damage to his throat, but that was okay with him. He could already start to feel changes as wounds began closing under his hands, and he could see bone and muscle beginning to knit back together through the openings in her chest cavity.

Even through the pleasure, John could feel himself growing weaker from blood loss, but he chose to simply trust her. Considering he was uninjured, it would take very little blood to sustain him until they could get more, and she was welcome to all that remained. Not long after, he felt her cease feeding and close his wounds, but she didn't stop there. There was a considerable amount of blood covering them both from her injuries not closing and her coughing it out.

She spent several minutes devouring every drop she could find on both their bodies while hissing slightly. It was a bit primal, but controlled, and John could see her legs twist into position with the reconstruction of her spine. The situation remained serious, so he was doing his best to not enjoy her antics too much, but it wasn't easy. Eventually, she simply lay with him, caressing his face with her remaining hand.

"I'm so sorry," she said, weeping softly into his neck and shoulder. "I never thought . . . I mean, I never really understood what you . . ."

John stroked her hair as she stammered. "I know, hon, it's okay."

They lay in silence for a few moments before shifting into their normal positions. She was out of danger, but he noticed her right arm was still missing. Considering how weak they both were at the moment, it was most likely a simple choice of priorities, and he decided not to mention it.

"I apologize for what happened. I am not certain how I lost control so easily. However, the point I was making still stands." John might have been a little confused, but he was no less angry about the situation as he was before losing control.

"He's right," Danielle agreed from her curled-up position. "You said we were different now, and we both notice it."

As I was saying before, the progenitor continued as if the last few minutes had never happened. *When the energy ceased, I did not recognize the two of you at first. The auras I am accustomed to seeing from you were different. Whatever happened to you altered you in some way,* the progenitor's mental voice was as soothing as he could make it, most likely in an attempt to keep John from getting angry a second time.

"I still find this whole thing hard to accept."

Danielle's agreement was evident by the way her grip on him tightened.

"How are we supposed to not consider this as just another attack or manipulation?" He was clearly pissed, but the progenitor could sense there would be no further loss of control.

Children, I can sense you're both already returning to what you consider normal. We have witnessed many things here we do not understand, and this could simply have been a strange side effect of this third entity saving you. Anything designed to simply heal can have a strange effect on a vampire, the medical nanites used on you earlier are proof of this.

Danielle shifted positions to simply sit next to her husband.

"I get the feeling you don't believe that to be the case though," she spoke, casting a brief glance at her half-regenerated arm.

My belief is not relevant. I wish to provide only facts since there has been enough confusion for one day. You mentioned the past, but this situation is different. While it is true I ended your struggle with the SOG, that is all I did prior to initiating contact with you. This entity was far more benevolent than I.

"Your people must have a different definition for that word than humans do." John's eyes grew hard. "Being manipulated is not a positive feeling. Why even bother us at all if whatever that new thing was could have destroyed the dark entity so easily whenever it wanted?"

You are making an assumption from a very biased and narrow perspective.

"It looked that way to me, and you said so yourself at the time." John was referring to his and the progenitor's powerlessness during the final confrontation.

I can answer your questions, but not without my own assumptions. At the very least, I have a great deal more experience to draw from, and I am more of an unbiased observer than either of you have been.

The progenitor took their shared silence as permission to continue.

First, we are at least agreed that something else saved you, and you have both likened that to my own interference in your brief war with the SOG?

They both nodded in agreement.

The biggest difference I see in the interference itself is that I could have done so whenever I chose, but you are only assuming that whatever saved you this time had that same freedom. I am uncertain of exactly when this other entity joined the fight at the end. I believe I sensed something "enter" you as you were pushing John away, but I am completely certain it had no direct involvement in your struggles until that point.

John raised his hand, and the progenitor would have rolled his eyes if he could.

"That's pretty much my point," he insisted. "It's messed up to make us go through all that for nothing, and definitely not my definition of the word *benevolent*."

Danielle was content to simply sit and listen while focusing on her arm.

Perhaps it had no choice.

"What do you mean?"

The progenitor hesitated since he hadn't wanted to go beyond facts, but there really wasn't much of a choice.

If we are to assume that entities of great power exist on higher levels or planes of existence, does that not have the potential to render all lower levels of life meaningless? If these great entities simply did whatever they wanted, whenever they wanted to do it, would that not make all of us simple playthings for them? No decisions or actions of any mortal or creature on our plane of existence would matter, since one of "them" could simply do or undo it in an instant on a whim.

"Um, okay," John said slowly. "But what's your point?"

"He's saying," Danielle interrupted, displaying her new arm to the group, "to assume that maybe something good was watching out for us, or at least aware of what was happening, but was unable to do anything. Then something changed, or certain conditions were met or whatever, that allowed it to save us in the end. It didn't simply interfere but used me as a conduit to do so." She wrinkled her nose as she thought.

"I am certain of that last part, and it matches what you both say you saw. Think about it, the whole thing, even the impossible parts, were all my honest ideas. I am starting to remember pretty clearly now, and while there was definitely something there, I felt in control. The progenitor's power wasn't enough to make my idea work, so something else simply did. I don't really understand the very end though." She grabbed John's hand.

"Once it was over, I was really confused. There was so much light and fire, and I could feel the burning," she said and shuddered slightly. "I remember calling out and then John holding me. The pain was terrible, and I figured we were both done for, but then we woke up, and then John lost control, and our bodies were different," she finished.

"I would like to point out that everything you have both said is effectively guesswork as to this thing's intentions. What makes your guesswork any more accurate than mine?" It was a fair question.

You are correct, but I believe the few facts we have point to benevolent intentions. Danielle was being assisted, not controlled, but what made this possible? Consider the amount of power she was wielding and her state of mind the instant this other entity chose to interfere.

I believe every decision you have both made, every battle either won or lost, and every bit of suffering you both endured culminated in creating the circumstances that allowed this other entity to use her as a conduit. John, even your attempts to stop her could have been needed as a way to distract her active mind and allow for another to enter her safely and unnoticed. Further, I believe if either of you had failed to give everything you had at any moment, there would have been no outside assistance. You had to fight and sacrifice to your own destruction so that something else could step in and remake you.

"Sorry, man." John wasn't convinced. "It's a nice theory and all, but you're starting to get a bit preachy for my tastes."

291

I am simply telling you what happened. How it happened remains a mystery, but my theory is just as sound as any other, unless you can disprove it. It is also a fact that you were both healed at the end. Danielle, now is a good time to ask the question you are holding back.

John turned to his wife, who looked slightly confused.

"Well, no big deal or anything, but I said I remember the whole final fight, right?"

John nodded and motioned for her to continue.

"I just don't know why I was saying the things I was saying. I mean, I remember everything I said or did, but I don't have a clue what I was talking about, and I am relatively certain I was not being controlled."

Danielle, do you remember facing the dark entity for the first time?

"Of course I do, why?"

Please tell us exactly what happened and what you remember.

John had the impression that Danielle's next response would be very important. He also suspected the progenitor already knew what it would be.

"Not much to tell, really," she said shrugging. "I mean, it hurt like hell when I absorbed it, but no big deal. I woke up in bed and pretty confused." She narrowed her eyes. "Everything was a bit jumbled, but pretty peaceful, until I saw the entity again in the stasis chamber. That's when I started saying and doing all that crazy shit."

Is this enough proof for you, John?

He was too busy gaping in shock to respond.

"Wait, why are you both looking at me like that?" She couldn't confirm the progenitor was actually looking at her, but she was sure he would get the meaning.

"Dani, oh my god, that's not what happened at all. You don't—"

That is enough.

Danielle was looking at her husband in confusion.

I had suspected this but was not certain until now. My daughter, terrible things were done to you, but it would seem they have all been removed. Your memories are not being blocked or protected. For you, that missing time never existed.

More interesting is that you had this time during your brief struggle with John. I sensed your bodies returning to normal after that incident, and it is my guess that is when they were taken from you. To me, this proves that the differences I sensed in you both once the entity left were done intentionally to encourage your final conflict.

"But why? I was on your side at first with the whole benevolence thing, but I'm starting to agree with my husband. I don't like people or things that mess with my head."

John put an arm around her as her eyes clouded a bit.

That is because you do not remember what was taken. You have been together for over nine centuries yet is it safe to say you have a better understanding of one another after seeing things from opposite sides.

"Well, I can't argue with that," Danielle agreed with the assessment, and John simply nodded.

Is it anyone else's fault that neither of you seem to be capable of learning a lesson unless it is beaten into you? There was a hint of mental laughter. *Daughter, do not worry about your lost time or memories, but you need to worry about your husband. You have stood on the other side of the glass, and he was not cleansed as you were.*

While your husband had to experience terrible things, they were experienced mostly as an outsider. Even his direct encounter with the entity was very brief. His burdens are heavy, but they can be handled and released, at least with the help of another.

Danielle took the hint.

You, however, went toe to toe with a god, at least from your perspective. You looked into an infinite abyss and experienced things mortal creatures were not meant to experience. Despite how badly you lost and suffered, I believe it was necessary to achieve final victory. Unfortunately, I do not think it would have been possible for you to truly live or even survive with those memories. I see their removal as a form of "payment" of sorts for your efforts.

"Your explanation has a lot of 'I believes' in it." John was shaking his head. "I just don't know."

Danielle placed a hand on his cheek.

None can deny that those memories and that time have been removed from her. My power cannot do such a thing.

"Does it really matter, love?" She turned his head to face hers. "I think we established that whatever it was, it doesn't want to or can't hurt us, and isn't that all you were worried about?" She kissed him gently. "I promise we'll talk about what happened, and I swear I'll help you any way I can."

"Okay, dear, I guess we can agree on benevolent intentions, I suppose."

See, I told you. To think I did not even have to mention the rest.

They turned to face him; eyebrows arched.

Well, I just meant the obvious reward you both received on top of everything else.

Neither vampire had a clue of what he was talking about and just continued staring.

Seriously? Wow, you really are as bad as children sometimes. You mean to tell me the two ancient powerful warriors have yet to properly examine their surroundings?

They glanced at each other briefly before slowly looking around the familiar cavern. Everything was as it should be, a little brighter than normal, but John had noticed that earlier.

Danielle was the first to look up, and John heard her sudden hiss as she reflexively dived for cover. His confusion grew, until he glanced upward himself and mirrored her actions. Neither of them had noticed the several holes in the cavern's roof, most likely a result of the amount of power released during the final battle with the entity. The added brightness in the cavern that John had noticed earlier was due to the amount of sunlight pouring in from above.

Will both of you please just calm down and think. You were unconscious for hours, not to mention how much time has passed since you woke up.

It was a fair point, and they stared at each other from their respective hiding places. Neither of them wanted to make the first move, but they couldn't remain hidden forever, and so they approached one of the areas receiving direct sunlight.

They knew that they should be feeling at least slight discomfort simply from being this close, but there was none. After a slight nod to each other, both vampires reached out with a single hand and slowly moved them into the light. The progenitor sent them a mental impression that they were being silly, considering how much time they had already spent in the sunlight, but he was unwilling to directly interrupt their moment.

"It feels a little weird, but there's no pain," Danielle was the first to speak. She had stepped completely into the light and was looking up to better feel the warmth.

That is most likely because you are unaccustomed to feeling the sunlight on your skin.

John had found his own spot to mirror Danielle's actions, although he didn't think to close his eyes before he looked up.

"Ow!" he screamed, reflexively jumping back into a shadow.

Idiot, even human children know not to look directly into the sun.
There was mental chuckling at John's foolishness as Danielle twirled in circles, ignoring them both.

"Yeah, yeah," he mumbled, allowing his retinas to heal.

As the initial shock of their newfound ability wore off, the full implications began to set in, and they both faced the progenitor.

"I was about to ask how this was possible," Danielle began, "but that's pretty much par for the course at this point, isn't it?" She chuckled at her own comment, even as she felt John throw his arms around her.

"Even if I don't fully understand, I guess neither of us can argue about benevolent intentions anymore." He could sense Danielle's agreement. "Can you tell if this is permanent and not just another temporary change?"

I cannot say with absolute certainty, but I sense no further changes occurring within you.

"This is amazing, but in a way, this just makes me even more confused about what we even are."

They had reverted to their preferred position, but this time they were sitting in the light.

You are what you are.

"That doesn't answer the question," Danielle replied while John rolled his eyes at the progenitor's typical cryptic response.

Only because you people, and the mortals you came from, insist on applying random meanings to even more random words. Words only mean what you want them to, and the meanings are frequently relative. For example, what you call "love," I would call "synergy." You have both spent centuries asking questions you insist are important to you, and yet you spent those same centuries blinded to the answers that were consistently provided.

This terrible dark battle you have been through, this battle fought in secret, this battle that no one would ever believe presented an opportunity for something to provide you with answers so directly, it nearly killed you both. Take the hint and stop asking stupid questions. When you ask what you are, I know you are referencing the creatures you have become. The answer is as irrelevant as the question.

They were honest enough to admit the progenitor might have a point, but it wasn't easy to let go of nearly a thousand years' worth of uncertainty.

The true answer to what you are is that you are two halves of the same whole. None of your powers or abilities are more important than that simple fact, and exactly what that "whole" might be is equally irrelevant. What matters is that you both need to continue striving to be as close to a single entity as possible for two living creatures. You both need to learn and understand how to share your burdens, all your burdens, and not just when they become too heavy for you as individuals. This, more than any other power or ability you possess, will allow you to survive the true darkness.

They both sat up a little straighter.

"You mean the Shakeeth, don't you?"

Yes. Since meeting you, I have entertained your unending foolish questions. Would you like for me to counter them with a question of my own? The question I have been asking for tens of thousands of your years?

They motioned for him to continue.

Why you? He allowed them to consider the simple question for a moment.

"You mean humans and not just us, don't you?" Danielle offered.

Correct. Why you? All life is but food for the Shakeeth, yet never in our history has our food done anything but rot in the ground. How is it that I managed to crash onto this pathetic little planet, which also happens to be home to the only race in the known universe to be affected in such a way by Shakeeth blood? Further, how did this new race of abominations, and to be fair, most of my children are just that, create the two of you?

"Wow," was all John could think to say as Danielle silently considered the implications. "Okay, you definitely win the best-question contest."

"Yeah, I don't know how to ever answer that one," was the best Danielle could offer.

I do not believe in what you humans would call fate, but I do believe that perhaps the universe is providing the opportunity to correct a mistake. The essence of my people is nothing more than immortal hunger. A race such as the Shakeeth cannot be allowed to exist, and someone must correct the mistake the First Ones made.

If my people do still exist, it is only a matter of time before they enter this area of space. There will be no secret battles then. There will be untold waves of starships and armies bringing fire and destruction, and everything will fall into true darkness as untold billions are extinguished and consumed.

The vampires shuddered slightly at the remembered images the progenitor had shared with them.

"Can your people even be stopped?" Danielle asked quietly.

No, I do not believe it is possible. It is for that reason the task must fall to you.

"Well, I'm not loving the level of confidence here, but you at least know we won't go down without a fight."

No amount of power will allow you to defeat them on your own. If victory over my people is even possible, you will only attain it by leading the mortals openly. All mortals.

Their eyes twitched slightly at the hint toward other undiscovered races amongst the stars.

Now, if you do not mind, I am very tired.

They looked at each other quickly, knowing exactly what the progenitor meant.

"Um, look," John began, "we don't want to kill you. I admit that these last experiences have given us a better understanding of why you want to finally sleep, and we are more comfortable granting your request than we were before. However, you said yourself how much you've enjoyed interacting with us and our family, so why not just stay with us?"

Danielle nodded her agreement. "Even if we can't find a way to allow you to be mobile again, we can promise that you'll never be alone," she added her statement to John's final plea.

Children, he started slowly, *your offer tempts me greatly and makes me wish I still had the ability to weep, but this cannot be. I have lived too long, and it is time for me to see what is on the other side. These final memories, I will take with me as a gift, one for which I am grateful, but it is time for me to go.*

I leave you both as stewards of this world, but to do this, you must have my power. To lead the mortals against the darkness, you must have the power of gods, but to prevail, you must never let power change what you are.

The progenitor was confident with his decision, but the future was never certain. He let his senses wash over the two beautiful children sitting before him and hoped he was making the right choice.

He was being honest when he said he did not believe it was possible to defeat his people. If they still existed at all, they would be legion upon legion of beings potentially as powerful as he was. It wasn't failure to defeat the Shakeeth that frightened him most; however, it was the possibility of his two children faltering. The power he was about to provide them would be enough to let them rule his people if they became corrupt. Rather than fight the dark, they had the potential to lead it.

I truly believe if you remain as one, there is a chance for all, but if you ever forget who you are, you will burn. This is my final warning.

They reflexively glanced at their wedding rings, nodding their understanding.

The time for words has now passed. Fulfill your duty.

John and Danielle slowly rose and moved to either side of the progenitor's frail form. She kissed his cheek, and they were both weeping as their fangs pierced opposite sides of his throat. Despite the purity and power of the blood, neither of them experienced even a hint of frenzy. They fed in silence, and it wasn't long before they felt his presence leave their minds as the body turned to dust.

John leaned against the stone wall, overwhelmed with a combination of power and sadness, while Danielle quickly knelt beside the pile of dust. He watched as she placed a hand on the pile and began mumbling. There was a small flash, and he crouched down for a closer look as the dust began to change. After a moment, the pile was replaced by two dark rings, and Danielle added one to the same finger as her wedding ring.

"So you're an alchemist now?" John inquired as he took the second ring for himself.

"Why not?"

He chuckled at her nonchalant reaction to discovering an amazing new ability. It was just that kind of day.

"How do you feel?"

"Honestly, right now I don't feel particularly powerful." She leaned against him. "More like total exhaustion, and I just want to go home." She was toying with the new ring as she spoke.

"Agreed, but we aren't finished yet. If he's gone, it means there's no longer a shroud protecting this place, right?"

John waited for her to nod in agreement since, in all honesty, he wasn't completely sure.

"Well, sweety, there's a whole spaceship, albeit a small one, in here we have to hide or take home before someone notices the changes to the area and starts to investigate."

"Yeah, I know," she answered tiredly.

"Don't worry, we'll take care of this, then go home and sleep for a week, and then we are due for a serious vacation."

"Promise?"

"Hell yeah. Remember, we really can have margaritas on the beach now."

Danielle smiled as he reminded her of the promise he had made what seemed like years ago. She leaned up to kiss his cheek, and then both ancients went to work.

EPILOGUE

Unknown

"Father is going to be mad at you," the voice came from nowhere.

"I disagree." A simple defense but clearly stated.

"You broke the rules," a second accuser sounded.

"I disagree."

"You interfered. The rules are clear. Father is going to punish you," a third accuser threatened.

"I corrected a mistake of our own making. The prisoner did not belong on that plane. It was our failure that made it so."

"The prisoner was one such as we. The power to destroy our kind does not exist. We could only weaken, contain, and banish, this you know."

"But by doing so, we created something that we have the power to destroy. We did not."

"By doing so, we created something that exists in the lower plane. The rules allow for no interference," the accusers echoed.

"We are the ones that put it there, the rules do not apply in this case."

"The rules apply in all cases."

"The prisoner was reawakening. I allowed it to be destroyed before it could challenge us again. That is all." It knew it had made the correct decision, no matter how many of its brethren disagreed.

"We can no longer be challenged by such a creature; the prisoner would simply have been banished again."

"And what of the damage to the lower plane?"

"It does not affect us, and that is only one universe of many in the lower plane. This you know. The rules are absolute."

"I did not interfere directly. I only allowed the defenders of light's plan to be successful." It knew the argument was lost but refused to relent.

"You allowed the creation of life and energy that did not exist. You allowed the destruction of the prisoner, one who cannot be destroyed by the lower plane. This is direct interference," the accusers' voices were growing louder.

"I removed the memories before I left. There is no proof on the lower plane that interference occurred."

"Father knows the rules have been broken, and you altered their bodies."

It had been hoping that the others didn't notice that last part. The alteration had been so simple but was unfortunately the one transgression for which it had no defense that the others would understand. It had simply wanted to do something good.

"If they are to defend the light, they deserve to stand in it." It knew the others would not care, but it needed to be said.

"They are not of the light; they are of the Shakeeth. They battled the prisoner only to protect themselves. You made a mistake. The rules exist to prevent mistakes. You will be punished."

"Why do any of you care? It was already decided that their universe will be lost to the darkness, just as most of the others, yet we cannot interfere. All I did was allow for a possible future where the Shakeeth are defeated. If we are of the light, why am I to be punished?"

"This is not what you have done. You made a mistake."

"I did not."

"The ones you call defenders are of the darkness. By allowing their survival and the prisoner's destruction, you have exchanged a single enemy for two."

"You said the lower planes do not concern us, so how can they be our enemy?" It hated how irritating and circular these arguments could become, but the question was met with silence. "You will answer me, or you will admit the error."

"They could challenge us."

"That is absurd." It could not believe its accusers' statement. "You worry not about losing so many of the universes to the Shakeeth, but you are concerned about a pair of lower beings."

"The Shakeeth are of the dark and cannot enter this plane."

"You said my defenders were of the dark as well, or are you prepared to admit the truth? To admit that they are blended with the light of the mortals, enough so to grant them access to this realm?" It was met with only silence. "As pleasant as the silence is compared to your voices, I still do not see the concern. Two lower beings cannot challenge us, even if they should be granted access."

"You were too busy breaking the rules to see."

"See what?"

"They have potential."

"All lower beings have potential."

"Their potential has no end we can see. We cannot predict what they will become."

Now it was its turn to be silent, for all lower beings had predictable limits.

"You may see and examine for yourself. The rules do not forbid observance, only interference. Though it may take eons of their time, if the two remain as one, they could grow to challenge even us."

It began to laugh at the others.

"You dare laugh at this?"

"You are all afraid. So yes, I laugh at the cowards you have become. Most likely they will be destroyed as their universe falls, but perhaps one day the future you fear will come to pass . . ." It paused for effect. "If beings such as they challenge you, then you deserve to be challenged. If that day should come, they will find an ally in me."

"*BLASPHEMY!*" the accusers' cry rumbled through the plane.

"*THEN BANISH ME!*" it returned in challenge. "Only Father is all-knowing, and he neither stops nor silences me. Now begone, I grow weary of your foolishness."

"You will regret your arrogance," its brethren threatened as one, but they left.

The debate was more heated than it had anticipated, but the entity scored at least a few points—not that it would matter. Nothing ever changed here anymore. Unfortunately, despite the harshness of its arguments, the entity knew it would never again be able to interfere.

It was likely the current transgressions would be forgiven, if for no other reason than the cowards would want to pretend the harsh argument had never happened. Additional transgressions, however, would most likely spark reprisals from the others, and that could be very bad for the lower planes. In fact, the entity would need to be forever on guard on behalf of the two he had saved. If the others were truly afraid, the day might come when they would ignore the rules, much as it had done.

That was okay. Eternity was better spent with a purpose, and it regret nothing. The mortals and lower beings of that universe deserved a chance, and the entity believed that the true light was in the lower planes and only granted to this realm at their behest. At least the lower beings fought against the dark, whereas its brethren simply hid behind rules.

Whatever happened, at least it was able to watch.

Montage Kapalua Bay, Maui

Isaac Keller knocked gently on the door of the penthouse suite, wondering how this eccentric couple could possibly require so much food. Of course, that was far from the strangest thing he had noticed in the week they had been staying here. He was no stranger to the odd tastes and actions of wealthy people, given how long he had worked at this resort, but these two definitely stood out. It would also be nice to know why they kept asking for him.

It started when they arrived last week, and he was simply on shift and the one bringing them drinks. That was normal enough, as guests could order as many drinks as they wanted as they lounged on the beach as easily as if they were in the attached bar. The strange part was that after that first day, apparently the couple had insisted to his superiors that he be the one to deliver them. No matter what his other duties were, he was randomly pulled away simply to serve drinks to them.

Everyone he worked with was curious, but the couple never spoke to him, so he had no idea why they liked him. In fact, neither of them so much as looked him in the eye. Yet not only did they insist that he, and no other, serve them, but they tipped him more money than he had ever seen at one time. In the last week, they had given him more money in gratuity than he had made in the previous year.

His shift this evening had ended over an hour ago, but his manager had forced him to stay simply to deliver their dinner. The phone call with his wife had not gone well, since he had promised to be home earlier than normal, but she would forgive him. There would be another mouth in their home to feed soon, so neither of them could say no to such a large increase in income. As he heard the door begin to open, Isaac shook his head free of distracting thoughts.

It wasn't surprising to see it was one of their scary-looking bodyguards; otherwise, what be the point in having them? There were enough rich and famous people always coming and going to the popular resort that the bodyguards themselves were not odd to see. The couple seemed to have a large number of them, however, and none of them ever got very close unless needed. As the multiple carts were brought into the room, at least he realized the number of guards explained the amount of food. He stepped in himself to better supervise and assist with the distribution of the meals.

The majority of the guards seemed to be gathered in an adjoining room. Isaac could see beer bottles, cards, and assorted other activities but not a whole lot of "guarding" being done. The husband was visible further into the suite, his back to the door as he watched some random program on the room's large television. The large sitting room where the carts were initially brought contained no one except the woman, simply lounging alone on a plush couch, and a single guard off to the side.

"Hello, Isaac," she said sweetly, causing the breath to catch in his throat.

She had simply never spoken to him before, and something about the way she said those two simple words had him mesmerized.

"Really now Isaac, a married man should not be so blatantly staring," she said grinning.

"Oh, uh, so sorry ma'am," he stammered. He realized he had, in fact, been staring.

She was doing nothing but simply lounging in one of the resort's robes, but there was just something about her that kept him from looking away.

"You just startled me is all."

"That's okay, tell me, which of these meals is the best?" It was such a simple question, so why did he feel so much weight behind it?

"Wow, that's actually hard to say, ma'am. It would seem you both ordered one of everything." He couldn't help but chuckle lightly.

"Which one is your favorite, Isaac?"

"To be honest, ma'am, I realize we're on an island and everything, but I'm an old-fashioned steak-and-potatoes kind of guy," he answered the harmless question.

She barely glanced at the single guard in the room with her, who immediately separated the indicated meal while motioning for the others to be brought to the next room. The filet meal was placed gently on the coffee table, but not directly in front of the woman. A bottle of beer was added, and a comfortable chair was brought closer. It was all very strange.

"That will be all," she announced.

The staff members began moving the empty carts back out while a guard went to the door to pass out generous gratuity.

"Not you, Isaac," she added as he turned to join the others.

Another staff member caught his eye, but he simply gave a small shrug.

"Oh, of course, ma'am," he said, realizing that despite all the food they brought, no dessert had been ordered. He quickly pulled out a pad, anticipating the need to take their order.

"Sit down Isaac," she instructed, and he immediately sat without thinking.

She seemed to be saying his name more often than necessary, yet every time she did, he felt more drawn to her.

"Please, enjoy." She waved at the meal he indicated as being his favorite.

"Ma'am, that's not appropriate." He was getting a bit nervous. "I really should return to my duties."

"Nonsense Isaac, your duties ended over an hour ago. You are only still here because of us, and we won't be having your pregnant wife slaving to make you dinner at such a late hour. After all," she smiled, "we aren't monsters."

There was something about the way she had phrased her final comment that sent warning bells off in his mind. Also, he wore his wedding ring around his neck at work, so how did she know about his wife or that she was pregnant?

Whatever strange thing was going on, this woman was clearly accustomed to being obeyed, so he began eating. Why not? It smelled delicious, and it was true that he had been extremely hungry. As he ate, she placed three beautiful but very old-looking ruby rings on the coffee table.

"Who told you about my wife, ma'am?" he asked after taking a drink of beer to clear his throat.

He noticed the husband was sitting with them at the table now. Strange, Isaac didn't remember seeing him change places. Her lips were moving, but he couldn't hear what she was saying, as she placed a hand over the rings.

"Isaac, give me your finger." She ignored his earlier question.

He slowly held out his hand, curiosity overpowering good sense, as a guard took away his empty plate. She gently took hold of his hand, and before he could say anything, he felt a small sharp pain as his finger was cut open. He hadn't even seen what she used to cut him, and her grip was as if her entire body was made of steel.

He knew he should be getting concerned or even terrified right now, but somehow he just did not feel that way. She carefully maneuvered his finger to allow blood to drop onto the stones of all three rings. Once completed, she leaned down and licked his injured finger gently, never breaking eye contact with him. Finally regaining his senses, Isaac pulled his hand back quickly, ready to demand an explanation, before noticing the cut was gone.

Examining his finger revealed no sign he had been cut, yet not only had he felt it, but he had also seen the blood dripping. He looked up to see the husband and wife repeating the procedure with their own fingers, making the cuts on each other with obvious claws that no human should have. Despite knowing he should be starting to feel fear, Isaac honestly felt perfectly safe. Just extremely curious. The rings crackled slightly with energy once the couple completed whatever it was they were doing, serving to increase his curiosity further.

"Isaac?"

"Yes, ma'am?"

"We have a very long story to tell you, Isaac." She was looking directly into his eyes, and he could almost feel himself getting lost. "It's an amazing story that you will not believe, and then we are going to prove it to you. Finally, after you hear it all and have been shown the proof, you will answer our question."

"Um, what question, ma'am?" Everything was sounding so strange to him, but he felt very strongly that he wanted to hear what they both had to say.

"There is a great and terrible darkness coming, Isaac," she started. He could see sadness in her eyes. "A very long time from now, but it is coming. All will fight, or all will be consumed. When this darkness comes, we will do all we can to protect you, but the humans must know we can be trusted."

Isaac thought he saw a tear in her eye, but it was red, and why had she said the word *human* in such a way?

"We will need human friends to help bridge the gap between us and the others."

They each put one of the rings on, and Isaac could have sworn he had seen fangs while she had been talking. She picked up the remaining ring and held it out to him, smiling sadly.

"Isaac Keller, would your family like to be our friends?"